PRAISE FOR *AGAINST THE INQUISITION*

"[A] stirring song of freedom."

—Nobel Prize laureate Mario Vargas Llosa

"*Against the Inquisition* delivers a message of solidarity and respect among human beings. This monumental masterpiece is worth a million speeches and op-ed pieces. We celebrate its publication in English: may its message of love and freedom reach the world at large."

—International Raoul Wallenberg Foundation

"*Against the Inquisition* is one of the greatest novels of the twentieth century. It combines suspenseful storytelling, poetic beauty, and admirable wisdom. Without straying from the plot, Marcos Aguinis creates an impressive portrait of the Spanish Inquisition and the colonial society of South America."

—*Lecturalia* (Spain)

"*Against the Inquisition* can be read as an exciting historical adventure with a dramatic ending, as the tale of a marked man who flees from his executioners while staying true to his beliefs risking torture and death, and also as a bitter testimony of our history that invites us to reflect. Only through understanding the abominations contained in our past can we have a future without errors."

—*El Mundo* (Spain)

AGAINST
THE
INQUISITION

AGAINST THE INQUISITION

MARCOS AGUINIS
Translated by Carolina De Robertis

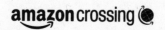

Previously published as *La Gesta del Marrano* by Plaza & Janes Editores, S.A. in Argentina in 1991. Translated from the Spanish by Carolina De Robertis. First published in English by AmazonCrossing in 2018.

Published by AmazonCrossing, Seattle
www.apub.com

Amazon, the Amazon logo, and AmazonCrossing are trademarks of Amazon.com, Inc., or its affiliates.

ISBN-13: 9781503949263
ISBN-10: 1503949265

Cover design by David Drummond

Printed in the United States of America

To Francisco Maldonado da Silva,
who heroically defended the arduous right
to liberty of conscience.

To my father, who enriched my childhood
with lively stories and would have
enjoyed this one.

Contents

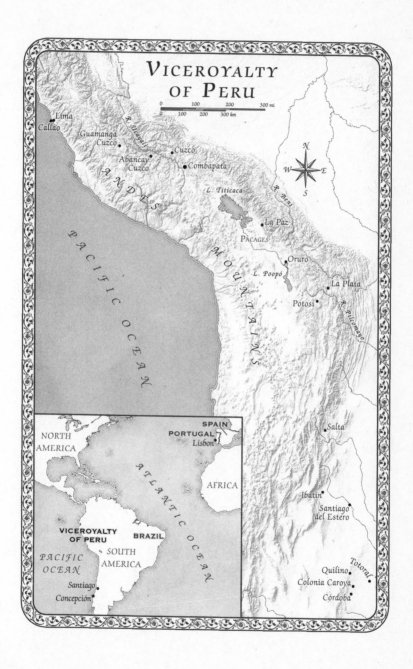

VICEROYALTY OF PERU

BOOK ONE

GENESIS

EMBERS OF CHILDHOOD

Prologue

Francisco—grimy, skin and bones, his wrists and ankles rubbed raw by the shackles—is an ember burning under rubble. The judges stare at him, vexed: a monstrosity, an utterly intolerable nuisance.

It's been twelve years since they locked him in secret prisons. They subjected him to interrogations and privations. They brought in scholars to accost him with loud arguments. They humiliated and threatened him. But Francisco Maldonado da Silva did not yield: not to physical pain or to spiritual pressures. Now, the tenacious inquisitors rage and sweat, not wanting to burn him at the stake until he's shown remorse or fear.

When, six years ago, the prisoner fasted in a rebellious act that almost dissolved him into a corpse, the inquisitors force-fed him, gave him wine and pastries, as they couldn't stand for this worm of a man to steal from them the power to control his death. Francisco Maldonado da Silva took a long time to recover, but he succeeded in showing his tormentors that he could suffer no less than a saint.

In his stinking dungeon, the ravaged prisoner often looked back on his odyssey. He was born in 1592, precisely one century after Jews were expelled from Spain and Columbus discovered the West Indies. He could still recall the light in the remote oasis of Ibatín, where he spent his early childhood in a house full of pastel colors and spots of blue.

Later, his family hastily moved to Córdoba, fleeing persecution that would soon catch up with them. They navigated perilous circumstances: Indians, pumas, thieves, astounding salt flats.

When he was nine years old, his father was arrested one wrenching afternoon. A year later his older brother was torn from their home. When Francisco turned eleven, his home no longer held any possessions, as they all had been confiscated and sold at a loss by the relentless authorities. His mother, defeated, half crazy, surrendered to death.

The scarred teenager completed his education in a monastery; he read the Bible and dreamed of reparations that were as yet unspeakable. He saved an apoplectic, rode through Córdoba's magnificent mountains, and came to know the most absurd flagellations.

Before turning eighteen, he decided to head to Lima to study medicine at the University of San Marcos. There he longed to reconnect with his father, who was still alive but shattered by the tortures of the Inquisition. He journeyed by wagon and mule across thousands of kilometers, from the infinite pampas of the south to the frozen altitudes of the Andes. Along the way he spent time with unexpected travel companions and made discoveries that changed his own sense of identity. He descended into dazzling Lima, called the City of Kings, to receive his final revelation. There, in addition to a dramatic reunion with his father, he met and helped Saint Martín de Porres, the first black saint of the Americas; took part in the defense of Callao against the Dutch pirate Spilbergen; and graduated in a radiant ceremony.

The persecution that had started in Ibatín and spread to Córdoba took hold again in Lima. He decided to embark for Chile, an eternal fugitive. There he won a place as senior surgeon at the Santiago hospital, as he was the first professional with legitimate credentials to arrive in the land. His personal library surpassed all the existing collections in monasteries or public spaces in Lima. He visited salons and palaces, rubbed elbows with civil and religious leaders, and received praise for his cultural refinement. And he married a beautiful woman. He became successful and esteemed; his well-being repaired the chain of past suffering.

A common man wouldn't have changed such circumstances. But in his spirit there shone a stubborn flame, a rebellion that rose from the depths. He knew that other people like him also roamed the world, keeping their secret beliefs inside. It was difficult, unsettling, shameful. Against the logic of convenience, he chose to remove his mask and defend his rights head on.

1

Half a century before that crucial moment, the Portuguese doctor Diego Núñez da Silva arrived in the southern oasis of Ibatín. He was born in Lisbon in 1548. As a boy, he had moments of happiness, but after earning his medical degree, he decided that he was tired of persecution and obsequiousness. So he fled to Brazil. He wanted to get away from the endless fires, the vertigo of horrible accusations, the basins of forced baptisms, the torture chambers, and the Acts of Faith—or sentencing hearings—that were devastating Portugal. On the way, he delighted in the ocean, enjoying its tempests, which seemed to erase the absurd storms of humanity. But when he disembarked in Brazil, he learned that it was best to steer clear of the territory dominated by the Portuguese crown: the local Inquisition was even more brutal than the one across the sea. So he continued his exhausting, dangerous journey toward the Viceroyalty of Peru. He arrived in legendary Potosí, where the silver mines were exploited until their veins showed unmistakable signs of depletion. He found other Portuguese people who, like him, had fled, and he struck up friendships that would later have terrible consequences.

Eager to practice medicine, he proposed the construction of a hospital for the native peoples, submitting paperwork at the town council of Cuzco. He did not succeed, as the Indians' health was not a matter of official interest. On learning that doctors were needed in the south, he took to the road again. He journeyed across plateaus, ravines, and spectral deserts until he reached Ibatín, where he met Aldonza Maldonado, a young woman with sweet eyes but no fortune. She was beautiful, and a clean-blooded Christian, meaning that she lacked any Moorish or Jewish roots, but, due to her meager dowry, she couldn't hope for a favorable match. She accepted the marriage offer of this mature Portuguese physician, who was poor and a New Christian (as these converts or children of converts were called), because of his trustworthy appearance and friendly manner; his boyish bearing and beautiful, carefully trimmed bronze-colored beard did not escape her feminine eye. The wedding proceedings were austere, as demanded by the financial circumstances of both bride and groom.

Don Diego felt blessed. He'd offered his services to all of Ibatín and to the scarce populations scattered through the territory of Tucumán, and had received a good response. He saved enough to build a home and, as he gazed at the courtyard of his new house made of stone, adobe, and cane roofing shaped by the Indians' hands, he felt the urgent need to fulfill a delayed obligation. It was a hot rectangular courtyard, full of untamed brush, onto which rooms let out on all sides. He had to change it to reflect what was in his heart.

He found out that there was an orange grove at the Monastery of La Merced. He spoke to the gaunt superior, Brother Antonio Luque. One chat sufficed to get him the help of a handful of kids, two Indians, and two black men, plus a collection of saplings. Under his supervision, hoes uprooted the brush, stalks and roots moaned, vermin fled. Next, picks and shovels removed the dens of viscachas and the eggs of reptiles. They scraped the damp earth, making grooves through which rainwater could run. Then they tamped down the dirt until the rectangle was as smooth as the skin of a drum.

He marked twelve points with the tip of his boot and ordered holes dug at each one. He kneeled and, refusing help, placed each orange tree in its respective place. He pressed the earth around the slender base of each trunk, emptied buckets as if pouring water for pilgrims, and, on finishing the task, called out to his wife.

Aldonza emerged with curiosity, her hands wrapped in rosary beads. Her beautiful dark hair reached her shoulders. Her olive skin contrasted with her blue eyes. She had a round face, like that of a doll, heart-shaped lips, and a small nose.

"What do you think?" he said with pride, gesturing with his chin toward the young trees. He explained that soon they would offer orange blossoms, fruit, and pleasant shade.

He did not tell her, however, that this splendid courtyard of orange trees was the embodiment of a dream. It brought to life his nostalgia for remote and idealized Spain, a place his grandparents had belonged to and that he'd never known.

2

The sumptuous fronds of the orange orchard were already housing the raucousness of birds when the couple's fourth child, Francisco, was born. His first cry was so intense that there was no need to leave the room to announce his vigor.

Francisco's three siblings were Diego (who, as the first-born son, bore his father's name, which was the custom in Spain and Portugal), Isabel, and Felipa. Diego was ten years older than the mischievous Francisquito.

This family had in their service a couple of black slaves: Luis and Catalina. Comparatively, owning two slaves was a decisive sign of poverty. Don Diego had bought them in a sale of faulty merchandise: the man limped, due to a wound inflicted on his thigh during an escape attempt; the woman was blind in one eye. Both had been captured in Angola as children. They'd learned basic Spanish, which they mixed with rough expressions in their native tongue. They also resigned themselves to baptism and the imposition of Christian names, although secretly they kept on invoking their beloved gods. The lame Luis fashioned a musical instrument out of a donkey's jawbone and a small sheep's bone; he scraped the jawbone's teeth with a hypnotic rhythm, as his voice unfurled a melodious drone. The half-blind Catalina accompanied him by humming, clapping, and sensually moving her whole body.

Luis told Don Diego that he came from a line of witch doctors. The physician recognized his intelligence, so he taught him how to assist in surgical tasks. This was seen as scandalous in the prejudiced town of Ibatín. Although some black and mulatto people already worked as barbers, and therefore performed the common procedure of bloodletting, they were not trusted to ease a fracture, drain an abscess, or cauterize wounds. Don Diego also placed Luis in charge of his medical instruments. Luis's limp did not keep him from following Don Diego through the streets of Ibatín or across its rocky outskirts, carrying a suitcase over his shoulder filled with surgical tools, powders, bandages, and salves.

Don Diego had acquired the habit of sitting below his orange trees in a cane chair to enjoy the cool evening air. Francisco himself often recalled him during his own fierce later years: When his father sat in the evenings, a small audience surrounded him, drawn by his enthralling stories. If he started telling a story, it was hard to get up; it was said that even the birds stopped moving. Don Diego's repertoire was inexhaustible, willing as he was to offer new tales of heroes and knights, or episodes of sacred histories.

One day the orange orchard was dubbed "the academy." The doctor didn't mind the irony. In fact, not wanting to appear daunted, he decided that in that very place he'd offer his family a systematic education. He deemed their scattered lessons insufficient. He persuaded the frail and friendly Brother Isidro Miranda—with whom he'd exchanged intimate family histories—to give lessons to all. He knew this would be frowned upon, because to learn something outside of catechism, in those times, meant the invasion of dangerous realms.

He put out a table made of carob wood and surrounded it with benches. The sweet-tempered friar suggested that he teach the four basics: grammar, geography, history, and arithmetic. His voice was warm and persuasive, his best attribute. His bony face, on the other hand, held eyes that had something excessive about them, as if caught in a constant astonishment or fear.

The students in the school included Aldonza, who'd already learned her letters from her husband; their four children; Lucas Graneros, a friend of the now-teenaged Diego; and three kindly neighbors. Aldonza, though descended from good ancestry, had not received instruction beyond the skills of knitting, spinning, sewing, and embroidery.

"Knowledge is power," Don Diego repeated to the motley group of students. "It is a strange power that can't be compared to the sword, or gunpowder, or muscle. He who knows is powerful."

Brother Antonio Luque, the severe superior who had provided the saplings from his orange grove, did not share this opinion. Luque was a coarse priest who'd been invested by the Holy Office of the Inquisition with the status of a familiar. As a functionary of the Inquisition, his task was to denounce people who threatened the faith, and to take the accused into custody on the tribunal's behalf.

He used a calm tone to deliver his response: "Knowledge is arrogance," he said, each word dripping with bile. "It is for wanting to devour knowledge that we were cast out of paradise."

And, referring to the doctor's courtyard of orange trees, he dismissed it outright: "It is an eccentricity."

As if he hadn't been clear enough, he added: "It is absurd for an entire family to study. A woman's education should be limited to manual labors and catechism."

Diego Núñez da Silva listened to him in silence. He understood the dangers of offending the authority of a familiar. After hearing each sentence, he lowered his eyes and even bent his head. The sullen priest was small and had a hurtful gaze. The doctor, in contrast, was tall and tender eyed. He had to cede to the priest's power, but not so much as to shut down his academy. He restrained himself to saying that he would reflect on these sensible words. He neither dismissed Brother Isidro, nor did he limit the hours of his classes or exclude women.

Brother Antonio Luque was still bothered. He summoned Brother Isidro Miranda to come and "inform" him about the "ridiculous academy." He asked a half-dozen questions, which Brother Isidro answered, his eyes bulging more than ever. Afterward, Luque reproached him: "What kind of notion was it to teach the four basics?" His gaze was brutal. "Those are subjects for qualified institutions, not for Ibatín."

Brother Isidro pressed the trembling cross that hung at his chest, not daring to reply.

"To teach such splendid subjects to miserable beings! It's like watering sand!" Luque rose and began to pace the dim sacristy. "What's more, you have committed an unforgivable omission: you overlooked theology, the queen of the sciences. If you and that highly suspicious doctor want to cultivate souls, teach them, at the very least, the rudiments of theology. The rudiments!"

The following afternoon, Brother Isidro opened a tattered notebook and taught his first theology class. At the end of the lesson, young Diego confessed that he wanted to learn Latin.

"Latin?"

"To understand Mass," he said in his own defense.

"You don't need to understand Mass," the priest explained. "It's enough to attend, listen, be moved, and receive communion."

"I want to learn that, too!" Francisco raised his little hand.

"'That' is called 'Latin,'" Brother Isidro said.

"Yes, Latin."

"You're not old enough."

"Why not?"

The priest approached the boy and pressed his shoulders. "Not everything can be known."

He let go of the boy, walked slowly around his students, and murmured, as if to the boy's father, "Knowledge, my friend, is not always power."

A couple of weeks later, he caved to their demands and began teaching Latin. Francisquito and his brother Diego studied it as if it were a game. They chanted declensions while jumping rope and playing hopscotch. When Brother Antonio Luque learned of this development, he let out a burst of astonishment. But suspicions still gnawed at his spirit.

Francisco has turned thirty-five years old. He uses the last names of his mother (Maldonado) and his father (da Silva). A few months ago he relocated to Concepción, in southern Chile, to avoid the lashings of the Holy Office. But he knows that they will reach him; his escape only makes their work more difficult, and in truth, he doesn't want to keep living like a fugitive: he's been one long enough already, just as his father, grandfather, and great-grandfather were.

He sleeps lightly, restlessly. He senses that it will happen one of these nights. He toys with alternative plans, but dismisses them as naïve. The two of them—he and the Inquisition—will have to face each other, fatally.

At last he hears noise around the house. His premonition becomes reality. He imagines the soldiers, with their implacable order for his arrest. He has arrived at the moment that will turn his life upside down. He gets out of bed in silence. He must not frighten his sleeping wife and small daughter. He dresses in the dark. Those henchmen usually act brutally, and he plans to surprise them with his calm bearing. Even though his heart has started beating in his throat.

3

Ibatín nestled at the foot of a mountain. The clouds lingered to water its slopes, transforming the otherwise arid land into a fantastic jungle. To arrive at this oasis, Don Diego had had to travel the same roads that, centuries before, the Incas had opened for the first time, and that the conquistadores had later worn down in small, suicidal armies inspired by delusions of a marvelous city built with silver walls and roofs of gold. Although they did not find such a city, they founded others, among them Ibatín and San Miguel de Tucumán, beside a river that wound sonorously down the Ravine of the Portuguese. They christened it *Río del Tejar*, or River of Tiles, after the tile factory they erected on its shores. It is unknown, however, after which Portuguese man or men the ravine was named; that name already existed when Don Diego Núñez da Silva arrived.

From the beginning, the residents of Ibatín had to struggle against two threats: the exuberance of nature, and the Indians. The breath of pumas, those tigers of the Americas, emanated from the jungle, and the river ran through astonishing gullies; in the rainy season its tributaries swelled rapidly and turned the river into a dark, aggressive monster, which once reached all the way to the threshold of the main church.

A perimeter of tree trunks surrounded the town. Each neighbor was obliged to keep weapons in his home, and at least one horse. They lived ready for battle. They had to take turns making the rounds of their insecure fortifications. Don Diego fulfilled this duty every two months, and Francisquito felt great pride at watching his father prepare, at the way he checked his firearm, counted his munitions, and placed a helmet over his copper-colored hair.

The main plaza of Ibatín was intersected by royal roads that led to Chile and Peru to the north, and the plains of the pampas to the south. The racket never ceased: the din of wagons, the braying of mules, the bellowing of oxen, the whinnying of horses, and the passionate haggling of merchants. At the center of all those swirling people, beasts, and vehicles there stood a Spanish cherry tree, also called the "tree of justice." It was the rustic axis of the city: a testimony to its founding and a sentry overseeing its growth. Its solid rootedness to the earth—"in the name of the king"—legitimized the colonists' presence and actions. The Spanish cherry tree was the site of floggings and executions. Prisoners met their severe sentences with rope around their necks, flanked by guards. The town crier declared each crime, and the executioner carried out the hanging. The Spanish cherry tree exhibited the corpse with a macabre pride; neighbors gazed morbidly at the body as it hung and swayed ever so slightly, as if bearing greetings from hell. On feast days and celebrations, the bodies had to be removed before they could fulfill their punishing, instructive role. Feasts for the birth of a prince, the coronation of a new king, or the designation of other new authorities—it was essential that Sundays and saint days never be contaminated with an execution. Not because executions themselves lacked festive elements, but because *Ecclesia abhorret a sanguine,* and it behooved good Christians to render unto Caesar what is Caesar's, and unto God what belongs to God.

The plaza was, then, a constant spectacle. If there wasn't a hanged man, accompanied by the swiftly arriving flies, there was secular revelry. If there wasn't a bullfight, there was almost certainly a procession: against the growing proximity of the river; against an epidemic, because of the lack of rain; because of the excessive rain; against the renewed threat of Calchaquí Indians; or to give thanks for a good harvest. During processions, the four religious orders paraded, each with their distinctive traits: the Dominicans, the Mercedarians, the Franciscans, and the Jesuits. The maniacal Brother Antonio Luque usually led the litanies and imprecations with his booming voice, and this allowed him to remind hidden heretics of his fearsome power as a familiar. He marched before the idols, eyes on the dust of the road because "dust we were, and dust we shall be," and every once in a while he glared irrefutably at whomever would soon be denounced. Later, there would be horse races and simple theatrical presentations on sacred themes, as well as poetry contests, in which Don Diego had once participated. As darkness fell, fireworks blazed. Once, Francisquito burned his hand in an attempt to light one.

This spare description would be incomplete without remembering that the town hall, the seat of local government, stood at one side of the plaza, a building composed of several rooms surrounding the requisite courtyard. Its whitewashed walls shone like snow on a high mountain. At the center of the courtyard stood a well, which was inlaid beautifully with tile. Across from the town hall, the main church loomed. There they stood, the two powers that struggled for dominion of Ibatín, the province of Tucumán, and the entire continent. Terrestrial power on one side, heavenly power on the other. And just as the first extended all the way to the cruel Spanish cherry tree, the second extended to other churches and monasteries. At the Spanish cherry tree, Caesar ruled (even those condemned by religion were turned over to the secular branch), and, in the temples, God reigned. But both frequently overstepped their bounds, because God is everywhere, and Caesar cannot accept being less than God.

On nearby streets the other churches rose, with their respective monasteries. The Franciscans built a taller church than that of the Mercedarians, and added a sumptuous chapel. The Jesuits would not be left behind: they constructed a nave with forty-meter-long transepts, and walls made of brick and adobe; they paved the floor with ceramic tiles, plastered the walls, and carefully tiled the roof; they put in a majestic altar and graced their temple with an admirably ornate pulpit. It was clear that the Jesuits had joined in the belligerence of their society.

———∿∿∿———

He pulls back the iron lock. The moment he cracks open the door, several hands push in from outside. They assume that Francisco, in his fear, will close the door. But Francisco doesn't move. The soldiers have to rein in their vigor, because here, in front of them, in the shadows, stands a broad-bodied man whom the lamplight has brushed with gold and indigo. They stare, perplexed. They almost forget what they were supposed to say.

The main henchman holds a lamp up and asks, "Are you Francisco Maldonado da Silva?"

"Yes."

"I am Juan Minaya, lieutenant for the Holy Office." He presses his lamp against Francisco's nose, as if wanting to burn him. "Identify yourself."

Francisco, half-blinded, asks the obvious. "Didn't you just say my name?"

"Identify yourself!" he growls with bureaucratic disdain.

"I am Francisco Maldonado da Silva."

The lieutenant slowly lowers the lamp, which now sheds light on floating, spectral dust in the air above it. "You are under arrest, in the name of the Holy Office," he declares with pride.

The other men take hold of Francisco's arms. They dominate his body, because prisoners often try to escape.

But Francisco is not thinking of that. It seems odd, but in that crucial moment his mind flies to his childhood town of Ibatín. He hears the sonorous River of Tiles, envisions the vice-patrons' chapel, recalls the cacophonous main plaza, sees under his eyelids the snowy peaks and slopes covered in jungle, the ceaseless wagon factory and the courtyard of orange trees planted by his father. He also recalls the books.

4

The denizens of the vast province of Tucumán were in the habit of accumulating goods known to build wealth: subdued Indians, land, black slaves, packs of mules, droves of pigs and cattle, and fertile fields. To these they added luxuries such as silver dishware, furniture, fine cloth, gold, and delicate utensils imported from Europe. But nobody thought of gathering treasures in the form of books. Books were expensive to buy and difficult to sell; what's more, they contained reckless thoughts. And thoughts troubled the waters in a manner that chairs or mules, for example, never would.

Don Diego was drawn to the eccentricity of a personal library, even though it didn't fit the mentality of his time and place. Instead of investing his savings in productive goods, he spent them on questionable tomes. He brought some from his native Lisbon and purchased the rest in Potosí. His collection would have drawn admiration in Lima or Madrid, where universities and intellectuals thrived. In backward Ibatín, however, it only made him more suspect.

The books lined thick shelves in a small room that he shut himself into for hours of study. There he also kept his case of medical instruments and a few keepsakes. Nobody could enter this room without his permission. The slaves had precise instructions, and Aldonza, ever understanding, made sure her husband's will was respected.

Francisco loved to creep into that makeshift sanctuary when his father read or wrote there. He took pleasure in keeping him company, and imitating him: he'd pick up a volume tenderly, wedge it on his chest like precious cargo, place it on the table, open the hard cover, and riffle through page after page of symbols that all looked the same. Colored panels and illustrations rose up from the unruly sea of letters.

Among those volumes, one stood out: *Theater of the Pagan Gods* by the Franciscan Baltazar de Vitoria. It was a spellbinding catalogue of pagan deities, bursting with tales of fabulous beings and the ridiculous beliefs that existed before the arrival of Christ. Brother Antonio Luque was against Francisco's looking inside such a book.

"He'll confuse it with religious material."

His father, on the other hand, believed the book would strengthen the boy's powers of reasoning.

"It'll help him not become confused—that, exactly."

The boy read it out of order. Heroes, gods, filicide, betrayals, metamorphoses, and miracles took place alongside realistic plots. He learned to respect crazy ideas: they had power, too.

When his progress in Latin allowed him to translate a few verses, he played with the *Anthology of Latin Poets* compiled by Octaviano de la Mirándola. His father told Brother Antonio Luque that the poems by Horace found in that volume unfurled a fantastic lyricism and that his phrases penetrated the mind like a welcome rain. But the severe monk was not interested in lyricism, only faith.

"Horace's morals," Don Diego continued, "are pleasing to Christian sentiment."

"Morals," Luque countered dryly, "do not need to be pleasing, only obeyed."

Between the medical and general sections of this personal library stood the six volumes of Pliny's *Naturalis Historia*. It would take Francisco years to read them in their entirety. Those fascinating volumes distilled the thirty-seven books written by that brilliant Roman, a hungry man who devoured all the knowledge of his time. Francisco studied without limits, starting with the origin of the universe and everything it contained; Pliny even knew Earth was round. Don Diego had boundless admiration for Pliny. By his count, this Roman scholar had studied a grand total of two thousand books by 140 Roman authors and 326 Greeks. His thirst for knowledge was so intense that he avoided walking in order to save time; he was always accompanied by scribes to whom he dictated his observations. His collection was intelligent and, despite his peerless erudition, he had the humility to cite his sources. A few of his observations were astonishing: he affirmed that animals are in tune with their own instinct, act in accordance with it, and in this manner resolve their problems, whereas man knows nothing about himself unless he learns it; the only thing he knows how to do innately is cry. Therefore, the duty of each human being is to learn and become aware, Don Diego added. After hearing that, every time Francisco cried, he said to himself, "I'm behaving like an animal. Now let's see how a man behaves."

Pliny dedicated many pages to fabulous beings. It delighted him to describe people with backward-pointing feet, mouthless animals who ate by inhaling scents, winged horses, unicorns, people with such colossal fingers that they could cover their entire heads with them, like hats.

"Is it all true, what Pliny wrote?" asked Francisco.

"I'm not even sure it was true for him," his father answered, stroking his beard, which was carefully trimmed and flecked with gold. "But he wrote it because it was true for somebody. He took on the task of compiling, not of censoring."

"Then how do we know if it's true?"

Don Diego shook his leonine head. "That's the great dilemma of all thinkers," he sighed. "Or of those who love thought."

5

Next to the cedar bookcase that held the beloved books, there stood a chest in which Núñez da Silva kept his best suit and a few linen shirts. At the bottom, hidden by clothes, the curious Francisco found a rectangular case covered in purple brocade, wrapped several times over with a cord and closed with a knot.

"What's this?" he asked his mother, having taken the strange object to her.

"Where did you get that?"

"From the chest. From Papá's room."

"With whose permission? Don't you know you shouldn't snoop through people's things?"

"I didn't go through anything," the boy said, afraid. "I left the clothes as they were. But I just—I found this."

"Put it back in its place," Aldonza ordered with sweet severity. "And don't go in that room when your father isn't there."

"All right." He hesitated, turning the case between his small, dirty fingers. "But—what is it?"

"A family keepsake."

"What kind of keepsake?"

"All I know is that it's a family keepsake." She glanced around her and whispered nervously, "A wife shouldn't ask questions that a husband doesn't want to answer."

"Then—it must be something bad," Francisco mused.

"Why?"

"Papá always answers. I'm going to ask him what this is."

Aldonza blushed. Nothing seemed to escape this child. "For now, put that case back exactly where you found it. When your father returns, try not to bother him with unnecessary questions."

"I want to know what this family keepsake is."

Don Diego had gone to the outskirts of a plantation to attend to sick Indians. The Indian overseer had come to him personally, full of worry: he feared the outbreak of an epidemic.

"What's an epidemic?" Francisco had asked as his father organized his instrument case.

"The rapid spread of a disease."

"How is it cured?"

"I wouldn't say it can be cured, only restrained." He gestured toward Luis to pick up the case, as, with the other hand, he made reassuring motions in an effort to keep the Indian overseer calm.

"Restrained? Like a horse?"

"Not exactly. It must be isolated. Locked in, with a kind of wall."

"Are you going to build a wall around the Indians who have the epidemic?"

Don Diego smiled at his son's persistent curiosity. "Only figuratively. First I need to find out whether what the foreman heard is true."

That night, as soon as his father returned, Francisco let loose another question. "What's in that purple case in the chest?"

"Let him unwind," Aldonza protested. She'd run to receive her husband with a cup of chocolate and some sprigs of mint.

"Is it an epidemic?" young Diego said, approaching.

Don Diego tousled Francisco's hair and addressed his older son. "Fortunately, no. I think the foreman jumped to that conclusion out of fear. That man is too cruel. He demands so much of the Indians that he ends up believing they'll unleash an epidemic to avenge themselves."

Francisco's eyes stayed glued on his father, who owed him an answer.

"I'll talk to you about what's in the case," he finally answered. "But first I need to bathe, all right?"

The little boy couldn't contain his joy, and he thanked his father in advance. He went out to the garden, picked some ripe purple and white figs and lustrous pomegranates—his father's favorite fruits—washed them, and arranged it all on a copper tray.

Don Diego entered the dining room in clean clothes, emanating freshness after his bath. His damp hair and beard shone, dark and bright. In his hand, he held the mysterious case. He placed it on the table. Francisco climbed onto the chair beside him; Diego, Isabel, and Felipa also gathered round, though Aldonza kept her distance, seeming uninterested in the matter. In reality, it unsettled her, but she didn't dare express this discomfort with anything other than silence.

"It's a family keepsake," their father warned. "Don't get your hopes up."

He untied the knot that held the thick cord in place. He stroked the worn brocade, which had no inscription of any kind. He looked up, seeking better light, and asked for the candelabra to be brought closer. The strong flames made the old cloth glimmer.

"This has no material worth. But its spiritual worth is boundless."

He lifted the lid.

"A key . . ."

"Yes, a key. A simple iron key." He cleared his throat, raised his eyebrows, and said, "There's an engraving on the handle. Can you see it?"

All the children leaned in closer as their father adjusted the candelabra. They made out an image.

"It's a three-pointed flame," he explained. "It might be the flame of a torch. That's what it looks like. A symbol, no? The engraving itself is nothing exceptional." He cleared his throat again. "So why do I keep this object in a case and consider it so valuable?"

Francisco leaned in until his nose was almost touching the key; he could smell it, but he couldn't decipher the mystery. Don Diego held it out to him, solemnly, as if it were a hallowed thing.

"Touch it. It's pure iron, no silver or gold at all. My father gave this to me, in Lisbon. His own father gave it to him. It comes from Spain, from a beautiful house in Spain."

Francisco picked up the key gingerly, holding it with both hands the way priests hold up bread and wine to consecrate it during Mass. The flickering light of the candelabra reverberated on its coarse surface. It seemed to emit a radiance of its own: the small three-pointed flame on the rusted handle gleamed.

"It belongs to the lock of a majestic set of doors once walked through by many princes. In that home there was a gorgeous room where gatherings were held around precious documents that were written there, and copied there. Look at the key's texture. It was made by a blacksmith known for his holiness. He used metal filings that had never been part of any weapon, that had never hurt a man. That faint yellow patina covering it is like a robe protecting something that's never tarnished. This key was stroked by great princes, remember, whose dignity and wisdom we can just barely hope to emulate. When those princes, against their will, had to stop going to that splendid place, and our ancestors had to abandon that house, they closed the sturdy door and decided to carefully guard the key. Yes, this simple and, at the same time, precious key symbolizes those documents, that room, that whole assembly of dignitaries, the magnificent home of our Spanish ancestors. I'll tell you more: my great-grandfather tied the key to his belt. He never parted with it, even though he had to weather storms that would have frightened the bravest among us. When the angel of death came to visit him, even in his weakened state, he would not loosen his grip on the engraved handle. His son, my grandfather, had to tear it from his hand, weeping as though he were committing sacrilege. That's when he sewed the case and lovingly wrapped it with brocade so that the shameful story of forcing a dead man's hand would never have to be repeated. My grandfather told my father to guard this object as though it were a treasure. My father said the same to me. And now I'm telling you."

A heavy silence fell. Don Diego's four children were bewildered. The candlelight streaked their cheeks with red.

Their father lifted the relic close to the faces of Diego, Felipa, Isabel, and Francisco, in that order.

"Take another look at the flame in the engraving. Doesn't it seem enigmatic? Can you imagine what those three points might mean? No? Look: they resemble three petals, each one held up by a wand, and those wands in turn rest on a thick horizontal beam."

He paused for further questions, but their astonishment left no room for opinions.

"One day you'll know." He brought the key to his lips and kissed it. "The princes and our ancestors believed they would return to that house. That's why we guard the key."

Finally, Francisco stammered, "Can we return?"

"I don't know, my son, I don't know. When I was little I dreamed of becoming one of those legendary princes and opening those majestic doors."

—⁓—

The young Alba Elena is startled awake by the noise and starts to cry. Her mother takes her in her arms. Francisco Maldonado da Silva tries to approach them, but the officials grasp his arms all the more tightly, their hands firm as shackles. His stunned young wife, holding their daughter, approaches the nightmarish group, which is illumined by the lamp of Lieutenant Juan Minaya.

"Don't be afraid," Francisco manages to say.

"Silence!" orders the lieutenant.

Francisco strains against them. The officials grasp him harder.

"I won't escape," he exclaims with unexpected authority, meeting their eyes.

The human shackles are paralyzed. A surprised doubt invades those military bodies. They suddenly remember that this man is a physician whom the authorities have honored, whose father-in-law is a former governor of Chile.

Little by little the rough fingers loosen, and Francisco frees himself. He recovers his poise and walks toward his beloved Isabel Otáñez and their daughter. He dries the mother's tears and kisses the child. He fears that he may never see them again. They will take him to war. To the most unjust of wars, the results of which are only known by God.

6

Francisquito's brother Diego invited him to go fishing. First, they would go and fetch Diego's friend Lucas Graneros, and then they would walk together to the River of Tiles. Lucas's father had a wagon factory that supplied the entire province. He had built an enormous enterprise. He'd been shrewd enough to channel the abundance of wood found in Ibatín into the large-scale production of the best imaginable transportation between the northeastern mountains and the port of Buenos Aires. He'd grown rich faster than many of the gold seekers. He owned 120 black slaves, as well as Indians and mestizos who skillfully worked the chisel and carpenter's plane.

Graneros had built his home in a neighborhood of artisans. There, as soon as dawn broke, the forges lit up and the workshops hummed with noise. Everyone knew the silversmith Gaspar Pérez, who created pieces for altars, as well as the shoemaker Andrés, who fashioned rustic boots, monks' sandals, and fine footwear with copper buckles. The saddler Juan Quisna repaired harnesses, polished saddlebags, and sewed saddles. The tailor Alonso Montero made doublets, ribbed jackets, habits for religious dignitaries, and suits for royal officials. The hatmaker Melchor Fernández molded the thick felt that covered the heads of captains, feudal public servants, and magistrates. Almost all of them were men with some mix of indigenous blood, though they were anxious to assimilate into the culture of the European conquerors. They dressed like Spaniards and strove to speak only Spanish.

The morning promised to be a hot one. Francisco was carrying a slingshot that the enslaved Luis had made for him with the bladder of an ox. He used it compulsively, aiming at any target: a wild fruit, a flower on a bush, a faraway pebble. He'd become infallible in hitting the lizards that darted like sparkling arrows. The first time he hit one on the head he buried it with honors, even making a cross out of two twigs to mark its tomb. "Anyone who kills lizards with a slingshot is not only agile, but also clever," his father had declared.

The neighborhood of artisans emitted a spicy scent, a mix of metal, leather, dyes, and wool. Behind the workshops, a pair of tall walnut trees marked the entrance to Graneros's factory. It was gigantic, so extensive that it had been nicknamed "a nation." Under an awning stood carpentry tables, boxes of tools, and scraps of copper and brass. Several wagons were finished, while others resembled the skeleton of a prehistoric animal. Curiously, the compact assembly could be achieved without a single nail, and the structure of these vehicles was so sturdy that they could carry at least two tons. The wheels were a marvel, more than two feet in diameter; two of them could sustain the entire weight of the wagon and its cargo, and they were joined by a single, sturdy axle. The center of the wheel was a solid mass carved from the center of a tree trunk.

Lucas told the brothers that his father had given him a spinning top for his birthday.

"It's this big." The boy demonstrated with his hands. "The size of a pear."

It had been made from light wood and a metal tip. Then it had been painted with bright colors.

"May I take this piece of wood?" asked Francisco.

"Of course," Lucas responded, as he examined his sack of bait. "What do you need it for?"

"To make myself a top just like yours."

Lucas laughed. He picked up another piece and walked toward a group of men. The conversation was so brief that when the brothers approached he could already tell them that the following day he would give Francisco a spinning top just like his own.

"With a metal tip, and nicely painted!"

He leapt with happiness.

"For now, I'll lend you mine," Lucas offered.

Francisquito took it, overjoyed.

They headed for the river, leaving behind the active commotion of the workshops, and took a path that was partially shaded by oaks. They arrived at the equally busy northern terrace, crammed with merchants, slaves hauling cargo, and packs of mules prepared to take new burdens. From the large inn, whose walls bore strange remnants of red paint, there spilled a group of strangers, while another group entered a grocery store shaded by the foliage of a carob tree. Beside the great gate in the fence, a small chapel stood watch. They went through the gate, into the deep, compelling jungle.

A few minutes later they arrived at the river; its waters resounded between the verdant shores. They climbed to the rocky edge that both Diego and Lucas considered the best spot for casting their lines. As they prepared their bait and tackle, Francisco played with Lucas's top. There were a few horizontal slabs among the rocks, like wide steps. He wound the string around the shiny wood, tied the end to his index finger, and threw it down at an angle. The metal tip drew sparks from the rock. The toy spun madly, its stripes becoming blurred rings of color. The top reached the stone's edge and fell down to the next level, still spinning. Then it tilted from side to side, as if uncertain, and lifted its metal tip as if it were an animal with a wounded foot. Francisco picked it up, rewound the string, and aimed to make the top descend more stones. He calculated the distance, pulled back his arm, lifted his opposite leg, and threw the toy at a slant. Its landing was sure: the top advanced quickly toward the stone's edge, leapt to the next one down, kept spinning, progressed to the next edge, leapt again, went on spinning, and Francisco began to shout and urge it on with palm fronds.

"Three steps! Come on! Let's go, let's go! The fourth!"

"The fourth!" exclaimed Lucas.

Diego became excited, too. He left the fishhooks and approached the toy, which kept spinning, though it was starting to show signs of fatigue. It grazed the edge of the fifth step, but it leaned too far and fell, landing upside down. It kept turning, as if angry with itself.

"What a shame."

"It was too good," Lucas said.

"It's going to fall off!" warned Diego.

It was true: the top was almost at the rocky cliff's edge. In an instant, they'd lose it to the river. Diego lunged to grasp it and slipped on a clump of grass. His foot jabbed right into a hole.

Lucas and Francisco rushed to his aid. The crevice was deep and sharp edged. They couldn't pull his leg out. Carefully, they turned Diego to realign his body with the hole's shape, until finally they could move his leg. They pulled him out slowly, sweating under Diego's screams. His ankle was covered in blood, and a chunk of flesh hung loose from his leg. Despite the pain, Diego had the presence of mind to ask Lucas to bandage the wound.

"With your shirt, with whatever you've got. Quick! It's got to stop bleeding."

Then they carried him: Lucas took him by the shoulders, and Francisco by the knees. They asked for help from a group of black men, who lent them their donkey. Everyone helped Diego mount; he wrapped his arms around the beast's neck. They walked home, followed by the retinue of men, who were afraid of losing the donkey. They put him to bed immediately. Aldonza ran in search of salves. Diego fought to mask his pain, insisting that it wasn't serious. The shirt turned tourniquet was now dark red. Luis brought in a washbowl full of warm water, undid the bandage, and carefully washed the skin, fearless at the sight of so much blood. He adjusted the hanging flap of skin and wrapped a clean bandage around the wound. He placed three pillows under the boy's leg so that his ankle would be higher than the rest of his body. Then he left in search of the doctor.

Lucas stayed with his friend until Don Diego arrived. Francisco blamed the accident on the spinning top. The doctor took a sweeping look at the prone body, and asked questions as he examined the limb. He requested more warm water, and for everyone to move aside so as not to obstruct the light. The slave lifted Diego's leg, and the doctor unwound the bandage almost all the way. The boy began to complain of pain, because the cloth had become stuck. Luis poured water while Don Diego maneuvered until he'd completely freed the ankle. He chose a pair of tweezers and extracted the imperceptible foreign objects that had insisted on remaining lodged in the gash. Then he approached the borders of the bluish flap of skin, and pulled it up. Diego gritted his teeth. His father covered the raw flesh with a milky powder, a blend of willow bark and zinc filings.

"You'll be fine in three weeks. Now you need repose. There's no need for a cast. You'll also take a teaspoon of this medicine."

He opened his medical case and took out a glass jar.

"This is a medicine used by the Indians of Peru. It calms pain and lowers fevers."

Turning to his wife, who was staring in anguish, he added, "Every time I've used this, it's been effective. Even more than mandrake."

"What's it called?"

"Quinine. They extract it from a plant called *quina*." He sat back down beside his son's bed, took the boy's pulse, and intensely studied his face. Then he gestured for the others to leave the room. Did he want to remove Diego's clothes and give him a complete exam?

Lucas took his leave. Aldonza and Francisquito accompanied him to the front door. But Francisquito wondered why his father would want to give Diego a full examination. It didn't make sense. He'd only injured his ankle, and the remedy had already been applied. Might he want to give him intimate medical advice that only boys could hear? Well, wasn't he, Francisco, himself a boy? A good opportunity to find out. He stealthily returned to the silent room, which was thick with the odor of unguents.

Don Diego stroked his son's forehead as his son gazed back at him with gratitude.

"I've never had such a bad fall before. It hurts a lot."

"I know. You're wounded in a very sensitive area. The quinine powder will help. I'll also prescribe herbal infusions that can act as sedatives. That's all that can help from the outside, and—" He broke off. After a little while, he repeated the last words. "From the outside—"

Francisco crawled along the dim edge of the room and managed to hide a short distance from the bed. He knew this way of introducing a difficult topic: his father sweetened his voice, stroked his brown hair or the edge of a table, and repeated certain words.

"Do you understand, my son?"

The boy nodded to please his father, but he didn't understand. Nor did Francisco.

Don Diego's mouth contorted. "What I'm trying to say, my son, is that not all the help you need comes from outside of you, like the healing powder, the quinine, or the infusions. You can also get relief from inside, from your spirit."

Was that the intimate subject he wanted to broach? Francisquito felt disappointed. But young Diego nodded again.

"I don't think you fully understand me," his father insisted. He wiped his forehead with a handkerchief; noon was a burning oven.

Was there something else, then? Francisco came closer, curled up like a cat. He couldn't bear to miss a single word.

"The most important cure, the definitive one, comes from the spirit. You should take strength from that cure."

Diego dared to confess his confusion. "I think I understand," he said, "and I think there's something I don't understand—"

"Yes." His father smiled. "It's simple, and it's not. It sounds familiar, obvious, like something you've heard before. But there's another resonance, a profound one, that can't be known without some preparation."

He searched the table for the bottle of blackberry water and took a long drink. Then he dried his lips and settled back into the creaky chair.

"I'll explain. We doctors use healing products drawn from nature. And although nature is the work of God, God has not consecrated it as the absolute resource, but rather has provided human beings, His beloved creatures, with mechanisms that allow them to make contact with Him. An edge of His infinite greatness lives always in our hearts. If we open to it, we can recognize His presence in our minds, in our spirits. No medicine is as effective as that presence."

He dried the sweat from his neck and nose with a cotton handkerchief.

"You wonder why I say this. And why I say it with a certain"—he snapped his fingers, in search of the right word—"solemnity. Well— because it's a matter that concerns my medical practice but—but you are not the same as other patients."

"I'm your son."

"Of course. And this means something special, almost secret. It means something to God, and to our particular relationship with Him."

Francisquito needed to scratch the back of his neck. He itched with confusion and impatience. His father wasn't undoing the knot.

"I should take communion?" Diego guessed, in an effort to unravel this enigma.

His father moved his shoulders to loosen his back. He was tense, but wanted to appear relaxed.

"Communion? No. That's not what I'm trying to express to you. The host slides from your mouth to your stomach, from the stomach to the intestine, from there to your blood, to the rest of your body. But I'm not talking about the host, or about communion, or about rites, or about anything that comes into you from the outside. I'm talking about the uninterrupted presence of God inside of you. I'm talking about God, the One."

Diego frowned. Francisco did, too. What new or secret thing was he trying to suggest?

"Don't you understand me? I'm talking about God, the one who heals, consoles, gives light, gives life."

"Christ is the light and the life," the boy recited. "Is that what you're saying to me, Papá?"

"I'm talking about the One, Diego. Think. Look within. Connect with what has lived inside you since before you were born. The One— do you understand, now?"

"I don't know."

"God, the One, the Omnipotent, the Omniscient, the Creator. The One, the One," he repeated emphatically.

Diego's face was turning red. He was prone in his bed, his father seated. Both were very tense. The father's figure seemed gigantic, not only because his body was higher, but because he was forcing his son toward an arduous line of reasoning.

Don Diego smoothed his mustache and his trimmed beard, freeing his lips to speak as he gathered himself like a person about to recite. In a slow and stately voice, he spoke. His words were incomprehensible: *"Shema Israel, Adonai Eloheinu, Adonai Echad."*

Francisco shivered. The only word he recognized was *Israel*. Was it a magical incantation? Did it have something to do with witchcraft?

Don Diego translated, in a tone of devotion. "Hear, O Israel, the Lord, our God, the Lord is one."

"What does it mean?"

"Its meaning is already inscribed in your heart."

The mystery had yet to be revealed. The swollen purple cloud that hid the sun was about to burst. A few of its drops already pearled Diego's forehead.

"For many centuries, this brief phrase has sustained the courage of our ancestors, my son. It synthesizes history, morality, and hope. This phrase has been repeated under persecution and amid murders. It has sung out between flames. It connects us to God like an unbreakable gold chain."

"I've never heard it before."

"You have heard it, of course you've heard it."

"In church?"

"Inside your own being. In your spirit." He extended both index fingers to mark the rhythm. "Listen, Diego. 'Hear, O Israel' . . . Listen, my son: 'Hear, O Israel.'" His voice fell to a whisper. "Listen, my son. Listen, son of Israel, listen."

Diego sat up, stunned.

His father placed his hands on Diego's chest and gently made him lie back down. "You're starting to understand." He sighed. His voice became more intimate. "I'm revealing a great secret to you, my son. Our ancestors lived and died as Jews. We belong to the lineage of Israel. We are the fruits of a very old tree."

"We're Jews?" A grimace deformed young Diego's face.

"That's right."

"I don't want to be—I don't want to be *that*."

"Can an orange tree not be an orange tree? Can a lion be other than a lion?"

"But we're Christians. And," his voice faltered, "Jews are traitors."

"Are we traitors, then?"

"The Jews killed Our Lord Jesus Christ."

"Did I kill him?"

"No." He forced a smile. "Of course not. But the Jews—"

"I am Jewish."

"The Jews killed him. They crucified him."

"Did you kill him? You are a Jew."

"God and the Sacred Virgin protect me! No!" Diego crossed himself in horror.

"If it wasn't you, and it wasn't me, then it's clear that 'the Jews,' that 'all of the Jews,' are not guilty. Also, Jesus was as Jewish as we are. Let me correct myself, Diego: He was perhaps even more Jewish than we are. He grew up, studied, and preached in cities that were manifestly Jewish. Many of those who worship him in fact abhor his blood, they abhor Jesus's Jewish blood. Their thoughts are filled with horse droppings: they hate what they love. They can't see how close to Jesus every Jew actually is, for the simple reason that they belong to the same lineage, the same history plagued with suffering."

"So then, Papá, we . . . I mean, the Jews, they—we—didn't kill him?"

"I did not participate in his arrest, or in his trial, or in his crucifixion. Did you? Or my father? Or my grandfather?"

The boy shook his head.

"Do you realize what an atrocious lie has been spread? Not even the Gospel claims it. The Gospel says that 'some' Jews called for the execution, but not 'all.' Because otherwise, my son, they'd have to include the apostles, as well as his mother, Mary Magdalene, Joseph of Arimathea, and the first community of Christians. Are they also irredeemable criminals? Absurd! Right? Jesus, the Jewish Jesus, was arrested by the powers of Rome, which had conquered Judea. It was the Romans who tortured him in their dungeons, in the same dungeons where they'd tortured hundreds of other Jews like him, and like us. The Romans invented the crown of thorns to mock the Jew who tried to become a king and liberate his brothers. Death by crucifixion was also invented by them, and it wasn't just Jesus and a couple of thieves who died on the cross, but also thousands of Jews in a time that started before Jesus was born and lasted long after his death. A Roman speared his right side and Roman soldiers drew straws over who would get his clothes. Meanwhile, it was Jews who faithfully brought him down from the cross and buried him with care and grace. It was Jews who remembered and shared his teachings. And still, Diego, and still . . ." Here he paused for a long time. "Nobody harps on what the Romans did, that the Romans and not the Jews mocked and killed Our Lord Jesus Christ. The Romans are not persecuted. And no one insists on blood free of Roman stains."

"Why so much rage against Jews, then?"

"Because they can't stand our refusal to submit."

"Jews don't accept Our Lord and Savior."

"The real conflict isn't a religious one. They don't long for our conversion. No. That would be easy. They've already converted whole communities of Jews. In truth, Diego, they're battling to make us disappear. That's what they want, for better or for worse. Your great-great-grandfather was dragged by horses to the baptismal waters and then they tormented him because he changed his shirt on Saturdays. He was forced to leave Spain. But he didn't give up. He brought the key with him, the key to his old home, and he had it engraved with a little three-pointed flame."

"What does it mean?"

"It's a letter from the Hebrew alphabet: *shin.*"

"Why that letter?"

"Because it's the beginning of many words: *shema,* listen; *shalom,* peace. But, above all, it's the first letter of the word *shem,* which means "name." That is to say, the ineffable Name of God. *Shem,* the Name, has infinite power. Many Kabbalists have studied the matter."

"Who?"

"Kabbalists. I'll explain it to you one day, Diego. The essential thing right now is that you understand the profound decision that many Jews have taken. The decision to keep existing, even if only through the conservation of a few rites and traditions."

Diego was confused. He could not absorb this flood of facts and arguments; he could only be astonished. Francisco, still in the shadows, didn't understand either. Both of them were disconcerted, shot through with an unfamiliar fear. Diego in bed, and Francisco in his hiding place, both of them breathing hard. Their father's words were an earthquake that fractured them into contradictory pieces.

"But we're Catholic." Diego couldn't let this go. "We're baptized. I've had my confirmation. We go to church, we confess. We're Catholic, aren't we?"

"Yes, but by force. Saint Augustine himself said something like, 'If we are dragged to Christ, we believe without wanting to believe; and one can only believe when one arrives to Christ through the path of freedom, not of violence.' We have had violence used against us, and it continues to this day. The effect is tragic. We appear Catholic on the outside in order to survive in the flesh, and we're Jewish on the inside in order to survive in spirit."

"It's terrible, Papá."

"It is. And it was for your great-grandfather, and your grandfather, too. As it is for me. What do we want? Simply, for them to let us be what we are."

"What should I do to—to become a Jew?"

His father laughed gently. "You don't need to do anything. You're already Jewish. Haven't you heard it said that we're considered 'New Christians'? I'll tell you our history, my son. It's an admirable history, rich and painful. I'll explain what's called the Law of Moses, which God gave to our people long ago on Mount Sinai. I'll explain many beautiful traditions that confer enormous dignity to this harsh life."

He leaned his hands on his knees so he could rise.

"Now rest. And don't tell anyone our secret. No one."

He looked at the bandage, touched it softly, and rearranged the pillows under his son's leg.

Francisco stayed on the floor, curled up in a trembling ball, until he was called for lunch. Then he snuck out without being seen.

7

The academy in the orange grove held class in the afternoons, after the heat of siesta time subsided. Brother Isidro would arrive punctually and take his place at the table made of carob wood. He would rub his bulging eyes and wipe a thin lock of gray hair from his face. He'd set out his materials and wait for his students to take their places. As befitted an instructor, he tried to be severe—his eyes helped with this—but he could not hide his tenderness.

One day, in early February, he arrived in the morning, as soon as Mass was over. It was the first time he'd ever come at that hour. He was empty-handed and his face was extremely pale, giving him a harsh look. He asked to meet with the doctor. "Urgently!" he exclaimed. Francisquito took advantage of the visit to tell his teacher that he'd succeeded in translating another verse of Horace: he could show it to him right this moment. The monk forced a smile and gently pushed him aside.

"First I must speak to your father."

"Yes, my father's on his way," the boy insisted. "I can read it to you while we wait."

The monk was in no mood to concentrate. Aldonza invited him into the parlor and offered him hot chocolate. He thanked her but did not drink and would not even sit. When the doctor appeared he sprang toward him with a frightening urgency. He grasped his arm and murmured into his ear. The two men left for the back courtyard. Francisquito looked questioningly at his mother, who had also turned pale.

They saw the way the monk waved his hands with unusual nervousness, but they couldn't hear what he was saying. The birds' cacophony in the cheerful orange grove seemed out of tune with the old teacher's anguish. Don Diego listened to him in shock.

When they came back inside, Aldonza offered the hot chocolate again, but the monk excused himself with a whisper and left swiftly, head down, clutching his crucifix with both hands.

All of a sudden, the placid morning burst into movement. The efficient and loyal Aldonza—at her husband's laconic instruction—ordered the preparation of chests, trunks, and boxes: they were cleaned, distributed, and packed with all the possessions in the house. "Understand? Everything. Take apart the large pieces of furniture and tie them as compactly as possible." Luis and Catalina listened, not believing their ears. Immediately, the four children and Aldonza herself joined in the tasks.

Don Diego got dressed and went out to visit the sick, as he did every day; he returned for lunch. When they sat down at the table he passed the bread around, made sure that all were served their stew, and said that he would now share the important news.

"We're leaving this city."

There could be no other reason for the madness that had rapidly overcome the household. Why are we leaving? Why such a hurry? Their father ate slowly, as was his habit. (Or was he eating this way on purpose, now, to transmit a sense of calm?) He dipped his bread in the stew as he explained that this change would be good for the family: he'd been planning it for a long time, almost hoping for it. (Was he lying?) The opportunity had arrived: this very night, a caravan was heading south and they would take advantage of it.

"Tonight?" Isabel and Felipa exclaimed in unison.

"Also," he added emphatically, determined to prevent panic, "we'll like our new home: we're moving to Córdoba."

"Córdoba?" Francisquito repeated, startled.

"That's right. A small and delightful settlement surrounded by gentle mountains, with a peaceful river running through it. More tranquil than this Ibatín, with its menacing jungle, its Calchaquí Indians, and all its growth. We'll have a better life."

Francisquito asked whether the place would resemble the Córdoba of his ancestors. Don Diego said yes, that this was the very reason the founder had given it this name.

Felipa wanted to know how long the journey would take.

"About fifteen days."

Isabel wasn't listening. Her chin had sunk to her chest and she was shaking with rhythmic intensity. Her mother embraced her. Between hiccups and tears she coughed out, "Why? Why are we leaving? We're fleeing something."

Aldonza dried her cheeks, sweetly, and closed her daughter's lips. Francisquito was irritated by his sister's lack of sense. And her lack of interest in the legendary city of their ancestors. But then, in a flash, he understood that she was right. They were leaving Ibatín forever and they were doing it fast, too fast. A lump rose in his throat.

Felipa also started to cry. The only one who stayed calm was young Diego. What did Diego know? Since his accident he'd started having long talks with his father, accompanying him on his medical rounds; at night, they read together in the private room. So, then, what did Diego know?

"Why don't we leave with a different caravan?" Francisquito tried to offer a proposal that would relieve everyone.

His father did not answer him and called for more stew. During the entire lunch Aldonza did not say a word. She was carrying out her husband's will with her usual submissiveness. She had difficult questions, but she kept them buried in her chest. She loved her husband

and her family, and, in addition, she'd been raised to be a good woman: sweet and obedient.

The siesta that afternoon was brief and uncomfortable. Chaos had invaded every corner. The events of the day brought anxiety; they hurt. Francisquito learned, at that tender age, that in the course of a single day a family and its essential possessions can be moved, a neighborhood parted with, explanations offered to satisfy the infinite curiosity of acquaintances, an executor hired to handle business affairs. This precocious experience, lived through as an innocent, would serve him many years later.

The wagon arrived in the evening, parking in front of the door. It had gigantic wheels and a colossal body, which was covered in leather. The two yoked oxen blared. Several laborers carried out the trunks and furniture. Aldonza, with undisguisable tension, begged for that desk to be lifted with care, and for this chest to be set down gently, for the curved edges of the armoire not to be banged, and for the armrests of chairs to be well secured by rope. An assortment of tables, pots, pillows, keepsakes, blankets, pans, beds, straw mattresses, clothes, candelabras, rugs, tears, sighs, chamber pots, suitcases, and urns made their way rapidly from inside the house to the wagon.

The rooms became empty and bleak. Francisco spoke to the echo, that new invisible presence that had taken his family's place. A few scattered candles illuminated their last night, during which no one slept because nothing was left, not even the rush mats. Their father extinguished the candles one by one, as if ending a ritual. The house was a dead being they were leaving respectfully, and with an unnamable oppressiveness.

When he thought everyone was asleep, Don Diego went out to the courtyard. A tenuous light poured through the foliage. He stayed still in his beloved orange grove, taking in its branches, its hidden fruit, its slow verdant breath. The trees formed an enigmatic awning, a weave through which the stars blinked. He focused on a very bright one.

And he confided his fears. Then, in a very low voice, he recited psalms that praised the beauty of the night and the scent of plants. Finally, he confided in a listening star that he still hoped to return; he had dreamed of settling in this place forever. This did not appear to be the will of the Lord. He walked closer to one of the trees and leaned against it. He stayed still, feeling its dampness. He made it his—the leaves and branches, the scent and freshness, as though he could transfer a physical temple into his spirit, transform it into something portable. He prayed to God for them not to be caught on the dangerous road.

They had to leave before dawn. The moon was still dusting salt over the rooftops. Don Diego returned to the naked rooms and started gently calling his family member's names: Aldonza, Diego, Isabel, Felipa, Francisco. The enslaved Luis and Catalina did not need to be summoned: they were ready, with the last bundles on their heads.

There was a last, terrible attempt at resistance from Isabel and Felipa: they clung to a doorjamb, crying, crouching, demanding to stay. Finally they entered the dark womb of another wagon, climbing the ladder attached to the back opening. Francisco followed them, full of curiosity, his way barely lit by a hanging lantern. Several straw mattresses were spread throughout the vast tube. A lattice, held in place by wooden stakes on both sides, was covered in leather. The roof was held up by arches made of flexible wood shaped into an oval structure, from which rain would likely run off. The enormous cylinder resembled a chapel, reduced in size and suspended in air. He looked for a place to sit between the soft bundles and people. He preferred to be near the front, where he could see the road. He tripped over a pile of blankets and a pair of legs.

Astonishment and joy ran through him: a man sat leaning against a stake. Despite the darkness, Francisco recognized him as the lantern glowed across one side of the man's face.

"Brother Isidro! What are you doing here?"

The old priest gathered his legs in so the boy could keep going forward. But Francisco decided to stay by his side.

Don Diego checked to ensure that his whole family was present, calling each person by name and straining to see them in the dark. He included the slaves' names. Aldonza distributed blankets. The wagon lurched into motion.

The axle squeaked and the ropes groaned. The wagon swayed spasmodically, until it settled into a rhythm, slow, unique, like that of a fantastic boat. They crossed the main plaza, which was deserted. The church and town hall gleamed like ghosts. The Spanish cherry tree where a thief had recently been hung was almost impossible to see. The oxen kept on, eastward, and then they turned toward the south. The wagon crossed the neighborhood of the artisan workshops, which were silent as tombs. They could not see the foliage of the walnut trees that marked the start of Don Graneros's property, with its prosperous wagon factory. Francisco hadn't managed to say goodbye to Lucas, though Diego had.

The long adobe walls grew distant. They arrived at the southern terrace, where the shapes of many other wagons could be made out, already in line. Herds of mules, donkeys, and horses held close to the caravan. A few armed officials were examining documents. Don Diego ordered his family to stay quiet inside the vehicle, covered in shadows. Happily, the officials had no interest in the passengers, only in the baggage and goods. They paid more attention to the second wagon, the one that held the family's trunks and furniture.

After half an hour the wagon shook again. The real journey was beginning. The caravan crossed Ibatín's fenced border through the great southern gate. A fine layer of silver covered the countryside. A breeze shuddered through the open space, carrying the scent of freedom. Don Diego touched the monk's hand, a gesture of understanding: for now, they were escaping the long arm of the Inquisition.

The rhythmic sway lulled almost all of them to sleep.

8

The sunny morning undid the coolness of the night. Blankets, shawls, doublets, and jackets were cast off like hindrances. Sweat gathered and glistened on the oxen's haunches. The laborer driving the wagon, seated under the front roof on a suitcase full of his own clothing, watched the animals move as if watching the movement of trees. Don Diego examined his gun and placed it between his legs. Then he said, "Near here is the road toward the City of Caesars."

He seemed about to say more, but then stopped to prick his ears toward the creaking of the stakes.

"What's the City of Caesars like?" asked Francisco, crossing his legs.

"They say that its streets are paved in gold," his father said, stretching, without disturbing the firearm. "All the homes are palaces. The residents have developed arts and agriculture, and they enjoy the best fruits and vegetables."

"Is it far away?"

"Nobody has been able to get there," Brother Isidro said.

"It's that far?"

"It's possible that the residents have been able to throw explorers off their scent," Don Diego explained. "It's possible that we've passed close by without realizing it. Who knows? Maybe certain tribes enjoy the city's protection in exchange for leaving clues to confuse seekers, and then, if someone gets too close, they attack and kill him."

"I'd like to go to the City of Caesars," Francisco admitted.

"When will we stop to rest?" asked Felipa.

"At ten o'clock."

The caravan was heading toward a small forest. They were now quite far from the mountain range, and from such a distance they could take in its majesty. In the foothills they could glimpse the blurry village of Ibatín. The jungle was a distant black strip with purple patches. There they crouched: the dangers of nature, the Calchaquí people, and the Inquisition.

Every once in a while the doctor and the monk exchanged worried glances. The implacable Brother Antonio Luque would not be satisfied with the disappearance of his suspects. He had already hunted down and arrested, in small remote La Rioja, the alleged Jew Antonio Trelles. It was likely that he would do the same with them.

The guides on horseback marked out a circumference, and the oxen left their path to obey this familiar prod. They were visibly tired. The guides pulled the wagons off the road, forming a great circle. While the travelers stretched their legs on the ground, a few laborers freed the oxen from their yokes so they could eat and drink. A few other laborers looked after the group of donkeys, mules, and horses. The break would last until four in the afternoon, waiting out the six hours of peak heat: the oxen could bear thirst, hunger, rain, darkness, and swollen rivers, but they could not endure heat.

The Núñez da Silva family's wagon was parked beside the one that held their possessions. Two laborers climbed up and placed a set of rungs from one wagon roof to the other. Over this makeshift frame they hung leathers to create a perfect hut under which they could enjoy drafty shade. There, they could eat and then take their siesta. At the center of their wagon circle, a campfire was lit to prepare the meal.

The laborers who worked on these journeys—a mix of black people, Indians, mulattoes, and mestizos, some enslaved, some free—were well trained, and fulfilled their tasks efficiently. By the time the passengers had unwound, the laborers had already slaughtered a cow and butchered it. Soon the redolent smoke of grilling meat hovered over the wagons. Luis unpacked several stools with canvas seats and a small camping table from the wagon, for serving lunch.

Suddenly, the pack of mules strained in many directions, having clearly sensed a threat. The laborers struggled to contain them.

"Pumas," Don Diego confirmed, reaching for his gun.

Brother Isidro called to Francisco and his siblings: "Stay close, don't move."

The fragrance of cooking meat had excited the wild creatures. The mules' terror spread to the rest of the animals. They had to be whipped, pushed, and surrounded to be kept together. Some of the passengers offered to explore the immediate surroundings. The pumas were likely hidden among the reeds, or behind the next copse, or perhaps in the grass. They wouldn't dare attack unless they were very hungry.

After half an hour, calm returned to the improvised corral and people began to relax again. The danger seemed to have passed. Catalina and Luis chose succulent pieces of grilled beef with the tips of knives, arranged them on a pair of trays, and took them to the Núñez da Silva family's table. Those who preferred could savor a stew of vegetables, potatoes, garbanzos, and meat. A small demijohn of wine sufficed for the whole family, with enough to share with the passengers of another wagon. Oranges were passed out for dessert.

The adults folded their jackets as pillows and lay down on the grass. Francisco, for his part, was still restless from all the excitement and preferred to devote this first respite in the journey to satisfying his curiosity. He studied the undersides of the wagons, as if they were intimate areas of a body. Crouched and alert, he stared at and touched the floor that seemed so firm when one was traveling inside, but which was actually made of a rough material pulled over planks. The wagon's body extended over a long beam that connected it to the yoke. He stroked the beam, which was smooth and stained with ox sweat and road dust. Then he walked to the circle of coals where the meat had cooked. The fire was going out. He went toward the group of oxen, near the stream. Nearby, the other livestock grazed.

"Why can't mules have babies?" he'd asked his brother Diego in Ibatín, as they watched a drove of them.

"Because they're born from a donkey and a horse. They're artificial. They can't propagate themselves. They weren't part of Noah's Ark."

"No?"

"No. They're an intrusive species. They didn't appear on the fifth day of creation, like the rest of nature's beasts. They appeared a long time after that, when a donkey, instead of coupling with a female of its own species, did it with a female horse."

"Is that wrong?"

"I think it's wrong."

"Then why does anyone raise mules? And sell them? And use them?"

"For that very reason. They're useful and strong. They're ideal for transporting cargo at a good pace, and for moving across rocky terrain. They're an invention that helps men get rich."

"And it's not possible to have a male and female mule together? To 'couple,' as you put it?"

"It almost never happens. And if it does, the female mule isn't fertile."

"Why not?"

"Because that's how it is. She's sterile. As I said, a donkey and a horse can make a mule, but mules have no offspring. They can't produce anything—not another mule, not a horse, not a donkey."

At that moment, Francisco's thoughts were interrupted. A few laborers came running.

"Over there! Over there!"

They ran toward the campfire, which had already been covered with earth—"Over there, over there!"—and on to the corral, where they formed a ring around the agitated animals. Those traveling with guns aimed them at the reeds. Three terrified donkeys had separated from the herd; they were trotting off, chased by a copper-colored brightness.

Out of the grass a puma shot up like an arrow.

In that moment, Francisco witnessed an extraordinary thing.

One of the three donkeys slowed down, while the other two kept on. It didn't turn to charge at the puma, but, rather, offered its rump while twisting its head, as if calculating how long it had before being caught. The puma, several meters away, leapt in a bright arc and landed violently on its victim's back. The donkey shook with the blow, but didn't change its posture, as its two companions gained a great distance. It waited, with incredible fortitude, until its ferocious rider had settled into place. Then it threw itself suddenly to the ground, waved its legs in the air, and crushed the puma with its back. It brayed with pain and joy. The puma struggled to escape the lethal trap. It opened its blood-soaked claws and beat its tail against the ground in despair. The donkey kept rubbing its wounded back as if seized with an itch, until it broke the puma's delicate spine. Then it flexed its legs, lifted its head, and rose clumsily.

Don Diego gestured at the other men to lower their guns. There was no need to kill the puma. The donkey was already doing it, in formidable bites, chewing at it with grace. Blood pooled around the animals and smeared their hides. At last, the exhausted donkey stumbled away from what was left of the puma before falling to the ground.

The laborers worked fast, exulting loudly. Shining knives cut the puma's precious skin, which, still damp, was displayed like a flag.

The donkey was gravely injured. Blood flowed rhythmically from its neck. Its jaws were covered in foam. It breathed rapidly.

"It'll have to be sacrificed."

Francisco couldn't bear to watch the crime. He ran back toward the wagon, but nevertheless heard someone say, "It's not worth wasting munitions. Cut its throat."

———————

The receiving lieutenant of the Holy Office pushes the chair that stands in his way. He walks for the door and, impatiently, orders, "Let's go!"

Once again, the officials close their fingers around Francisco's strong arms. They pull him away from his wife. She tries to resist: she moans, shouts, begs. She holds out her daughter, who is bathed in tears—it's all useless. They take Francisco out to the dark road.

"Where are you taking me?"

They push him and, after a few minutes, Lieutenant Minaya tells him, "We're going to the Monastery of Santo Domingo."

9

They resumed their journey after four o'clock. The wagon circle unwound into a long line of twenty laden wagons. In front, as always, the guiding horsemen rode on their agile horses, exploring the terrain ahead and riding back with information.

The family began to talk about the heroic donkey. How it had defended its companions. How it bore the pain of claws and fangs. How it ended up killing the predator with its teeth. How it fought in spite of its own fear.

"But they cut its throat!" Francisquito protested.

His father shook his head and reminded him that the donkey was already dying, that it would have been crueler to abandon it in such a condition of suffering. But the boy couldn't contain his sobbing. Aldonza reached for the earthen pitcher and, trembling, filled a small jug of water. She, too, thought what had happened was an injustice.

The countryside became bereft of trees. The farther they got from the mountain and its seething jungle, the greater the emptiness around them. Grass carpeted the land, at times yellow, at times verdant, while the copses became ever sparser. A fox ran beneath the wagon. In a few stretches, *ñandús* approached, provoking the sudden flight of other birds. The wagon's driver, swaying on his worn suitcase, pointed at crows circling in the sky: in an archaic rite, they were celebrating the death of an animal, and soon they would fall on the carcass to feast.

After several hours of travel, the caravan resumed its wagon circle. Dinner had to be prepared before night fell.

Isabel and Felipa found bushes of wild berries between the bay laurel trees. Their lips turned black as they sampled the fruits with gluttonous speed while also filling a cooking pot with them.

Their dinner was frugal, lit by candles. The berries were served as dessert.

Their stop was brief. The laborers put out the fire and soon the wagons were back in their line. Twenty swaying towers moved in the darkness along a route that had already been assessed by the guiding horsemen. Night was the best time for travel, as the oxen suffered less.

Francisco lay between Don Diego and Brother Isidro. Through the front opening he could see the stooped driver on his old leather suitcase. From the ceiling, a lance-like cattle prod hung like a mythological finger. Through the back opening he saw the black cloth of the firmament stretched over everything, sparking with light. Francisco already knew a few of the constellations. There, for example, was a tail of the Milky Way. There, the Three Marias that formed Orion's Belt. There, a planet. Yes, it was a planet, because it didn't blink: it was round and large like one of Brother Isidro's eyes. He'd been taught that astrologers could diagnose illnesses and predict the future by reading the stars. For them, it was like a kind of text. Why not? God could make a snail of stars one letter, and a snake of stars another. Was the terrestrial alphabet perhaps invented in the image and likeness of the celestial one? Francisco tried to shape an *L, O, C, T, P,* or *M* in the blanket of the stars.

Before going to sleep, he sat up to drink some water. That's when he noticed how the countryside mirrored the firmament. It was an incredible sight. Millions of insects had lit their lamps. They laughed and their lights winked. They laughed and sang. The dark grass was enchanted. It seemed full of diamonds. He reached his hand out, wanting to catch the fireflies, but his brother pulled him back by the belt.

"You're going to fall."

Francisco remained captivated by the feast of lights. It occurred to him that these myriad insects also formed an alphabet. They were the book that God had written into the countryside, just as He had written another one with the stars. Perhaps the one in the countryside was about simpler things. Out in the distance a cluster lit up in the shape of an *A*, and another in a *T*, quickly replaced by a *V* or an *F*. Only those with very good training could read such a book.

He slept.

At dawn, milky vapor rose from the land. The caravan coiled up near a river for the breakfast rest, after having traveled for almost ten hours without pause. The animals needed a break. There was just enough time to heat the chocolate and fry up a meal. Again, the wagons circled up and the oxen were unyoked. The ground was damp. The men ran to hide behind some bushes. The women went in the opposite direction. The animals watched the humans' prudery with bemusement as they went about relieving themselves without concern.

The tributary of the Dulce River that they had to cross this morning had swelled. While breakfast was prepared, the guides surveyed the terrain. They investigated animal tracks, gorges, and the sporadic rocky clearings that offered the safest route. Several passengers who had made this journey before affirmed that though the river ran fast, it wasn't very deep.

One of the bosses selected three guides and ordered them to attempt a crossing. Their horses protested: they bucked, turned, whinnied. Finally, shaking, heads raised high, they entered the turbid waters. A few meters in, their bellies were already wet. The riders spurred them onward. The horses sank deeper. A little farther and they'd reach the shore. Only half of each horse was visible over the choppy surface of the water. They pushed on. The ground seemed firm. The current pressed one horseman to the side; he would take longer to reach his goal. The others started climbing upward. Immediately, the third rider also succeeded. Now they knew the depth of the river. They could cross. Eah! Everyone to their place! Onward!

———————

In the Monastery of Santo Domingo, a hooded monk guides Francisco and his captors down a narrow corridor. The lieutenant walks in front with his lantern, two of the officials grasp the prisoner's arms, and the third one keeps watch from behind, hand on his knife's hilt. Their steps echo gloomily in the darkness, as though they came from a multitude. The monk opens an arthritic cell door. Lieutenant Minaya gestures with his chin and his subordinates push the captive into the tiny black room.

Francisco puts up his hands to keep from slamming into the invisible wall. Immediately, shackles encircle his wrists and ankles. The shackles are soldered to long chains attached to the wall.

The door closes. A key turns and the lock slides into place. The footsteps recede. Francisco touches the damp plaster around him. There is no window, no bench, no table, no mattress. He sits down on the bare, uneven dirt floor. He waits. He will have to wait many hours, perhaps days. He will have to wait in a crouch, blind and defenseless, as the fierce puma leaps onto his tenacious back.

10

During nocturnal travel, candles were forbidden, as they could set the wagon's wood or rush weaving aflame. However, the lantern stayed lit beside the driver as he yawned up on his old suitcase. The vehicle's motion allowed for sleep when a stable rhythm was established, but there were often strong, sudden shudders; the route was full of stones and animal tracks. At times the wagon became stuck, and the driver descended, called for help, wielded logs or dry branches, had the vehicle pushed, and pressed the oxen into motion to free the wheels. Nobody slept through the night.

Meanwhile, the voices of the night offered partial news of its mysteries. The whistle of cicadas was sliced by the screech of an owl, the creak of wagon wheels barely hid the clamor of beasts, and dark wild boars prowled in search of prey. Snakes slithered, viscacha rodents ran, otters congregated, and hares darted around. The long-suffering oxen hauled their yokes at a steady pace while, all around them, the invisible fauna attacked, fled, devoured. There was another risk as well: the cruel Indians of the Chaco.

At dawn, Francisco would glimpse the rosy awakening of the horizon and the moon still hovering high above. Soon the breakfast wagon circle would begin. The morning routine would repeat itself, after which the caravan would resume for a few more hours, until ten o'clock, when the implacable sun attacked the countryside, permitting lunch and siesta. Then they would all do the same things they had done yesterday and would do tomorrow. Later, they would resume the march until the horizon turned purple. Wagon circle, campfire, dinner. They would keep on if the night was clear and the guides could see their way. The caravan was more tired with every passing day. But their destination was close.

One day, at noon, they stopped in a small forest of quebracho trees, the last such forest on their journey. It was said that the wood of quebracho trees never decayed. It was so hard that it exhausted all axes. It was the most vigorous wood in the world.

Rain began to fall and the laborers built a tent so they could keep on cooking. In the late afternoon it rained again. The oxen pressed on, stepping firmly through the mire, not frightened. The river crossing had been worse. After a while, the rain was nothing more than a memory. It would not return for the rest of the journey.

The arid landscape prevailed in the end. The heat and dust increased dramatically. In the afternoons the wind picked up, its whistle often torturous. Wild animals ran through the bare expanse, searching for brush to hide in. The scarce greenery that had accompanied them at the start of their journey had withered into amber and zinc. The lethal salt flats were close. Judging by the birds of prey that glided above them, the caravan seemed to have stalled. The oxen were mere ceramic figurines in the infinite wasteland. They breathed in sandstone. Francisco asked whether they could get lost and end up circling forever in this hostile plain. The answer was no, but his question clearly unsettled the people around him.

Now water had to be rationed. A bony whiteness stretched out before them. Just looking at it made one's eyes hurt. The oxen entered a flatland of endless salt. The evening sun lit the spiny edges of shrubs. The night grew cold, faster than before. The wind scraped, carried voices. Francisco covered his head. Something slid into his nightmare. When he woke he heard his father running after the horses, accompanied by several men. He made to step down to the salt ground, but his mother grabbed him by the arm.

"Don't go!"

That's when he saw a couple of slaves lying prone. Their motionless bodies were dark against the milky ground. A red pool expanded beside them.

"They were killed last night," said Aldonza.

"Why?"

She shook her head. "By thieves, I suppose. They were right beside the wagon with our things."

Francisco broke free and approached the corpses. They were facedown, with wounds on their backs. They had been killed while they slept, or while they kept watch. Brother Isidro stood beside them, worrying his rosary. The laborers murmured among themselves, rowdy, bewildered. One of them told Francisco that his father had been one of the men who went out in search of the criminals.

"Murderous sons of bitches! We'll hang them!" swore a few traders.

"My father will get the thieves and they'll be brought to justice right here," Francisco said.

"If there are no trees a wagon roof can be the gallows," a trader said as he handed a mulatto some rope to try it out. The mulatto smiled slightly and climbed up to the cattle prod, where he secured the rope with skill and pleasure.

"Papá will get those thieves," Francisco said again to his mother.

She rubbed her eyes, as if to wipe away salty sandstone, or tears, or fury.

"Papá was in front. He's brave."

"He's impulsive," she said. "He shouldn't have put himself at risk. It's dangerous." She looked at Francisco and added, "They're criminals. Didn't you see what they did to those poor men?"

Francisco glanced at the inert bodies.

"Your father is a doctor, not a soldier."

Catalina offered them cups of chocolate.

"I know what got him riled up." Aldonza stroked her cup with both hands. "He was called on to tend to the wounded. He couldn't do anything because they were dead, but he saw that they fell beside the wagon that held our things. He realized that a chest was missing." She took a long sip. "Not just any chest—for him."

The chief of the caravan called for the burial of the corpses. He chose the place, and two enslaved men began to dig the hole. No earth came up, only salt. White salt with dark marks slowly piled up. A scrawny vein of water appeared, resembling dirty milk. One shovelful threw a dead weasel into the air; it fell heavily onto the heap. Who knew how long it had been buried in the place that would now be occupied by these two men. It was still whole, revoltingly intact under the sheath of salt that had crusted its worn pelt. They lifted the dead and placed them on cowhides, then, pulling the edges of the hides, slid the bodies into the grave. Other hides served as covers. The soft coffin was quickly covered by the shovelful, while Brother Isidro led the muttering of litanies. Two crosses were nailed over the mound.

The sun burned. Its incandescent breath was reinforced by a sporadic, stifling breeze. The travelers lay in a paralyzed siesta. Their dry lips had to bear the strict rationing of water. That afternoon they would have to go on no matter what, they said, because otherwise the grave for two would become everybody's tomb. "The riders will reach us," one of the foremen said reassuringly, as he ordered the laborers to harvest the fleshy leaves of a cactus. The fat, spiny leaves offered a slight reprieve from thirst.

At three o'clock they began to prepare for their departure. A few specks danced on the horizon. Aldonza gestured to them with excitement. They were not a mirage, promising water and vegetation. They were the riders. They seemed to fly just above the briny plain. Their helmets shone like blue spheres. Where were the thieves? Had the riders killed them and left them for the vultures? The improvised noose awaited a neck around which to close, and did not want to be disappointed.

Don Diego and his companions entered the wagon circle, covered in salt. They were so hoarse that, at first, they could barely speak. They were each offered half a jug of water, and then they unspooled their report in faltering voices. They had not caught up to the murderers. No. The thieves had had too much of an advantage. They'd fled the camp at least an hour before the crime had been discovered. The tracks they'd left at first seemed dependable, and then they didn't. They had separated, to throw off their pursuers. There had been three of them, at least. They had abandoned the trunk during their flight, disappointed in its contents. Here, Don Diego smiled. The thieves had thrown books from the trunk as they'd rummaged through it. They'd disregarded the first layer of volumes with the hope of finding, beneath them, valuables or jewels, and then they sloughed off the second layer. And so on. "These salt flats have never read so much as they did today . . ."

The mulatto untied the noose and, shrugging, returned it to the angry trader.

A few books broke when thrown, while others lost pages, Don Diego told them. He gathered them up, devotedly, as if they were wounded children, while his companions grew impatient because they longed to catch the thieves. They argued, threatening to leave him alone with his ridiculous task. And they did so, but after a while they retraced their steps, as it was not possible to catch up to the criminals. Then they helped him finish collecting his things. That way, they at least wouldn't return empty-handed.

At last, a key penetrates the lock. How long has he been locked up here? He sits up, dizzy. He leans his palms against the cold wall. His shackled wrists and ankles hurt. The door creaks and a shaft of light penetrates the cell. The lamplight undulates, advancing stealthily. The uneven plaster is stained with rust and soot.

He hears another set of steps. As they approach, a black man brings in two chairs and opens a folding table. Then he stands still beside the door, next to a servant holding a lamp. Two monks enter. Their habits are black and white. One is the local commissioner, Martín de Salvatierra. He is accompanied by Marcos Antonio Aguilar, a notary of the Holy Office. They sit. Brother Aguilar readies his inkwell, quill, and paper. Brother Martín de Salvatierra takes out a rolled parchment, opens it, and says, "Doctor Francisco Maldonado da Silva?"

"Yes, Brother Martín."

The commissioner ignores the fact that they know each other, bothered by the prisoner's inappropriate familiar manner.

"Do you swear by the Father, the Son, and the Holy Ghost, and by this sacred cross, to tell the truth?"

Francisco continues to hold his gaze. This same scene has already scorched his nightmares: the functionaries of the Holy Office order and he answers; they demand and he concedes. He makes fists. His wrists have blistered under the iron shackles. He feels as though he's being watched from a great height.

"Forgive me," he coughs.

The monk blinks.

"What is this?"

"I will swear to tell the truth—"

"Then do so."

Francisco continues to hold his gaze. "But not like this."

The notary knocks over his inkwell. One of his servants rushes to his aid.

"What are you saying?" the commissioner growls.

"I will only swear by God."

Thunder shakes the cell.

11

The increasing greenery surrounding the caravan marked the end of their trek. Soon they would arrive in Córdoba, where a new home awaited them, along with new friends and, according to Don Diego's predictions, a more peaceful life. Espinillo trees covered the friendlier, undulating landscape. Blue mountains emerged in the distance. Among the bushes, modest snakewood shrubs showed off their juicy rubies. The first copse of carob trees made for a tempting natural rest stop: the trees extended long branches like the ceiling of a church. Hours later, acacia trees blooming golden flowers appeared. The sudden inclines made it necessary to yoke more oxen in front when going up and then in the back when going down. The air cleared itself of salt and dust. Valleys multiplied between hills and ramparts.

A solitary ranch beckoned them for their midday rest. The travelers hurtled toward the earthen pitchers and the corrals. The ranch dwellers sold lambs, chickens, eggs, and squash. From the well arose one bucket after another of clear, cool water. Prickly pears poked between the stone garden walls, and the travelers collected the flavorful fruit in pots.

The next day they camped beside a river. They were already in the valley that let out onto the city of Córdoba. Hills rose gently on either side of them, thin streams visible between their undergrowth. The narrow road snaked between colored rocks, quartz stones, and green groves. They passed the posts of Quilino, Totoral, and Colonia Caroya. They were one step from their destination.

12

"Isn't it beautiful?" Don Diego exclaimed. "They say it resembles the city of our ancestors. This river is identical to the Guadalquivir. And, close by, the mountains ripple gracefully. Look at how varied and lovely they are!"

Córdoba—the New World one—was far from Lima, the capital of the Viceroyalty. Because of this, it offered the hope of being a good refuge, far from spies and denunciations. But the arm of the Inquisition did not lose strength through distance, and could lengthen like elastic to pursue heretics across mountains; it could cross deserts and leap over the widest canyon.

Don Diego Núñez da Silva had arranged for his family to move into the home of the Brizuelas, thanks to the fact that Juan José Brizuela would be moving to Chile with his wife and two children. With the money he'd receive from his house in Ibatín, Don Diego could pay for the new one in Córdoba. José and Don Diego had known each other for years, and they knew of each other's fears. As a result, the arrangements had been easy to make. They were received warmly and invited to rest under the grapevine while the servants packed up one household to make room for another. The two families lived together for ten intense days.

The house was more modest than the one the Núñez da Silva family had left behind in Ibatín. The young Francisco suffered a disappointment over this, as well as over the lack of orange trees. Instead of an intimate grove, there stretched an awning covered in sumptuous grapevines. The front door was made of two planks linked by strong iron hinges and a rusty knocker someone had brought from Toledo. A hall with an oval ceiling led to the rectangular patio, which was overhung by grapevines; in its center stood a well, decorated with ornamental tiles. The living room opened to the right; it was dark, but the floor was graced with a flowered rug. Several chests and an armchair stood against the walls. Beside the only window, there gleamed a desk. It was upholstered in blue cloth, a sign of luxury. Chairs and colorful cushions invited relaxation. The furnishings were complemented by a religious image on each wall and a couple of framed mirrors. The living room led to the dining room, with its long walnut table, two benches, and four chairs. Further on, the almost bare bedrooms. Behind the patio of the grapes stood the kitchen, the servants' quarters, a small garden, and the animal pen.

Marcos, the Brizuela family's youngest son, was taller and hardier than Francisco. They became fast friends. Francisco told him about Ibatín, the enchanted jungle, the river full of fish, the ferocious Calchaquí Indians, the white chapel of the vice-patrons, the largest wagon factory in the world, the fight between the donkey and the puma on their journey, and the original academy in the orange grove that his father had invented. Marcos listened with undisguised astonishment and, in a gesture of reciprocity, tried to surprise him as well: he described the docility of Cordoban Indians, and recounted a scandal that had recently surrounded the beautiful mulatto Elisa. In addition, in Córdoba, there was something without equal in the world: the wintering of thousands of mules brought up from the pampa and later sold in the north at spectacular gains. Francisco wanted to see this marvel, but his friend offered him something even more compelling: a perfect hiding place. It was a cave behind the animal pen. He took him through the wooden fence, parted a blackberry bush, moved a triangular stone, and, squatting, invited him to slither a few meters under the interwoven branches. They entered a damp chamber. The thick growth around them muffled outside sounds. In the hiding place, a sacred silence reigned. Marcos made him swear that he wouldn't show it to anyone. Not even to Lorenzo, the son of Toribio Valdés, captain of the Lancers, who lived nearby.

⁓

The notary of the Holy Office scrapes his quill across the paper and verifies Francisco's possessions. In this first phase, it is required to compare his declarations with the actual inventory. The Holy Office is strict in its adherence to the law. It leaves nothing to the caprice of men; the defense of faith is at stake.

When Martín de Salvatierra deems this phase complete, Francisco asks, with false naïveté: "May I know of what I am accused?"

The commissioner glances at him briefly, with a mix of irony and surprise. The notary rolls up his documents. They both leave without answering. The official oversees the black men as they remove the table and chairs. Then he closes the door behind him and turns the key. Finally, he shifts the unbreakable bolt into place.

The startling darkness, the silence, and the cold return.

13

When the Brizuela family left, Francisco grew closer to the Valdés boy, Lorenzo. The two became companions for dramatic adventures. He was the captain's only legitimate child, though he had some alleged siblings and suspected that some of the mestizos and mulattoes bore a likeness to him. A wine-red stain covered the left half of his nose and reached to his lower eyelid. It was believed that the mark could be traced to a craving his mother had indulged when she was pregnant. Lorenzo was clever and aggressive. He jumped rope facing this way and that, with side steps, on one foot, in a squat, and moving backward. He climbed trees like a cat and could shimmy his way onto the thinnest, highest branches. When they groaned and threatened to break, he would fly through the air and end up hanging from another one. He lent his rope to Francisco so he could learn the difficult jumps. Together they roamed the streets, leaping through the spinning ring their rope formed in the air. He also taught Francisco to quickly scale the enormous carob tree near the main plaza. Their aerial pirouettes frightened some monks, who ordered them down immediately. But the boys fled through the knotted branches, pretending to be invisible. The monks did not tolerate such disobedience and they marched with outsize anger to the home of Captain Valdés, who listened to them and, to calm them, promised to reprimand his son. Lorenzo listened to the lecture but later told Francisco that, as his father told him to stop climbing that tree, he also laughed about the looks on those monks' faces.

Captain of the Lancers Toribio Valdés was admired, hated, and feared. He was unpredictable. In his youth, in his native Spain, he had knifed the village blacksmith to death for sullying his honor. He liked to proudly recount the story, how forcefully he'd sunk his blade into the burly man's belly until blood formed a thick pool into which the dying man collapsed, crying out for a priest. When the priest arrived, the blacksmith could no longer speak, and he left for the next world without confession. Toribio Valdés had the opportunity to keep the smithy, but he wasn't about to commit the blunder of starting to work. That degradation was reserved for those who lacked noble blood.

Toribio left his village when he learned that the troop marching up and down the main road was about to join a military regiment. It was comprised of vagabonds, prostitutes, and fools who hoped to improve their luck through the Eighty Years' War. He entered the army's ranks, doled out wounds, penetrated enemy territory, and discovered his military vocation. Soon he was wearing a uniform and bearing powerful arms. Later he embarked to fight against the Moors. He learned to hoist sails, load cannonballs, and storm a boat on the high seas. He visited Venice and almost reached Istanbul. He lost three fingers on his left hand and one on his right in an African prison. He managed to escape, first by land and then by sea. He ate snake meat and drank water from infested puddles. He returned to Spain bearing proud scars and sacks full of hate. He volunteered to travel to Peru: he wanted the riches that the Orient had denied him. But Valdés had to wait a year. Meanwhile, he killed two men over new offenses to his honor; he no longer recalled these offenses, but that didn't matter since he'd cleared his name. Finally, he received his orders and ran to the port. The ship rocked intensely in the stormy Atlantic. Near Portobello, the worst fears of ocean travelers were met: they were shipwrecked, and half the crew died.

Toribio Valdés finally succeeded in reaching Lima. He searched for the gold that his empty purse demanded, but, to his shock, he discovered that gold could not in fact be gathered on the streets. So he asked to be sent on surveying expeditions, or punitive expeditions, or any kind at all that involved monetary gain. He was placed on a list of volunteers and had the opportunity to direct his attacks at Calchaquí bodies and traitorous Calchaquí arrows; for this, the governor decided to reward him, naming him captain of the Lancers of Córdoba, a title that came with a house, deputies, servants, a salary, and additional privileges both spoken and unspoken.

When Don Diego Núñez da Silva went to greet the captain, he offered his medical services to him, his family, his military subordinates, and his slaves. The captain of the Lancers, who had put on boots, short silk trousers, a brilliant vest, and a sword sheathed at his waist to receive him, thanked Don Diego for the deference. Francisco and Lorenzo, spying from behind the door, smiled with satisfaction.

14

Córdoba had seven churches. In the main plaza stood the cathedral, and to the side—as if their powers didn't face off in reality—stood the town hall. The many blocks around this plaza included solid, well-built homes, some of them with second stories.

The Cordobans made up for their isolation with vainglory. They bragged about their supposed lineage: Ladies and gentlemen of dubious origins competed to describe their noble genealogies. They claimed to be human jewels in the middle of this country peppered with brutish indigenous people. Their assertions went unquestioned because no one was imprudent enough to challenge his or her neighbor. An understanding reigned that proof was not to be requested, and the registries that could have provided evidence did not exist. Plus, it wasn't difficult to forge a false document. Feverish ambitions aimed to affirm a noble court as incandescent as the one in Madrid.

While the laypeople accumulated titles, the monks brought vigor to their own mandates. They did not want to fall behind. The three established monasteries, with space for meditation and extensive land for agricultural exploitation, were called Santo Domingo, San Francisco, and La Merced. Brother Isidro Miranda locked himself up in the Monastery of La Merced. He conveyed his long ecclesiastical experience and was accepted. It was good for an old man who had preached, performed conversions, and taught in these lands to bring his wisdom to the order that did so much to rescue the faithful among the bloodthirsty Moors and who, now, in America, suffered a kind of disorientation because there were no Moors, only Indians.

The Franciscan monastery was the largest, and it was preparing for the visit of an exacting supervisor whose saintly reputation had spread to the outer reaches of the colony. This just man was known to visit the untamed tribes with a crucifix in one hand and an out-of-tune violin in the other. It was said that he'd worked miracles. He was so thin that he sometimes seemed invisible, but his voice was powerful. His name was Francisco Solano. Don Diego had met him in the city of La Rioja a few years before.

Finally, there stood the sturdy Monastery of Santo Domingo, home of Brother Bartolomé Delgado, who had been given the distinguished title of commissioner for the Holy Inquisition. Brother Bartolomé was bald, obese, and of an indeterminate age. His black-and-white Dominican habit floated around his rotund body; to make it, more cloth was used than that required for half a dozen other monks. He treated the neighbors kindly and appeared at their homes without warning. Sometimes he arrived for lunch, sometimes for dinner; he also stopped by to say good morning at the early breakfast hour, or good night when it was almost time for bed. He greeted people with a smile and went directly to the table where a dish was being served, or dessert, or simple fruit. But his goals were not limited to appeasing his constant appetite; he also liked to talk. He was a master of the art of conversation, of witty, amiable, interminable chats.

Brother Bartolomé was aware of his abilities, and in no way felt indebted for the wine and food he consumed. In addition, he believed that these tireless visits did not spring from idleness or gluttony but formed part of a daring mission. He was a member of the valiant Dominican order that had, since the beginning, been a privileged instrument of the Holy Office. Nothing was more correct than to enter into people's privacy, their courtyards, dining rooms, haciendas, and even their bedrooms in order to detect subtle signs of heresy. The conversations about adventures, gossip, business, and fantastical stories allowed him to glimpse tastes, inclinations, or even secret guiding rituals.

When Francisco met him unexpectedly, he suppressed a scream of shock at that mass of flesh, which resembled a mountain more than a human. He had been playing hide-and-seek with Lorenzo and, while his friend counted to ten against the wall of the corridor, he ran off to disappear in the carpeted living room. Francisco arrived there, agitated, and froze when he saw people. His father was in one chair, and in the other, a black-and-white giant. Both turned at this unexpected intrusion. Francisco raised his hands to defend himself from the cat that bristled on the clergyman's lap. It was a large animal, snowy white. His father called him over, introduced him to Brother Bartolomé, and asked, "What should you do before a dignitary of the church?" The boy bent to one knee, took the man's huge, flabby hand as it extended toward his face, and kissed it, keeping half an eye on the cat's threatening jaws.

"You may return to your play," the commissioner declared.

Francisco lingered a moment before leaving so as not to be spied by his friend. The two men were talking about food. The priest wanted to know what ingredients were used in Lisbon, and what spices in Potosí. He reciprocated with a brief recipe he'd learned in Córdoba, from neighbors and travelers, involving grilled quail and duck *a la marinera* flavored with pepper, garlic, and saffron. Then they both attempted to re-create the formula known as "white food" invented by one of Felipe II's cooks. They knew it included minced poultry cooked over a slow fire, but there was nothing exotic inside the special sauce, only milk, sugar, and rice flour. Brother Bartolomé praised Don Diego's ample cultural knowledge, which pleased little Francisco, because it was true.

Later, he saw his father accompanying the clergyman and his cat to the door, promising to invite him for dinner along with his powerful neighbor, the captain of the Lancers.

"Medicine needs the support of religion as much as it needs the military," Don Diego laughed before saying goodbye.

Brother Bartolomé walked away pensively. His eyes were on the ground, and his white cat moved beside him as if glued to his robe. His mind sifted through every word of his encounter with the Portuguese doctor, from the style of his greeting to the last goodbye. During their conversation about delicacies, Brother Bartolomé had thrown out a few incompatible or unpleasant combinations as a kind of trap, but no indication appeared of rejecting pork, fish without scales, or the mixing of milk and meat. He also weighed the courtesy with which he was received, and the fluid command the man had of Catholic doctrine. The commissioner had also not missed his chance to glance at the books lined up near the desk. He was impressed by the wife, an Old Christian, and clearly devoted. It did not escape him that Diego Núñez da Silva, since his arrival in Córdoba, had attended religious events and participated in processions with his entire family, including the two slaves. He went to confession, listened to Mass, and received communion. An excellent dissimulator.

When he arrived at his monastery, he crossed the cloister and went to his room. He dipped his quill and recorded his impressions. Every once in a while, going over them, he found clues that he himself had written down without realizing their meaning.

Imprisoned in the black, damp cell of the Dominican monastery in Southern Chile, Francisco awaits the next phase while blowing on the burning wounds opened by the shackles.

He hears steps. The commotion returns: iron, keys, the lock, the door creaking open, the shaft of light. Two soldiers enter and stand on either side of him, as if they fear his escape. A black man approaches and offers him a pot of warm milk. Francisco can barely move his stiff, cold arms. He tries to take the pot without trembling. His chains jangle. He drinks. The warm liquid caresses his throat and spreads through his muscles like a benediction.

This time, there are no words. The black man retreats, then the soldiers, and they leave him in the dark, alone again.

15

Don Diego believed he'd earned the commissioner's trust. He was not so naïve as to consider himself safe, but he did feel calmer.

He asked his wife to make her best dishes and prepare a painstaking service. The meal with Brother Bartolomé and the captain of the Lancers, Toribio Valdés, could mean the beginning of a lasting bond. His prestige in Córdoba depended on this relationship, as did his success, and, above all, his freedom.

Don Diego suggested to Aldonza that she make pork chops, an array of vegetables, and milk puddings, and that she also buy some wine. For this occasion, it was worth drawing on one's savings. Aldonza worked hard to create the most pleasing possible menu.

The walnut table was covered with a cloth that Aldonza had embroidered as a maiden. Catalina cleaned the ceramic dishware and made their few pieces of silver shine. She put out platters, saltshakers, jugs, spoons, and knives. Each place setting had an embroidered linen napkin. She arranged fruit in a wicker basket and filled an earthen pitcher with blackberry water. The humble dining room shone, fit for a palace.

Toribio Valdés arrived wearing his suit reserved for special occasions. Was he honoring his splendid medical neighbor? Was he honoring the commissioner? He never missed a chance to dress with pomp. He took off his pointed hat and bowed as if greeting a royal court. While they waited for the priest, he told Don Diego a few details of his battles on the high seas against the Turks.

Brother Bartolomé entered without knocking, as was his habit. He was a man of the church who could only bring good fortune; it wasn't necessary to ask permission. The colossal cat accompanied him, tangled in the folds of his robes. The feline's corpulence matched the priest's; it could have been mistaken for a sheep.

Don Diego went to meet him. The priest lingered to gaze at the grapevine, whose juicy branches were already weighed down.

"I've harvested the best ones," the host said, smiling.

The three men sat down at the table. The captain began sampling delicacies, while the monk studied everything carefully. The man of the house felt content: he had brought two powerful men together in his home. In Ibatín he had been cautious, but now he felt more capable. Nevertheless, none of this opulent meal would remain in his memory except one brief, painful fragment.

"Did you buy this silverware from the wife of Antonio Trelles?" Brother Bartolomé asked as he studied an engraved knife.

"Part of it," he answered, surprised. "Only a small part."

"Aha!" The monk closely inspected the blade and the handle.

Don Diego's forehead started to shine with sweat.

"How did you guess?" he asked, attempting to make his smile look innocent.

"I didn't guess," he responded. "I knew."

"You knew?"

"Of course. Don't you recall that I am the commissioner of the Holy Office?"

"But of course!" he said, laughing loudly.

A few years earlier, Antonio Trelles had been detained in La Rioja for suspicions of practicing Judaism, and he'd been subjected to a famous trial. Don Diego had met him in Potosí, and when he visited La Rioja as a doctor, he tried to help him. A serious mistake: the crime of Judaism deserved no mercy, only repentance and harsh sentences. Helping a Jew was also a crime. As was showing sympathy when the atrocious sin had not been recognized. A tall Franciscan with a vague gaze, who occasionally played a small violin, took him aside and advised him that if he wanted to escape the same fate, he should leave immediately without saying a word. The Holy Office proceeded to confiscate all the prisoner's possessions, and the Trelles family sank into destitution. Don Diego had been reckless enough to approach the wife and buy part of her silverware, using almost all the money he was carrying. It was the only thing he could do to help alleviate her sorrows.

Brother Bartolomé changed the subject and began enjoying his lunch. The host, meanwhile, was swallowing stones.

Is it day or night? Once again, the steps in the corridor, the irons, key, lock, creaking door, shaft of light, soldiers bursting in full of hate.

Between the soldiers, the black-and-white presence of a monk.

Francisco unglues his rheumy eyelids. He recognizes Brother Urueña, the kind clergyman who had so warmly received him in this Chilean town of Concepción.

He tries to sit up, but finds it difficult. His body is a bundle of pain.

The soldiers part. A servant brings in two chairs and leaves. The soldiers follow him out. They leave a lamp on the ground and close the door. Only the monk remains. Now there is enough light.

"Good morning."

Is the Dominican smiling? Is this possible? Can miracles happen in the depths of a dungeon?

16

Catalina ran through the streets, gripping her skirt in fistfuls to keep it from slowing her down. Francisco recognized her from where he sat up in the carob tree and conveyed his surprise to Lorenzo. What was the matter with Catalina? Despite her agitation, she was able to say that Doña Aldonza had ordered her to fetch Francisco, and she didn't know why. Her face brimmed with fear.

"What's the matter?" Francisco pressed.

She couldn't understand it: there were people.

"People? What people?"

They ran toward the house.

At their front door a soldier stood watch with a steel spear and a heart-shaped shield. He tried to block their entrance, then assessed their insignificance and looked away. There were about ten people in the courtyard, three or four of them clergymen. At the living room door stood another armed soldier. Aldonza, flanked by Isabel and Felipa, was pacing with her chin sunk down to her chest and a white handkerchief twisted in her hands. Francisco received her long, trembling embrace. That was when he learned that Brother Bartolomé Delgado and Captain Toribio Valdés had entered solemnly to "arrest the physician Diego Núñez da Silva, in the name of the Inquisition." They were accompanied by a retinue of the king's soldiers and familiars of the Holy Office. As was the custom, the procedure had to take place in the presence of a notary. They had locked themselves up in the living room.

"They're going to take him," Aldonza sobbed. "They're going to take him."

Francisco tried to approach his father, to be with him, to hear what they were asking him. The soldier blocking the door refused to let him pass. Nobody could enter—no exceptions. The Holy Office preferred secrecy.

He returned to the three women, who were circling the well in despair, clutching the beads of their rosaries. Lorenzo, who had followed Francisco home, shook his hair from his face and tried to get a more detailed explanation. Francisco, with a knot in his throat, stared at the severe men as they spoke in sullen tones, the kind one might imagine people of high purpose and proven pure blood would use. He made out a few strong words in the muffled conversation: Marrano, the lapsed Law of Moses, epidemic, witchcraft, dishonesty, murderers of Christ, Sabbath, cursed race, purification by fire, swindlers, New Christians.

He went to the second courtyard, where he found Catalina sitting on a heap of dirty clothes. She was weeping. The slave's sobs intensified Francisco's fear for his father. He went farther off and entered the hiding place that Marcos Brizuela had shown him. It was the perfect cavern, a place where he could lie still and think. Maybe, after a few days, Brother Bartolomé would change his mind and then his father could go free. Or perhaps he should escape on horseback in the middle of the night. Captain Valdés had the fastest horses in the city; Lorenzo could help him get them. He returned to where Catalina sat. He wrapped her plump face in his hands and turned her to look at him. Her eyes were red.

"We're going to save him!" said the young Francisco.

He whispered to her to prepare clothing and food for a journey. He returned to the hiding place and cleaned it out. When he went to rejoin his mother, the interrogation was still going on.

"Where is Diego?"

"He went to get Brother Isidro," answered Felipa.

"What is Papá accused of?" Isabel asked again.

Aldonza broke into sobs again. She squeezed her handkerchief against her eye sockets. What she knew or suspected could not be spoken.

"How many times are you going to ask the same thing?" Felipa scolded, so upset she barely finished her sentence.

The soldier at the living room door moved aside. The retinue approached, anxious for an update; they would have the privilege of being the first to hear the news, and would spread it across the city. But it wasn't time yet; the soldier held his lance up and they returned to their places.

Diego arrived, tense and frustrated. His eyes blazed.

"He won't come," he told his mother.

"He won't . . . ?"

"He's insisting that it's useless. That it would make things worse."

"Brother Isidro won't come?" Isabel repeated, as incredulous as the rest of them.

"He's not a member of the Holy Office, or even Dominican. His intervention would only complicate things."

"He's abandoning us," Isabel said with a shudder.

"It's prudent," Aldonza said. "He sees more than we can."

"Yes! He sees better with his devil eyes! What can the eyes of devils see, eh?" exclaimed Diego.

"My son!"

"He's a coward! A traitor!"

The soldier in front of the door adjusted his position. The retinue approached him again. So did young Francisco. The white cat appeared and, close beside it, the giant figure of Brother Bartolomé. His face had become severe. Then, Don Diego emerged, looking infinitely exhausted.

The captain of the Lancers followed him, along with the monk who fulfilled the role of notary.

Francisco ran toward his father. A lance detained him coldly. A murmur arose. Brother Bartolomé asked the soldier to lower the lance and allow the boy to embrace his father. Then, with exaggerated slowness, he announced that Doctor Núñez da Silva stood accused of Judaism, and that the Holy Office had ordered him, Brother Bartolomé, to investigate his possessions during the interrogation in the presence of the good notary, who had created the legal document. The result of these proceedings now allowed him, Brother Bartolomé Delgado, commissioner of the Inquisition, to turn over the prisoner to the secular branch of power, captain of the Lancers Toribio Valdés, in order to arrange his immediate removal to Lima. In the capital of the Viceroyalty, Don Diego would be judged by the High Tribunal of the Holy Office.

Aldonza exploded into sobs that were impossible to silence, not even by stuffing her handkerchief into her mouth. Her daughters tried to comfort her, but they were crying, too. The familiars of the Holy Office mumbled a prayer. Francisco stared at them; they seemed like specters of the nightmare that the world had become. The young Diego, on the other hand, stayed rigid, fists tight.

Aldonza dragged her fear and despair toward her husband. But instead of reaching him, she fell on her knees before the commissioner of the Holy Office. Brother Bartolomé rested his wide hand on the woman's head, as though giving her a blessing. He mumbled a few words in Latin and told her in a low voice that her husband would be in Lima for a few months, that they should accept divine justice, that if Don Diego expressed sincere remorse and the judges determined it to be real, he would be absolved and return home. This was definitive, the will of God.

Captain Valdés ordered the soldier not to leave the prisoner unattended for any reason.

Francisco ached to tell his father that he had a safe hiding place and that, with Catalina's help, he had prepared provisions. He could rest a few hours, eat, and then, during the night, flee on the best horse in town. It wasn't a fantasy; everything was almost ready. But the soldier wouldn't leave his side, and the quiet familiars of the Holy Office weren't leaving.

Brother Bartolomé was brought paper and quill. An assistant carried his inkwell as he went through the house, followed by the prisoner. His duties included a thorough inventory. He told Don Diego to turn over all his cash, as well as any jewels in the house. The commissioner explored the dining room and the bedrooms. Don Diego didn't say a word; Aldonza cried continuously. Francisco would not unclasp from his father; he had to explain the escape plan. It was critical.

In the bedroom, Brother Bartolomé ordered the chests to be opened and their contents to be spilled onto the rug. Blankets, bedcovers, pillowcases. And a case covered in brocade.

"What is that?"

"A family keepsake."

"Let's see it."

The doctor undid the knot, opened the case, and took out the iron key. Brother Bartolomé fingered it, seemed to measure its heft, held it up to the light, and returned it.

"Fine."

Francisco, propelled by a fiery current coursing through him, reached out his hand and took the relic from his father. He was part of a heroic chain. He took charge of putting it away, lovingly, sliding it into the case and wrapping the hemp string around it. He tied a solid knot. Meanwhile, his father gazed at him with infinite gratitude. Francisco took advantage of the commissioner's distraction to whisper his plan. Brother Bartolomé saw him and called over Captain Valdés. The boy feared that he'd been overheard.

The captain's steps rang out with authority.

"I've completed the first part of the inventory," he said. "You can take the captive."

"Papá," whispered Francisco, "let's escape now!"

"There is no escape," he answered into his ear, squeezing his shoulders with affection.

"Yes there is!"

"It would be worse."

He was irritated by this sudden resignation; it was unknown, unacceptable. His father was too valiant to give up.

They went out to the courtyard. More soldiers arrived, and they pushed Don Diego into the street. Francisco, with his throat tighter than ever and his nerves driven to frenzy, forced his way through and tried to protect his father, but an official pushed him aside roughly and he fell to the ground.

Endless curious onlookers had gathered; it was the great show of the neighborhood, just like the men hung from the Spanish cherry tree in Ibatín. Dozens of horses and mules stood by.

It was clear that the operation had been planned in advance, without actually waiting for the interrogation's results. The persecution of Don Diego, they would later learn, had been ordered when they still lived in Ibatín.

They told Don Diego to mount his mule. Before doing so he looked back at the inside of his home through the open door: Aldonza and their daughters stood frozen by the well, like statues in a cemetery. He asked to say goodbye to them. The soldiers did not listen; they did not want to listen. Fury rose into Francisco's head. Two soldiers drew their blades.

Brother Bartolomé called for calm. "Wait."

He went inside and spoke to the women. He explained that they could say goodbye to the heretic, because they were linked by blood. They listened with astonishment, hung their heads, and walked behind him, full of shame. At that moment, Francisco had an absurd thought:

that painful trio of women dressed in black, pale and helpless, were the three Marias of the Passion. They moved with intense suffering toward Christ the captive, Christ the ridiculed, surrounded by soldiers. Christ was his father, whom these women loved and yet could not help. The soldiers did not understand this, and, in mocking tones, allowed the prisoner to embrace all the members of his family. Don Diego clasped Diego, his mature oldest son. He looked at Francisco, picked him up, and hugged him fiercely.

They parted—the doctor in the center, an official on each side. The march had an exhibitionist quality to it. They took the main road, as a form of punishment, and as a warning to others. The news had already spread like fire to every corner of the city. All of Córdoba came out to the street, to their doorways, their front halls. It was important to demonstrate the strength of the Holy Office, and to remind the people that its long arm could reach the most distant lands.

The figures grew small in the distance. They turned a corner. Their disappearance unhinged Francisco, who leapt onto one of the horses tied up by his house and bolted off. He was too fast to be stopped. He galloped through the streets and caught up in a few minutes. His father, stunned, stopped his mule. The officials reached for their weapons.

"Papá, Papá!"

Francisco's horse disturbed the tidy formation.

"Get out!" they shouted.

He reached out his arms and tried to embrace his father again, but the soldiers struck his knees, grabbed his reins, and pulled on his stirrups. They almost threw him off his horse. Finally, he managed to reach his father's side. They pressed each other's wrists, and stared at each other with intense despair.

An angry, cruel blow from a shield pushed them apart.

"Get out of here!"

The officials surrounded the doctor, as they had before.

"I'll go with you . . . I'll go with you," the boy begged.

The formation moved back into place. His father turned to stare at him with a broken heart as his captors forced him to keep moving. Francisco would not give up, and followed them at a close distance.

They arrived at the edge of the city. The soldier in charge turned and faced the boy, frowning. "It's over, idiot. Now go home."

His answer was to lower his eyes and stay silent. But without any sign of obedience.

His father intervened. "Go back, Francisquito. Go back. Take care of your mother and your siblings."

He shuddered. His father was serious. This was the irrefutable voice; he was whole again, as before. Francisco lifted his gaze and saw his father. He saw him moving calmly. He saw him raise his right hand, gently, to wave at him for the last time. He saw how then his father spurred on his mule, to end the goodbye, and moved away more swiftly. The soldiers pressed their horses on behind him. His father looked like the man in charge, not like a prisoner.

He remained in that spot for a long time. Then he looked out at the blue mountains that his father loved so much, and retraced his steps, sad and helpless. What would they do to him? What would they do in Lima? What would they do before arriving in Lima? He had heard rumors that the prisoners were abused on the journey so that upon arrival they would put up no resistance.

He dismounted in the middle of the rowdy crowd that still blocked the door of his house. He was scolded for having galloped off. The horse's owner tried to twist his ear, but he freed himself. Insults were hurled his way. Then he turned toward Lorenzo's home. His friend seemed strange. What was the matter with him? He approached, and his friend backed away.

"Lorenzo!"

He didn't answer. Was he ashamed of his own father, the captain? Did he feel guilty about the terrible fate his father had forced on Don Diego?

"Lorenzo!"

Lorenzo waited.

"Your father—" Francisco began.

Lorenzo gave him a look that he'd never seen before. It was terrible, full of contempt. The stain on his face glowed like a lit coal. Lorenzo stepped forward defiantly and spat at him. "Jew!"

Francisco was paralyzed, and then shattered into pieces. He could not grasp this new monstrous, shattered reality: Lorenzo's father had just arrested his own, and now Lorenzo was insulting him. The tongues of fire that had been rising and falling in him for hours now devoured him completely. With the force of a hungry tiger, he threw himself on his former friend, toppling him, punching, kicking. Lorenzo fought back with his head and teeth. They rolled, grabbed, pushed. Between gasps they hurled insults. They saw the blood on each other's lips and started to loosen their grips. They stared at each other in shock, both battered, short of breath. They rose slowly, their guards up. Another attack was possible. But they ended up moving away from each other, growling, eyes full of hatred.

As he dried his wounded face with his arm, Francisco went around his house, to the back. He parted the bushes and crawled into his hiding place. "This is where Papá should have hidden." He lay down in the cool shadows. The smell of dirt was pleasant. But he still felt oppressed. The horrific scenes of the day would not stop running through his head. He tossed and turned, as if he were in bed and unable to sleep.

He finally sat up and decided to leave. No place, not even this one, could offer him solace. From the corral, two mules observed him with large almond eyes. That's when he realized that he couldn't walk because of the intense pain in his knee.

Diego looked him up and down. "Francisquito!"

His torn clothes, the bruises on his forehead, and the blood on his cheeks made for an astonishing effect. His brother approached to help him. Francisco had a mad urge to cry at the top of his lungs, but he was asphyxiated by shame. He couldn't explain this. A claw slashed at his throat. Diego slid his hands into his brother's armpits, lifted him, and leaned him against his chest.

—— ⁓ ——

Brother Urueña sits in a chair and offers Francisco the other one. Francisco can't believe it; this man's appearance is angelic.

The monk caresses the cross that hangs on his chest. He seems pained by the damaged state of the friendly, cultured doctor.

"I have come to console you," he murmurs sweetly. Brother Urueña used to visit him in his home. Sometimes he stayed to dine. He told anecdotes about doctors, surgeons, and (in a low voice) certain priests. Francisco corrected his Latin, and the monk pretended to be angered, then promised to improve, only to make the same error the next time. Together they had strolled the beautiful shores of the majestic Bío-Bío River.

"How is my wife? And my daughter?" He cannot hide his anxiety.

The priest keeps his eyes lowered. "They are well."

"Have they—have they frightened them? Have they—"

"They are well."

"What will they do with me?"

Their eyes meet for the first time. Brother Urueña seems sincere.

"Please believe me. I am not permitted to provide information."

They are silent. From the corridor, he hears the muted sounds of the officials who keep watch, alert to the probable aggression of the hungry, shackled prisoner.

17

An atmosphere of mourning spread through the house. Even though Aldonza came from an Old Christian lineage and had ample evidence thereof, she had married a New Christian who would now be put on trial by the Holy Office. Her four children had wretched blood in their veins.

The home was rapidly dismantled. Brother Bartolomé oversaw the plunder. All prisoners of the Inquisition ran up costs, he explained: there was the travel, the food, the clothing, and, once in Lima, the fees for the prisoner's maintenance in jail, as well as the creation and repair of instruments of torture, the torturers' salaries, and the price of candles. Where would all those resources come from? From the prisoners themselves—it was only logical. They were the sources of evil, forcing the Holy Office to work so tirelessly. This was why their possessions were confiscated. Any remaining funds would be returned at the end of the trial. "The Holy Office was not established to accumulate wealth, but, rather, to protect the purity of faith."

On the first day, the commissioner took what was left of their money. On the second day, he chose silver and ceramic pieces from among their dinnerware (including those that had belonged to the ill-fated Trelles) and only left the jugs, platters, and plates made of tin or clay. On the third day, he went through the religious images, pillowcases, cushions, and chairs with armrests. Then he left the family in peace for a week, because he couldn't find any buyers for what he'd taken so far. He reappeared to look at the books; curiously, however, he hadn't come to take them but to order Aldonza to lock them in a chest.

"First wrap them with a blanket," he said, "so their pestilence doesn't seep out."

He associated the books with the fate of Don Diego. "They filled his spirit with perverse ideas. They ruined his reason. Their pages do not transmit the word of the Lord, but, rather, the tricks of the devil."

Aldonza listened with close attention and hope. He was the authority who had torn her husband from her; perhaps he could also bring him back. It was he who would determine her children's future. The scope of the harm he'd inflicted conveyed the scope of his power. Aldonza had been taught to bend in the face of power. And so she bent before the words of this monk, this commissioner, who in recent days had started to insist that his intention was to help.

He extended his index fingers, musing, "Like this, straight, is the path of faith."

He stirred his fat fingers in the air. "Twisted and unstable, like this, are the digressions of heresy."

Aldonza hoped that her good, submissive conduct would be appreciated by the commissioner and that he would positively inform the Tribunal of Lima so that the judge might be merciful with her husband. For this reason, instead of wrapping the books with one blanket, she used two. She hated those books, and yet she touched them lovingly. Each of them had accompanied her husband for many hours.

"They won't leak any more pestilence," she murmured, slamming the chest closed.

"Nobody will read them. I never liked them."

Brother Isidro offered to resume lessons, as a form of distraction and solace. Diego resisted. The rest of the family was wary.

"I've discussed it with Brother Bartolomé," he explained. "There are no objections."

Diego got up angrily. He did not hide the repugnance on his face.

"Brother Bartolomé will help," the monk continued, as if he hadn't seen, "to maintain the path of faith. He will supervise the lessons, and we'll go over catechism each day." •

"The straight path," Francisco mocked, extending his index fingers.

"If Brother Bartolomé has requested it, we'll do it," Aldonza decided.

The following afternoon they sat down around the table. Brother Isidro moved from one subject to the next with the goal of raising his students' spirits, but he failed. They were distracted, hard to engage. Then he suggested they read an edifying story from *Count Lucanor.*

"Bring us that book," he said to Felipa.

"There are no more books in this house," Aldonza said uneasily.

"What?"

"They no longer exist for us."

The monk scratched his wrists under his wide sleeves.

"You didn't know?" Felipa couldn't hide her surprise. "Brother Bartolomé didn't tell you?"

"You weren't informed by the sacred commissioner?" Diego added in a mocking tone.

"If someone offers me money for them," Aldonza said with fury, "I'll sell them. I'll sell them all. That very instant."

But who was going to waste money on such useless and dangerous volumes? They were locked away and destined to rot for having brought disgrace to the family.

Francisco saw things differently. His sadness propelled him to visit the chest. It was a reunion with his father. When no one was around, he sat on the floor and gazed at it. Inside that chest there beat the heart of an immortal life. He saw it in the tenuous glow of the painted wood. Inside, mythological beings formed by letters communed with each other. Surely the corpulent Pliny was recounting part of his *Naturalis Historia* to sensitive Horace, and the inspired King David sang his psalms to the archpriest of Hita. His mother didn't understand this, Brother Isidro would have been scandalized, and Diego would have made fun of him.

〜〜

Brother Urueña rattles out a prayer. Francisco watches him tenderly; what a shame that soon he'll have to leave and he, Francisco, will be alone again in the stinking cell, bitten by the steel shackles. They had just reminisced about the few months he'd been living in the city. He had traveled south from Santiago de Chile with his wife Isabel Otáñez and his daughter Alba Elena. It was a similar trajectory to the one his family had taken from the oasis of Ibatín to luminous Córdoba just before he turned nine. His father had sensed the long arm of the Holy Office grazing the nape of his neck, just as he himself recently had.

"The Holy Office looks after our well-being," the monk insists. "I want to help you. We can talk for as long as we need."

Francisco doesn't answer. His eyes glitter.

"You are an erudite man. You cannot fool yourself. Something is clouding your heart. I've come to help you—truly."

Francisco waves his hands. The rusted chains clank together.

"Tell me what's the matter," the Dominican encourages him. "I will try to understand."

For the captive, these words are a caress. The first affectionate gesture since he was torn from his home. But he decides to wait a few minutes before speaking. He knows that an intricate war has begun.

18

A shadow spread across the walnut table. The five students and their teacher startled at the sudden appearance of Brother Bartolomé. The class continued under his watch.

At the end, a weary Aldonza offered the commissioner chocolate and fig pastries. Diego excused himself, gathered his things, and left. A few moments later, his sisters Isabel and Felipa did the same. The commissioner did not seem troubled; he stroked his cat and kept on smiling. Francisco preferred to stay in order to hear his mother's conversation with the two men. He slid to the floor and pretended to focus on a map.

"Are they still put away?" Brother Bartolomé asked between noisy sips of chocolate.

"Yes, put away, exactly as you instructed."

"They are dangerous books," he insisted, mouth full of pastry. "There are too many."

"My husband," Aldonza said timidly, "used to say there were too few. That they were nothing compared to the libraries of Lima, Madrid, or Rome."

"Well, well!" he laughed, crumbs flying from his mouth. "Such comparisons make for absurd conclusions. We are not in Madrid, nor are we in Rome. We live in miserable lands full of sin and infidels. Nobody owns a library. It's an eccentricity!"

Brother Antonio Luque, that small, harsh man, had said the same thing. Aldonza lowered her eyes, still swollen from crying.

"It is a collection that evokes other collections." Brother Bartolomé shook the crumbs from his cassock and raised his eyebrows. "That is true. Despite everything—" He cut himself off, took another bite of pastry, and immediately swigged chocolate to wash it down.

"Despite everything . . . ?" Brother Isidro tried to remind him of his interrupted thought.

"Ah!" He shook off crumbs again. "I was saying that, despite everything, it is a valuable collection."

Aldonza blinked. Francisco looked up from the colorful map and turned toward the black-and-white mass.

"Valuable?"

"Yes, my child."

"I'll sell it now, Father. You know that I'll sell it."

"There's no need for haste," he said, stroking the cat's plush fur.

"I don't want that library in our house anymore," Aldonza protested. "I'm afraid that it might hurt us, might bring on more disgrace. It's poisonous. You said so."

"If you sell it, you might poison whoever buys it." He pulled the feline's fat tail.

Aldonza bit her lips. A lock of hair fell to her cheek. She hid it quickly beneath her black head scarf.

"We need money, Father," she implored. "I have to feed my family. I'm alone with four children. That's why I suggested selling the books."

"We'll find a way." He drained the cup of chocolate, licked its inside with gusto, and placed it back on the table.

"I can't see the way. I can't imagine it." Aldonza wiped sweat from her forehead with the back of her hand.

"For now, don't mention the books to anyone. Are they hidden in a chest?"

"Yes, yes."

The monk leaned his head toward her, whispering, "You have to keep them hidden until the right moment."

Aldonza didn't understand what moment he was talking about.

"The moment to sell them, or turn them over, or trade them for something, or give them away. Without their affecting anyone."

"We'd be better off with a few coins to show for them," she lamented.

"How many? Who would give you five, who ten, who twenty? Do you know how to negotiate? I will help you negotiate." He turned suddenly to Brother Isidro. "Do you agree?"

The monk was taken unawares, and his terrified eyes bulged from their sockets, darting everywhere. "Yes, of course!"

The woman picked up the empty cup and carried it to the kitchen. She had to do something; this commissioner was disconcerting. In the kitchen she pinched her arms to punish herself for lack of composure, until the spiritual pain turned into the cheap tears of physical pain. It was easier to control physical pain. She returned in a better state.

The commissioner waited for her to sit down again, then knitted his brows to share a profound revelation. "Aldonza, I have come here to comfort your soul."

She shrank back like a small animal before a predator.

"I have always been a devoted Catholic—"

"I don't doubt it. But the Lord has decided to test you. He chooses men and women to give testimony. And each of those who are chosen should feel flattered. Don't forget that you are an Old Christian. Your blood is free of impure ancestors." He raked his gaze over Brother Isidro, who instantly pretended to be focused on his wooden crucifix. "God loves just people, the best people, and makes demands on them."

She leaned her elbows on the table and her chin on her fists. Her face was full of distress.

Brother Bartolomé pressed on. "Don't you understand? It's easy: only the best can reach the extremes of fidelity and obedience. Only the best, with their suffering, augment the glory of the Lord. Sinners and the unworthy, they don't know suffering. They even commit the blasphemy of trying to reject it. God has chosen you, my dear Aldonza. And so something has happened to you—we know what."

She began to tear up. Brother Bartolomé let out a long sigh, put his hands on his knees, and rose. The cat fell to the floor and walked insolently over Francisco's map, which made him want to pull out its whiskers. Brother Isidro and Aldonza also stood up. The two priests left together, and the house sank back into emptiness.

Francisco tries to touch kind Brother Urueña's hand, but the chains make it a herculean effort.

"What do you want to say?" the monk asks encouragingly.

"A priest is prepared to keep secrets, right?"

"That is right, my son."

"If someone asks you to do so are you even more obliged?"

"The secrecy of confession is inviolable," he says.

"Before I confide in you," Francisco says slowly, "I have to ask whether you will keep the secret I am going to tell you."

The clergyman fingers his cross. "I am a priest, and I am obliged to fulfill the commands of the Lord."

Francisco sighs again. Deep in his anguished soul he does not believe him. But the war presses him forward. He stretches his shackled legs, puts his hands on his chest, looks up, and starts to draw back the heavy veil.

Brother Urueña's mouth hangs open and his eyes grow very, very wide.

19

The books stayed in the trunk for six more months, untouched. Six months. Francisco counted them in the church almanac.

One morning, Brother Bartolomé's servant arrived to announce that, in the afternoon, the monk would be paying them a visit. Strange—he never announced his visits. But this time he was doing so because a learned man who recently arrived from Lima would be accompanying him. A beam of optimism lit up their house. Finally, they would have news of Don Diego. Of course he would be bringing them something; why else would a learned man visit the bankrupt home of an impure family?

Later that day Brother Bartolomé, with his cat walking under his hem, made a gesture, and the esteemed learned man crossed the threshold. He paused a moment to study the courtyard, the grapevine, and the well, then searched for the way to the living room, which was usually found to the right in most homes.

He wore a black pointed hat, fine cloth shoes, and an ample jet-black cape. Without greeting anyone or acknowledging those who were watching him expectantly, he went to the living room and sat down. His bored eyes roved across the coarse walls that once held mirrors and paintings. He did not rise to greet Aldonza, restricting himself to a movement of his head. She, in her consternation, offered to serve him something but the learned man coldly asked to be shown the books.

"The books?"

"Yes, the books you are selling. Brother Bartolomé told me about them."

The priest put his cat on his lap and, stroking his fur, made a gesture of approval. His gaze seemed to say, "Hurry up, woman, I've brought your buyer." But Aldonza sought news of her husband. Had he gone to trial? Would he return soon? Her children were clustered in the doorway, also anxious.

The gentleman scratched his neck and said that he knew nothing about her husband's fate, and so had no information for her. Aldonza, crossing her fingers, begged him not to be upset; she wasn't asking for information, just some kind of news. The gentleman added that he had not come to Córdoba to deliver the mail. He could only tell her— and this he said disdainfully—that word had spread in Lima about a Portuguese doctor who had been thrown into the Inquisition's secret prisons. "That could be the same man."

Brother Bartolomé moved his head and thanked the man for such an important and amiable service. Then he addressed the distraught woman. "The chest of books, my child. We're going to show them to him."

Diego summoned Luis, and the two of them carried in the heavy trunk. Aldonza found the key and slid it into the lock. She looked at the priest. She didn't dare lift the lid: it was a tomb full of pestilence. Brother Bartolomé lost his patience and angrily demanded that she open it. She did so, clumsily, afraid that poison might spill out or the devil's claw might spring up at them. The gentleman was surprised to see an earth-colored shroud. Luis and Diego pulled out the heavy bundle with both arms. Brother Bartolomé unfolded the blankets and the room lit up.

The arrogant learned man twisted his head back and forth like a jeweler appraising a gem and reached for the closest book. He picked it up, gauged its weight, looked at its covers, and flipped through the pages. He chose another one, read a paragraph, traced a finger down its spine, reread the title, and placed it beside the pile. He picked up the next book and went through the process again.

Brother Bartolomé relaxed. He stroked the cat and wondered whether the learned man would place more importance in the title, the author, the condition of the book, the quality of the printing, or the perversity of the paragraphs trapped inside. And he wondered, too, how much money he would offer.

Diego returned to the group of siblings spying from the door. Silence reigned in the living room, disturbed only by the gentleman from Lima paging through the books. Aldonza stood nearby, watching uneasily. He was rummaging through her absent husband's intimate things; it was as if his very eyes, teeth, neck, or nose were being touched. When he put down the last volume, the stranger started to separate out a few, until six were in a pile.

"What have you decided?" asked the priest.

The learned man stood up. "We'll talk."

He bowed slightly and went to the door. Brother Bartolomé walked briskly to keep up. The learned man had six volumes under his arm. He was buying them, or so it seemed.

The room had emptied. This was how a city must feel after an invader's departure: fear still in the air but mixed with the happy certainty that the threat was gone. Francisco approached the brilliant pile. He recognized some of the books by their size and color. They breathed again. He sat beside them. He didn't try to open them. He wanted to caress them, to caress his father. Aldonza let him do it.

<hr/>

Francisco explains to the stunned Brother Urueña that he has decided to completely embrace his faith, and that, for many years, he has been practicing it in secret. This allowed him to satisfy the demands of his conscience.

"I have the living sensation of God!" he exclaimed.

The Dominican begs his saints to provide him with arguments to refute this heretic's demonic elation; he has to break apart the shadows that have overtaken his soul.

"You are saying," the monk interjects, "that you have the lived sensation of God."

"Yes."

"And yet you deny Him."

"Deny?"

"You deny God. You deny Our Lord Jesus Christ."

Francisco Maldonado da Silva's arms fall to his sides. The chains shake noisily.

"This man hasn't understood a thing." He sighs to himself. "I've been speaking to a puppet."

20

They never found out how much money the learned man paid for the six books; the funds weren't for the family, but to "defray the costs of the prisoner." They would go directly to the treasury of the Holy Office.

Diego muttered through gritted teeth, "I want to kill him. I'll kill him one day."

"Me, too," said Francisco.

"Boys, boys," Aldonza begged.

Diego clapped his brother's back. "Let's get out of here." He gestured to Luis. "Bring the mule and a sack."

"Where are we going?" asked Francisco.

"To the killing place," he whispered.

They took the path to the river. Against the sky rose the olive groves the Jesuits had planted soon after settling in Córdoba. An ox dragged the water carrier's cylindrical wagon. Behind it walked a group of slaves bearing bundles of clean clothes on their heads, keeping a steady pace and balancing so as to keep their heads still and their cargo fragrant and fresh. Luis, limping, smiled at them.

The street's edges dissolved. Brush grew between the hoofprints. They caught sight of the river. Watercress carpeted the ground and cornstalks waved. They turned onto the eastern path that followed the river. There Luis fulfilled a ritual he had brought from Africa: he handed the mule's reins to Diego and hopped on one foot down to the shore. He was very strong and balanced on that single limb, while the other served as a disabled companion. Francisco watched in fascination as he picked up a wide stone and kneeled. He pulled up blades of grass, rubbed his head with them, passed them over both shoulders, and scattered them in a crescent shape over the water. Then he cupped his hands and drank. He threw a few drops behind him. He mumbled words he'd been taught as a child. He didn't know their meaning, but they brought good luck. He recovered the mule's reins and the walk continued. The drops stayed on the nape of his neck for a good while, as they were gradually seeping good luck into his long-suffering body.

They heard a distant rumble, like the sound of battle. The winding path led to a rustic edifice at the top of a hill. Stinking gusts announced the proximity of their destination. They undertook the ascent. The mule protested and Luis steered him by the harness. The resistant animal smelled danger. Luis slapped its rump and successfully urged it on. Several black people appeared and announced that the wagons were waiting by the willows. Oxen and horses grazed around them. The air reeked of excrement, urine, and the smell of raw meat. A bloody vapor rose from the back of the rectangular building. The path ended at a dilapidated gate. Diego already knew this place but wanted Francisco to see where these transactions occurred.

The slaughterhouse functioned on a kind of plateau where men with sweaty torsos and large knives worked hard at butchering. Powerful hooks awaited the gushing cattle, and dogs sniffed between the great wheels in hopes of getting something for themselves. A destitute nobleman—just as Diego and Francisco now were—shooed the dogs by throwing stones. They were his hungry rivals.

A vehicle began its departure; the slaves had finished filling it so the oxen were urged into motion. A bundle of intestines slipped through the rear opening, uncoiling like a pink snake; the dogs leapt on the innards and ripped them to shreds. The nobleman attacked the dogs with a long cane; he could not tolerate the sight of them eating.

In the pasture, the commotion of pigs and cows mixed with the butchers' laughter. Francisco also laughed when one of those men fell in the mud in pursuit of an escaped baby pig, which fled toward an empty pasture, believing this would save him. The man, a paunchy mestizo, rose with a howl and resumed the chase. Mud stained his face and chest. The man cursed, pointing his knife at the creature. The terrified animal ran back and forth, searching for a way out. The mestizo hemmed it in, caught it again, but, once again, it got away. For the butcher this was no longer a job; it was revenge. Black people, mestizos, mulattoes, and the few Spaniards who were there gathered around to watch the filthy show. The butcher was fighting with a pig for his honor. It was a parody of a bullfight. He approached the animal stealthily, then chased it, shouting. He stabbed it once in the side and another time in the foot. A scarlet ribbon slashed across its black hide. The animal broke free from its aggressor and kept running on three legs. The improvised audience cheered for the pig. The mestizo's round belly was covered in mud and blood; his mouth foamed. He brandished his knife in the air, blind with fury, and charged his enemy. The pig flailed its head and the knife flew from the butcher's hand. The man rolled, then stood immediately, like a monster rising from a swamp. He shook his head to fling the dirt from his eyes, recovered his weapon, and leapt at the beast again. He embraced it with his legs and punched and stabbed it. The blade pushed in and out between streams of blood. He pulled its ears and managed to open a deep cut along its throat. The pig crumpled and fell, while the butcher collapsed at its side. The animal's neck was a crater spitting red lava. Francisco pitied the victim. The smeared butcher sat up painfully, raised his arms, and let out a triumphant roar. He leaned over the still-warm body and took to enjoying his work and his revenge. He dragged the pig and hung it up, opening it down the center and taking out the innards. He cut off its head and put it on his own, like a crown.

"Marrano!" the crowd shouted at him from the fence.

"Marrano!" Francisco shouted along, caught up in the brutal comedy.

The mestizo's teeth shone behind layers of filth. He struck up a dance and leapt around for his audience, which cheered and yelled obscenities. He made as if to throw the young pig's head at a black man's face, then at a mulatto, and then he put it over his genitals. Finally, he hurled it forcefully across the fence. The crowd's focus shifted to the head as if it were a ball. Francisco realized that neither Diego nor Luis was with him anymore. Nor were they in the horde now fighting over the useless head. The destitute nobleman came running with his hands full of stones to throw at the dogs. A Spaniard shouted at a group of slaves, calling them "shitty and lazy," demanding that they finish loading a wagon.

Diego appeared at his side. "We're leaving."

They began to walk away from the slaughterhouse. They passed through the ruined gate and started to descend toward the river.

"What about Luis?" asked Francisco.

Diego put an index finger up to his lips. He was walking with long, hasty strides. Francisco trotted to keep up with him.

"And the mule?"

Diego insisted on hurrying and not talking.

Soon they heard the insults.

"Marranos! Marranos!"

"Run!" said Diego.

They left the path. The bushes hid them well. They burrowed into them, prickly branches scratching their arms and heads. They heard the threatening voices a few meters away. Knives gleamed. *"Marranos! Marranos!"* They stayed down until their pursuers were gone. Relief arrived slowly, a kind of awakening. Birds sang nearby, and one circled above them.

"What happened? Why were they chasing us?"

His brother slapped his shoulder, sighed, and smiled.

They opened the curtain of bushes and returned to the path.

"Let's run," said Diego.

"Why?"

"To reach Luis."

A few minutes later they glimpsed the mule and Luis limping at its side. He saw them approaching but did not slow down. It was critical to arrive home as soon as possible. Diego gave him a sign of approval: the mule was carrying a sack full of meat. The operation had been successful.

"A small compensation," Diego said as he evaluated the amount of stolen food. "Not enough for even one of the candelabras the commissioner took from us."

"I want to kill him," Francisco said, tightening his forehead. "I'm serious."

"Who? The commissioner?" Diego shook his head. "I want to kill him, too. Strangle him. Stab him. But who can kill a pig like him? He's the king of pigs. In every sense."

"He's a *marrano.*"

"Francisquito."

"What?"

"Don't say *marrano* again."

"Why not?"

"Call him a pig, a hog, a swine, or the son of Satan. Just don't say *marrano*, that word for young pigs—that ugly word."

Francisco was perplexed.

"*Marrano,*" his brother explained, his face going dark, "is what they call us. *Marrano* is what they call our father."

<hr />

"How could you think I'm denying God?" exclaims Francisco. "Didn't I just explain how hard I've worked to study His word and do His will?"

"You deny Him, my son, you deny Him," the monk responds in despair, suffocated by the airless cell and the captive's words.

"Please remember the Gospel of Saint Matthew," Francisco urged. "That's where Jesus says, 'Not everyone who says to me, "Lord, Lord!" shall enter the kingdom of heaven, but he who does the will of my Father in heaven.' I do the will of the Father. And for this I am punished by the Inquisition."

Brother Urueña dries his forehead. It is very difficult to vanquish Lucifer. "This man will end up burned alive," he thinks.

21

The captain of the Lancers headed toward the Núñez da Silvas' home with firm steps, accompanied by Brother Bartolomé. His accusatory mood could be felt from afar. He entered full of hostility, without asking permission. The priest tottered behind him, carrying his heavy cat. They sat down in the living room and demanded that the family appear. Aldonza, as usual, offered to serve them sweets. Valdés rudely turned down the offer. They'd come regarding a grave matter. Diego made a calming sign toward Francisco; he knew what this was about.

"There are devout acts and aberrant acts," the monk began with hoarse severity. His pupils burned under thick eyelids.

The captain nodded.

"Aberrant acts can be corrected with devout ones. On the other hand"—he paused, and silence blazed across the room—"what can be expected of those who commit aberrant acts while they are under the suspicion of sin?"

The ruined family looked like a group of small animals about to have their throats slit.

"Captain Valdés has received a report of theft," the monk said with distaste.

The captain nodded again.

"Debtors have committed theft. Have you so quickly forgotten that the Holy Office is now spending time and effort to recover a heretic's soul? Is this how you repay the authorities and dignitaries here and in Lima who devote themselves to preserving the faith?"

The captain frowned; he was focused and satisfied. "This is how it's done," he thought.

"This theft, this aberrant act—"

Isabel murmured, "What theft?" But Aldonza asked her not to interrupt the priest.

"This theft. This aberrant act," he repeated, "is proof of the bad habits that have reigned in this family. We had assumed that, except for him"—he would not mention Don Diego by name—"the rest of you would be safe from corruption."

He paused and stroked his cat's fur. Then he raised his burning eyes again.

"But it is not so! Therefore," he said, lowering his voice, "I have called for the lessons with Brother Isidro to stop. They have only offered empty knowledge and have not improved you. The soul, to be perfected, needs other kinds of exercise."

The captain adjusted himself in his chair. He thought to himself that this monk had a golden tongue.

"Diego and Francisco," he continued, "will come to the Santo Domingo monastery. We will teach you to be good. As far as the girls' education, I will be in charge of that."

The punishment was disconcerting. The captain also seemed surprised. What kind of penitence for violating property was this? A simple change of school and of teachers? Was the commissioner joking?

"To cover part of the costs of this new teaching," the priest went on without softening his brow, "you will need to offer my monastery a contribution."

"We don't have anything left to offer!" Diego protested.

"Silence, fool!" cried the commissioner. "There are always offerings when the heart desires it. If there is not enough in the material realm, one gives from the spirit."

"Yes," Aldonza said, wanting to soften her son's inappropriate outburst.

The monk glanced at her with a glimmer of tenderness before returning to his role of inquisitor. "There are still valuable possessions in this house."

Diego pressed his fists and quietly muttered, "You want to keep exploiting us, you son of a bitch."

Brother Bartolomé turned to the submissive Aldonza. "Call for the box that contains your husband's instruments."

Don Diego's box of medical and surgical instruments contained scalpels, valves, knives, saws, burins, and lancets, some made of steel, others silver. Luis was in charge of cleaning them, sharpening them, and keeping them organized. He did this enthusiastically because only the insurmountable barrier of his race had impeded him from studying and practicing his vocation as a doctor. He would boil the pieces, polish them, and, before setting them in their places, indulge in a pretend game of physician; he'd lift a lancet as if it were a pen to open the vein of an imaginary apoplectic person, or he'd grab a scalpel and dig an arrowhead out of another invisible patient's shoulder. He would also brandish a scalpel to scare off Francisco when he tried to play with the saws or burins. Don Diego had bought those instruments in Potosí. After his arrest, it was up to Luis to guard them.

Aldonza ordered him to bring the revered suitcase, but the enslaved man seemed not to understand. Aldonza repeated her order. It sounded incredible, as nobody had requested it for months. Luis leaned forward, then left the room with his broken gait, crossed the grape-trellised courtyard, and headed to the servants' quarters. Francisco hoped he would flee and hide in the secret cavern, disobeying his submissive mother and that fat man who had sold six books at a loss (or to his gain, his own dark gain) and who now wanted to get his hands on the medical instruments. Those voracious tiger fangs of his wanted another piece of his father. Hopefully Luis would not return, or else he'd hide the suitcase and say he couldn't find it, that it must have been stolen. His hope, however, melted. Luis returned with the heavy suitcase on one shoulder. His weak leg seemed like it would buckle under the weight.

Brother Bartolomé gestured for him to place it on the table.

"Open it," he asked Aldonza, coldly.

She looked at Luis. "Do you have the key?"

"No."

"What? You don't have the key?"

"The doctor has it."

"Are you saying that the doctor took the key with him?"

"Yes, *Señora.*"

Brother Bartolomé burst between them, gripped the padlock, and tried to rip it off. He twisted it. He pulled without success. He angrily ordered Luis to try to open it. The enslaved man hunched forward between the priest and the soldier. He also pulled and twisted.

"What's the matter?" the priest scolded. "Haven't you opened it before?"

"No, Father. Only the doctor would open it."

"Weren't you the one in charge of cleaning and sharpening the instruments?" His mouth twisted with suspicion.

"Yes, Father. But only the doctor would open and close the case."

"Tell me how he would open it, then!" the priest shrieked, arms trembling.

"Like this," Luis said, inserting an imaginary key.

"Allow me," declared Captain Valdés.

He pushed Luis aside. The warrior struck an elegant pose and made delicate movements, aiming to create a friendly connection with the stubborn padlock. He spoke to it in a persuasive tone. But in a few seconds he was already forcing it with rage. He struck the table. He struck it again, more vigorously, and his hair fell into his face. He began to sweat. He forgot that he was being watched by a family and the powerful commissioner of the Holy Office. His tongue hung from his mouth; he swore and contorted. Brother Bartolomé begged him not to get so overexcited. The captain cursed all locks and their whorish mothers, named a saint, and invoked shit to fall on the eleven thousand virgins. The commissioner's calming words had the opposite effect of inflaming the captain's resentment, and, out of his mind, he raised the suitcase over his head and hurled it to the floor. The cat saved its tail by a miracle. Its meow mixed in with the general terror. The captain stomped on the resistant suitcase, adding emphasis with insults involving the genitals of cows, mares, and parrots. The monk sweat at what he was hearing but he could not stop the man. Francisco thought that the captain was no different from the butcher who had chased the young pig; he was only missing a knife in his hand. The stomping was so ruthless that his boots managed to dent the lid. He let out a cry of triumph, just like the butcher. He only stopped short of crowning himself with the victim's head.

"Pick it up!" he ordered, gasping.

Luis lifted the wounded case and placed it on the table, in the same place where it had been before being violated. Toribio Valdés broke the lid into fragments. The old suitcase was ravaged in front of the horrified family. The captain carved an irregular orifice, his teeth gritted. He slid his hand in, smiling, and felt around furtively. His face shifted from joy to surprise. He pulled his fist out and opened it: a stone. He started at it, stupefied, and gave it to the monk. The monk turned it between his fingers, holding it to the candelabra's light, and placed it on the table. The captain took out a second stone. A third. A fourth. Faster and faster. He passed them all to the commissioner, who stared at them with growing rage and piled them beside the ruined suitcase. The captain took out all the stones as he reprised his catalogue of curses, in which he now included the patron saints of Tucumán. Brother Bartolomé,

Aldonza, and her children all crossed themselves after each blasphemy. Valdés picked up the empty suitcase, turned it around, and shook it with such hatred that it almost fell from his hands. From the hole poured a trickle of residual sand.

Brother Bartolomé glared at Luis, his eyes full of poison, and the captain took this as permission. He pounced on the slave and hammered his head with his fist, shouting obscenities. Luis doubled over and fell to the floor, covering himself with his arms. Diego and Francisco leapt at the aggressor and tried to stop the hurricane of blows. Valdés's spite was going to demolish the world. The slave slipped away between the man's legs, spitting blood. The captain chased after him. They fell in the courtyard, near the well. The scene from the slaughterhouse was being repeated. Luis's face was bleeding, and he was crying. Brother Bartolomé intervened energetically and ordered the captain to calm down.

"Enough! I will interrogate him!"

"Interrogate?" The captain dragged Luis to a pillar and tied him to it. He unhooked the riding crop from his belt and began to whip him.

"One!" he roared.

Luis collapsed against the pillar. A red stripe glowed on his back.

"Two!"

"Let me interrogate him!" the monk insisted.

"Three! So that he tells the truth."

"Don't hit him!" Aldonza begged, hands clasped as if in prayer.

"Four!"

"Stop, that's enough!" the monk implored. "He will tell the truth."

"So he tells it quickly—five!"

"Stop, stop!" Felipa screamed, covering her ears.

Luis fell against the pillar and lay in an unnatural position. Drops of blood grew on his back. He was a curled-up ball of pain.

Brother Bartolomé asked Francisco to bring him a chair. He was ready to start the interrogation. An inquisitor should always be seated.

"What's the point of sitting there," the boy thought, "when it's more logical to untie poor Luis and interrogate him in the living room." But the priest had his reasons: he considered it effective to ask questions right there, without freeing him from the pillar or untying his hands, without letting his body unfurl from that crushed position to which he had been reduced by blows. Francisco brought out the chair. He was in obvious distress. The monk leaned close to the bruised head and whispered the prescription of a ritual. He interrogated him in a low voice, almost in the mode of confession. Luis moaned and said, over and over, "I don't know, I don't know."

Catalina stood trembling behind Aldonza. She held a washbowl full of warm water and healing herbs. She wanted to devour time so she could reach her husband's side and ease his suffering. Brother Bartolomé sighed, his face ruddy, eyes violet. He turned to Valdés with a look of defeat.

"I think he must have taken the instruments with him."

"Who? Núñez da Silva?"

He nodded and, with great effort, rose to his feet. He adjusted the folds of his robe and told Diego to untie the slave.

"You believe he took them to Lima, then?" the captain asked incredulously.

"That's how it seems." He scratched the bulky nape of his neck. "But—how could we not have noticed? Why didn't he tell us?"

"Why?" the captain exclaimed. "To shit on us!"

Catalina kneeled and with infinite love began washing the blood from Luis's head and torso. Then she rubbed salve on the wounds. Felipa and Isabel approached, in solidarity, full of emotion. Luis moaned, eyes half-closed. Francisco caressed his strong arm. Luis gave him a sad smile of gratitude. They picked him up and, together, carried him to his room at the back of the house. He lay down on a hay mattress. His back was a dark page crossed with purple lines.

Francisco wanted to offer him some additional reparation for such an unjust punishment. He went in search of a tray, one of the few still left after the Inquisition's thorough pillage. He filled it with fruits and returned to the small room. He squatted down and showed it to Luis, who teared up again, mumbling, "Just like for the doctor."

"Yes, Luis. Just like we did for Papá. He liked for me to serve him this when he came home from work."

"He liked it—" he confirmed hoarsely.

After a while, he asked about "them." Francisco assured him that the house was now free, for the moment, of the elephantine monk and the violent captain.

———— ‹∿› ————

Brother Urueña rises, exhausted.

"Son." He joins his hands imploringly. "Do not allow yourself to be dragged away by the devil. Do not let yourself be tricked by his devious arguments. I beg you, for your own good." The monk's mouth has gone dry.

"I only listened to God, and to my conscience."

"I have come to console you. But, above all, I have come to offer my help. Do not cling to your own deafness," he insists. He is pale and hoarse. He pulls the chair back and moves toward the door. He asks for it to be opened.

Francisco's brow furrows. "Don't forget your promise."

The clergyman blinks, bewildered.

"You promised to keep my words a secret," Francisco reminds him.

Brother Urueña lifts an arm and makes the sign of the cross. The door creaks, a servant removes the chairs, a soldier takes the lamp away.

22

Brother Bartolomé had said that he would personally oversee the education of the Núñez da Silva girls. To "oversee" meant to impose his own will.

He came in the afternoons to talk to Aldonza, sitting in the half-empty living room. He savored her chocolate and fruit pastries. Catalina had to obtain the ingredients from some neighbor or another, especially the flour.

"How can he enter that room?" Francisco thought with uncontrollable hatred. "He himself ordered the removal of the mirrors and icons, the cushions and armchairs, and for the chests and candelabra to be sold."

"What does he want to take from us now?" Diego murmured each time he saw the monk enter their house with his huge cat.

Aldonza was deteriorating. She could endure great physical suffering, but she could not bear such profound moral subjugation. Her husband had been torn from her; before their betrothal he had told her that he was a New Christian, but he had never confessed to practicing Judaism. Was it true? If he had committed heresy, how should she behave now as his wife and as a Catholic mother?

When Brother Bartolomé came to call, Diego would immediately flee, as the man's presence repulsed him. Francisco, on the other hand, did the opposite: he tried to approach. In this fat, friendly, and severe commissioner there was something mysterious that Francisco had to discover. At the very least, he was the one who could best inform him about his father's fate. Because, in Córdoba, from the bishops on down, the only response ever uttered on this matter was "I don't know." His father had been taken to Lima to await trial. But for how long? "I don't know, I don't know." The commissioner could not say, "I don't know"; he was the commissioner.

The monk would enter with his belly swaying and his white ball of a cat at his side. Aldonza, as always, offered him something to eat as proof of her submissiveness. With his thick fingers he broke off pieces of fruit pastries, then threw his head back as he stuffed them into his mouth so as not to lose a crumb, sucking the ends of his fingers. He would immediately drink chocolate, as he liked to mix the pastry and the liquid on his tongue. His cheeks would puff intermittently as though he were practicing his swigs. Snorts of pleasure escaped him as he chewed and swallowed. His robe stank of sweat, and his cat of urine.

When he finished, Aldonza would offer him another round.

"Later," he would sometimes say, suppressing a punctual burp.

Then came a monologue on his favorite topics: food and faith. Completely oblivious to the privations she suffered, he told the anguished woman about outlandish combinations of meats, sauces, vegetables, and spices. Meanwhile, Francisco kept his ears open as he traced shapes on the ground.

Why did he come so often? A few days earlier, Diego had said, "To plunder us."

"To eat," Felipa said, indignant.

"I come to prevent the resurgence of heresy in this house," said Brother Bartolomé that afternoon, emphatically, as if he had gotten wind of the insults spoken in his absence.

Aldonza stared at him with zealous hope, making herself believe his every word.

"Do you suppose, my child, that it did not hurt me to take him away?" he asked, without mentioning Don Diego's name. "Do you believe that it didn't affect me to send him to another city in chains? Did I not suffer when I had to confiscate some possessions?" He leaned back on the creaking chair and placed his huge hands on his round belly. "I did it for Christ. I suffered as I did it, my child, but I did it with firm conviction."

Francisco almost retched when his nose inadvertently touched the robe and grazed the cat. The animal did not flinch. The commissioner's hand descended to the boy's bronze hair and gently rubbed his scalp. This had a somnolent effect. He understood why the cat was always dozing. But Francisco did not want to sleep; he wanted to accost the man with questions. He would do so that very afternoon. And, as he waited for the right moment like a stalking beast, he learned about his sisters' fate.

"Do you see, my child?" the monk repeated. "It is what's best for them, for you, and for all of you."

"Where will I get the dowry, Father?"

"We shall see, we shall see. But first things first: Have you decided?"

Aldonza twisted her fingers. Brother Bartolomé leaned forward and irreverently patted her knees, while his left hand kept on stroking Francisco's hair. There was something in that gesture, an excessive confidence, that scared the boy.

"Remember that danger looms over them," he added. "Their father is being prosecuted by the Inquisition, and—"

"What will they do to Papá?" Francisco burst out, pulling away from the hypnotic hand.

The monk froze: his fingers, tongue, breath. Only his eyes moved, searching for the boy in surprise.

"What will they do to Papá?"

The man crossed his fingers over his mountainous chest.

"I will explain it to you another time. Now I am speaking with your mother."

"But—"

"Go, Francisco. Go and play," Aldonza begged.

"I want to know."

"Another time." The monk now spoke with a caveman's tone.

"Go, Francisco."

The boy lowered his head. He was glued to the floor. This time, he would not obey.

"Fine," the monk said. "He may stay, but he must not interrupt."

Brother Bartolomé touched the feline with the tip of his shoe. The animal opened its golden eyes and, with a single leap, settled on the man's warm lap. He stroked him lavishly; all of his tactile love was now for the cat.

"Do you understand?" he continued, addressing Aldonza. "Your daughters are in danger. Let us use the word 'danger,' as it is the correct one. However devoted they may be, however pure your own blood, they bear the contamination of a Jew. That is not the case for you; nobody questions your legitimacy as an Old Christian. But the children you created with him—yes, they are questionable."

"Where will I get the dowry?" she asked again, full of anguish.

"The other danger is that, exactly—that of poverty. What can you do with these girls if you barely have enough money to subsist?"

"Oh God, God—"

"And the third danger—why emphasize this!—is the temptation of the flesh."

The woman crushed and ground her rosary.

"All right, I have decided!" she exclaimed. "But—what about the dowry?"

"We will begin to speak of that tomorrow. For today, it is enough to have made a decision. It is a good decision, worthy of a good mother."

He rose, making the universe creak, as was his custom. Francisco clung to his black robe.

"Tell me about Papá."

"What do you want to know? There is nothing to tell—not yet."

"What are they doing to him?"

"What do you think they are doing?"

"Nobody tells me, no one explains. Why hasn't he come home? When will he be back?"

The monk gazed at him with unexpected tenderness and leaned his heavy hand on the boy's shoulder.

"Your father has committed heresy. Do you know what that is?"

He shook his head.

"Your father has betrayed the true faith, and has exchanged it for the dead Law of Moses. Do you know what the dead Law of Moses is?"

He shook his head again. The hand was hurting his shoulder.

"Better for you not to know. Better that you never know! And that you never stray from the righteous path," he sighed.

"But—but what will they do to him?"

He stroked his double chin and took a deep breath. "They will try to make him return to the true faith. That is what they will do."

He walked to the door. Aldonza followed him like a soul doing penance. Francisco ran to his side, tripping over the cat and stepping on its tail.

"He will return!" Francisco shouted with the falsetto that broke through whenever he was on the brink of tears. "He will return here and he will return to the true faith! I'm sure of it!"

Aldonza crossed herself.

"He will return!" he called out over and over, pulling on Brother Bartolomé's robe.

The monk picked up his cat and murmured, "That—only the Lord can know."

Francisco stamped his feet briefly and then ran to the back door, toward his impregnable hiding place.

———◊◊◊———

The notary Marcos Antonio Aguilar unrolls a sheet of parchment and dips his quill, while the commissioner, Martín de Salvatierra, listens closely. Brother Urueña fulfills his duty by testifying to his terrible conversation with Doctor Francisco Maldonado da Silva, word for word. While he may have failed in his goal of reforming the prisoner, he can offer the Holy Office an accumulation of horrific facts and conclude that the man is a most persistent rebel.

23

The prolonged sobs of a dog in the night would not have had any special significance if Aldonza hadn't linked them to the sudden deflowering of their peach tree. "This portends misfortune." Her children tried to minimize the drama of it; the dog was from the neighborhood, and had been stepped on by a horse.

"It portends misfortune," Aldonza insisted, standing in the sea of pink surrounding the bare fruit tree. A brief spring gust had torn off all its petals.

Francisco thought that the only misfortune this could prophesy was his father's death. Diego asked Aldonza to move away from the peach tree. She raised her darkened gaze and said that she was tormented by a horrible premonition.

"You should leave, my son—although it hurts me to my soul, you are the one who should go far from Córdoba as soon as possible."

Diego's mouth twisted. "Leave?"

"Yes, before we come to regret your not doing so."

"I don't understand. Where would I go? When?"

She reached out her trembling arms and embraced him like a small child.

Diego thought that suffering might teach one how to see the future. His mother had reasons to worry, even if she didn't know the whole truth. Perhaps he should go to La Rioja, near the Andes, for a few months.

Brother Isidro arrived unexpectedly. Aldonza was alarmed, thinking that he, too, must have had the premonitions, but he said no; he had felt the need to visit them simply because he missed them, and because he knew they were sad.

That afternoon, Brother Bartolomé came to the house. Aldonza received him with her customary gestures of submissive obedience. In a few minutes, the monk's fingers were pinching pastry and his voracious lips were slurping chocolate. She mentioned her awful feeling. The commissioner said that he hadn't heard any dog's prolonged sobbing, and he was not at all concerned with superstitions over a blossoming tree. However, he did ask to speak with Diego. Aldonza dropped the tray that held the rest of the pastries.

"Diego?"

Francisco was tracing another map at the priest's feet; he offered to go find his brother. He searched the courtyard, looked in the garden, and asked the servants. Diego was nowhere to be found. "How lucky," he thought.

"He's not here," he told the commissioner.

Aldonza had already begun to pinch her rosary. Brother Isidro gritted his teeth, caressed his crucifix, and said to himself, "Thank you, Lord, for saving him."

Brother Bartolomé's mood changed. His round figure no longer expressed goodwill, but uneasiness.

"If he flees, it will only make things worse," he murmured.

The woman seemed about to fall to her knees. She managed to stutter, "Flee? Why would he flee?"

"Captain Valdés is waiting on the street." The commissioner pointed toward the front door. "If he doesn't appear immediately he will be taken by force."

Aldonza burst into tears and Francisco ran to the back. Captain Valdés and a couple of assistants marched into the courtyard and stationed themselves before the doors. The atmosphere from a year ago, when Don Diego was arrested, had been brusquely re-created.

Brother Bartolomé became extremely severe, the captain overbearing, and the family terrified. Behind the henchmen, the lugubrious familiars of the Holy Office appeared; they had been informed and invited to witness the edifying task. The only ones who hadn't been apprised were the prisoner and his family. Just like one year earlier. The Holy Office made a cult, an exercise, out of secrecy. They did the same with insensitivity, when purity of faith was at stake. Aldonza's despair didn't matter. She fell to the ground and clung to the commissioner's sandals. They were unmoved by the absence of the head of the family or the ruined state of this home. They went through the rooms in search of Diego. They pulled off the tablecloth to inspect under the table, opened the few trunks that remained, dragged aside beds bereft of mattresses, and scoured the servants' quarters. Finally they found him in the corral, from which he had been trying to escape next door. A fierce struggle broke out. The accused refused to submit and shouted at them to let him go. Four men dragged him to the first courtyard, where Brother Bartolomé awaited. Diego was shaking like a ship at sea. He fought his captors every way he could, but did not escape. The captain put a dagger to his neck.

"You'll behave decently, you stinking Marrano!"

The young man became still. They let him go. He straightened up, pushed his hair back from his face, and pulled at his ripped shirt.

"Come closer," Brother Bartolomé ordered from his chair.

Diego looked around him. He took two slow steps forward. Then lightning struck—he pushed one of the familiars of the Holy Office against Captain Valdés, kicked a henchman's shinbone, and disappeared down the street. He mounted a horse and flew off at a gallop. By the time they ran out after him, nothing was left but a cloud of dust.

The soldiers crashed into each other, searching for their mounts, and chaotically prepared to pursue him. Helmets clanged; the men cursed. "That reptile will pay for this," the captain kept saying.

Brother Bartolomé abandoned the house in a majestic rage, followed by his court of familiars of the Holy Office. Aldonza fell into the chair the monk had left empty. Francisco glided to the back of the house, and, when he'd confirmed that no one was watching, he entered his hiding place. "He can hide here if he comes back." He lay down on the cool earth. He imagined his brother galloping toward the slaughterhouse and, there, in the fray of animals, wagons, and slaves, he could change horses. He imagined his pursuers, who, on recognizing the horse without a rider, would think that he was trying to throw them off the scent by running barefoot, making them hunt through the whole fetid place. They would go through the pastures, beat the laborers, and slip in the blood and fat. Meanwhile, his brother would gain leagues of distance as he headed toward Buenos Aires.

Before dark, Catalina served a frugal dinner. Francisco stroked his mother's hand, wanting to transmit that the misfortune was not so bad; Diego had managed to escape, galloping in the direction of the ocean. But he couldn't sleep that night. When fatigue finally subsumed him, he was startled awake by a noise. A strange brightness approached, and iron clanged outside. He leapt out of bed and found his brother, dirty and shaking, between guards. They were tying him up beside the well. The light from their lanterns revealed bruises on his face and a bloody streak on his ruined shirt. They pushed him toward the living room, while one of the soldiers sent for Brother Bartolomé. Aldonza rushed toward her son, but they held her back before she could cross the threshold. She fell to her knees.

The wait became an eternity. Aldonza begged for her son to at least be allowed a drink of water. Francisco went to the well, filled a jug, and tried to put it to his brother's lips without permission. An official snatched the jug from him and poured its contents at the prisoner's feet.

A murmur arose, and the commissioner entered with his drowsy cat. An official who had just pulled Francisco's ear for his insolence now followed the monk. Brother Bartolomé settled pompously into a chair in the bare room, adjusting the folds of his robe and straightening the cross on his chest. He ordered the soldiers to bring the captive closer. The notary prepared his inkwell, quill, and parchment.

"Identify yourself," he said.

The young man stammered his name.

"Profession."

In Diego's dizzy vision the commissioner hovered in the air above him like an immense globe.

"Profession," pressed the monk.

"I don't know."

"Possessions. State your goods."

Diego hung his head. "Goods." The word sounded strange. "Goods. Good. Good and evil. My goods." He was weakened by exhaustion.

The commissioner counted on the fingers of his left hand. "Money."

He shook his head.

"Land. Silver objects. Horses. Mules. Slaves. Gold objects."

The notary's quill moved sonorously. Diego stood, with ropes around his body, moving like an elm in the wind. Brother Bartolomé gripped his cross and leaned close to the prisoner, forcing him to raise his gaze.

"Have you practiced Judaism?"

Diego shook his head.

This was not enough for the commissioner. "Answer! Have you practiced Jewish rites?"

"No—no. I'm a devout Catholic." His voice trembled. "You know that I'm a devout Catholic."

Brother Bartolomé let his cross fall back against his chest.

"In any case," he said, suppressing a yawn, "you will be put on trial by the Inquisition. You will be taken to Chile, and from there you will board a ship to Lima."

Aldonza's suffocated sobs were the only sound to fill the room. The hearing was over. The notary quickly finished the legal document while the henchmen untied Diego and gripped his arms. The officials formed two lines of honor around the corpulent commissioner and picked up their lanterns.

The few hours that remained in the night only sharpened the sorrow in the house. The following morning, the first son of Don Diego Núñez da Silva would go to be reunited with his father (or with his father's corpse), and Brother Bartolomé would return with a scroll to once again take stock of the assets of this impertinent family. In the end, he would take every last tattered rag.

Francisco didn't fall asleep until the break of dawn. His tangled thoughts had been shot through by a question that cut like a spear: "When will it be my turn?" He had just turned ten years old.

The familiar sequence: steps, lock, key, creak, a strip of light. Several soldiers enter.

"Get up!" they order.

His body is weak, riddled with pain.

They open his shackles. The rusted rings break off shreds of his skin and drops of pus. His wrists and ankles are startled by their sudden freedom. But a rope is tied around his waist. Long, thick, firm.

"Walk!"

"Where are you taking me?"

"Walk, I said!"

He staggers toward the door. Two soldiers tie his arms back; they hold and guide him. He enters the corridor. At last, something else will happen.

24

They went to church frequently. Aldonza, held up by one daughter on each side, walked with guilty steps. Francisco zigzagged restlessly, in front and behind, sometimes resembling the guide, sometimes the family dog. People did their best to avoid them. They exuded sadness and misfortune. This was how alone the three Marias must have felt when Christ was crucified, the boy thought again. "Christ was spurned like my father and my brother, and those who loved him were spurned as well. The ones who killed Christ and the ones who now refuse to greet us are the same in their malice."

Francisco liked the sermons of Brother Santiago de La Cruz, the spiritual director of the Dominican monastery, because he did not emphasize threats. He neither stirred fear with talk of the punishments of hell, nor did he describe them in morbid detail, as did most priests. He preferred to expand on love. Francisco was captivated by his explanations of Christ's kindness. The spiritual director pulled up the wide sleeves of his habit and leaned his fingers on the wooden rail. He offered moments of pleasure rather than a beating. "Although today is not Holy Thursday," he would say, "on which the sermon of the Last Supper is given, I will refer to it because, truly, it should be present in all sermons. Remember the ceremony in which Christ kneeled and washed the feet of His disciples, including those of Judas Iscariot, and said, 'I give you a new commandment: that you love each other, as I have loved you.'"

With simple examples, Brother Santiago de La Cruz demonstrated that love is more than a formula. "An upright Christian is he who loves others." And: "At the end of His life, Christ offered us a synthesis of His mission, because, in loving each other, we love Him. All imitation of Christ should begin with the practice of love for our mothers and children, our brothers and sisters and fathers, our relatives, our neighbors, the poor, the saints, and the sinners. Each human is marked by Him as a recipient of our affection." He raised his index finger for the first time. "To fail to do so is to mar the success of His divine mission."

Jesus hung over the altar. Blood clung to the crown of thorns. Blood streaked his nailed hands and feet, and a ribbon of blood trickled from his wounded side; blood also dripped from his knees and other parts of his furiously whipped body. He had suffered for the happiness of mankind. "He suffered for us, for my father, and for my brother Diego," Francisco thought. "If we're meant to imitate Christ, we're definitely imitating him now with our suffering."

25

Every day, Francisco went to the Santo Domingo monastery to attend Mass, fulfill tasks of penance, and study the catechism. He returned home in the late afternoon. On the way he gathered the fruit that hung over garden walls. He kept his mother and sisters company as they embroidered in silence. To break the atmosphere of mourning he told them about his encounters, about the artwork of Agustín and Tobías, who'd come all the way from Cuzco to carve marvelous reliefs for a new altar, or about the benefits of this or that sacrament, according to what he'd learned in class.

Then he would go out for a ride on an old and skillful mule, the only one they had left. He headed toward the river, then took the path in the direction of the blue mountains. The sunset warmed the colors of the sky. Birds circled overhead, calling out messages. Fragrances rose into the growing quiet. Looking back, he saw the cluster of houses near the sandy shore of the river.

On this day he dismounted, as the mule seemed hurt. Its front right foot was bleeding. He parted its hairs; the animal flinched in fear. He stroked it, and, taking its reins, led it back home. They had gone a long distance. Far down the road, two men and a mule appeared. They seemed to be in a hurry. It was obvious that they wanted to reach Córdoba before nightfall. He recognized them as Franciscans from the color of their robes. One of them was slim and was in the lead. The second man followed, pulling the mule; he was hunchbacked, with a beard so thick his nose was barely visible. They caught up to Francisco and asked how far they were from the city.

"You are already in Córdoba. As soon as you pass that next bend in the road, you'll see it."

The tall monk was walking rapidly, moving his arms like oars; he had a mad look about him. His stained habit was covered in the dust of a long journey.

"Did you come from far?"

"From La Rioja."

He tried to adjust his pace to that of the hurried monks. He told them that he'd never been to La Rioja, but that his father had been there. At this, the thin one smiled lightly, and asked who his father was. He answered that he was a doctor by the name of Diego Núñez da Silva.

"Diego Núñez da Silva?" The monk approached Francisco and put an arm around him, long as a tentacle. "I met your father—yes, I met him, and we spoke about medicine, among other things. We need doctors in these lands, do you know? I could not continue my studies because I was sent to Montilla monastery and then to Loreto monastery. Your father was struck by my stories about the bubonic plague in Spain. Do you know what the bubonic plague is?"

Francisco shook his head.

The monk explained as they kept walking. It was clear that he liked to chat; it had been a long time since he'd talked to anyone beyond his assistant. They followed the bend in the path, and there, in the diminishing light, a handful of towers stood beside the pearly ribbon of the river. The cicadas let out a great noise of welcome. The travelers paused for a moment to take in the landscape. The skeletal monk breathed through his mouth, smiling, allowing the breeze to ripple through his beard.

Francisco went in front to help guide them in the growing shadows. Soon he heard a clean, marvelous sound. It was the melody of an angel, something he'd never heard before. He looked back and saw the tall monk with an object that he held against his neck as he rubbed it with a stick. Francisco tripped against the mule, because he could not walk normally in the thrall of that music. It was like a giant butterfly scattering gold and sapphires. He felt the urge to leap. The thin stick rose and fell delicately as the fingers of the monk's left hand pressed the different strings.

The assistant noticed the boy's fascination and glided to his ear. "He is a saint. This is how he expresses his thanks to the Lord."

When they arrived at the outskirts of the city, the monk stopped playing his mysterious lute and put it away in one of the bundles on the mule's back.

"Could you tell us how to reach the Franciscan monastery?"

"Yes. It's close to my house."

"I am an inspector general of monasteries. Tell your father that I would like to see him tomorrow. Tell him my name is Francisco Solano."

The boy swallowed. How could he tell him that his father had been arrested as a Jew?

"What's the matter, my boy?"

Francisco hung his head.

The monk kneeled. He kneeled before a child! He placed his closed hand under Francisco's chin, and gently raised his gaze. "What happened to your father?"

His throat ached and he just barely managed to tell him that his father was gone, that he'd been taken to Lima.

"I understand," whispered the monk.

He rose pensively, scanned the starry sky, looked at his assistant, and asked to continue forward. They arrived at the royal road. Francisco felt the light, warm hand on his back. It was the sign of a miracle. He wanted to hug the man's knees.

Before the door of the monastery, the tall monk bid farewell with the following words: "Tomorrow I will bless your home. Go with God."

Francisco mounted his mule and, despite its wounded foot, forced it to gallop the short distance home. He burst into the room, found his mother, and threw himself at her feet. He leaned into her and said, "Tomorrow we will be visited by an angel."

Aldonza had heard talk of a monk who played a three-stringed instrument, and who was credited with marvels, but she did not believe that he would deign to visit them. "Why would he give us his time and his blessing? Our house is cursed."

The following day, at noon, Catalina came home from washing clothes in the river, full of excitement; the only gossip of the day was about the violin-playing saint who had come to town. The fantastic versions of the story coincided: he enchanted people with his music, understood the ways of animals, and performed miracles. The sleeves of his habit were wider than usual because, after dipping them in the river and taking them out full of fish, he had fed a hungry caravan; his sleeves remained wide as a testament to that marvel. All these wonders had Francisco spellbound.

At the end of the day, Brother Andrés, the violinist's companion, appeared. The boy recognized him from his hunched back, though he'd now been neatly shaved by the monastery barber. Since his superior had not yet completed his work duties, he explained, he thought it best to come and let them know. Aldonza offered him pastries and a cup of chocolate. The monk accepted a pastry and asked whether the whole family was present.

"Yes, all of us," the mother said.

"There are so few of us left," Felipa added.

Brother Andrés nodded; he was aware. This kind of news was shared immediately. The portrait of a mother with three children, two slaves, an empty house, and the oppressive uncertainty of the fates of her husband and eldest son—it must have made for a catastrophic effect.

He ate the pastry, leaning over the tray, emphasizing the deformity of his back. It was clear that he was not interested in the body, but in Francisco Solano. He began to speak of him and did not stop until night had fallen. Of course, he was captivating. It was like a beautiful story from a book. But it was not a fantastical story—Francisco Solano existed, and this deformed Andrés was living proof.

Aldonza offered him more pastries. But Felipa discreetly removed the tray—she did not want Francisco Solano to arrive to nothing but crumbs.

When he crossed the threshold, everybody rose to their feet. The man, a blurred figure in the twilight, quickly approached the mother. He blessed them and sat down. His hood fell onto his back and his long body glimmered with the radiance of the candles that Catalina respectfully placed at his side.

26

That night, Aldonza felt compelled to tell Francisco Solano about her husband's arrest, contradicting the urgings of silence that she herself had given her son that morning.

Francisco Solano inspired trust, despite the withered state of his flesh. He told them that, once, as he walked through Indian territory, he had become exhausted, and the people there had built him a kind of chair and carried him on a frame.

"I traveled half asleep," he laughed, "and occasionally I felt like a fraud imitating the pope. A terrible sin of arrogance, of course. But I let them do it because the help they were giving me, and which I truly needed, did them good. They were incredibly happy; they felt strong and generous. If I, to protect my virtue, had rejected this spontaneous offering, it would have been a selfish act. Paradoxical, no?"

At the end of the simple dinner, he surprised them.

"My brothers expect me to sleep in the monastery tonight. They have made splendid arrangements. But I won't go. Their monastery should always be beautifully kept, not only during an inspection. Nor will I explain my reasons. I will allow you to deduce them yourselves."

"Where, then, will we spend the night?" asked Andrés.

"You, in the monastery. And, if this family agrees to it, I prefer to sleep here."

"Here?"

"Yes. In this house. I wish to keep you company and convey my affection."

"It's an honor we don't deserve!" Aldonza exclaimed, bewildered. "We'll prepare the best room for you."

"No, no," he said, shaking his long head. "Do you want to chase me away? I only need you to lend me a basket. I'll sleep under a tree, under the open sky."

"Father—"

He extended his arms in a cross, with an air of resignation. "Every once in a while I give myself the pleasure of sleeping uncomfortably."

He said goodbye to Brother Andrés.

Catalina cleared the table and Aldonza went in search of a basket. She returned with three, so that the monk could choose. But Francisco Solano asked her to put them to the side, to replace the diminished candles with fresh ones, and to sit with him and her three children to converse. They formed a nervous circle. His peaceful courtesy did not erase his status as an extremely respected minister of the church. It was hard to understand his warmth for this disgraced family, unless he was looking at them through the lens of paradox, to which he seemed inclined.

The frogs began to croak and fireflies lit up the dark corners. The only dissonance—disruptive, unsettling—was Aldonza's cough.

The monk told them about his encounter in La Rioja with Doctor Diego Núñez da Silva, whom he called by his full name. He talked about the famed trial of Antonio Trelles, which began because he had tried to practice medicine without formal certification, and ended in the not entirely proven crime of being a practicing Jew. Part of his dinnerware had been acquired by Don Diego at a high price, as a way of helping the defenseless wife. "This reveals," he said, "that Don Diego has a noble heart."

His words set off a new wave of coughs from Aldonza. She choked on phlegm and tears; it was the most comforting thing she had heard in her life. Isabel and Felipa went to her side, embraced her, and dried her cheeks. Francisco felt miserable. His beautiful father was so far away, perhaps mutilated by torture or perhaps hung from a Spanish cherry tree in Lima.

Francisco Solano raised his large hand and placed it on the woman's head. He murmured a prayer and said that she should continue to nurture hope. And that she shouldn't feel disqualified from her faith for having married a New Christian. "All of us, the new and the old, are children of the Lord. This difference is unfortunate. Listen, the apostles themselves were New Christians. The receivers of the sacred Epistles were all New Christians. And who is more of a New Christian than Saint Paul himself?" The clergyman settled back into his chair and, fingering the long cord of his habit, spoke of the recent and dangerous division. "Before, people spoke of Christians, Moors, and Jews. But since the mass conversions, only the Christians remain. These Christians may be saints or sinners, but they are not good for being old or bad for being new. It is a serious way of impeding those who've joined the Christian faith from enjoying the same dignity as those who were already part of it. The Indians who were baptized—what are they if not New Christians? That the blessed acceptance of our faith should imply a new kind of sentence—this is absurd."

"The Indians are New Christians like our father?" Isabel asked, stunned.

"What else could they be?"

He gestured with his hands, sleeves waving along with them. Francisco had the fleeting impression that fish from the river might swim out right then and there. The monk spoke of New Christians who should be humbly imitated by many Old Christians, such as Juan de Ávila, Luis de León, Juan de La Cruz, and Pablo de Santa María. They all came from Jewish families full of rabbis. "In La Rioja, my vicar was a New Christian. He helped me a great deal, even though he was a persistent sinner. Every day he committed a minor sin. Every day! What a man! I pleaded with him, reprimanded him, and even threatened him. Useless. I came to think, and I believe I was correct, that the Lord was using this man to show that I was not as persuasive as they say I am."

"Brother Bartolomé Delgado will arrest you," Francisco blurted.

"Why?" The monk looked astonished.

"Because you criticize those who persecute New Christians. You defend the New Christians themselves."

"But not heretics," he said loudly, his face filling with a military glow. An uncomfortable silence followed.

"Not heretics," the monk repeated, returning to his normal tone.

"My father is a heretic?" Felipa stammered.

"I don't know. That will be determined by the High Tribunal of the Holy Office."

"You said he had a noble heart."

"I did say that. But heresy is another matter. Heresy is an attack on God, and an alliance with the devil. It is extremely serious."

"You told us not to be ashamed," Isabel ventured timidly.

"I said it, and I will say it again. Do not be ashamed, and be strong so as to resist temptation. If Doctor Diego Núñez da Silva has sinned, we shall know it. He can repent. If he has not committed any heinous crimes they will offer him reconciliation."

"What does that mean?" Francisco asked.

"Forgiveness, after an adequate penance."

"Then our mother and my sisters and I will be able to safely walk the streets again."

"You can do so now."

"No," Francisco replied, "we cannot. People say ugly things to us."

"Child, be quiet," Aldonza protested, fist to her mouth to suppress another cough.

"My mother and sisters do not dare go out anymore," added Francisco. "It's humiliating to walk to church, to Mass."

"Ridiculous!" exclaimed the monk.

"It's true," Francisco insisted, turning to Felipa. "What happened the last time?"

"People threw fruit rinds and eggshells at us," she said.

A cool, damp stillness kisses his face. Several mules and soldiers wait at the monastery door. The arms that grip Francisco help him mount. He hears the words "Sergeant," "equipment for prison," "Santiago."

Is he being taken to Santiago de Chile? An official says the name "Maldonado da Silva." The word "Silva" echoes.

"Silva," Francisco recalls, "from the lineage of Hasdai and Samuel Hanaguid."

27

An uproar greeted the dawn. Francisco Solano had not exaggerated when he said he'd share his breakfast with the morning birds. He broke his pastry into small pieces and attracted a hungry flock. Catalina, by now an expert at trapping small birds to enrich her stews, pounced on this fantastic crowd with her hemp net, which horrified the monk. She thought he had been using those crumbs as bait, and meant to help him catch them. Francisco Solano pushed her; Catalina imagined that he was angry because she had only captured a few so she leapt with renewed energy at another cluster of frenetically pecking birds. The monk shouted at her to move away, and she replied at the top of her voice that she was doing her best.

There was no more pastry for breakfast so Isabel served the monk some fruit. He ate a few white figs and left for the monastery. He wanted to arrive in time for Mass. Before he left, he mentioned that in a few days he would continue on toward Paraguay. He then offered to return the following morning to walk with them to Mass. This way he would teach the bad Christians how people who've been through difficult situations should be treated.

That afternoon, Brother Isidro appeared. He had heard about the Franciscan's visit. The whole city had found out, he said hyperbolically.

"He explained why he doesn't like for us to be called New Christians," Francisco said, unable to contain himself.

"Your mother isn't one."

"My father is, and so am I, and my sisters and brother, too," Francisco went on emphatically. "He taught us that it's a name used against Jews."

"That could be." His protruding eyes searched for someone else to speak with, to escape the siege.

"Who are the Jews?" Francisco asked.

Brother Isidro stepped back in surprise with a hint of fear. He ran his hand through his sparse white hair and then traced his hairline with his middle finger.

"Why do you want to know?"

"Because I've been called a Jew—a Marrano Jew."

"Who has called you that?"

"I'm asking you what it means, and you ask me who said it."

"I cannot answer you. You'll know in due time."

"I need to know now! Please—"

"Impatience is not a—"

"What impatience, Father!"

"What do you want to know?"

"Is it true that they worship a pig's head?"

"What? That's ridiculous! Tell me, who has told you such nonsense?"

"Lorenzo."

"The captain's son?"

"Yes."

"They don't worship a pig's head. They don't worship any animals, or any images."

"Lorenzo says they do. In that case, why don't Jews eat pork?"

"Because their laws forbid it. Those two things are completely unrelated."

"Then why are Jews pigs—*marranos*?"

"These things are unrelated. I just told you that."

"Why did people shout at me, call me a *marrano*?"

Brother Isidro pressed the boy's shoulders with both hands and shook him. "Because that is the way ignorant, irresponsible Christians talk."

"You're not telling me the truth."

"The truth! It's so complicated—how to explain it to you? Look, your father is a New Christian and the Old Christians don't like that."

"Does that mean he's Jewish?"

"They want to keep labeling him as Jewish. Didn't Francisco Solano tell you?"

"He was a Jew, then. Or *is* a Jew?"

"His ancestors were Jewish."

"They didn't eat pork."

"No. But they didn't worship—what you've been told they did. They worshipped no image."

"What do they believe in, then?"

"Only in God."

"What makes them different from us?"

Felipa's arrival allowed the monk to free himself from this dialogue. The girl said that her mother felt unwell and begged him to see her. The clergyman, before departing for Aldonza's room, ordered Francisco to say ten Our Fathers and ten Hail Marys. "They will comfort you."

Francisco Solano kept his promise. He came the following day with his hunchbacked assistant to accompany them to Mass.

Aldonza seemed smaller and more stooped than before, a black shawl hiding her hair, her forehead, and part of her cheeks; only her blue eyes could be seen clearly. The monk asked her to walk to his right. That distinction caused, in her, a new shortness of breath. Isabel would walk to his left. Young Francisco would be in front, Felipa behind. Following Felipa, to close their entourage, Andrés the helper. They formed a cross. A human cross going to church with an exhibitionist spirit. The monk's bony head towered in the center, causing rumors to ripple out. This lesson about solidarity was only understood by some.

―――

Martín de Salvatierra spies the small group of men from a barely open window in the thick wall of the Dominican monastery. At the group's center, dutifully tied up with rope, is the prisoner. His beard and hair are disheveled. His arrest, interrogation, testimonies, and transfer have all been carried out with effective discipline.

"May the Lord help him to rediscover the truth," he prays. "May the long journey to Santiago de Chile work on his soul as the path of Damascus did on the soul of the apostle."

28

The fates of Isabel and Felipa were resolved by Brother Bartolomé. He considered it necessary for them to join the novices who would form the core of a new convent for nuns. The bishop Trejo y Sanabria was determined to open it soon. It was advantageous to help the bishop, and, as a commissioner, it was a triumph to have the descendants of a heretic commit to the true faith. Custom demanded that the future wives of Christ approach the divine nuptials with a dowry. Where to get that sum, when their assets had been confiscated and sent to Lima? Divine providence came to their aid. In effect, Juan José Brizuela, owner of the house where Aldonza and her children lived, had just been arrested in Santiago de Chile. The property would have been paid for by Don Diego with what he earned from selling his house in Ibatín. But this residence had already changed hands at a good price, thanks to the intervention of the implacable Antonio Luque; the monies arrived by well-guarded mule to the treasury of the Inquisition. Núñez da Silva was in no condition, then, to fulfill his duties. The arrest of Brizuela in Chile made it necessary to sell the Córdoba property to a third party, as money was required for the cost of the trial. And here Brother Bartolomé displayed his skill: he turned to the Indian overseer Hernando Toro y Navarra, whose recent riches were out of tune with his shabby home, and proposed an advantageous procedure in the name of the Holy Office. Brother Bartolomé could sell him Brizuela's house at a low price if he donated dowries for Isabel and Felipa to the future convent. It was not difficult to reach an agreement, and, with his cat and a smile, he went to deliver the news to the sorrowful women.

Upon learning of the arrangements, Aldonza clasped her hands anxiously and wondered where she and Francisco would live. "At least your sisters will be safe," she consoled her son, coughing as she spoke. "They will have food, shelter, and dignity."

A date was set for Felipa and Isabel to go to the home of Leonor Tejeda, the widow who had donated her assets and her home to build the first convent for nuns, dedicated to Santa Catalina. The sisters were instructed to take all their possessions with them. In their new home, they would be told what to do with each item: the clothes would be mended, reshaped, and either kept for daily use or donated to the needy.

Isabel and Felipa went through the few trunks they had left and prepared their limited trousseau. Catalina helped them sew and mend where it was called for. The enslaved woman didn't know where she would end up, either. She and Luis prepared a farewell luncheon. She went through the neighborhood and filled her basket with whatever fruit, vegetables, or grains she could find on her path. Luis arranged to fill a pitcher with red wine at the Mercedarian monastery, with the essential complicity of Brother Isidro. Aldonza, struggling against the weakness that tugged her toward bed, took out the only embroidered tablecloth she had left, which, thanks to a stain, had not been sold. Felipa and Isabel set out what remained of the dinnerware: one ceramic plate and three tin ones, four jugs with crooked lips, three nicked knives, the saltshaker, and a clay serving bowl. Aldonza gathered flowers from the potato plants in their garden and placed them at the center of the table.

During the sad meal Felipa joked about the flowers her mother had set out, comparing them to hyacinths. Isabel laughed at the clay serving bowl, which traveled frequently back to the stove to bring new servings. Francisco pretended to cut his own throat with the knife; its dents did nothing but tickle. Aldonza ate slowly, interrupted by her cough, smiling at her children's silly antics. That afternoon they were to appear at the home of Leonor Tejeda.

Isabel and Felipa arranged the bundles on their heads, like slaves. They set out toward their new home, accompanied by their mother and Francisco. In the street, adobe walls extended their shadows like long puddles of ink. A few passersby turned to watch the woman, who seemed like a widow, and her children of wretched blood. They murmured but no longer hurled insults. It was known that the girls were headed for the novitiate; they were purifying themselves of the heresy their father had committed. Francisco glanced at the onlookers from the corners of his eyes and saw expressions of hatred, approval, pity, and disdain. Every neighbor felt entitled—and obliged—to have an opinion regarding the relatives of a Marrano.

A nun with a wrinkled face welcomed them. She had come from Castile, Spain, by mistake, and she'd been sent to this mansion to help Leonor Tejeda found the convent. She had the virtue of going unnoticed, and this modest way of hers served as an example of how a bride of Christ should behave. She looked at the group with mousy eyes and invited them in. She ordered Francisco to stay outside.

"No men allowed."

She wore a large black habit with V-shaped sleeves. Her snow-white scapular conveyed her obsessive cleanliness. A jet-black belt slung around her waist and a rosary with pale wooden beads hung around her neck. Her starched wimple trembled on her head. She was withered, hunched, and half blind, and yet she exuded a strange vigor. She walked ahead of them down the short hall and turned left at the colonnades of the first courtyard. A couple of novices asked if she needed anything.

"Light," she answered coldly, gesturing at her visitors to sit on a carob wood bench. A candelabra was brought in.

"For them," she said. "I see better in the dark."

Isabel and Felipa placed their bundles at their feet and folded their hands on their laps. Aldonza coughed and apologized.

"These girls," the nun said, "have been honored by the church. I do not like to flatter in vain, but I do want them to feel grateful."

"We are," Aldonza assured her. "We are."

"Brother Bartolomé told me of these girls' virtues."

"That man is a saint," Aldonza said.

"And he told me that their dowry has already been paid."

"Thanks be to Our Lord and the Sacred Virgin."

"Now these girls must learn how to live in the sacred retreat of a cloister."

Night was falling sweetly. A few candles lit up in the austere rooms of the convent. A warm scent of resin and honeysuckle spread through the air.

"You may bid your daughters farewell."

Isabel and Felipa waited stiffly between their mother and the nun, between their known world and the world they were to discover. They would be releasing their pasts, which, despite the bitterness, had given them love and their shares of happiness; they now entered an exalted yet highly regulated future. Behind them lay their childhood and their dreams, which included the arrival of some handsome, magnificent gentlemen. Before them lay their new role of disciplined service to God. They stared in anguish at the plants in the courtyard, the flowerpots shrouded in darkness; for many years to come they would see this same courtyard, these same flowers. They would sit on this carob wood bench again and again, and remember this moment. They also stared at the few novices who glided noiselessly through the halls, like ghosts. They would do the same.

Aldonza reached for her daughters' hands. She caressed them. Then she began to cough up phlegm, and cough tears, and, without waiting for her cough to subside, she embraced them fiercely, touched their backs, necks, and arms, saying over and over between ragged breaths and eruptions, "May God bless you." Felipa's cheeks were drenched. She asked the nun for permission to say goodbye to her brother. The nun assented and guided them back to the front door. She slid back a creaky bolt and opened the door. A shaft of outside light invaded the floor. Francisco had been crouching against the coarse wall; he sprang up and embraced his sisters. Never had he so powerfully felt that they belonged to each other. He hadn't imagined that the separation would hurt so sharply. Were all his relatives going to fall away, like a leper's fingers? He had to imprint them into his body. But Isabel and Felipa pulled away, shaking and afraid.

Aldonza and Francisco walked home with heavy steps. She murmured Hail Marys. Francisco only thought of the greatest son of a bitch in the world and his revolting cat; that man had shattered his family into pieces. Back home, he felt the house to be more empty than ever. He lay down on a mat. He gazed at the sky through the window of his bare room. He attempted to read the stars. He longed to recapture its mysterious alphabet. Perhaps the celestial bodies that didn't twinkle were the vowels. Venus could be the *A*, and Jupiter the *E*, for example. The stars themselves were the consonants. There were too many consonants. "No, I don't think I can resolve the enigma that way." The wise men of ancient times studied the illumined heavens as a living body. "The constellations assemble and gather themselves into shapes," he thought. At the same time, parts of those shapes were part of other shapes; they were superimposed. Like peeling back skin to find muscles, and bones under that, and inside those bones the marrow. The brilliance rose from the simultaneous display of all those planes; a living body that allows its innards to be seen along with its surface skin. He wondered whether he should read it like *Treatise on Anatomy*, his father's book.

In his rage, he searched intensely for an encouraging sign, but could not find one. His interrogation of the stars continued on the nights that followed, and into the years that followed.

29

One winter morning, Hernando Toro y Navarra, the strong and brutish Indian overseer who had acquired Juan José Brizuela's property and donated Isabel's and Felipa's dowry, arrived to claim the property. His boots were dirty, but he wore a silk shirt, a blue velvet vest, and a wide-brimmed hat. The contrast reflected his farmer origins and recent wealth. He could not read but could make any mathematical calculation in an instant. He took delight in punishing his Indians and commiserated with the sick.

He went through the house and ordered that personal items be cleared out. A squadron removed the last trunks, furniture, and objects in a flash, piling them in the muddy servants' quarters. Toro y Navarra looked back out through the bedroom, now stripped bare, and saw the woman and her son seated on a log under the naked grapevine. Soon the furniture from his previous home had filled the house; it seemed new compared to the junk swept to the back.

Brother Bartolomé influenced the Indian overseer to let the mother and son remain in the house for a few more months, at least until the end of winter. The newly rich man relegated them to the servants' quarters. Luis and Catalina, meanwhile, could not stay and were added to the legion that labored in the Dominicans' giant orchard.

The cold and the rain forced them to keep the braziers lit and dry their clothes inside the house. Francisco went to the monastery every day to fulfill his tasks of penance; before returning to his mother's side he managed to hide fruit, cheese, bread, and cured meats under his clothes. Not that he was any good at stealing; rather, some of the monks looked up at the sky as he gathered his provisions.

Aldonza's piercing cough rang out like a bad omen. At night, Francisco covered his ears so he wouldn't hear it. He imagined her sitting in the dark, the veins in her neck swollen, her face discolored. One morning she woke with a sharp pain in her chest, as if she'd been stabbed by a knife. Francisco helped her search the straw mattress, but there was nothing there except the stench of death.

She said, "It's not a knife; it's the call of death."

The boy ran for help. Toro y Navarra's wife came in, responding with unusual mercy to what she saw. Frightened, she called for a doctor. Cold cloths were placed on Aldonza's head. The doctor sat on a stool and calmly took her pulse, looked into her pupils, touched her cheeks, and asked for the urine in the chamber pot to be poured into a glass jar so he could examine it in the light. He recommended daily suction treatments, vegetable broth, and the application of leeches to remove the bad blood. Francisco offered to search for all that was needed: vegetables for the soup, leeches, and someone to skillfully apply the suction. He flew to the convent and returned with good news.

On a table at Aldonza's side there appeared a dozen cups made of thick glass and a candle. She was told to lie facedown, and her back was undressed. An expert neighbor was to perform the treatment. With her left hand the neighbor held the glass cup, and with her right hand she inserted the candle's blue fire. Before the flickering flame could go out, she placed the glass facedown against the skin. Aldonza let out a cry of surprise and burning pain. The neighbor covered her entire back with those objects that sucked at her flesh. Through the glass, she checked that the skin was being pulled forcefully; pores were opening and the skin turned red and gleamed with sweat. She was covered with a clean blanket. The glass cups had to work for at least ten minutes. The void inside them would "suck out" the illness. When ten minutes had passed, the able neighbor began to move each cup back and forth in order to lift an edge from the skin; air rushed in and the glass detached. She removed the twelve cups in the blink of an eye, and Aldonza was left with twelve bulging red circles ringed with black. She rolled to her side, laboriously.

"In a while, she'll feel better," the neighbor predicted.

The procedure was repeated every day. As was the bloodletting through leeches. The wife of Toro y Navarra visited her in the afternoons. Two of her slaves prepared the patient's food.

Francisco, on returning from the monastery, found Aldonza up, wearing a long serge nightgown. She took advantage of her fledgling recovery to make some arrangements. But when Francisco learned the finality of those arrangements, he was pierced with anguish; his mother had finished sewing her shroud. She placed it at the head of her bed, neatly folded. Over the shroud she draped the silk sash she had worn at her wedding. On top, like a paperweight, she put the crucifix that her mother, now dead, had given her years ago. She stared at the lugubrious pile with satisfaction, almost with hope. She asked Francisco to help her lie back down. She had grown thin and old. Every motion magnified her pain. She moaned involuntarily.

"My son, I wish to confess."

He set out in search of a priest. Keeping out of puddles, he went to find Brother Bartolomé. He couldn't have explained why his steps led him there. He could have found the Dominican monastery with his eyes closed. He entered through the gray gate, crossed the disharmonious cloister, and stood before the enormous commissioner, whom he found reading a report, the cat on his knees.

"Father—"

Bothered by the interruption, the clergyman looked at him, brow furrowed, and made no move until the boy explained the urgency of the matter. It took him a few moments to respond, as if he hadn't understood.

Then he put his papers down and stood up heavily.

"Let's go," he said.

He had never walked so fast. His belly bounced madly and his double chin puffed with heavy breathing. The cat ran a few yards by the monk's right foot, then a few by his left. Their rush to reach the dying woman eased Francisco's hostility toward them both. He glanced at the cat's neck and decided that he wouldn't cut it after all, and he wouldn't slice through Brother Bartolomé's double chin. The duo exuded a certain inexplicable kindness. But when they reached the sick woman's side, something incredible happened.

"Thank you for coming, Father," Aldonza murmured weakly. "I don't wish to anger you, but I will confess to Brother Isidro."

"I am ready to receive your confession, my child," the commissioner insisted, his bulky face awash with surprise.

She shook her head with a sad smile.

Brother Bartolomé turned pale. His double chin trembled. The knife that had cut into Aldonza's chest a few days before now sliced into the monk's heart.

"Well done, Mamá," Francisco cheered without speaking, "that's exactly the answer I've wanted to hear from a saint like you." And he ran again, this time in search of the monk with the bulging eyes and cowardly spirit.

Isidro was not startled; he was resigned to the arrival of calamities, like links in a chain. Without a word he gathered up his vestment and his sacred oil. He sensed that Aldonza would need something more than a confession. His walk contrasted starkly with Brother Bartolomé's. It was almost solemn. Brother Isidro assumed the power of his sacred role, while Brother Bartolomé had lost touch with it in his arrogance.

Isidro felt clean and peaceful, while Bartolomé felt guilty and murky. Isidro behaved, on this terrible occasion, the way Don Diego would have wished him to.

He entered the room, which was warmed by the smoky brazier and the vapors of herbs. He made the sign of the cross and was left alone with the sick woman. Brother Bartolomé was invited into the living room by the man of the house, as it was too cold to be outside. The room was now decorated with new, luxurious furnishings.

Francisco went into another room, beside his mother's, where an enslaved woman was ironing clothes. He curled up on the floor. The black woman removed the ashes from the iron and filled it with coal, then closed it and shook the thing vigorously to heat the base. She sprinkled water on the clothing and began ironing. With her left hand she pulled the cloth taut, and with her right she erased the wrinkles, glancing intermittently at the grief-stricken boy. Outside, the naked trees received a light, freezing rain.

Brother Isidro appeared, eyes red with tears. He walked slowly under the needles of rain, hunched over, arms limp at his sides. Francisco wrapped himself in a sackcloth and went to him. They clasped hands and embraced each other in the icy cold.

He went into the room and approached his mother. Her body was covered in a blanket, and she emanated calm. Her thin cheeks seemed made of quartz. Her forehead, now free of the furrows of suffering, shone with a cross of sacred oil. She would no longer respond, and she would not cough again. She had become a piece of eternity. Francisco advanced cautiously, scared of committing a desecration. He kneeled beside her. He stared at her in sorrow. His fingers shook as they reached for her still, beloved hand. He touched it, pressed it. Then he began to cry in a blend of animal sounds and suffocation. He cupped her face, still warm from fever, and kissed her forehead, her flaccid cheeks, her nose, lips, chin. It was horrific to confirm that she was dead.

BOOK TWO

Exodus

The Journey of Bewilderment

30

Lorenzo Valdés attended Aldonza's funeral and walked behind Francisco in the drizzling rain all the way to the cemetery. They embraced and teared up together. They were friends again.

The following week, Lorenzo went to see him at the Santo Domingo monastery, where Francisco had been sent to live. Lorenzo invited Francisco to go with him to a corral. On the way, Lorenzo credited his own great skill in mounting horses, climbing trees, and walking on ropes to early training.

"You have to start by subduing mules in order to know how to subdue Indians," he said, repeating his father's declaration.

He had grown accustomed to visiting the thunderous corral to handle two or three animals and impress the laborers. He invited Francisco to come see him. The corrals blended viciousness with valor. They were a good school for men who would have to face the adversities of this savage continent. The captain of the Lancers celebrated his son's cruelties. "Mount, beat, and domesticate! That's how a good soldier does it."

Lorenzo knew mestizos and a few impoverished Spanish gentlemen whose job it was to tame wild beasts for little pay. He asked for a lasso and boldly entered the corral. The animals, in their keen sensitivity, registered the intrusion and began to buck. A seismic undulation rippled through the gray mass. A few began to run, while others whipped around in circles, pushing at their neighbors. Their hoofs stirred clouds of dust and manure. Lorenzo ran after the most spirited ones. Cries arose, along with the whir of the spinning lasso. Finally, he cast the rope and a damp mule fell forward. The creature tugged convulsively, dragging Lorenzo behind him. Several laborers came to his aid and managed to take her down. The beast kicked and tried to bite. They tied her legs, while others held her head down with a prod and blindfolded her eyes. She rammed her head against the ground, wounding her own eyes and teeth. They placed a second harness on her feet and left her to think she was free. She rose with a furious howl. Blood dripped from her head. She seemed determined to exact revenge, but because she was held by two harnesses, movement only tangled her. Her despair increased; she turned, arching her back, and let out blaring sounds.

The captain's son leapt onto her. The outraged beast flexed her spine wildly. The rider leaned toward the nape of the creature's neck and gripped her ears as if they were handles. His legs grasped the sweaty abdomen and would not let up the intensity of their grasp for any reason. The offended mule thundered, spun, and hurled herself against her slippery enemies. As her struggle was fruitless, she decided to bolt. This always happened. Lorenzo was ready, legs tight around her belly, hands on the verge of pulling off the creature's ears. The animal attempted to run, but the laborers who held the harness had seen it coming and stopped the attempt. She strained her neck angrily against the sudden tension of the reins. She was dazed. Then she charged at the laborers like a bull. Lorenzo dug in his spurs. One, two, six, ten times in a row, with as much rage as he could, until he drew blood. The mule lost her sense of direction and turned in abrupt circles in an effort to buck the machine wounding her mercilessly. Lorenzo did not detach; he savored this war.

Francisco watched uneasily. Standing at the log fence, he jolted in time with his friend. Lorenzo was flung into the air and mounted the mule again, though she kept on bucking. He twisted her ears and shouted obscenities. The mule, now sheathed in dust and sweat, was about to fall in exhaustion, but first she received yet more blows.

When she seemed at the edge of collapse, they took the blindfold from her eyes. The skillful rider let go of her ears, which were, miraculously, still attached to her head. The mule foamed at the mouth and turned as if drunk. Finally, Lorenzo led her to the foreman so he could confirm that she had been subdued.

"Well handled," he acknowledged, caressing her damp mane. It was the first caress this animal had ever received.

The rider made a gesture of triumph and dismounted. He deserved to rest for a while before domesticating another beast. He walked to the fence, slipped between its logs, and sat next to Francisco. He was agitated, still breathing through his mouth like a male dog right after dismounting a female. He hugged his knees. Francisco admired him with some inner conflict, as he felt no desire to subdue animals.

"Come on! Don't you dare to?" Lorenzo laughed. "You'll do it one day. It's easy."

Meanwhile, the task continued. It was a virile pleasure that did not seem like work. That was why there were no Indians involved. They were not permitted to participate, as they were considered slow and clumsy. Whenever one of them obtained an untamed beast at a low price—thin, sick, or possessing weak veins—he would take it to his hut and tame it with a method that differed greatly from the Spaniards' way. Instead of giving the creature a bloody beating, an Indian would tie it to a tree trunk surrounded by bare land. And there he would leave the beast for twenty-four hours without food or drink. Then he would touch its back to see whether it was tame. If the animal still possessed some spirit, he left it for another twenty-four hours in the same conditions. When asked the reason for this method, the Indian would answer, "It wants to rest."

Francisco was not drawn to Lorenzo's passions, but he celebrated his bravery. Talking with him, and seeing him, produced an inexplicable sense of well-being. His own increasing passion, on the other hand, was for something more reprehensible: books. It bothered him that they were only grudgingly allowed at the monastery. The local representatives of the Inquisition were still wary as to the purity of faith that reigned in his heart.

After insistent begging, Francisco gained permission to read the prayer book. And instead of savoring it slowly at a pace of a few pages a day, he devoured it in half a month. His reunion with the written word gave him hours of forgotten joy. He found reprieve from his own helplessness. A few sentences made him smile, while others made him cry. When he finished, he went to request another book, but he was refused. He began reading the prayer book again from the first page, and had read it five times through when finally Brother Santiago de La Cruz, somewhat more confident after these good seeds had been sown, gave him an apologist's biography of Santo Domingo, or Saint Dominic, the founder of the order to which the monastery belonged. Domingo Guzmán had been born in Spain—"like my ancestors," Francisco thought—and the members of the Dominican order had, since the beginning, been pursuers and suppressors of those dirty heretics the Albigenses, and for this reason they became the strong arm of the Inquisition. Domingo Guzmán traveled to many countries and even went as far as Denmark; he gave captivating sermons and practiced what he preached. Barefoot, sheathed in a worn robe, and eating little more than crusts, he opened hearts with entreaties and a certain amount of humility. He died at the age of fifty-one, consumed by the demands of his ministry.

Francisco transmitted a few enthusiastic comments about the saint to his spiritual director. De La Cruz did not allow himself to be impressed (education was also a kind of taming, though a subtle one).

"Read it again."

The boy stroked the book's covers and immersed himself again in the exemplary story. Every one of Saint Dominic's journeys and sermons had a concrete goal: to convert, to sanctify. He did it for the people of his time, but he also did it for those who were still to come. He did it so that he, Francisco Maldonado da Silva, would learn and reflect and adhere more closely to Our Lord Jesus Christ. "So that I, Francisco, should not be lost."

The spiritual director thought it opportune to offer him another work: the life of Saint Augustine. This legendary doctor of the church was born in Africa, in the year 354. Christianity was just emerging from the pagan multitudes. His mother was no less than Saint Monica, and his father was a pagan. It must be said, then, that this eminent father of the church was a New Christian, Francisco thought. In his youth, Augustine had avidly traversed the whole sewer of sinful acts. "I tried to satisfy the ardor I felt through the most vulgar voluptuousness," he would acknowledge in his *Confessions*. Later, after a great deal of reading and seeking, he converted. He was already an expert in philosophy. He was named bishop of Hippo and soon astonished people with his startling virtue. But he astonished people even more with his writing, which soon became a torrent. He produced books about religion, philosophical treatises, works of criticism, law, and history. He wrote to kings, pontiffs, and bishops. He refuted heresies with unparalleled brilliance. Finally, he completed *Confessions*, a jewel Francisco would have liked to have read in its entirety, not just in the fragments doled out in the biography. He longed to emulate the man, to write treatises and epistles.

The spiritual director made no more demands; the boy had gained his confidence and seemed well "tamed." "Like the mules in the corral," the boy might have added.

The next day, with a conspiratorial look, the monk offered a new book, a summary of the life and works of Saint Thomas of Aquinas. He referred to the man as a colossus. Francisco burned with excitement.

He was at a loss to convey his gratitude. Santiago de La Cruz did not act arbitrarily; he regulated the boy's education wisely. When Francisco returned the volume on Saint Thomas quoting some of his maxims, the spiritual director opened his hands.

"I have nothing more to offer you."

"Nothing?"

"I have no more books," he apologized.

Francisco thought of telling him something, but didn't yet dare. It could be taken the wrong way. For months, he had longed to read it. It was a prize that he perhaps did not deserve. The book was in the monastery chapel. But no, better to stay quiet. It was too much.

"In the monastery chapel," he whispered, his own voice unrecognizable.

"What about it?"

"In the chapel—" he began to sweat.

"Speak."

"There is a Bible."

"Yes. That is true. So?"

"I wish to read it. I wish—"

"It is too much for you." He gave the boy a sidelong glance.

"Just a little each day," Francisco implored. "The parts you choose for me."

"Only the parts I choose!" he exclaimed, quickly regretting his words.

"I promise."

"No spying in the Song of Songs, or in Ruth, or in the part about Sodom and Gomorrah."

"The parts you choose," Francisco said.

"Well then, to make things easier you'll read only the New Testament."

"All of it?"

"Yes. But not one page of the Old."

Hours later, a love affair began. The boy took possession of the enormous tome that was kept in the chapel. He opened the robust cover and went into ecstasy over the pages bejeweled with illustrations. He entered a familiar garden. He read and contemplated. The letters formed a landscape full of streams and hills. He savored the four Gospels, the Acts of the Apostles, the Epistles, and Revelations. His longing to learn gathered power with an irrepressible need to believe.

In his prayers he addressed Our Lord Jesus Christ, his Immaculate Mother, and the saints whose lives he had studied and admired—Dominic, Augustine, Thomas—asking them to help him become imbued with the true faith. But, above all, he prayed for them to help dissolve the drops of poison mentioned by the familiars of the Inquisition, in case it was true that his father had injected them into his soul.

When the spiritual director grew used to finding Francisco immersed in the verses of the New Testament and had seen sufficient evidence of his obedience, he lowered his guard. The young reader did not break his promise. He memorized the genealogy of Jesus according to Matthew and Luke, as well as many of the words spoken by Our Lord in his years of sermons. He could recite the facts to be found in one Gospel that went unmentioned in another, as well as a dozen of the terrifying images described in Revelations. In the Epistles of Saint Paul, he was particularly pleased and impressed by the one addressed to the Romans. He read it several times, but only fifteen years later would he understand the reasons for his enthusiasm.

He did not break his promise for fear of reprisal. It would have been intolerable for these secret pages to be taken from him. As he memorized the New Testament, and as his rereading increasingly became a test of his memory, his urge to dive into the voluminous Old Testament grew, but he would not do it without permission. He said as much to Santiago de La Cruz.

"Only to reinforce my faith in the fulfillment of the divine promise," he begged.

"The Old Testament contains the Dead Law of Moses," the spiritual director said with a penetrating gaze.

"But it also holds the promise of the Messiah," Francisco remarked.

"Whom the infidels do not recognize."

"They must not know how to read."

De La Cruz smiled. "They read with other eyes."

"Yes—infidel eyes."

He smiled again, patted Francisco's back, and raised his index finger authoritatively. "I accept, but on one condition."

"Please tell me."

"Any doubts that appear, you'll discuss with me."

"It would be a privilege," Francisco said, flushing with happiness.

"It is a duty."

The boy kissed the spiritual director's hand and ran to the chapel. The peaceful space was more beautiful than ever. The altar candles raised their still flames toward the polychromatic images. Francisco kissed the thick volume's embossed spine. He stroked the first page and read in fascination: "In the beginning, God created the heaven and the earth. And the earth was without form, and void . . ."

31

Santiago de La Cruz confirmed that reading the Old Testament was not undoing Francisco's beliefs. The questions he posed demonstrated his sharp intelligence, but no weakening of faith; the harshness of Moses, for example, or Samson's eroticism, the sins of David, Solomon's transgressions, or the ineffectiveness of prophetic sermons were all announcements of the errors the Jews would commit against Christ. He rapidly absorbed the drier chapters, including the boring genealogies and the interminable prescriptions of Leviticus and Deuteronomy, but he said nothing about verses that contradicted Christian dogma. On the contrary: he was excited to recognize moments that foreshadowed Christ, or concrete prophesies that His kingdom would arrive. The boy's unique talent prompted the man to take an unusual step—to introduce him to the bishop of the province, who was paying Córdoba a visit.

Bishop Fernando Trejo y Sanabria was a Franciscan obsessed with education. He was trying to create a college for higher education with a faculty comprised of Jesuit priests. He wanted to offer a range of degrees, from baccalaureates all the way to doctorates. He was Creole, loved the Indians, and dreamed preposterously of founding a university in these lands.

Francisco was enthralled by His Illustriousness. He had imagined a gigantic being with a thundering voice and menacing gestures. The man who received him, however, was of medium height, with a gaunt face, small hands, and a threadbare gray habit. He was a warm candle whose flame burned brightly but was rapidly consumed. His sickly appearance suggested that he had little time left among the living, which was why he burned with such an urgent call to offer mass sacraments of confirmation to the residents of Córdoba.

Francisco returned to the monastery full of wonder, hungry to partake in such an occasion. His spiritual director would help.

Santiago de La Cruz accepted the challenge and made arrangements for the boy to sleep from then on in a cell beside his own. There was just enough space for a rush mat, the leather suitcase that held his meager possessions, a table, and a chair. The director wanted him close day and night. He was trying to convert him into a *doctrinero*, a parish priest for the Indians, because his love of reading should translate into some kind of useful work.

Sitting beside Francisco, near the well, he began to emphasize the value of sensory signs.

"A sign is that which reminds us of something," he explained. "For example, the olive branch is a sign of peace, the robe I am wearing is a sign of priesthood, and a footprint is a sign that someone has stepped in that place. Sensory means that one registers the sign through the senses: sight, smell, hearing, touch, or taste."

He raised his right hand and approached Francisco, trembling slightly. He brushed the boy's cheek with the tips of his fingers.

"Touch," he murmured. "You feel that I am touching you."

Francisco was struck by an unfamiliar shudder and pulled his face away.

Santiago betrayed the hint of a smile. "You don't only feel," he added. "This contact transmits something, says something. It is a signal, a sign. It speaks to our bond."

The director's voice went hoarse. He stared at his disciple with intensity and then stood. Francisco rose as well.

"Stay here," he said.

The boy watched him walk away, toward his cell. He closed the door behind him. After a brief while he heard the whistle of a whip. Francisco counted the lashes: four, six, seven. The whistle of discipline was accompanied by a muffled cry. Why did he go to punish himself right in that moment? Did he deserve those blows for having made an error in the description of signs? But had he actually made an error? Francisco felt a vague fear. Should he keep waiting where he was?

The monk returned. He was pale but relaxed. He gestured for the boy to sit on the ground, while he himself sat on the bench in order to face him. Or to be less close to him than before.

"When a bad thought invades the mind," he explained, "we are sinning. This is what happened to me."

Francisco was moved by his sincerity and humility.

"You too should flagellate yourself before your confirmation," he advised.

The boy wondered what bad thought the director may have had. Something prickled in the monk's heart. Perhaps he was concerned that he might be offering too much attention to a heretic's son; perhaps— this would be the worst thing—perhaps he went to punish himself because of my sins, because of the bad thoughts I have that only he can sense.

"I will prepare myself properly for confirmation," Francisco promised. "I will fast, and flagellate myself."

"These are good regulations for the body. Correct. But do not forget the regulations of the spirit: prayer, seclusion, and affirmation of the doctrines."

"I will do all of that."

"You should prepare yourself to receive confirmation the way the apostles prepared to receive the Holy Spirit. For fear of the Jews who killed the Lord and also wanted to kill all of His disciples"—Santiago de La Cruz intentionally emphasized the point—"the apostles shut themselves away in Jerusalem. They prayed and fasted. They knew how much Jesus had taught them, but they were not yet valiant soldiers. On Pentecost, when the Holy Spirit descended on them, they were transformed into an invincible army. They proudly proclaimed their identities as Christians, and went forth to preach."

Francisco smiled at these resonant words, but his head echoed with "the Jews who killed the Lord and also wanted to kill all of His disciples." He would have liked to ask, with the turns of phrase his father had used with Diego, whether he, Francisco, had really killed the Lord and wanted to kill all Christians; or whether it wasn't true, after all, that the first disciples were all Jews. But he maintained his smile and kept listening to the lesson.

This disconcerting sequence of events reoccurred on other occasions. The spiritual director would approach the boy in an affectionate manner, gaze at him tenderly, take his hand, press his shoulder, run his fingers through his copper-colored hair. He taught him the truths of the faith in a warm voice. He was the captivating preacher who penetrated his chest as if with a spear. But then he'd suddenly be shaken by an invisible bolt, and would step away to breathe deeply, or would go into his cell to whip himself. He'd return changed, cleaned of the bad thoughts that had invaded his mind.

Francisco prayed, ate little, and almost never left the monastery. He also helped out in the orchard, cleaned the sacristy, rested in the shade of the central fig tree, or lay on the mat in his cell. He went over what he'd learned in his mind using a question-and-answer format; he wanted to absorb the entire catechism. If he could achieve this before confirmation, God would reward him.

"What are the sacraments?" he asked himself in the privacy of his cell.

"They are effective sensory signs of the grace established by Our Lord Jesus Christ to sanctify our souls," he'd answer.

"How many sacraments are there?" he continued.

"Seven, like the seven days of the week."

"Name them," he would order himself. "Each one is extremely important."

"Baptism, confirmation, the Eucharist, confession, last rites, the priesthood, and matrimony."

"How many elements constitute each sacrament?"

"Two."

"What are they?"

"Matter and form. Matter is the physical thing that is utilized: oil, wine, water. Form is the words that are used to apply the material."

"What are the materials of each sacrament?"

"For baptism, natural waters." He counted on his fingers. "For confirmation, the holy chrism. For the Eucharist, bread and wine. For confession, sins and penitence. For last rites, oil."

"What is the principal effect of the sacraments?" he asked himself, raising his voice.

"Divine grace that flows toward the believer," he responded with aplomb.

Santiago de La Cruz entered and tried to confound him with another question. "Do you know what sanctifying grace is?"

Francisco raised his eyebrows.

Before he could respond, the clergyman said, "It is the supernatural gift that makes us friends of God."

He gathered his robe around his knees and sat beside the boy. He continued sweetly.

"We commonly say that we are in friendship or in a state of grace with someone when there is a bond of love, when we give and receive help, when there is trust. Between you and me, now, there is friendship. On the other hand, if there were hatred, insults, quarrels, we would say there is enmity, or that one has fallen into misfortune with regard to the other. Well, the same occurs with the Lord. When mortals fulfill His mandates, we are in friendship and grace with Him; if we sin, we enter misfortune and enmity. Remember that Jesus says in the Gospel of Saint Matthew, 'Not all who say "Lord, Lord" shall enter the realm of heaven, but only those who do my Father's will.'"

Francisco longed to ask him why Jesus constantly referred to the Father while Christians disregarded His example, referring only to Jesus, except in the prayer Our Father. Sometimes, Francisco wanted to think about the Father, but fear arose that this might be a sin because it might mean brushing against the Dead Law of Moses, as Brother Bartolomé and Santiago himself had both pointed out before.

An hour later, his face severe from having inflicted the usual whipping on himself, Santiago added, "Do not confuse sanctifying grace with actual grace." His voice was metallic, and his eyes were hard. "Sanctifying grace is permanent, a supernatural aid that illumines our spirit and implies friendship with God. Actual grace, on the other hand, is transitory; it is help to practice a particular virtue or to resist temptation. I just received actual grace with a few lashes to break off the sinful thoughts in my mind. But at no time did I lose the sanctifying grace I received at baptism."

"Yes." The boy blinked.

Santiago stared at him, eyes glittering with fury. "Now go over everything I've taught you about confirmation. The date is almost here. I don't want you to disappoint our bishop."

"Very well."

"Don't you 'very well' me," he pressed. "Tell me right now: What is the sacrament of confirmation?"

Francisco tried not to be disturbed by the baseless hostility. "It is a sacrament that imprints on our souls the role of a soldier of Christ."

"What is its material?"

"The sacred chrism, a blend of oil and balm."

"Why the oil?"

"It spreads gently and penetrates the body, leaving a lasting mark. It invigorates the limbs. The ancient fighters would anoint themselves for strength," he added, hoping to pacify the man.

"Why the balm?"

"It is a fragrant liquid that preserves against decay. The people of ancient times used to 'embalm' the dead."

"What is the form of this sacrament?"

"The words uttered by the bishop: 'I mark you with the sign of the cross and confirm you with the chrism of health.'"

Francisco fell to his knees and raised his eyes to the ceiling. He prayed to Our Lord Jesus Christ to help him receive this sacrament with devotion and reverence so as to become His valiant soldier. And for Him to bestow strength, so as never to be tempted by cursed heresies.

Santiago de La Cruz nodded. He said "Amen," and left.

32

"Brother Bartolomé Delgado is dying! He is dying!" A black man rushed across the courtyard in search of help. The servants sprang up like frogs after the rain. They were black people and mulattoes, and they went back and forth chaotically, without direction. The priests didn't know what to do either. They found Brother Bartolomé at the threshold of his cell, lying faceup and struggling for breath. His face was red and more swollen than usual.

Santiago de La Cruz patted his fat, sagging cheeks. "Brother Bartolomé!"

The only sound in response was a death rattle. He raised the edge of his robe and dried the foam from his mouth. He moved his head to the side to help him breathe easier.

"Summon the surgeon Paredes."

Several servants bolted off.

Francisco crouched beside the immense commissioner. The cat was sorrowfully licking its owner's temples. Francisco appreciated the feline's loyalty, but he felt no pity for the man.

Prayers rose in muttering voices around the mountainous body. Without divine powers he would soon die. But Santiago de La Cruz did not limit himself to prayer; he had to do something while they waited for Tomás Paredes. He thought it might help to raise his head with pillows.

"What will the surgeon do?" Francisco asked.

"A bloodletting, certainly—that's the first thing that's done in cases like this one."

"We can't find Paredes," a servant announced, still catching his breath.

"What?"

"He left for a ranch," another explained, sweaty and also breathing hard.

The clergymen glanced at each other, unsure. Francisco thought, "If only Papá were here." The cat let out a meow, sensing catastrophe.

Santiago saw his brothers' helplessness, and exclaimed, "I will do the bloodletting. Bring me a sharp knife."

This decision broke off the litanies. One of the monks shouted at an enslaved man to bring a knife and a bowl. Another rolled up Bartolomé's wide sleeve and placed the silver bowl below the elbow, to catch the blood. Santiago de La Cruz pulled up a chair and began to open the vein. Brother Bartolomé's arm was elephantine. Filth streaked the damp folds of his elbow, and no vein could be found. The spiritual director gauged where the vein might be and cut into the skin. The sick man shuddered; he was still half-conscious after all, and this generated optimism. But the cut did not hit the mark; only a few drops of blood fell. Brother Santiago tried again. He was emboldened now, and he stabbed without subtlety. He searched for the elusive vein shrouded in flesh but failed again. He was sweating hard.

He tried a third time. He displayed not only recklessness, but also anger; that blood-filled vessel was as fat as the rest of that monumental body, and yet it put up too much resistance. The knife slid in at least five centimeters, slashing left and right; he cut muscular tissue and reached the bone. But could not perforate any vein. The blood that spilled from the wounds was meager. Santiago de La Cruz muttered words that surely must have been a prayer, though they sounded like insults. Exhausted, he handed back the knife.

"It's impossible."

Francisco wished to intervene. He had watched his mother's bloodlettings, but he feared that Santiago would be offended. The dirty elbow had an irregular cut edged with a scarlet stain. The bowl had barely received a few meager drops. The sick man inhaled deeply and let out an alarming, suffering sound.

"Would you let me try?"

Santiago de La Cruz stared at Francisco in surprise. Then he looked at Brother Bartolomé's swollen face, and gestured for the boy to be handed the knife. Francisco asked for water and a short cord. He washed the ankle and tied the cord tightly a few inches above it. He had seen that the surgeon proceeded this way when performing bloodlettings on the weakened Aldonza. He felt around the flesh to assess his options, and chose the vein that felt the widest. He inserted the steel blade's tip and gave it a twist. A thick stream of dark blood fell resonantly into the container. Sighs of relief erupted around Francisco like air bubbles. The Lord had worked a miracle through this orphan. The bad blood that was poisoning Brother Bartolomé flowed out in a continuous stream. His head would soon be less congested.

"Tomás Paredes!"

The surgeon hurried in. Francisco stepped back carefully, without letting go of the bleeding foot. Paredes approached.

"You made this incision?" He examined the cut from one side and then from another. Then he looked at the bowl, shaking it slightly to study the blood's density and color. "Who taught you? Your father?"

"I've seen him do it."

"Very good!" He beamed. "Very good, indeed."

Brother Bartolomé blinked; his eyelashes fluttered. His cheeks seemed less red.

"That's sufficient," the surgeon decreed.

He rolled a piece of bandage into a ball and applied it to the wound on the fat ankle.

"Hold it here, like this. I will return to check up on him and give him a proper bandage. Look, he's already waking. Let's see, Father! Open your eyes wide! Wide, I say!"

He turned to Santiago de La Cruz and gave out additional instructions.

"Prepare a vegetable broth with a boiled frog. Frog skin has many beneficial nutrients. He should drink ten spoonsful now and more later tonight."

An hour later, Francisco was once again glued to his bench, repeating the questions and answers that a believer must memorize when about to receive the sacrament of confirmation.

33

The spiritual director gave him a neatly wound knotted rope, his personal whip. He lent it to him as demonstration of his paternal affection. It was the color of excrement, with dark stains, traces of blood that testified to the energy of the scourge. He instructed Francisco to apply severe discipline on this night so he could enter the church in a pure state the following day. All of Córdoba was in a state of excitement over the imminent mass confirmations.

Caravans were already arriving from nearby towns. At the gates of the city, as well as in the main plaza, there grew encampments of Indians, mestizos, mulattoes, and black people, both male and female, brought by overseers and priests. A festive atmosphere reigned. The banners of religious orders waved, recalling the fervor of processions. The catechists gathered their people to count them, watch over them, and reiterate their teachings. Despite their heterogeneity, they were a replica of the apostles before Pentecost: fearful, naïve, wretched.

Francisco also waited on that eve of the great event. The doubts that often shuddered through his chest would be erased when the sacred chrism and the bishop's words filled him with grace. He retreated into his cell and lit a wick. He pushed the table and chair aside and rolled up the mat. He needed space to remove the impurities. He bared his torso. He took up the whip and prayed an Our Father as he unrolled it. He thought of his sins, desires, and moments of imprudence or intemperance. He evoked his father's face, the iron key, the lost library: there was Satan with his tempting disguises. He grasped the handle and lashed his back. He doubled over. "Take that, devil!" he exclaimed, smiling. For strength, he prayed another Our Father and hurled a challenge at Satan. "Show yourself again, with your tricks!" He saw the enigmatic engraving on the Spanish key. He lashed out again. His assaulted skin opened its pores. He had no air, no words. Those beloved images weakened his drive.

He had to humiliate himself, deserve the punishment. "Sinner! Wretched one!" He whipped himself a third time, but more softly. He paced the rectangle of his cell, eyes and whip lowered. He understood that he was a coward, full of vice. He repeated, "sinner, sinner," but it wasn't enough to excite him. "Coward." That didn't work either. "Unworthy boy, son of a heretic, that's it, son of a heretic, filthy Marrano, that's it, filthy Marrano. Shitty Jew!" He lashed himself forcefully. "Shitty Jew! Apostate! Murderer of God!" Another lash. Another. And another. He succeeded in unleashing a kind of madness, an intimate ferocity. The whip whistled and his mouth spat out curses. His shoulders and back filled with cross-shaped marks.

Suddenly, the door creaked open and Santiago de La Cruz entered. He found his disciple in a disheveled state, dripping sweat, whip hanging from his right hand. "This figure barging into his cell," Francisco thought, "could be Christ or Satan." His self-flagellation could invoke either one of them. In either case, he needed to continue; the greater one's offering to the Lord, the greater one's disobedience of the devil.

"Shitty Jew!" He cringed under a formidable lashing. "Apostate Marrano!" Another lash.

Santiago de La Cruz flexed his fists. His inhibitions melted. He opened his mouth, his eyes, his arms; he took off his robe and rushed toward the half-naked, profusely wet, hurting boy. He embraced him tightly.

"Enough!" he said. "That's enough."

Francisco did not resist. His lungs moaned, depleted, broken. He stared at the ceiling, stunned, as if birds were singing down to him.

"My dearest angel—" the spiritual director whispered, caressing his arms and neck. He pressed his torso against the boy's. His lips approached the agitated mouth and kissed it.

Francisco shrank back. Was this Christ loving him, kissing him, rubbing his body? An ax split his head in two. He grabbed the spiritual director's hair with both hands and pulled him back violently. Francisco's eyes blazed. He gathered his last strength and hit him, howling. The monk's back sank against the wall; he put his hands up to defend himself. He prayed with hoarse, incomprehensible words. Francisco raised his whip, prepared to break open the man's face. But he hesitated a moment, just long enough to see the chaotic situation more clearly. There before him, shamed by lechery and impotence, was not the devil, but his spiritual director, who was also breathing hard, and also visibly horrified, fingernails digging into the adobe behind him. His judgment had been undone by the cruelest of temptations. The monk grabbed the whip from Francisco and gave himself a brutal lash. Another one followed immediately. On his head, his left shoulder, his right shoulder, his waist, frenetically, with hatred, murmuring insults against himself. It was a storm of rough blows that seemed more of a massacre than a form of discipline. He seemed to want to destroy himself, to shatter his body into pieces, to reduce himself to dust. Francisco watched, stupefied, because his own flagellation had been a caress compared to this one.

The director's knees buckled. He was mad, ricocheting from the walls. But he kept on doling out fatigued lashes and murmuring curses. He inhaled deeply, gathered himself, and delivered the final blow. Then he collapsed.

His disciple stayed glued to a corner. Nausea rose in him. The body from which beautiful sermons flowed, and which belonged to his esteemed spiritual director, lay like a corpse gnawed by wild beasts.

His wounds were holes through which the pestilence in his soul would escape.

His breath was ragged and shallow, as his cracked thorax couldn't properly expand. Between hoarse moans, he begged Francisco, "Go to my cell and bring me the brine and vinegar."

Francisco thought he must be delirious. The monk repeated his words and, seeing the boy's hesitation, added grimly, "That is an order."

When he returned with a jar in each hand, he found the director back on his feet, supporting himself with great effort by holding the edge of the table. His torso was dripping with blood.

"Put brine and vinegar on my wounds," he said in an exhausted voice. "Do what I ask, even if I faint."

His student furrowed his brow.

"I must be punished more." A stitch of pain cut off his breathing; he raised a hand to his side. "Help me."

Francisco helped to hold him up.

"No, help me to suffer more, to purify myself—first the brine, then the vinegar." He bent to reveal the striped vermilion of his back.

The brine triggered burning pain. He gritted his teeth to swallow back his howls. He shook. He pinched his arms.

"More! More!" he implored.

Francisco emptied the jars. Santiago de La Cruz shook his head, no longer in his body.

34

Columns of barefoot men and women, dressed in wool or colored blankets, entered the church, which was profusely lit. There were also children over the age of seven. Priests, Indian overseers, and dignitaries would act as godfathers. Banners were raised to coordinate the placing of each column in accordance with the people's places of origin. Women gathered to the left of the nave, men to the right. All the lights had been ignited: the altar candles, the candelabra that hung from a woven rope, the torches in the choir area, the lanterns and innumerable oil lamps along the walls. The smell of melted tallow blended with the smoky clouds of incense.

The space filled with people, smells, and heat, as if animals had been gathered rather than people. More than a congregation, the church resembled Noah's Ark. The place reeked of grass and dung, pig and ox, mule and goat, urine and dog shit. Lice, bedbugs, and fleas swarmed. These were the true people: oppressed, disoriented, searching for salvation and solace. Some adolescents dripped snot and pus. It was the universe in a stable, which surely pleased the Lord.

The bishop appeared. His presence impressed the faithful, as he wore all the pontifical vestments: the surplice, stole, and cope. His head was crowned with a mitre. In his right hand he held the tall crosier, symbol of his authority. Men and women pushed each other to better see this radiant figure, who resembled the saints in the alcoves. Trejo y Sanabria explained the rite they were about to celebrate. He synthesized the teachings that the priests had been delivering. He extended his hands and everyone knew this signified the invocation of the Holy Spirit, so that it might bring the seven gifts. Then he approached those who would be confirmed, in their uneven rows. In one hand, he held the silver container that bore the sacred chrism. He dipped his thumb in the liquid and drew a cross on each forehead, all the while pronouncing sacramental words.

Francisco felt the thumb's contact and the imposition of the mark. When the cope grazed him he shuddered, as if brushed by the sacred tunic of Christ. The material manifestation of the sacrament, oil and balm, had been placed on his head, and the bishop spoke the words that gave it form. Both elements joined to bring about their transformation; divine grace flowed to him, granting him the role of a soldier of the Holy Church. In his ears, the formula resounded that assured him of the presence of the Father, the Son, and the Holy Spirit. The bishop, the godfather, and the confirmed person made a human trinity in the service of the sacred trinity that had created the world. The bishop then gave the boy a slap on the cheek; this was a symbol of the disposition that he must have to endure the affronts directed at the Lord. He looked into the boy's eyes, smiled, and greeted him as Jesus had greeted His disciples: "Peace be with you." The confirmed one lowered his head and focused on his desired emotions.

After almost an hour, after having confirmed all those who were present, the prelate returned to the altar and prayed on behalf of the congregation. Finally, he addressed the multitude filling the church. He was pale, on the verge of falling.

"The Lord blesses thee from Zion, so thou may see the good of Jerusalem for all the days of thy life, and that eternal life may be thine. Amen."

He invited the people to join him in praying the creed, an Our Father, and a Hail Mary. From the choir area surged the strains of a motet. The voices, accompanied by harp and guitar, emitted a melody that was soon accompanied by the same melody in another key, a torrential counterpoint. Heads turned to find the origins of the music that echoed through the vaults. Francisco clasped his hands and kneeled in the cramped, odorous forest of legs and sandals. He prayed that the gifts of the Holy Spirit might fill him with strength to prevent him from straying from the right path. That he might not be ashamed of his Catholicism, but rather of the heresies committed by his father and his brother. He recalled the words of Jesus in the Gospel of Luke: "For whoever is ashamed of me and of my words, of him shall I also be ashamed on Judgment Day."

35

Lorenzo confessed that he wished to travel. He was sick of living surrounded by mountains and monotonous salt flats. He wanted to see the ocean, for example, with its gigantic foamy waves, and to take part in battles on the high seas. He wanted to fight against the scimitars of the Turks and the sabers of the Dutch. He had too much energy and strength to keep on chewing boredom among the brutish Indians of Córdoba. "They're unbearable, obedient, and dumb; they've forgotten the art of war; they're like mules after they've been broken, useless for anything except carrying loads." He preferred the Calchaquí Indians or the terrible nomads of the Chaco; against them he could wield his blade and gun. He also wanted to experience the mule fair of Salta.

"It's the biggest assembly in the world. That's what Papá told me. Half a million animals gather in that valley. Like ants."

Lorenzo overflowed with enthusiasm. Instead of filling himself with thoughts of books or monks, he collected information from travelers. He knew that in the heights of the Andes, among the snowy peaks, there flowed an infernal canal of water that sprang from the center of the earth. Nearby there glowed the wondrous Potosí, built from solid silver. And then came the capital of the Viceroyalty: Lima, the City of

Kings, where noblemen and their beautiful wives rode in carriages of gold. And there was Callao, its port. The ocean! At the port swayed galleons, frigates, caravels, and launches. "I'll embark toward Panama and then on to Spain. And to the land of infidels! I'll kill Moors with the techniques for killing Indians."

Lorenzo Valdés was exultant about his plans.

"You have to come with me, Francisco."

36

Isabel and Felipa still lived in Doña Leonor's mansion. Soon it would officially become a convent bearing the sacred name of Catherine of Siena. Francisco had to tell them of his plan, as it meant leaving his sisters even more alone.

Their activities followed the strict model of Spanish convents. They aligned themselves with an ancient Roman schedule, for its mystical resonance. Their day commenced at dawn with first prayers. Then they attended Mass. At eight, they had breakfast. Prayers followed, after which they began their tasks in the labor room. They sewed, embroidered, spun, and wove. Here it was also crucial to hold back words and voices, though winks and muffled giggles erupted over the smallest incidents. At twelve, there were more prayers, followed by lunch. As the spoons and knives clinked, ears dutifully absorbed readings from a sacred text. At three, it was time to pray again, then siesta, and then catechism for the rest of the afternoon. At seven, evening prayers. Then they had their frugal dinner, said their night prayers, and—to sleep! Fridays were different because they took time to examine the errors they'd committed, and penance was given out; the pupils had to humiliate themselves and publicly denounce their morbid desires. They also had to list their minor offenses, such as distraction during catechism or irritation with sewing.

Santiago de La Cruz arranged the visit, which was not easy to obtain. Francisco thought his sisters seemed painfully mature and distant. Isabel looked more like their mother every day: short, timid, with bright, clear eyes. Felipa was a feminine version of her father; her nose had grown along with her stature and she exuded a certain hardness and exaggerated gravity. They both inspired respect. He gathered his strength and breathlessly told them of his plans to go to Lima to study medicine at the University of San Marcos. After a few seconds of silence he added that he might not see them again for many years. The young women stared at their brother with a neutral expression and invited him to sit on a bench among the colonnades.

The ensuing silence was interspersed with comments about life in the future convent, as a way of evading painful topics: loneliness, resentment, fears, humiliation. The young women worked their rosary beads and he ran his fingers through his hair. When they ran out of time, they stood. Francisco wanted to absorb the sight of them. He knew that very soon he would be longing for this moment. His sisters lowered their eyes with the modesty their new circumstances demanded. Felipa had lost almost all of her funny impertinence. Nevertheless, she did express one irritating thought.

"Be careful not to do the same thing as Papá," she warned him.

They looked at each other with a mix of affection and suspicion. The curse that had befallen their family had cast a shadow on their faces. They said nothing more. The three of them blinked back tears. Francisco embraced them for a long time, and when he left he did not dare turn back to look at them. When he arrived back at his cell, he dipped his quill and wrote on parchment, "As soon as I get the money, I'll bring you with me."

He also bid farewell to Brother Bartolomé. The obese commissioner had recovered from his stroke. He was on a strict, disgusting diet meant to detoxify his colossal body. The monk was swallowing medicine, holding his nose. He asked Francisco to tell him of his plans, when he had devised them, who had made suggestions, how he would bring them to fruition. He spoke in a friendly tone, truly wanting to help, but he could not avoid his natural prosecutorial style. Francisco, for his part, managed to respond with certainty despite the foggy nature of his hopes. He said that he had artfully used a pointed blade to perform a bloodletting, and he liked to help the sickly. He supposed that those who preferred weapons had a soldier's vocation, and those who preferred only to tend to the sick had the vocation of a priest. But he who had both tendencies had a doctor's vocation. For this reason, he wanted to study in the City of Kings.

Brother Bartolomé's thick lips pursed into a frown, unconvinced by this reasoning. "In any case," he conceded, "you are inspired to a useful purpose. What matters," he added with sudden solemnity, "is the health of your spirit. I don't want any more heretics in your family."

Francisco hung his head, humiliated.

"When you arrive in Lima, go to the Dominican monastery. Ask for Brother Manuel Montes. He will help you when you tell him who you are and who sent you. He will take you to the university."

Francisco's head was still down.

"Will you do it?" the commissioner asked.

"Yes, of course."

A hand touched him. Though the monk was fat, his skin was cold. The cat let out a very sharp meow, which resounded like an echo. Then Brother Bartolomé raised his right hand and made a cross in the air.

"I bless you in the name of the Father and the Son and the Holy Spirit."

The monk lay back on his armchair. He had proceeded adequately, with warmth and paternal firmness. The boy, however, would not leave. He stayed standing, in silence, his gaze fixed to an invisible point on the ground. Something was unfinished.

"What is it?" the priest asked.

"I need your authorization."

"You already have it."

"Not for my trip."

Brother Bartolomé frowned, not understanding.

"To say goodbye to Brother Isidro."

His expression clouded over. He drummed against his armrest and shook his head.

The boy had sensed this answer coming. Brother Isidro Miranda had been confined in the Monastery of La Merced since an evil spirit had invaded his brain. He engaged in long conversations with deceased bishops and accused almost all the clergy in the region of being Jewish. He had been locked up in his cell and was only visited by the order's superior.

"No," Brother Bartolomé said. "You cannot."

Francisco turned and slowly moved away, still waiting for something.

"Francisco—"

His heart raced.

"Come," the commissioner said.

He returned to the convalescent's side and listened.

"You will find what you are seeking."

"I don't understand."

"Yes, you do understand. You will find your father."

It was as if an open hand had struck his face.

The cat's phosphorescent gaze stayed motionless. The serious gaze of the commissioner's did, too. Francisco's chest, on the other hand, was a wild drum.

"I—"

"He's in the port of Callao. That's where you'll find him."

"How do you know?"

"Now you may go." He closed his eyes. "May the Lord bless you."

37

On the eve of the journey, Francisco filled his leather suitcase with his belongings. To the left side of his belt he tied the sling that Luis had made him out of a bladder, and on the right side he tied a small bag containing the coins he had saved during those years of monastery labor. He used a coarse linen shirt to wrap the thick book Santiago de La Cruz had decided to give him at the last moment, after a period of arduous meditation, to Francisco's amazement: a Bible. Less beautiful and almost devoid of artistic illuminations, but a complete Bible, beginning with Genesis and ending with Revelations, containing the Song of Songs and the Epistles of Saint Paul, all the prophets and all the gospels, the history of the patriarchs, and the Acts of the Apostles.

He lay down on his rush mat for a few hours of sleep. He wondered whether he'd make it to Lima safe and sound. He was familiar with the first part of the trajectory, as it retraced the path his family had taken nine years earlier. But a creak interrupted his thoughts: it was the rats, taking advantage of the night. The next creak was no longer usual. Francisco opened his eyes and saw a silhouette in the opening. He sat up quickly and felt for a match.

"Who is it?"

"Sshhhh!"

The silhouette approached slowly. Its clumsy lateral movements spoke volumes. Luis squatted. Noiselessly, he put down a heavy sack.

"How did you get in here?"

"There was no other way to see you," he whispered. "I climbed over the garden wall. It's dangerous, I know."

"I'm happy that you came. Do you know that I'm leaving for Lima?"

"That's why I'm here."

Francisco pressed his forearm. "Thank you!"

They stared at each other in the darkness. Luis smelled of earth.

"Do they treat you well, Luis?"

"I'm a slave, boy."

"Did you miss me?"

"Yes. That's why I'm here."

"Thank you again."

"And also because I have this, for the doctor."

"My father?"

"Isn't it true that you're traveling to Lima?"

"Yes, but—will I find my father?"

"You'll find him."

"I hope so!" he moved over to give Luis more space. "How do you know?"

"I'm a witch doctor's son."

"You were very small when you were captured."

"As small as you were when the doctor was captured."

"They didn't capture him. They arrested him."

"Is there a difference?"

They exchanged a kind of radiance. In that cell shrouded in silence, the two bodies heard each other's heartbeats.

Francisco touched his shoulder. "What have you brought for my father?"

Luis glanced around him, an unnecessary precaution. In a low voice he whispered, "His tools of sorcery."

"His tools? Didn't he take them to Lima?"

"No. I hid them, so they wouldn't be stolen. A sorcerer's power should never be stolen."

He brought the sack closer and made him feel through the jute cloth. Francisco recognized tongs, lancets, tubes, scissors, saws, cannulas. He untied the knot, inserted his hand, and stroked the silver instruments.

"Incredible, Luis!"

"Sshhhh! The monks might hear you."

"They almost got the secret out of you," Francisco said, smiling.

"When the captain beat me?"

"He almost made you confess."

"But I didn't confess."

"You're brave, a worthy son of a witch doctor. My father would be proud of you."

"Thank you, my boy. But—touch the instruments, why don't you. Touch."

Francisco continued to move his hand through the bag.

"The case!"

"Aha!"

"The case with the Spanish key. You hid that, too! Luis, you are a marvel, an angel."

Luis caressed the coarse sack and then murmured, "I want to travel with you."

Francisco was moved down to the marrow. "I wish you could come with me, but I'm afraid it's not possible. They won't tolerate your escape. They'll hunt you down and punish you. I can't buy you or care for you. They'd make us both come back. And then they'd also get the instruments."

Luis shifted position; he leaned his back against the wall and gathered his legs in, a reflex of suffering he had learned on the slave ship. He vigorously scratched his neck, sweating with rage. "I want to fly like a bird, but I can't. I want to work as a witch, with the doctor."

Francisco pressed his forearm again. The cry of an owl cut through the night; to the Indians, owls were a sign of blessing. Francisco thought of something.

"Listen, Luis. I went to say goodbye to my sisters. Do you know what I've decided?"

Luis strained his eyes in the darkness.

"I've decided that as soon as I get the money I'll bring them to live with me."

"In Lima?"

"Yes. I'm going to reunite the family."

"Are they happy, your sisters?"

"They don't know about my plan. I didn't dare tell them it. But now you know it."

Luis nodded, stretching out his legs.

"You should also know this."

Luis raised his head.

"I'll buy you. You and Catalina. And you'll come with my sisters. We'll all reunite."

Luis lunged forward and clumsily embraced the son of his former owner. Francisco caressed his hair. At the end of a few minutes they stood up and pressed each other's hands until they hurt. The boy opened his suitcase and inserted the jute bag containing the treasure he would return to his father.

38

Before dawn broke, Francisco left the monastery that had housed him for seven years. He passed through the rustic gate and walked the empty road, carrying his suitcase. The fresh, spicy air filled him with enthusiasm. He reached the area where a score of wagons were lining up little by little, while herds of mules were guided toward the path. Laborers had taken their places at the front of wagons, under lanterns that hung from cattle prods. Oxen moved slowly, obeying prods and shouts. Enslaved workers hauled loads onto the giant tubes through the back openings, while overseers, lanterns in hand, supervised the labyrinth of people and animals.

Francisco boarded a wagon and waited for the journey to begin. After half an hour, departure orders were shouted out. The tower on wheels received an energetic tug and began to sway. The caravan headed north. The guiding horsemen rode in front. On Francisco's wagon there traveled a married couple from Buenos Aires with two young daughters; they were headed to the city of Cuzco. The man looked like he could be his wife's father. There was no sign of his friend Lorenzo Valdés.

An officer remained in the area until the final herd had left. Then he went home, drank a cup of chocolate, and went to the captain of the Lancers' house. He walked at a calm pace, enjoying the freshness of dawn, satisfied by his efforts. His tenacious presence had discouraged the disobedient young man. He struck the door with the iron knocker. A pearly brightness was rising over the horizon. The servant showed him into the living room. After a while, the captain of the Lancers entered, and the officer rose to his feet.

"No news, my captain."

"Chá!"

Valdés gestured for him to sit back down. He ordered the servant to serve them both chocolate. The officer didn't dare tell him that he had just finished drinking a cup in his own home.

"And so—all is in order!" Valdés repeated.

"Effectively so. I watched the departure of the weekly caravan. Your son was not there."

"Aha!"

"He did not leave."

"Are you sure?"

"Yes, Captain."

"You have been surveilling them for a month now."

"Effectively so."

"Help yourself to the chocolate."

"Yes. Thank you, Captain."

"You drink without gusto. Don't you like it?"

"I like it, Captain." He ingested a long, noisy sip; obedience had to be demonstrated.

"So he did not leave—"

"Effectively so."

"Aha! But it is not so. My son left."

"What do you say, Captain?"

"That he left. Right under your plugged-up nose."

"I have supervised wagon after wagon. I felt through the bundles, watched the herds."

"Aha!"

"Your son was not there, Captain."

"Nor is he here."

"He must have escaped on horseback. I'll race to reach him, with my men!"

"Finish your chocolate. That won't be necessary."

"He's made fools of us!"

"Of you."

"Of—of—"

"He knew you were spying on him. He planned for you to be convinced that he would travel on this caravan. The departure of Francisco was good bait, wasn't it? He tricked you in style. I want to tell you, officer, that Lorenzo has been gone for a while. I don't know how, but he's gone. He had the kindness to leave me a respectful note. He's a skillful boy."

"Yes, he is skillful."

"And you are not."

The officer coughed and a few drops of chocolate fell on the captain of the Lancer's boots. Valdés looked at him scornfully. He was proud of his son, but worried about the inefficiency of his subordinates.

39

The young friends were reunited several leagues north of Córdoba. The overseer of the caravan accepted Lorenzo into the wagon where Francisco traveled, and allowed for his horse's reins to be tied to the vehicle.

He introduced himself to his fellow passengers. The girls were called Juana and Mónica. Their mother, about twenty-five years old, was named María Elena Santillán. The mature father, José Ignacio Sevilla.

"Sevilla is not a Portuguese surname," Lorenzo said after hearing him speak.

"My distant ancestors were Spanish," the man admitted and then asked Francisco to pass him a basket of oranges, more interested in changing the subject than in eating them.

Mónica hugged her mother's neck and whispered in her ear about why the young man had a wine-colored stain on his cheek and nose.

"Because my mother wanted to eat plums when I was in her belly!" Lorenzo responded, playfully tickling her navel.

"Where are you headed?" the woman asked.

"I to Cuzco, or to Guamanga," Lorenzo answered. "A big indigenous rebellion has broken out, like an epidemic. It's called 'the singing sickness.' It's a return to idolatry; the Indians are breaking crosses, pulling corpses out of cemeteries, murdering priests, and changing their names. We have to stop them. I'm going to join the exterminating militias."

"But that happened a long time ago!" Sevilla exclaimed.

"A long time ago?"

"Of course. Some Indian preachers announced the return of the *huacas*, the ancient gods of nature, and pressed the people to rise up against the authorities. But they were suppressed. Who gave you such outdated information?"

"Some magistrates."

"You must have misunderstood. That's over."

"The Indians aren't rebelling?"

"Yes, they're rebelling. They're also idolaters in many cases. But there's no massive rebellion anymore. I'm sorry to disappoint you. There won't be anyone for you to wage war against."

"Then I'll go to Portobello," the captain's son proclaimed, "and from there I'll sail to Spain and follow the troops marching to Flanders, as my father did, or I'll battle against the Turks in the Mediterranean, or against the Moors in Africa."

"Do you have a way to pay for your travels?"

"Pay? They'll pay me! And if not, I'll beg for a while and steal from infidels. What else would a good warrior do?"

Sevilla's expression was resigned. "And you, Francisco?"

"I'm going to Lima. I want to be a doctor."

"Ah. You'll study there. It's another kind of adventure, then."

"Yes."

"Doctors are needed everywhere. The few to be found anywhere in the province come from Spain or Portugal."

"His father was a doctor," Lorenzo explained.

"Yes? What was his name?"

"His name *is*—" Francisco corrected, "it is Diego Núñez da Silva."

"Diego Núñez da Silva?"

"You know him?"

Sevilla rubbed the right side of his nose, clearly holding back his response.

"You know him?"

"We met years ago. And someone who's also traveling in this caravan will be very happy to speak with you."

40

After crossing the salt flats, they stopped at a relatively welcoming spot, where bald trees offered a simulacrum of shade. The habitual wagon circle was created, the mule herds were enclosed in a corral, the servants set about grilling meat from a just-slaughtered cow.

María Elena led her daughters to the brush where the women gathered. Lorenzo wanted to stretch his limbs by climbing trees, and Sevilla took advantage of the moment to take Francisco's arm and introduce him to his Portuguese friend.

He was near the campfire; a man of medium height. He wore a flowing gray shirt and wide linen trousers; a shiny belt held his leather bag and a sheathed knife. A thick silver cross hung from his neck. His face had a vigor to it, with thick eyebrows muffling the impact of his wide, penetrating eyes. His upturned nose, however, gave his round head a friendly look.

"Here he is," Sevilla said.

"I'm happy to meet you," said the man before turning back to the servant who was grilling his meat. "I told you to take those tumors off."

The servant grasped the edge of the beef with his hand, right over the coals, almost burning himself, and carefully sliced away the swollen parts and ganglions.

"They don't realize that it tastes better without those disgusting bits."

He moved away from the people who were coming to claim their portions. Sevilla and Francisco followed him. After checking to confirm that nobody could hear them, he began to speak.

"So you're the youngest son of Diego Núñez da Silva?"

"Yes. And you—who are you?"

"Who am I?" His teeth showed in a bitter smile. "I'm Diego López. And as I come from Lisbon, they call me Diego López de Lisboa."

"My father was also born in Lisbon."

"That's right."

"Do you know him?"

"More than you'd imagine," Sevilla put in.

Francisco directed a questioning gaze his way.

"You want to know?" Diego López asked, picking up a dry stick.

Francisco nodded.

"Your father and I"—he stared at him intently, seeming to doubt for an instant—"we met over there, in Lisbon."

"In Lisbon?"

He stirred dead leaves with his stick as if he preferred that over stirring memories.

"Then—" Francisco stammered.

Sevilla shook his head. "It's useless," he sighed. "My friend prefers to forget."

"I prefer?" López shot back. "You think I prefer it? Or do I have to do it?"

"We've talked about this. Many times."

"But you're still not convinced."

"Memory isn't erased by will alone."

"But one must will oneself to erase it."

"Have you been able to do that?"

López broke the stick and looked up at the sky. "God help me!"

"You see?" Sevilla softened his tone. "On that path, you'll never reach the port."

"And yet, it is the best path. If only the alchemists could discover the filter of amnesia. Then one could choose it."

"I return to my thesis: you prefer to forget, but you don't forget, because if you did you would not be the same person."

Francisco listened to them. Sensing the pain and fear behind their words he strained to decipher the hidden meaning of their strange debate.

"My opinion is so different," Sevilla said, "that before leaving I finished my tenth chronicle."

"Congratulations!" López exclaimed ironically. "I hope those chronicles don't bring you tragedy."

"Everything that happens to us deserves to endure." He turned to Francisco. "Writing chronicles, I learned history. History is one of the oldest sciences. The Greeks invented a special muse in its honor. History breathes with meaning and value. I love it."

"History is a useless burden. Worse—a deadly burden," López growled.

They returned to the campfire, unsheathed their knives, and took good pieces of meat. They chose a large loaf of bread and a wineskin and then retreated to the shade.

41

Young Francisco found himself in an incredible tunnel of time on a trajectory brimming with bewilderment. Although he was eighteen years old, he felt much older. He recalled that in the courtyard of orange trees, now faded in his memory, he'd been told about an Arab book called *One Thousand and One Nights* that consisted of a series of stories told by a woman to a caliph in the course of a thousand nights. José Ignacio Sevilla and Diego López de Lisboa did something similar: in the course of fifteen siestas they evoked and discussed, in front of him, as if he were the privileged caliph, another succession of stories—their wounds, their unknown dignity, and their shrouded terror. They were part of a loose network of individuals in a permanent state of flight. They were irrigated by wretched blood and had to take great pains to win the respect of men. It was not enough to seem to be Christians; they had to erase the impurity of their origins. But, what were these origins, which were so execrable?

"Our origins are not only Spanish. They are Spanish and Jewish. The term 'Jewish' is a sign of evil," López said.

Francisco felt the vertigo that was driving those men mad. A mix of hatred, love, and guilt. Spanish Jews—a group to which he, too, belonged—were considered criminals. He opened his ears wide to drink in an utterly sad story: that of Spain's Jewish people. Sevilla, despite everything, loved the story. López de Lisboa abhorred it.

Once upon a time, the Jews arrived in Spain in King Solomon's ships and baptized the new nation Sefarad, which in Hebrew means "land of the end," or "land of rabbits." They planted Biblical sprouts: vines of grapes, trees of olive, fig, and pomegranate. Spain offered them a replica of the land they carried in their spirits; the rivers evoked the Jordan, the high mountains recalled snowy Mount Hermon, and the plains bore resemblance to the desert of the prophets. They lived in peace alongside the natives, and when Christianity became established, there were no confrontations; seeds were gathered the same way with Hebrew or Latin blessings. The blessedness of those centuries was intruded upon by the Third Council of Toledo, which unleashed a general anti-Jewish offensive, prohibiting mixed marriages, and if such unions did result in offspring, it was required that those children be taken to the baptismal bowl. Jews could no longer hold public roles, and they couldn't bury their dead intoning psalms that the neighbors could hear.

Nevertheless, the tolerant disposition of the people predominated over the severity of priests. The Visigoth kings' allegiances swung arbitrarily— some honored, others persecuted. One of them, for example, declared that the Jews of Spain were slaves in perpetuity.

In the year 711, a small Arab army successfully crossed the Strait of Gibraltar and in a few years almost the entire peninsula became dependent on the splendid caliphate of Córdoba. The capital city turned magnificent; its court drew philosophers, poets, physicians, and mathematicians. Parks sprang up with tranquil ponds and palaces full of fountains. For three centuries there reigned an atmosphere of fellowship. In that era, Jewish princes appeared in Spain.

"Jewish princes?" stammered Francisco. He couldn't believe it.

The first Jewish prince of Spain was called Hasdai. Many families claim to belong to his lineage, including those with the last name of Silva. The Silvas came from Córdoba, and surely from Hasdai. (Francisco thought of the rusted iron key.) *The brilliant Hasdai lived just before the first millennium. He spoke fluent Arabic, Hebrew, and Latin, and was a doctor and a diplomat. The emperor of Germany declared that he had never met a keener man. The emperor of Byzantium, for his part, sent him precious gifts, among them a book by Dioscorides, whom Pliny quotes, and whose works form the foundations of pharmacology. Hasdai rendered the text into Arabic. Throughout the caliphate, the study of the healing powers of herbs came to flourish. To this must be added the portentous discovery made thanks to Hasdai's ties to the Byzantine court: in the Orient, a Jewish kingdom had formed, the first independent Jewish kingdom since the catastrophe caused by the Roman legions. Its very existence proved that there was no eternal curse against Israel. Hasdai sent several missions, a few of which succeeded in striking up the desired ties.*

Later on, when the caliphate fractured into a mosaic of small kingdoms, another Hasdai arose—Samuel Hanaguid. Hanaguid means "the prince." He was also born in Córdoba, and with him, too, many families— including the Silvas—came from his lineage. He had mastered mathematics and philosophy and could speak and write seven languages. The vizier of Granada solicited his services, made him his secretary, and, years later on his deathbed, chose him to take his own place. It was the highest role a Jew had ever achieved in the palace of Alhambra. He governed for thirty years, built a vast library, and took the time to teach at a respected university.

In Córdoba, where the Silvas came from, there was also born a prince who did not only belong to a single state, but to humanity—Maimonides. He was the greatest of the philosophers of his time, and the doctors of the church bowed before him.

"A Jew before whom the church doctors bowed!" Sevilla declared.

He was named Aquila Magna, Doctor Fidelis, et Gloria Orientalis et Lux Occidentalis. *Without him, there would have been no Saint Thomas of Aquinas, or his* Summa Theologica. *He was the Saladin's personal doctor, as well as the physician requested by Richard the Lionheart. Those were wondrous times. Unfortunately, the quarrels between Muslim kingdoms grew, and hordes of fanatics arose. A preacher declared that the Jews had promised Mohammed that, if at the end of the fifth century after the Hegira the Messiah had not yet arrived, they would convert to Islam. The zealot addressed Jewish communities, exhorting them to keep their ancestors' vow. The Muslims couldn't tolerate the Jews' survival, despite the positive fruits of their past coexistence.*

Meanwhile, what was happening in the Christian kingdoms north of Spain?

"When the Islamic persecutions began, the Jews were displaced to the Christian kingdoms to the north, logically, just as they had fled from them before," Sevilla said.

"No refuge on Earth is final," sighed López de Lisboa, his round eyes emanating sadness. "Refuges are transitory. Worse—they're illusions. The solution is to abandon the refuge."

Sevilla and Francisco sensed that mournful words were coming.

"To abandon the refuge—" he cleared his throat. "The solution, then, does exist. It's to stop being a Jew. Permanently."

42

The trek to the north continued toward Santiago de Estero. Then they would travel through beautiful Ibatín. Francisco recognized this route, which he had traveled nine years before as a sheltered, happy child.

He gazed at Sevilla's little daughters, dozing against their young mother, and saw them as just as sheltered and happy as he had been on his last wagon journey. That is to say: precariously sheltered. They did not know that their father was a secret Jew, a man who could be arrested and burned alive. If that happened, they would lose all protection as well as their resources, because the Inquisition would confiscate all the family's money and belongings.

He breathed deeply to undo his unease. Was it the right thing to tell one's own family the truth? His father had not told his mother that he was Jewish. Of course, if he had done so, Aldonza might not have agreed to marry him. Then he would have been condemned to solitude, to suffer all the more intensely as a cursed man.

His father's marriage, and Sevilla's as well, were paradoxically mixed marriages—between Christians—New Christians who married Old Christians. At the time of betrothal, only one half of the couple knew the entire truth; the other was deceived, or opted to deny reality with the hope that it might not result in misfortune. Mutual consent was therefore impossible; in reality, it was two men marrying one woman.

Was there no solution? Diego López de Lisboa, sick of suffering, found the only one, a terrible one: "Stop being Jewish. Permanently." Francisco thought that if his father had opted for that logical path when he'd disembarked in the Americas, he would not have maintained his mistaken beliefs and would not have been arrested. He, Francisco, would have been able to enjoy the presence of his whole family. Perhaps his mother would not have died so young. They would not have lost their possessions, and would not have had to submit to the denigrating custody of Brother Bartolomé. He, Francisco, would not now be traveling to Lima.

From the time that his father had founded his eccentric academy, he had insisted that knowledge was power. He had a great deal of knowledge and had read more books than many of the know-it-alls of the Viceroyalty. Nevertheless, at the crucial moment when it mattered most, his knowledge had not served him. Nobody even recognized its power.

As Francisco considered these thoughts, the face of Jesus rose in his mind's eye. He relaxed his back against the wagon's beams and murmured portions of the catechism. An idea strained to emerge, but he crushed it with others, until it burst open. There was a parallel between Jesus and his father! Jesus was God; he had all the power. But the soldiers of Rome did not believe him, and mocked him, demanding that he prove it. Christ stayed silent, like his father. They beat him, pushed him, insulted him. Where was his dignity hiding—where were his lightning bolts, where was his strength? If he was capable of destroying and rebuilding the temple in three days, why didn't he expel his tormentors with a single breath? He was nothing more than a weak man. And the villains took advantage of the moment to beat him and have fun at his expense. They did not see that, behind his weakness, there hid an infinite force. They did not see that the pain was only making him more beloved in the eyes of the Father.

Francisco covered his face, shaking his head in horror. He had to be alone, somehow, in the midst of the wagon. Such confusion! Might the pain of the Jews, profound as it had been throughout the course of time, be a mysterious virtue that could make them immortal? Might Judaism be a way of imitating and realizing the Passion of Christ?

43

The Indian José Yaru, hired by José Ignacio Sevilla in Cuzco, behaved like the other carriers of loads, but his face and certain attitudes suggested a subtle difference. Just like the others he was obedient and silent, moving like a ghost. He could stand close behind someone and follow him for a long time without being noticed, or could disappear for long stretches. Once, the caravan left without him but he reappeared at their next stop. When he was asked about this, his answers were so laconic and evasive that it made the speaker want to stop talking to him. His facial features suggested tension, a deep tension that he hid with a guise of indolence and stupidity.

The Indian load carriers were not slaves, though they seemed to be such. Their work was hard and poorly compensated. Like the others, he followed the caravan on foot, slept under the open sky, and maintained a prudent distance from the Spaniards and the enslaved black people. He was not bothered by shouts or reproach; this was the natural way of receiving instructions, the treatment appropriate to his station. Was he resigned forever? He came from the heights of Cuzco. There, the Incas had reigned, touching the clouds. Cuzco had been the capital of a vast empire, the magnetic core to which the territories flowed that later would form the Viceroyalty of Peru. The great Inca was a child of the sun and, as with that great star, he could not be looked at directly. His reign was short and intense. The Indians trembled upon hearing of him. José, however, on being asked what he thought about the Incan Empire, about the people and customs of the Incas, invariably responded, "I do not think."

Sevilla knew that one of José's brothers had become a talented painter of churches. He reproduced the punishments the Jews had inflicted on the Lord Jesus Christ. But the Jews wore Spanish clothes, and on various occasions he had painted them with a gold cross on their chests. Sevilla also knew of an aunt who had been condemned as a sorceress because she had hidden idols and fed them *chicha*, a corn drink, and corn flour.

José Ignacio Sevilla met José Yaru right there in Cuzco. He had hired him to carry his packages from one store to another through the alley of the merchants. He was reliable and efficient. When Sevilla ended their contract because he was returning to Buenos Aires, the Indian lowered his hard head, clasped his hands over his belly, and asked point-blank to be taken with him.

"Why?" Sevilla asked in surprise.

"Because of a family war."

"You want to flee?"

"I have a family war."

Sevilla could not pry any more information out of him. What did "family war" mean? Was his father-in-law persecuting him? Did a brother-in-law want to kill him? Had he committed bigamy? Had his relatives spurned him? He needed to escape. Sevilla took pity on José and also calculated that in granting this favor, he would be gaining a good helper. He was taking responsibility for a fugitive, certainly; but he was not fleeing because of the religion, which would be a serious matter, but rather because of theft, murder, or adultery. Sevilla knew he might never know the truth. He tried to see into the man's stubborn mind. As he found no weighty obstacles, Sevilla assented.

José Yaru never removed his leather bracelets. Every once in a while he intoned a funereal song. His melody was like a ribbon undulating toward some mountain.

"I'm nostalgic for the heights," he would say by way of explanation.

The other Indians would listen to him in silence. During breaks, circles of load carriers would form. Though José was the same as the rest of them, he seemed to become the center of the group, as though he bore a dignity that only his brothers recognized.

44

Diego López de Lisboa was traveling in a different wagon and was not accompanied by his family this time. He had four brilliant children, one of whom, Antonio, excelled at writing in secret codes.

"I cannot reprimand Antonio," López mused bitterly during his talks with Francisco. "He takes my choice of rootlessness further than anyone; he won't allow himself to be called 'López,' much less 'de Lisboa.' He wants to stop being Jewish. He repudiates my heritage and, paradoxically, received it, because the main thing in the inheritance I have to offer is to be finished with the burden of Judaism. He goes so far as to invent a story of his own birth. He declares that he came into the light in Valladolid, even though he's never been there. Why should I reproach him? He'll be freer and safer than I have been, because I, sadly, am infected with a Jewish core that will only die when I'm buried. The same thing is true for Diego Núñez da Silva. His Jewish core was detected by the inquisitors and now he's imprisoned in Lima.

"Did I already tell you that we met in Lisbon? We were young, and we could run faster than our pursuers. We shared horrors. Then we learned to share, too, the uncertainty caused by the changing behavior of monarchs; at times the authorities became benevolent and raised hopes of coexistence, and at other times they were torn through by storms of hate.

"When the king of Spain signed the Edict of Expulsion in 1492, one hundred Jews emigrated to Portugal, as almost all of them dreamed of soon returning to their Spanish homes. But those dreams would not come true. With their places of permanence destroyed, many had to embark and suffer new misfortunes. A few were even sold as slaves. When the Inquisition succeeded in reaching Portugal it became clear that peace would not return. Thousands of people tried to flee the country that, at some moments, had seemed to hold some affection for them.

"Diego and I agreed to flee to Brazil after my parents were burned in an Act of Faith. We could not stay in that city. He helped me endure days and nights of fever, of madness. I tried to stab myself with a dagger because I could not get the images of charred bodies out of my mind. I stopped eating and drinking, until I lost all sensation. After a few months of insomnia and terror we traveled to the New World, where many of the persecuted were settling. The distance from central power allowed for the founding of free communities, and we hoped we'd be able to forget. And be reborn. But our information was incomplete; liberty had already provoked Inquisitorial visits, and the repression began here as well. We did not find a peaceful Brazil. No. Diego, after weighing his options, chose to risk a journey to the west, toward legendary Potosí. I, on the other hand, thought I would be safer in the recently founded Buenos Aires, as it was farther away from Inquisitorial powers than any other city.

"It was paradoxical: He, the doctor, without any economic ambitions, went toward the most frenzied center of wealth in the New World. And I, a merchant who knew the value of money, headed to flat Buenos Aires. He arrived in Potosí and then relocated to Ibatín to practice medicine. I took trips to Córdoba to initiate commerce in local fruits. In Córdoba, around the year 1600, my old friend appeared with his family, hounded by misfortune. I found out that he was not well, that he was fleeing the Inquisition. You were there, Francisco.

"I, on the other hand, was doing well. I had bought a small boat, *San Benito*. I exported flour to San Salvador de Bahía, Brazil, and there I took in cargo of olives, paper, and wine. The secret Jewish community of San Salvador was a trustworthy partner. I made money. And to evade the Inquisition's blows, I began to seek someone who could sell me a certificate of pure blood. In Córdoba, false titles abound. There are true artists of falsification and I have great respect for their skill. To combat the skepticism that sometimes assaulted me I was able to obtain a certificate that was so beautiful, it resembled an heirloom. Despite the coat of arms signified by that parchment loaded with wax seals and the signatures of dignitaries, I'd considered it risky to keep my main home in Buenos Aires—the young city was filling with Jews from Brazil. And so I moved to Córdoba, where, thanks to my loquacity, money, and initiative, I was quickly named a councilman in the local government. I then arrived at the painful conclusion that there was no use in cultivating my convictions in secret but that I should abandon them forever. Holding on to them would neither resurrect my parents nor give my children happiness. On the outside, I'm Catholic; a silver chain hangs from my neck with a thick cross, I attend religious functions, and I confess. I have to correct my inside, not my outside. My image is the right one. But I'm tired of fleeing. If I could, I'd study theology and become a priest like Pablo de Santamaría, who was a rabbi and became one of the most zealous advocates of the church. There's no point to Jewish martyrdom anymore; it's none of men's business and it doesn't move God. Why continue it?"

45

Sevilla, on the other hand, continued to tell the excited Francisco the history of Spanish Jews. The harsh Christian kingdoms of northern Spain decided to favor Jews when the Muslim states in southern Spain began to persecute them. However, this reception did not forge a cordial bond between the synagogue and the church. The church still needed to consolidate, and the presence of those who had been the chosen people raised questions about the solidity of some traditions. At that time a very dangerous kind of tournament began to grow in popularity—namely, the theological argument. Christians had no interest, deep down, in convincing Jews—they could always convert them forcibly en masse; rather, it was the Christians themselves who needed convincing. For this reason, theologians from both religions were summoned for public discussions that could help clarify the truth. In practice, if the Christians did not win the debate, a storm would erupt that included assaults on the Jews.

One of the famed polemicists on the Jewish side came from the south. He claimed to be descended from the legendary Prince Hasdai, the magnificent Samuel Hanaguid, and other Cordoban families brimming with artists and wise men. His name was Elías Haséfer, which means Elías "the book." The book, obviously, was the sacred writings. (It's possible that Séfer ultimately became Silva, as the Jews of this surname like to claim.) The tournament took place in Castile, in great pomp. Princes, noblemen, and gentlemen attended. On the church's side the bishop attended, along with superiors from the religious orders, doctors of theology, and scholars. Elías Haséfer had the right to consult a thick Bible that was placed at his disposal, but he startled the audience with long streams of verses recited from memory. The philosophies of the church and the synagogue clashed like swords. Each side excelled, and the first round ended in a tie. The second and third rounds gave the Christian theologians an advantage, as they overwhelmed Elías with unexpected arguments. The gentlemen began to strike their shields to express their joy. In the fourth session, Elías Haséfer, seeming weakened, relaunched each of his arguments as if from a catapult and turned his adversaries into ridiculous half-wits. The gentlemen no longer wanted to strike their shields, but rather longed to wield their swords. In the fifth session there was a close tie, and in the sixth session Elías Haséfer triumphed again. The king consulted with the bishop in a low voice. A seventh session was convened, but the monarch did not authorize debate. He clarified that this was an entertainment, not a trial; the truth of the church was not subject to doubt and did not require the defeat of a Jewish sophist. The king then offered gifts to all the participants. As he gave an exquisite chest to Elías Haséfer, he exclaimed, "What a shame you're not an advocate for Christ!" This outburst was obviously another gift, perhaps the most valuable one. But the next day the Jews of Castile had to mourn Elías Haséfer, who was murdered a few steps from his house.

Despite these tragedies, the Jewish ghettos still gave rise to astronomers, translators, mathematicians, poets, and doctors as brilliant as those formerly produced in the Islamic kingdoms, Sevilla explained to Francisco. Many luminous ascents, however, ended in falls. One example was that of Samuel Abulafia, who became as great a prince as Hasdai. He served as minister to Pedro the Cruel, King of Spain. His exceptional life is an example that exalts and terrifies, which is why Jews continue to remember him with ambivalence. They would have preferred to forget. Or, even better, that he might never have existed. Abulafia resolved the kingdom's financial ailments and gained favor among the powerful. He built the famous synagogue of El Tránsito, which still exists in Toledo, with beautiful Hebrew inscriptions around the Holy Ark. His residence was known as "the Jew's palace." He was weakened by political intrigues. His loyalty to the king stirred both admiration and hatred. His rivals sought revenge through attacks on the Jewish neighborhood. In one of those furious assaults, about 1,200 people died, including children. Finally, they wore down the monarch's trust. Pedro the Cruel succumbed to their slanders and ordered the imprisonment and torture of his formerly beloved minister. The torturers gloated over the prince's corpse after he died during their torments.

In this pathetic history, even this fact was defining. Just as in the distant era of the Visigoths, the people had more capacity for tolerance than for disdain. The Spanish took longer than the rest of Europe to assimilate their hatred. So much so that the ghettoes enjoyed autonomy, and the manuscripts of that period revealed a certain optimism. Philosophical and moral thought produced notable works; in the thirteenth century, in Christian Spain, a book was published that would become one of the most disconcerting to many men, *Zohar* or *The Book of Splendor*. It forms the core of the Kabbala.

"Have you ever heard speak of the Kabbalists, Francisco?"

The word was not unfamiliar to Francisco; he had first heard it when his brother was lying in bed with a wounded ankle, and his father had unveiled his profound secret. On the handle of the old Spanish key there was an engraving. They were not three petals, or three small flames; it was the first letter of the word *shem*, meaning "name." The Kabbalists attributed an infinite power to the Name, and, by manipulating letters, gained access to the depths of the mysteries.

Only in the fourteenth century—"Very recently," Sevilla emphasized, "considering the long history of Spanish Jews"—did intolerance clearly prevail. The fanatics gained territory with their cruelty. When epidemics broke out, they blamed the Jews. Sometimes it wasn't even necessary to speak the accusation—the masses ran right to the Jewish ghetto to kill and steal. Monks began to urge the extermination of infidels from within; at the head of excited mobs they broke into synagogues, profaned the altars, and enthroned an image there. Conversion was borne by Jews as a further offense. But a few converts, in their terror, mutated into extremist Christians as a way of erasing the stains of their own origins. One notable case was that of Pablo de Santamaría, the former rabbi whom Diego López de Lisboa admired, whose scandalously Hebrew name had been Solomon ha-Levi. The Levis descended from a Biblical tribe devoted to priesthood. The convert dove into theological studies and achieved the titles of archdeacon and canon of the Cathedral of Seville. Still not satisfied, he ascended to the roles of Bishop of Cartagena and Archbishop of Burgos. In this city, he composed an incendiary work: *Scrutinium Scripturarum*. He began to be called "the Burgosian," and his manual was used to pulverize Jewish arguments during debates.

"There are copies of the *Scrutinium*—in Buenos Aires, in Córdoba, in Santiago. And of course, there are several copies in Potosí, Cuzco, and Lima," López said. "For the Inquisition's officers and commissioners the book is a sword." He cleared his throat, as he did every time he was assailed by sadness. "And, without a doubt, it is a sharp sword."

In that year of mass conversions, 1391, the mob invaded the ghetto of Seville and killed four thousand men, women, and children. The synagogues were knocked down or transformed into churches. Months later the Jewish quarters of Córdoba were set on fire and approximately a thousand corpses were strewn on its streets. The murders spread immediately to beautiful Toledo and, from there, to seventy towns in Castile. Then crimes sparked up in Valencia, Barcelona, Gaona, and Lérida.

Francisco listened and absorbed, shaken.

46

The travelers admired lovely Salta, built on swampy terrain, as if it were a kind of squat castle. Hernando de Lerma had founded it on water like the Aztecs of Mexico. It had been his dream to build such a metropolis. Around the city stood the vast corrals where more mules were brought together than in any other part of the world.

The caravan reached the end of its journey. The wagons could not continue northward; the heavy oxen could only walk flat paths, from the pampas around Buenos Aires to remote Salta, at the foot of the plateaus.

López de Lisboa would remain in Salta at the home of a merchant friend and focus on his business transactions. Then he would return to Córdoba. He called Francisco over.

"I want to say goodbye." His upturned nose was red. "Perhaps you'll meet my son Antonio, if you return to Córdoba."

"Or if he goes to Lima."

"You're staying in Lima?"

"I'm going to study medicine. Then—God will provide."

"I sense that Antonio will also go to Lima." He sat down on a bundle. "When you embrace your father," he suggested, as he wiped his neck and forehead with a cloth, "you'll tell him that we've talked a lot, and that I agree with him."

Francisco's face turned into a question.

"Yes. I agree with him," he said. "I've received news that he has renounced Judaism. Permanently. He did the right thing."

"Are you sure?"

"The Inquisition gave him a light sentence. That only happens for those who truly repent." He sighed. "You see? So much suffering, for nothing. It's not history anymore, just butchery."

"Can history ever have an ending?"

"Theologians have demonstrated that the Jewish people existed, and were chosen, to announce and prepare for the arrival of Christ. Once that mission was accomplished their history was over. Their survival offends the divine plan."

"But the reality is that—"

"Reality must submit to theology, which is the truth." López de Lisboa wiped his face again, then folded the handkerchief and put it in his pocket. "I can't justify the stubbornness of José Ignacio, for example, who prefers an impossible path."

"It's not stubbornness." Sevilla appeared beside them, gazing at them with pity. "It's not stubbornness, my dear friend—it's conviction."

"Were you listening?" López de Lisboa said, annoyed.

"Only at the end, don't worry. Besides, I don't think you've said anything new. Only, perhaps, it seems to me, you've said it more emphatically."

"Because I no longer have any doubts."

"I'm sorry to disappoint you. You'll keep on doubting—that's why you needed the extra emphasis."

López de Lisboa just sat there and said nothing.

"We live in trying times," Sevilla said to console him.

47

Francisco noticed that in Salta some people wore kerchiefs around their necks, in what seemed to be a local form of coquetry. He felt disappointed at their lack of glamour. Lorenzo, on the other hand, burst into laughter because the goiter so endemic to these people struck him as funny. Francisco did not like him making fun of an illness. Lorenzo didn't think about illness. In his eyes those people were monstrous, and some monsters existed simply to entertain those who were not. In any case, he wasn't interested in the goiter wearers, but in the women of Salta, whose beauty excited him. Some wore their hair loose and thick, while others wore shining braids; their skin was soft, their gaze confident.

He found the brothel where he could put his fingers in the forest-like hair and take delight in the beautiful skin. That's how he told it. But, in reality, he bedded a mestiza who worked for a mean old woman and who almost stole his money pouch as he rolled around on a dirty straw mattress. With that urgency satisfied, Lorenzo brought his focus back to his next objective: to obtain free mules. "Spoils of war cost sweat and courage, not money." He told Francisco that he only needed one night to get half a dozen. The next morning they'd be able to embark on their journey toward Jujuy. Francisco didn't want to take the risk so Lorenzo agreed to meet him on the road. "You've spent too much time with monks to know how to steal," he said, punching Francisco's shoulder amicably.

In wide Lerma Valley, corrals full of animals stood ready for auction. They were built out of tree trunks and thick branches from nearby copses. Some unruly mules dug holes to get past the fences and had to be moved to reinforced corrals, while others were tricky and agitated their neighbors. Mounted on his blond horse Lorenzo resembled a rich merchant prepared to make honest transactions. He rode around the edges of various corrals, lingered to listen to the negotiations of sellers, asked the distracted mule drivers questions, mingled with other riders, examined shortcuts, and waited for the cloak of night. A fine drizzle, presaging the season's rains to come, helped facilitate his task.

The Sevillas and Francisco left at dawn. They hoped to arrive in Jujuy that same afternoon. It was best to plan the legs of their journey with precision, so as not to be stuck out in the open air; bad weather was coming. Sevilla had contracted a pack of mules from several traders, and the Indian José Yaru continued with him as a helper. It rained for half an hour when they were already far from Salta. Their baggage was covered with tarp, and the travelers pulled their ponchos up over their heads. The barefoot Indians tugged at the animals' harnesses. It was essential to keep advancing no matter what. These rainstorms would be frequent visitors from now on. When the rain ceased, the shimmering path seemed covered in broken glass, and an intense scent rose to the clouds, through whose tangled fleece the blue sky began to reappear.

Then they spied Lorenzo, descending laboriously from a mountain, dragging three mules. He had not obtained such abundant spoils.

48

So much loose rock abounded that the mules and Lorenzo's horse could no longer trot. Altitude sickness brought on dizzying stomach pains and fatigue. Every once in a while, they drank water or sipped a bit of broth with garlic. Sometimes they walked beside their animals so as not to overwhelm them.

Only José Yaru looked healthy, despite his constant sullenness; this was his homeland and the atmosphere sat well with him. He was marching toward an encounter with himself, a progressive harmony arranging his relationship to the world. His well-being was connected to terrible deeds—as well as splendid ones—that he could not communicate to anyone.

Francisco gazed keenly at the spectral landscape. They were closer to the heavens and, perhaps, to God. His father had come through here in his youth, escaping Portugal and Brazil. He imagined Don Diego arriving from the east, through ferocious jungles, and finding himself suddenly on this extremely arid high plateau on the road to Potosí. Even back then it was said that, in only ten years, the Spaniards had milked more precious metals out of those mountains than the Indians had in two thousand. Many thousands of Indians were buried in the mines by the system of forced labor known as *mita*.

Francisco reached the boisterous streets of Potosí. Neither were the walls made of silver, nor its rooftops of gold, but there were splendid carriages, and the men and women wore colorful clothing. The rich spent some of their earnings on vainglory and stashed the bulk of it in chests. Two entertainments dominated: brothels and puppet shows. The first one was condemned by the church, the second by the Inquisition.

Almost all the sermons were devoted to sins of the flesh. Priests insisted that Satan took delight in the bordellos. From the pulpit they glared reproachfully at the irresponsible males and at shameless women, because all of them attended church, including the brothels' madams.

The Inquisition, on the other hand, focused its attacks on puppeteers. It held that it was evil to make dolls talk. Weak minds would confuse inert objects with the Spirit and might end up believing in the power of a profane image. Not long before, the entire region had been shaken by a plague—the song sickness. Thousands of Indians had surrendered themselves to esoteric singing and dancing because they had heeded a call to return to the *huacas*, ridiculous gods of nature: lakes, mountains, stones, trees. Even worse, they had been taught that the gods no longer lived in objects, but, rather, that they sprang into the mouths of Indians and entered their innards to make them dance frenetically for days and nights. The filthy preachers said that the huacas were returning to battle Christ. The song sickness—*Taki Onqoy*—rattled the mountain. Expeditions had to be sent to suppress it. A large number of sorcerers, sorceresses, and chiefs were discovered to be complicit.

But the Inquisition was not only concerned with idolatry. The puppeteers were, above all, insolent people who tried to stir laughter at the expense of dignitaries. In oblique ways they referred to the minor sins of magistrates, the bribery of a judge, the mishaps of a bailiff, or the temptations of a priest. Abhorrent! These stories weakened faith. As a consequence the Inquisition prohibited puppets, but some daring practitioners still nurtured their craft in absolute secrecy.

Lorenzo was not about to miss out on such revelry. A good warrior needed entertainment. His virtues began with kissing the cross and bowing to the sword, but good spirits called for ass, tits, wine, and laughter. That's what his father used to say right in front of Brother Bartolomé's round face. Nobody could convince him otherwise. Soldiers had a tough profession and deserved thorough compensation. The pay was remitted in taverns and brothels during times of peace and with rapes when war was raging. This was a well-known, accepted fact consecrated by custom.

He dragged Francisco with him. The bordello blended in with the houses around it, though it was lower and darker. It was at the edge of the crowded city. The green door had a knocker shaped like the head of a monster sticking out its tongue. They were led to the parlor by a mestiza and invited to sit down. There, they met men who were busy receiving the caresses of several women, all of them laughing softly and playing with each other's hands. A mulatto woman offered small glasses of pisco. Francisco and Lorenzo began to drink. Two women approached them immediately. The pearly-skinned one gently placed her hand over Francisco's; she was tender and intoxicating. Francisco felt a current rush through him. Damp eyes watched him from behind dark eyelashes. Her rouged cheeks were as smooth as petals. Her painted mouth murmured turbulent words. She made him drink another little cup and recognized him as a novice, a rare thing. It would be fun for her to seduce him.

Lorenzo, on the other hand, took his companion by the waist and asked her point-blank where they could be alone. She guided him to the courtyard that led to the chambers with straw mattresses.

Another woman approached Francisco, very fat, missing teeth, wrapped in a cloud of lavender. The young man feared that she was coming to replace the young woman who had touched his hand. The old woman smiled and her wrinkled mouth became a horrific black circle. Francisco backed away. She massaged the nape of his neck.

"My son," she said, to calm him, "I'm here to charge you. I want you to have a good time. You like our beautiful Babel?"

He looked at the young woman and nodded. The fat woman extended a hand that was heavy with rings and bracelets. The young man dug into his money pouch, while the prostitute and the old madam watched him carefully. Loud laughter burst out at the opposite end of the parlor and a man in a silk doublet ran after two women who were fleeing toward the courtyard.

"Do you want to chase me?" the girl whispered.

"What's that?"

"You chase me and—when you catch me—you catch me!"

"I catch you?"

"Yes." She half closed her purple eyelids in an imitation of defeat. "You do what you want with me. What you'd like to do to me."

Francisco stared at her, stupefied.

"What would you like to do to me?" Babel asked.

Francisco shrugged and smiled.

"What would you like? Come on, tell me." She brought her hot cheek closer. "Would you like . . . to touch my face? Would you like to touch my neck? Look." She raised her head and stretched her snowy throat.

He was tense. A shudder rippled through his belly. His feet were cold, his hands sweaty.

"Would you like to put your fingers under my skirt? If you catch me, I'm yours. That's the game."

"I don't want to chase you," he said hoarsely.

"Caress me?"

Francisco looked at her with mistrust, excitement, and rage. Rage against himself. She touched the back of his hand again. Her fingers made soft spirals there and then they ventured to the palm. It tickled. Francisco laughed a little. She seized the moment to place the shaking hand on her naked throat.

"Touch," she invited him.

His eager hands lost themselves in the warm smoothness of petals and, as directed by the kind and charming Babel, they touched her nape and shoulders, then slipped cautiously toward the marvel of her breasts. Francisco's head became inflamed. He had to possess, press, kiss, spill out. He clumsily embraced Babel and bit her hot plum lips. She put her hands under Francisco's shirt and rummaged under his breeches. She confirmed that he'd ejaculated.

They slowly let each other go. Francisco was ashamed. The dizziness that had been drowning him now loosened its grip. She tried to get up, but he held her back.

"What do you want now?" She tidied her hair. "What do you want? Again? You'd have to pay Doña Úrsula again."

As if Doña Úrsula had been watching the scene, she appeared, large hand extended. Francisco did not hesitate. He was calmer now and could imitate Lorenzo.

"Let's go where we can be alone," he demanded.

Buxom Babel guided him to a small room. There, in the candlelight, he finally had full access to the vibrant body of a woman.

As they lay on the woolen mattress she asked him about his recent virginity.

"Are you proud of having taken my virginity?"

"I didn't take anything from you!" She laughed. "You're the one who lost it, in any case."

"Why were you baptized Babel?"

"It's not my name, just my nickname."

"And how did you get such a strange nickname?"

"I know words in many languages. I learn them immediately: Quechua, Tonocoté, Cacán." She began to dress.

49

José Yaru requested permission to spend one of their two days in Potosí visiting some relatives who had come from Cuzco years before. Many Indians had been brought through persuasion or force to serve in the silver mines. Some were obliged to work through the night. Any rebels were whipped, sheared of their hair, and sent to harsh prisons, not only to return them to their underground workplace in a tamed state, but also to maintain a state of terror in the others.

The mines devoured the workforce so that more Indians were requested from Indian overseers and other nearby communities. They were to pack their rustic clothes and a single animal skin blanket, say goodbye to their neighbors on a sad drunken night, and take the path to slavery. They were received like cattle to be examined and redistributed. The men—and vigorous boys—were pushed toward the tunnels, and the rest formed marginal neighborhoods in their tiny cabins, barely more than holes in the mountain slopes; a reserve that was occasionally visited by priests, there to teach them to be good Catholics.

José knew the place. His feet touched the gravel that the conquerors had turned into an inferno. Not a tree, not a plant. Nothing but a few giant cacti standing like candelabras. Males were only seen on Sundays, when everyone had to attend Mass. The women glided like punished souls; they tended the few narrow corrals, ground with the mortar and pestle, and distilled the chicha corn drink. They did not look up as José passed them in the winding alley. Nothing happened nor could happen to change their destinies. They waited for their men's fleeting returns, a joy as brief as a passing comet. The children grew against their mothers' wills. When their muscles were ready they would join and replace their fathers in new legions of laborers for the mines to consume.

The doors of the shacks were so low that one almost had to crawl to enter. They were protected by nothing more than a rush curtain. José separated the fibers and looked inside. The rancid smell spread through his body; he crouched against the outer wall. The small space before him, all the way to the wall of the next hut, was dotted with little black pellets of goat feces. After a while, an old woman's head looked out. She dragged herself out of the squat hut and sat down beside the Indian. They did not speak. After several minutes she rubbed her face, which was as dark and wrinkled as a grape. José waited, ecstatic. Then she put her hand in the folds of her skirt and took out a white bundle. It was a shawl that she slowly unfolded on her knees, uncovering a few pieces of black fleece. She murmured a few words and reached under the fleece to reveal an oval-shaped stone.

José gazed at the stone, spellbound. The sorceress turned it as though she were a priestess holding the sacred host. Then she reached back with her left hand and grabbed a bottle full of chicha. She closed one eye for better aim and poured the liquid over the stone.

"I've already fed it," she said, breaking her silence. "Now it needs chicha. Look how it drinks, how it likes it."

José nodded with respectful gravity.

"I found it for you. You asked for it." She wrapped the stone in fleece and then wrapped the whole mass back in the white shawl. "And don't forget the requests. I fed it well—it has spoken to me."

They went silent. The air whistled in that miserable labyrinth. A few children dripping with snot passed them like shadows.

"What did it tell you?" José asked after a while.

"That the time of the huacas has arrived. The huacas are resurrecting by the thousands. They will defeat the Christians and return us to freedom."

The children passed again. This time they lingered for a moment, staring at the still figures leaning against the wall and at the white bundle the old woman held with both hands.

"Did you ask them why they haven't already won?" José pressed.

She turned to him with an air of reproach.

"Because they haven't finished entering all of our bodies," she said. "When every one of us has a huaca inside of us, we'll be invincible."

"What should I do?" He gestured toward the wrapped stone with his chin.

"Feed it with more maize and chicha." She handed him the bundle. "Serve it. In Cuzco you will give it to the Indian chief Mateo Poma. It's a powerful huaca and it wants to be in Poma's body. The huaca will thank you for this service."

José affectionately pressed the deity and slid it under his clothes. It was the vehicle for a boundless force. The huacas were returning to restore justice in the world. José and the sorceress lingered until twilight unfolded its poncho over the hills. Many huacas slept there, and beyond those hills there were more mounds and peaks and amazing ravines. There were streams and rivers; there were tears. Each of these was a huaca. They were all descended from one of the two greats: Titicaca or Pachacámac. All the huacas had once been alive, until the Incans took power a few centuries ago, establishing the cult of the single Sun and abolishing the worship of huacas. In that remote time, were they defeated, or did they allow themselves to be so? The sorcerers said that they allowed themselves to be beaten so that the people would not be harmed. They decided to surrender to a slumber deeper than a lizard's. They seemed dead, but they were not, as each huaca is an immortal god. The Incas failed when the sun god abandoned them. Then the white men arrived on horseback, rising to the peaks. They killed the Incas and destroyed the altars, imposing their rule and exhorting all to obey a new god called Jesus Christ. They ordered memory to be lost, for

Indians to change their traditional names and take on ugly new Spanish names, and for them to bury their dead at the church instead of keeping them with corn seeds in comfortable clay pots, and for them to kneel before a doll nailed to a stick. The conquistadors turned the world upside down, bringing illnesses, killing people, offending, and raping. So much pain penetrated the slumber of the huacas that they awoke. The desolation around them stirred their rage. Each one set about resurrecting the next one to come to the aid of a people subjected to tyranny.

Their first manifestation occurred in the region of Ayacucho, near the criminal mines of Huancavélica. Shamans possessed by visions of huacas barged into the diocese of Cuzco and Lima, describing the rituals that should be performed in the face of imminent change. They instructed the people: "Don't believe in the god of the Christian, or in his commandments, and don't worship the cross or any of their images, don't enter their churches, and don't confess to their priests." They also ordered, "Purify yourselves with traditional fasts, don't eat any salt or garlic, don't copulate with your women, and only drink the feverish chicha." They had to be strong for the great battle.

They said, "The god of the Christians is powerful because he made Castile and the Spaniards, and because he supported Pizarro when he arrived in Cajamarca and conquered this kingdom, but the huacas were also powerful because they made this earth and made the Indians and the things that grew here, and because they were patient enough to wait in slumber until this moment in which they will battle and win." One potent preacher was called Juan Carlos Chocne. He promised, in the name of the huacas, that "It will go well, your children will be healthy as will your crops." And he said those who remained doubtful and submissive would "die and their heads will be on the ground and their feet to the sky. . . . Others will turn into deer, guanacos, and vicunas, and will fall from mountains." Many huacas began to manifest in men and women who suddenly emitted falsetto sounds or growls, while others surrendered to interminable dances. Hundreds of mouths intoned songs that were not from this time, or from that of the Incas, but, rather, that came from the time in which the huacas sustained the harmony of the universe. This was the *Taki Onqoy*, the song sickness.

The white men were infuriated. What seemed like another idiotic indigenous custom now threatened to become a revolt, and they denounced it with one terrible word: idolatry. For them, the resurrection of the huacas could be reduced to a disgusting cult. They didn't want to know about the deep feelings that were stirred. They only knew to do one thing— stamp it out! The song sickness was a plague. The Indians were not only denying the true faith but were also attempting to reclaim their pre-Incan roots. They were changed by a hope so ridiculous that it could only feed Satan. That's when the ruthless persecution began. The ecclesiastical leader Cristóbal de Albornoz launched a merciless war, overturning sorcerers, chiefs, and preachers. Juan Chocne, along with other accused leaders, was taken to Cuzco, where they were all subjected to the torments of the rack.

The defeated preachers stopped speaking the truth; they begged forgiveness and said that they had lied. Many were sentenced to lifelong hard labor building churches. The punishments included insults; they were feathered, shorn of their hair, and mocked in public. The repression cracked down on thousands of indigenous people, and all rites involving the cult of huacas were prohibited.

The god of the Christians reestablished his unjust order. But not forever. José was sure that the huacas had not been defeated; they had merely starred in a first skirmish, a warning. The renewed cruelty of the tyrants would be doubly punished. Every Indian in the Viceroyalty was still "conversing" secretly with the invisible reality. Behind their trivial appearance the huacas hid a wondrous power. In the valleys and mountains, along the coast and on the high plateaus, a great battle was coming. José had had to flee the raids unleashed by the exterminators of idolatries. His trip to the south had been providential, as his family war was the war of the indigenous family of this part of the world against the usurping family that had arrived from the high seas.

50

Francisco's nightmare re-created the walk of monks through the Dominican monastery in Córdoba. Santiago de La Cruz was offering him a chain with which to flog himself, but on taking his hand, Francisco saw that it was a lancet, with which he immediately opened a vein on the apoplectic Brother Bartolomé; then the shouts around him conveyed that he was dead. He felt afraid, and said, "I didn't kill him." The monstrous cat stared at him with its yellow eyes; it grumbled, showed its teeth, and was about to leap on him when the fat hand of Doña Úrsula massaged the back of his neck. He turned violently and woke up. Other men were sleeping around him. Coughs and wheezes echoed through the collective bedroom of the tavern, and the cold air barely curbed the smell of flatulence. The pale dawn slipped in through a skylight. The fragments of his dream still clung to him, along with images of Babel's smooth face. He rubbed his eyes. He had to go back, to touch and possess her. He adjusted his erect member and sat up, irritated to discover his reality.

"I should confess." He tidied his shirt and fastened his belt. "Yes, I should confess."

He made for the door and Lorenzo squinted one eye open.

"Where are you going?"

"I'll be back in a little while."

He washed himself in the bowl placed outside to catch rain and went out to the streets that, from the earliest hours, had been overflowing with urgency and lust. Potosí was Sodom, Gomorrah, and Nineveh all rolled into one. The black servants had already begun their labors. A few carriages traveled in search of officials or Indian overseers. The dawn stripped soot from the elegant buildings and pebbles rolled in the harsh cold wind.

He entered the first church he found. The atmosphere of protection and the scent of incense comforted him. The warm house of God produced an instant sense of harmony. He kneeled and made the sign of the cross at the end of the corridor. At the front stood the main altar, with its resplendent custody of the sacred sacrament. An altarpiece gilded in gold and silver was flanked by a set of mahogany chairs that culminated in voluminous pulpits. The building was more imposing and luxurious than it seemed from the outside. Its ceiling was decorated with colored panels joined without a single nail, like the wagons made in Ibatín.

He prayed an Our Father. Then he sought the confessional. A woman sobbed on her knees, while the priest, hidden in the discreet chamber, absorbed her human errors and forgave her in the name of the Holy Trinity. Francisco waited for her to finish. When he saw her make the sign of the cross, he took his place. He was lost in thought. He needed the priest's voice, his absolution. He approached with his head down and fell to his knees.

"Francisco Maldonado da Silva!"

It was a cold, emphatic voice that called his name from behind him. It hit him like a puma on his back. The voice did not come from the confessional. In the half light he recognized the small, energetic priest.

"Brother Antonio Luque!"

The superior of the Mercedarians of Ibatín, and feared familiar of the Inquisition, looked at him with glacial eyes.

"You recognized me," Francisco said after a few seconds, with a forced smile, after stammering a few other sounds that refused to coalesce into words.

"You look just like your father."

"With less of a beard." He touched it, grimacing.

"What are you doing here?"

"I came to confess."

"I realize that. I'm asking what you're doing in Potosí."

"I'm passing through."

"You're traveling to Lima, right?"

"Yes."

"You're looking for your father?"

"Yes."

The severe priest hid his hands in the wide sleeves of his habit. His face was not kind. He looked Francisco over many times, from his copper-colored hair to his worn boots. He used that roving gaze to intimidate his interlocutors, especially when they were taller than him. He did not speak, or welcome words to be spoken. After some time, in a voice so low the young man had to lean in to hear it, he spilled his bile.

"I know about your trip. In Lima, you'll find your father—and the Tribunal of the Inquisition."

Despite the cold that reigned in Potosí, sweat dripped from Francisco's head.

"You should have stayed in the monastery in Córdoba."

"I want to study medicine."

Brother Antonio Luque furrowed his brow. "Like your father."

"He's not the only doctor."

"A doctor like your father." Luque frowned. "And you'll probably be other things like him, too—are you already a practicing Jew?"

The unexpected accusation hit Francisco in the gut. He moved his head. He didn't know how to answer a priest who was allowed to attack him so unjustly.

"I—I've come here to confess. I'm a good Christian. Why are you insulting me?"

"You cannot confess."

"What are you saying?"

"You cannot confess. You are impure."

Francisco thought that the bitter monk might have seen him enter the brothel.

"I've come here to purify myself. That's why I want the absolution of the sacrament," he implored.

"You are impure; your blood is impure!"

The young man felt another blow to his stomach.

"Do you understand what I say?" Luque said, unmoved. "You are the son of a New Christian. You are filthy with Judaism."

"My mother is an Old Christian!"

"Was—she is dead," he continued in a low tone, monotonous, humiliating. "You didn't stay near her tomb; you travel toward your father, toward the prisoner of the Inquisition."

"I'm a Christian. I'm baptized. I also received confirmation. I believe in Our Lord Jesus Christ and His Holy Mother and in all the saints of the church. I want to save my soul! Don't close the path of salvation to me. I'm a Christian and I want to keep being a Christian," he said without stopping for breath, his lips dry.

"Those who have impure blood, like you, your father, and your brother, must do more penitence and acts of virtue than those of pure blood. Also, in leaving the monastery you have shown your paltry disposition toward sacrifice for the faith. I have reasons, therefore, to distrust you and to demand that before you benefit from the sacrament of confession, you tell me the whole truth of your purpose. I want what is best for you."

Francisco twisted his fingers, unable to find the best way to react to a man who was exceeding the authority of his role. It was obvious that he had no right to refuse him divine absolution, but he had plenty of power. He had the power to change Francisco's plans, retain him here in Potosí, defame him, and send him back to Ibatín or Córdoba. There was no other choice but to bow down.

51

Francisco was finally able to kneel in the confessional and unload his sin of fornication. He was absolved in the name of the Father and the Son and the Holy Spirit. The penitence of prayers the priest gave him was not burdensome, but rather gratifying. His ears echoed with the phrase, "Go, and sin no more."

But the accusatory image of Brother Antonio Luque stayed in his soul. The priest's steely eyes had seared with an unshakable contempt for his father, his brother, and, surely, all their descendants. Francisco wondered what he could do for God and His ministers to love Him. With what sacrifices could he stop them from constantly reminding him of his origins? Would Antonio Luque pursue him all over the earth, reminding him of his abominable condition? Just as he had appeared here in this church in Potosí, could he also find him later in Lima? Would he once again look at him with disdain and demand more degradations from him than from any other mortal?

He described his difficulties to Sevilla, who calmly explained that he should not feel weighed down by the contempt of Luque and the many who were like him; they were fanatics who behaved like beasts, with pure aggression and irrationality. His wife María Elena—her name as beautiful as she was herself—knew about these convictions. That was when Francisco discovered that this woman, too, observed Judaism.

She was a New Christian and had married Sevilla to preserve her faith. Their two daughters were not yet old enough to learn of this dangerous duality.

On departing from Potosí, Lorenzo rode between Sevilla's mules and his friend Francisco, resembling a gentleman flanked by squires. He had no problems of identity or purity; for him, everything was simple. He had toughened up in preparation for future adventures, and now he looked forward to some grand fun at the hot springs of Chuquisaca.

The Indians walked barefoot beside the mules and ran at a good pace when the animals were able to trot. In silence they invoked their gods when the Christian god grudgingly gave them air. They kept their ears open for orders, because obedience was what guaranteed their precarious well-being. Among them walked José Yaru, who did not talk to them, as words almost never flowed from his mouth, and, also, because it outraged him that they were so oppressed. Under his shabby tunic he carried the huaca that he was to give to the Indian chief Mateo Poma in Cuzco. The stone, wrapped in wool, firmly pressed to his skin, filled him with a supernatural power. José could prove how real this resurrection of the old beloved deities truly was; he was sleeping better, he was less tired, he had a healthy appetite, and he had plenty of energy for carrying bundles, pushing mules, and running for miles between these hills as towering as castles that would one day belong to him again.

52

Ciudad de la Plata de la Nueva Toledo was true to its name and received the travelers festooned with flags, as there was always an excuse for celebration. Its large homes were magnificent. The house of the president of the Royal Court was completely covered in tiles and silver plating. Almost all the buildings were large and sumptuous, as befitted powerful people.

The climate was milder here. Beautiful women moved through the streets, escorted by black servants. The esteemed members of the Royal Court could be recognized by their luxurious capes and the greetings they received as they went about their days. There were also many learned men.

"Diego López de Lisboa," Sevilla said, "wants to come here to study theology."

"He said that?"

"Don't you remember? He wants to deepen his Christian faith to erase his roots. But he won't be able to do it. It's an indelible mark."

"A curse?"

"Well—neither Job nor Jeremiah called the tests of the Highest One a curse."

The inside of the cathedral abounded with mirrors. Large silver pieces surrounded the main altar. Extremely tall candleholders lit the spacious nave by day. Francisco prayed to the Lord that He might shorten their trip; he was dreaming of Lima and of being reunited with his father.

They continued on to Oruro, where bars of silver were melted. Lorenzo tried to seduce several coquettish women. He was unsuccessful, though he'd been assured that they were quick to hide with a man and quicker still to lure him into matrimony.

They ascended to La Paz. On the path, some Indian women wrapped in colored ponchos sold them very cold eggs. Francisco learned that before the Spanish conquest these indigenous people had not known that eggs were edible, and they still refused to ingest them. They also saw groups of women examining sieves in the streams, searching for nuggets of gold that they would later turn over to their masters. The yield was negligible. La Paz, nevertheless, glowed like a rich place, its houses laden with decorations. Velvet and jewels were everywhere.

The caravan moved onward. The travelers took lodging in the pampas of Pacajes, where the columns of forced laborers were gathered before being taken to the mines of Potosí. It was a sad and varied multitude. Each Indian took his wife and children with him. The condemned formed groups identified by a flag; that was the sign they were to follow, the emblem of their tragic destiny. They carried bundles on their backs and dragged a few rams and vicunas with them.

Sevilla ordered a halt. José had lagged behind, transformed into a statue. Watching that imprisoned, resigned crowd filled him with profound pain. He could neither approach them nor flee, and the mere sight was a torment. Sevilla went in search of him while Francisco thought of him with pity and an ineffable solidarity.

53

At Lake Titicaca they were on the roof of the world. Dense caravans lined the edge of the water. The lake was as vast as the sea. Along its glassy surface glided small cane rafts that Indians had been making since time immemorial. The shores were pocked with garlands of mud, like wet cotton.

José continued acting strangely. One night, he rose quietly, went to a clearing, and kneeled to watch the moon; the cold penetrated his scalp. With one hand he stroked the bundle tied to his chest. Lorenzo remarked on this eccentricity to Francisco.

"Does he do that every night? Is he worshipping the moon?"

José dawdled in obeying orders and kept his distance from everyone, including the other Indians. One day, Francisco watched him move away toward the reeds surrounding the lake. The Indian was glancing around him, acting anxious. Had he stolen something? Francisco followed him and bore witness to an alarming scene. José squatted, reached under his stained tunic, and took out a white bundle. He untied it, opened a dark ball of fleece, and delicately took out a stone. Then he rubbed it with corn flour and poured chicha over it. Murmuring something, he placed the white shawl on the damp grass, undid the fleece, and placed the stone on top of it. He gazed at it for a long time, so still that it was as if he himself were also a stone. Then words resounded in falsetto, in

Quechua, which made him shake as though operated by springs. His head, shoulders, and legs trembled. Then calm returned. After a while, José returned the stone to the fleece and wrapped the fleece in the shawl. He tied the bundle to his chest and hid it under his tunic.

This act of sorcery shook Francisco. He had seen something abominable and damning. It would be best to leave and pretend the episode had never happened. But it was too late. José had noticed Francisco and pounced like a feline, knocking him down. José had turned ferocious, like a Calchaquí Indian, shoulders immense, head swollen.

"It's idolatry—" Francisco stammered as he tried to break the man's bestial grip. "It's dangerous—they'll burn you alive."

José pressed Francisco's throat with both hands, trying to strangle him. His calloused fingers sank in to the bone. He wanted to kill. Suddenly José released him and stepped back a few paces. His face was awash with fear. Fear that his crime would be discovered and the bundle at his chest wrested away from him.

"Are—are you going to report me?"

"It's idolatry, José," Francisco insisted as he massaged his neck. "But I won't report you."

The Indian could not overcome his suspicion.

"I won't report you, calm down," he repeated. "But don't sin again."

54

One of the last stages of the journey passed through the Cordillera de Vilcanota mountains. Sevilla warned that crossing them would be difficult. And, in fact, as soon as they entered the treacherous rocky terrain, rain and hail began to fall. One night, snow covered the entire landscape. The shapes of the mountains guided them. The streams dragged chunks of ice; the wind hurt their skin. They took refuge in a cabin where the proprietors knew the value of a pot full of boiling beans, cabbage, and mutton. The fire and hot soup comforted them. María Elena and her daughters wore so many layers that they looked like swaddled babies.

The ascents and descents finally delivered them to a gentler climate. They stopped at a couple of posts before arriving at the town of Combapete, which was famous for the longevity of its residents. Many of the people there were over a hundred years old. They laughed with all of their teeth and walked without canes. This marvel announced what followed: Cuzco, the capital of the formerly splendid Incan Empire.

The sun broke its rays against the towers of the ancient imperial capital. The landscape was magical. The streams had been transformed into canals. The fields stretched out in geometric terraces connected by long stone walls. Short lines of Indians converged there from surrounding areas, bringing food on the backs of llamas.

They advanced on the zigzagging path until they entered the alleys that in previous times had shuddered with the traffic of Incans and their majestic courts. They crossed several small plazas lined by houses with limestone façades and roofs with rosy tiles. Between the houses stood stables with lambs, llamas, pigs, and chickens. In the main plaza stood the magnificent cathedral. Dozens of mestizos were building a stage in front of the great door, for the great Feast of God.

Sevilla had proposed that Francisco and Lorenzo stay with him in the spacious residence of his friend Gaspar Chávez, who owned a business that manufactured cloth for many of the region's merchants. It would be no trouble for Chávez to host them for a few days. José and the rest of the Indians would also find enough space to sleep and eat in the sheds. José was more tense than ever; he had to deliver the huaca.

Chávez wore a blue felt hat that he never removed, not even to eat or sleep. He'd clamped it on when he went bald, he said, laughing at himself; he'd even learned to bathe with it on. He was missing two lower incisors and, when he spoke, his tongue would escape through the gap. He compensated for this unpleasant feature with his boisterous warmth. He received the Sevilla family with exclamations that could be heard far and wide. He kissed the girls and said that, of course, the two young men could live in his house for as long as they wished to stay in Cuzco.

"I suppose you're interested in the Feast of God." His tongue poked out between his teeth.

"Yes," Lorenzo answered.

"It's magnificent! A feast of God from the church and the good Christians," Chávez said emphatically, moving his tongue in a manner that seemed obscene.

"Have you known him for a long time?" Francisco asked Sevilla later, out of their host's earshot.

"Gaspar? Let's see," Sevilla said, thinking for a moment. "How old is your brother Diego? Almost twenty-eight?"

"Yes."

"Then it's been about thirty years since I met Gaspar Chávez. A good chunk of time, right?"

"Here, in Cuzco?"

"Near here, on the mountain. Your father was there when we met."

"Tell me."

Sevilla smiled. "You want more stories?" He winked conspiratorially. "Look"—he put his hands on his shoulders—"the surname Chávez has a particular origin. Its sound and spelling hide it, but not too much. It comes from the word 'Shabbat.'"

"He's Jewish?"

"Shhh! To everybody else he's a good Christian. Didn't he just praise the Feast of God?"

Francisco glanced at him sidelong.

"He goes to Mass," Sevilla said, "he confesses, he participates in the processions, he gives significant donations to the church. What more can you ask of him?"

Chávez's manufacturing had spread to the neighboring houses. They were hives full of bustling courtyards and covered corridors, arranged so that the rain would not disturb the work of the Indian and mestizo employees, or ruin the hundreds of looms in a constant state of activity. Between the looms, fires crackled to keep the space warm through the winter.

But the work was not only by contract or compulsion; it was also to fulfill sentences. Francisco learned that the authorities worked with the manufacturers in the area to put thieves and other criminals to work. In this way, they earned their keep and reduced the cost of being watched over. They wore iron shackles on their ankles and if they were seen to have good behavior, they received better rations and could be promoted to the status of voluntary workers.

The strong smells of wool and urine were eased by the slaves who circulated between the looms with brooms, ashes, and buckets of water. But neither water nor ashes nor the brooms could eliminate the strongest odor: that of deaf rage at the carriages, at the needles, at the inks and the cloth, rage that would spread through the Viceroyalty.

The Feast of God, meanwhile, had been in preparation for weeks, with processions and functions at the church. The Indians were receiving more catechism, bells rang anxiously, and priests took the faithful to the cemeteries. In the artisans' neighborhood, workers hurried to make new crosses, flags, and banners, while in the outlying neighborhoods, chicha was fermented and masks were painted.

Impatience grew in José's chest. He had been instructed to find Chief Mateo Poma. Unfortunately, the chief had left for Guamanga, but would return for the Feast of God. It was worrisome; it sounded like a bad omen.

The multitudes began to gather in Cuzco's central plaza. The rows of the faithful stood under flags that curled like snakes. The bells rang out again and many people fell to their knees. The parade of religious orders began: first the Dominicans, then the Mercedarians, Franciscans, Jesuits, and Augustinians, and then the nuns, each with their own banners. A short distance from them were the commissioners and familiars of the Holy Office of the Inquisition, their candles aflame. Behind the ecclesiastics came the secular government officials and the nobility in their splendid clothes. The gentlemen walked behind them, arrogant, closing the procession. The feast began.

A cacophony of bells tore the clouds open and a cascade of sunlight bathed the great door of the cathedral. In that miraculous instant, the bishop, enlarged by his mitre and chasuble, appeared with the sacred monstrance in his arms, covered by a mantle held by clergymen and the city's most prestigious secular residents. Among them walked Gaspar Chávez, his face solemn, bald head shining. (It was not true that he never removed his hat.) The altar boys swung incense in time with each other between the rows, while from balconies, flowers were thrown and aromatic waters sprinkled. The bishop paused intermittently so that the people could kneel before the sacred monstrance. Litanies floated up from the waves of devotees.

This first part of the festivities contrasted starkly with the next. Proceedings called for several hours of containment before unleashing the beast. The bishop returned to the cathedral with slow majesty. The monstrance was put away, the mantle rolled up, and the crosses well covered.

José was exhausting his longing eyes in search of Chief Mateo Poma. His huaca spoke to him again; a catastrophe would occur if it was not immediately transferred to the Indian chief's body. It even caused pain in José's legs, warning his bones that they might break.

Sevilla had attended this feast on other visits to Cuzco. He told Francisco to prepare for a pagan spectacle. "Tolerated by the church," he whispered in irritation. "There are incomprehensible concessions made to 'save the souls' of the indigenous people. They give the name Feast of God to a local rite, which is the heart of it. The procession we saw and other superficial details are just the wrapping, and barely so. You'll see."

The ululations of new rows flowing to the main plaza announced the beginning of abandon. Among the gentlemen, nobility, and clergy, Indian dancers appeared, covered in adornments, such as brightly colored linen, gleaming plates of metal, and trinkets. The people opened the way for this irrepressible delight.

"What's making them so happy?"

"Not God, exactly," Sevilla said, scratching his ear, "but gods. Their gods."

"Idolatry?"

"They're going to perform the struggle of good against evil. They've been doing this since before Christopher Columbus was born. But now they have no choice but to portray good as the archangel Gabriel and evil as the devil. This feast is so indigenous that it includes a wife of the devil because in their primitive religion there is no supernatural power without a feminine counterpart. They call her China Supay."

A whirlwind of monsters rolled toward the center of the plaza. Shouts broke out when, among the costumes, an enormous mask appeared with undulating horns, bulging eyes, and a half-open mouth with outsize teeth, all wrapped in a luxurious embroidered cape. Two-headed snakes and lizards erupted from its head. It was the devil, and the people cheered for him, especially when he threatened to catch whoever was nearby. China Supay skipped and leapt at his side, dressed as an Indian woman, a trident in her hand.

The shouting became even louder the instant that a thick snake of raucous, costumed dancers reached the center. With synchronized turns, they cleared the space before the raised seating area that now contained the civil and religious authorities of Cuzco. The multitude ceded an ample semicircle to them, and the actors did a circle dance as a form of greeting. Accompanied by local instruments including *cajas, erkes, quenas,* and *sikus*, they performed rhythmic steps until they formed a spiral, at whose center vibrated hell. The devil, China Supay, and the gods of pleasure romped, surrounded by that spiral. Their contortions were passionate and sensual. The Indians who inundated the plaza joined in from their places in the crushing crowd, with an elation verging on trance.

All of a sudden, from the raised seating area, the slender figure of the archangel Gabriel appeared in flowing white robes. He hurled himself down to the plaza and charged against the fence that protected the demons. The dancers closed ranks against his daring steps and the archangel, brusquely stopped, became a victim of temptations. One after another, the boisterous mortal sins tried to seduce him. They did so with gestures, contortions, shouts, expectation. But the archangel defeated them one after another, in successive struggles acted out in dance. Finally, he broke through the wall and scared off the devil and his followers. The dancers raised the archangel to their shoulders and formed a five-pointed star. Instruments and voices joined in to accompany the dance of triumph. Ponchos undulated like a condor's wings. But the devil, irredeemable, returned to attack him from behind. The archangel turned and struck him a decisive blow with his sword. The devil rolled acrobatically and, near the raised seating, took off his mythological mask, accepting defeat to deafening applause.

The devil was Chief Mateo Poma.

José recognized him by the white scar along his neck. He made his way through the multitude and embraced him.

That night, as the traditional drunken festivities unfolded around campfires, the Indian chief welcomed José at the door of his hut. Beside him lay two rabbits that his faithful had brought him as a tribute, condiments made from corn paste and llama fat, just as the old sorcerers prescribed, and jugs of chicha. José took out the white bundle and opened it. The stone was transferred solemnly to Mateo Poma's hands; he rubbed flour on it and poured chicha over it.

"What did it tell you?" he asked José.

"That I should find you immediately and tell you that the huacas are coming in great numbers to break the Christians' bones."

The flames of the fire made brushstrokes of light over their intensely focused faces. Mateo Poma stroked the scar at his neck; he, too, sensed the imminence of an earthquake.

That night, the ecclesiastic inspectors and their armed helpers carried out their raid. Those captured would be subjected to interrogation, torture, and sentencing for the practice of idolatry. Some would be subjected to the rack and have their bones broken. Among those rounded up in the raid were Chief Mateo Poma and José Yaru.

It was the end of the rebellion.

Meanwhile, the fireworks spilled out snaking colors and lit up the ecstatic eyes of the faithful. It was the end of the feast.

55

"Seven days from now, you'll arrive in Lima," assured Sevilla, who would be staying in Cuzco.

"I want to be there already," Francisco sighed. "This journey has been too long."

"I understand. But now the route poses no serious difficulties. From here to Guamanga, the hustle and bustle of cattle will continue. You'll find slopes, gorges, and a few muddy reed beds but, as I said, they aren't significant obstacles. You'll cross the beautiful bridge at Abancay, made of a single arch, built by the first conquistadors to facilitate transit from this part of the Viceroyalty. Ah, and then you'll see something fun."

"What?"

"Something fun and crazy. An isolated hill where a church is being built to the Virgin. Can you imagine? A solitary church in the middle of the desert. No faithful around. Usually, the population comes first, and then the temple is raised. Or both at once, but not the reverse order. The reason for this extravagance? They say that a pilgrim went there with a sacred image and its weight suddenly increased. He thought it must be a miracle—that the image wanted to stay there. And so they began to build a church in the middle of a wasteland."

Francisco shook his head.

"Well then. From Guamanga to Lima, you won't have any more curious stops. You'll become impatient."

"I'm already impatient."

Francisco pressed Sevilla's rough hands and gazed at his wise old face for a long time. For an instant, he thought he saw the ocean in his pupils. Then he went to say goodbye to María Elena and their daughters.

The girls were exchanging jokes about the adventures of their journey. Mónica recalled the salt flats near Córdoba, and Juana wanted to talk about the incredible concentration of mules in Salta. Mónica mocked her sister for confusing turkeys with crows. And Juana got even by reminding her sister of her fear of getting burned in the baths of Chuquisaca. Mónica said that she was no longer bothered by the mark on Lorenzo's face, and Juana dared to touch Francisco's arm and confess that she would miss him. The sudden tenderness was like a lightning bolt. Francisco kissed them, as if he were kissing Felipa's and Isabel's cheeks.

Sevilla's wife took him aside.

"José Ignacio told me that you're impatient to get to Lima. I want to offer you hope." She smiled, as Aldonza had done so many years ago. "You'll find your father. And together you'll be able to pray to the Lord."

"Thank you so much. Truly."

"When you're reunited with him, remember us."

"I will. I know that I will."

"We're brother and sister, you know."

Francisco responded with a conspiratorial wink.

"Brother and sister in history, in sacrifice, and in faith." She stared at him intently. "Hear, O Israel"—she added, in a prayerful tone—"the Lord, our God, the Lord is one."

"My father said that a long time ago, tending a wound on my brother."

"Those words are emblems of our strength. They sustain us, Francisco. They sustain us like the gigantic elephants that mythically sustain the world."

56

On the final leg of the journey, Lorenzo and Francisco recalled José Yaru. Lorenzo rode on his blond steed, Francisco on a mule, while the remaining mules carried the baggage. They were crossing plains fenced by lilac hills.

"They'll quarter him," Lorenzo predicted, unperturbed. "Unless he has the good sense to repent and beg forgiveness on his knees, with sincere tears."

"It's possible. They've arrested many people, though they won't kill all of them."

"José is an obstinate Indian, and idolatry is entrenched in him. He'll be punished harshly."

"How do you know that?" Francisco asked, bothered.

"Did he get up at night to look at the moon?"

"That's idolatry?"

"What else! He talked to it; I saw him."

"He talked to a stone."

"Really? That's even worse!"

"Worse, how?"

"The moon, at least, is enchanting, mysterious. A stone—" Lorenzo's mouth twisted in disgust.

"Or a piece of wood, or a lake. The universe."

"Yes, they see gods everywhere. They believe in anything. They're brutes, ignorant. They don't want to learn."

"Or they're poorly taught."

"Could be," Lorenzo acknowledged. "The priests round up the Indians and make them repeat the doctrine. Bah! They repeat it without understanding. Imagine. Even I don't understand the whole doctrine. What can they expect from those half-wits? When one of the foul-mouthed among them explains things, who knows what they say! The clergymen are reassured, hearing them repeat words or seeing them cross themselves. They want to believe that they're converted. They need to believe, it's easier that way. Because they can't be such idiots as to really swallow the story."

"What story?"

"That they're already converted. The Indians were idolaters and they're still idolaters. The only things that can stamp out their idolatry, the only things, listen well, are the rack, the noose, and the whip."

"It's been years since the eradication of idolatry started with all those methods." Francisco had a visceral revulsion for them.

"That's right."

"And they haven't stamped it out."

"Not completely. But there's less of it than before."

"I'm not so sure," said Francisco.

Lorenzo loosened his hold on the front of his saddle. "No?"

"I believe, Lorenzo, that this stubborn idolatry and the famous plague of *Taki Onqoy* have a deeper cause than the ignorance of Indians."

"The devil."

"It's not just about evil."

"What, then?"

"I don't know, or I can't explain it."

"There's nothing deep about idolatry, Francisco. It makes people believe in superficial things, in what the eyes or ears can sense. It's the devil's trick."

"You know what? Even though I'm disgusted by idolatry, this idolatry of the Indians doesn't revolt me. I'd say that . . . it moves me."

"Are you crazy? What makes the Indians' idolatry a better kind?"

"It's not that it's better. It expresses something."

"That they're all brutes."

"Listen. They abandoned it for the sun god that was imposed on them by the Incas. Then they abandoned the sun for Our Lord Jesus Christ, who was imposed on them by the Christians. Now they're abandoning the god of the Christians to return to the beginning." He was reasoning with great effort, selecting each word, uncertain.

"What are you getting at?"

"I don't know," Francisco said, shrugging. "Maybe that those gods affirm their identity, their roots. Those are their own gods, not the ones imposed on them by others."

"A stone affirms identity?" Lorenzo laughed.

"Many stones, and mountains, and trees. All the earth that they know, and their ancestors and their suffering. They need to be expressed through a religion of their own. Belief in those absurd gods fills them with something, something like . . . importance. They are gods who protect and respect them. Our Lord Jesus Christ, on the other hand, respects and benefits only Christians. So why should they love Him?"

"Your ideas are ridiculous. They confuse and disturb."

"I haven't worked them all out quite yet."

"Better to forget them." Lorenzo drew his riding crop and whipped it against Francisco's ribs. "Eh, monk's little pet! You'd better forget all that, seriously. Think about something else. Think about women. Now that we've almost reached Lima don't even think about defending those heresies out loud!"

From a hillock they could see the straight blue sash of the Pacific Ocean. They both knew that their greatest adventure was about to begin.

BOOK THREE

Leviticus

The City of Kings

57

Lorenzo Valdés and Francisco Maldonado da Silva entered Lima from the south and came across a cavalry brigade mounted on tall steeds with golden metal gleaming on their harnesses. The procession raised clouds of earth as it advanced toward the Plaza de Armas. The colorful parade, with its vertical pikes and standards raised high, made people on the street stand at attention, whether or not they admired the luxury and elegance. Two-wheeled, mule-drawn buggies moved away down adjacent streets or backed into doorways when they saw the troops were near. They were told that the cavalry brigade was searching for Marquis Montesclaros, Viceroy of Peru, to escort him in his travels, and nobody could obstruct them. Francisco and Lorenzo watched them go down the thunderous street of swordsmiths and decided to follow them, as a way of getting to know the city. Forges and hammers straightened sheets of steel and molded artistic handles on an array of swords and shields. Gentlemen and low-ranking nobility, examining the merchandise, grudgingly made way for the viceroy's officers. The harnessed steeds turned into the alley of the luggage makers. Here, there stood pyramids of chests, trunks, wardrobes, and suitcases. The cavalry then took the spacious street of the merchants, crammed with shops selling cloth, spices, wine, shoes, cordovan leather boots, dyes, jewelry, dinnerware, oil, candles, saddles, and hats. Slaves hurried to push the tables of wares aside to prevent them from being overturned by a soldier's spur. Lorenzo took advantage of the chaos to pocket a deck of playing cards.

Finally, the cavalry reached the colossal Plaza de Armas. It faced the viceroy's palace, whose sober lines belied the luxury inside. The cathedral stood beside them, in the same place where the first primitive church had been built at the orders of Lima's founder. On the other side, the town hall. The political, religious, and municipal powers touched, jostled, competed. The same display as in Ibatín, Santiago, Córdoba, and Salta.

The plaza dazzled Lorenzo and Francisco. It not only served for processions and bullfights, as in other cities, but also for the Acts of Faith.

"This is where my father was reconciled."

"I wish I could join the cavalry," Lorenzo sighed, fingering his pilfered cards.

"I don't wish to arrive at Callao, where he is now," Francisco thought.

Behind them, the wheel of a buggy grazed the edge of the canal that ran down the center of the street and overturned. The next carriage tried to avoid it, but its bronze foot rail got caught and the vehicle became stuck. Immediately, an array of carriages piled up against each other. Two officers made their way through, weapons held high. Furious faces and a few fists poked through the windows. Several gentlemen ran up to watch the incident unfold. Their elegance was striking; they wore short trousers gathered at the knees, with epaulettes three fingers thick on their shoulders, double-soled shoes to better protect from the damp, and gold chains that hung from jacket buttonholes, bearing toothpicks also made of gold.

Francisco asked for the whereabouts of the Santo Domingo monastery, where he was to find Brother Manuel Montes, just as he'd been instructed in Córdoba by Brother Bartolomé Delgado.

Within a few minutes they arrived at the church, with the monastery attached. They entered with the solemnity demanded by a sacred place. The altar gleamed; at the opposite end was the choir's balcony made of engraved cedar. Francisco made the sign of the cross and prayed. Then he walked toward a side door and slid back the bolt noiselessly. A forest of lights assaulted him; where he'd thought he'd find the courtyard he instead saw sapphires and rubies shining on panels of gold. He blinked, blinded. At the center of the cloister rose palm trees flanked with potted blue, yellow, and red flowers. He advanced, afraid of breaking a spell, approached the wall, and stroked the cool surface. The tiles had been made in Spain, and had only recently been installed.

Lorenzo swayed at the sight of the treasure, and grazed it with his nails; perhaps he could pry out a gem or two that seemed concealed beneath the glaze. Disappointed, he urged his friend for them to return to the main plaza, where it was more fun.

"You'll find your monk soon enough."

No priest appeared so Francisco followed his friend to the noisy street.

They crossed a fabulous stone bridge, arrived at the Alameda refreshed by the trees and fountains, and gazed on the majestic passing entourage of Viceroy Montesclaros and his court of nobles, pages, and gentlemen who competed for proximity in order to say a few words in his presence. Then they went down to the Rímac River and drank alongside their mounts. The viceroy, on his way back to his palace, lingered at a turret of the bridge to read his name and titles etched into the stone. Then his gaze roved down toward the water carriers, the black washerwomen, and the two friends beside the Rímac.

Lorenzo saw him. In a low voice, he proclaimed, "He saw me! The viceroy laid his eyes on me!"

He already felt that he belonged to the royal militia. His future was assured.

58

It anguished Francisco to reach Callao, even though the port had been the goal of his long journey: it was where his father was. He was anguished over finding Brother Manuel Montes, but he had promised to do so. He did not want to pass the fearsome palace of the Holy Office, even though curiosity devoured him. Finally, he decided to face all three challenges.

Lorenzo wished him luck. He gave him a mule as a gift, as the two that remained and the beautiful horse were enough to present himself with dignity before the chief of the militia. Lorenzo understood that the gaze the viceroy had bestowed from the bridge was already his certificate of admission. He was going to eradicate idolaters, fight against pirate raids, and domesticate rebellious Indians. He would have a brilliant military career.

They embraced, and then Francisco, tugging at his mule, headed toward the place he had tried to imagine in his nightmares—the Palace of the Inquisition.

He walked along the street that his father and brother had surely traversed on their way to jail. It was an active road, with no traces of the captives. On the mule's back he had securely tied the saddlebags containing the medical instruments, the case with the Spanish key, and the Bible. On turning a corner the mule stopped, and Francisco felt the same shock. The building was extraordinary. Below the elevated religious image glittered the maxim *Exurge Domine et Judica Causam Tuam* (Rise, Sir, and Defend Your Cause). A pair of spiral columns guarded the carved panels of the colossal door, through which dignitaries and their fearful powers came and went. A black-caped figure approached the door, which half opened to allow swift entry. The door closed. The air around Francisco turned chilled; he had seen no one less than the famous inquisitor Gaitán. Francisco was afraid and automatically raised his hand to the mule's back—the medical instruments and the key were gone! He felt for them again, loosened a rope, inserted his hand. No. They were there. His forehead was beaded with sweat and his heart beat against his ribs.

A long and sinister wall extended from the palace. "That must be where the torture chambers were," Francisco thought, "and the infinite dungeons."

Oppressed, he returned to the monastery. He crossed the church and entered the luminous cloister. The tiles burned. This time, he found Brother Manuel Montes, who welcomed him with restrained courtesy. Had he been expecting him? His skin seemed like a mask of death. His eyes, hidden in the depths of their sockets, seemed covered by a whitish film. There was something mummy-like in his appearance. Why had Brother Bartolomé ordered him to present himself to such a cold, disagreeable priest?

Brother Manuel, without asking questions, guided his young guest to a cell at the very back of the monastery, devoid of objects—no mattress, no mat, no bench, no table. It was a narrow hole in the wall with a single high window.

The clergyman entered first, and stared at the packed dirt floor as if counting tiles that did not exist. Then, with a slowness that increased the oppressiveness, he examined each of the four walls, whose adobe seemed to shrink back in shame. What was he looking for? Finally, he studied the cane ceiling crossed by a few beams.

"You'll sleep here," he said without emotion, his voice as funereal as his face. "After three days you'll go to Callao." He paused and looked him in the face for the first time. "And in half an hour you'll dine in the refectory."

Francisco placed his bundles on the floor and went to wash up. Why did he have to wait three days longer to be reunited with his family? On the way to the fountain, he discovered a corridor that led to the monastery hospital. It had a good reputation, according to what he'd heard in Chuquisaca and Cuzco. His father had wanted to create one in Potosí, for the Indians, but he could not get enough support. This one, on the other hand, was for monks and, especially, for the prelates and important men of Lima. He moved timidly down the corridor, which let out on an inner courtyard lined with patients' rooms. He saw the pharmacy—a room full of bottles, jars, urns, pots, and tubes. On a table stood a scale with a long handle and an hourglass. To the side, water tubes twisted and turned.

He felt someone breathing at his side. A hallucination? It was a black man dressed in the habit of the order, looking at him with tranquil eyes. Could a Dominican monk be black? Were the norms so different in Lima? The hallucination spoke, amicably. He asked whether he could help with anything.

"N-no. I was just exploring—I'll be staying the night, at the invitation of Brother Manuel."

"It's all right, my son."

He was not black, but rather mulatto. And he wore the tertiary habit, the one worn by the lowest rung of the order, with a worn white tunic, black scapular, and black cape, but without the hood of a priest. His African roots surely prevented him from becoming a regular monk.

"Do you need some kind of remedy?" he asked.

"No. I just wanted to see the hospital. I've never seen one."

"Oh, it's very simple. I believe all hospitals are the same. I am the barber of this one."

"Yes? I also want to become a barber, or surgeon, or doctor."

"Congratulations! We need pious doctors and surgeons. There are many charlatans, do you know? And they do great damage." His eyes shone brightly. "Are you studying?"

"I want to start."

"Congratulations, my son. Congratulations."

"Brother Manuel ordered me to go to the refectory. Forgive me, I'm going to get ready."

"Very well. You should do so."

Francisco returned to his cell and took out the clothes he had washed on the road. He changed and went to dinner.

He looked for Manuel Montes and the mulatto. Another monk showed him where to sit, as if they had reserved his place. Did the whole order know of his presence? Dozens of eyes looked his way. Why were they staring so gravely? Was it possible that they were already accusing him of something?

He was familiar with the rituals of refectories. He had partaken in them at the Dominican monastery in Córdoba. But this dining room was more sumptuous and brightly lit by large torches. Here the benches were made of carved wood and the floor was smoothly tiled. There were also more clergymen. The monks stayed standing beside the tables, faces hooded, hands hidden beneath their scapulars. A monk intoned the *Benedicte*. Another sang the *Edent pauperes*. They all sat down.

As a priest read aloud in Latin from a pulpit, servants glided silently with their laden trays. They carried casserole pots full of steaming animal innards. The diners' spoons began to move after the benediction and a special prayer for the recovery of the order's prior, Father Lucas Albarracín.

The word of God descended monotonously, interceded by the slurps of hungry mouths. Francisco glanced from side to side, confirming that the monks were still watching him.

He found Brother Montes. Not the mulatto, who entered later with a tray. He was a member of the order, but he also worked as a servant. They called him Brother Martín.

59

After the service, Francisco returned to his desolate cell. He found a candle, moved his baggage to the side, and lay down by the wall. The damp roughness eased his feeling of helplessness. The adobe wall felt, to him, like a mule's back: tough and trustworthy. Did a few steps' distance separate him from another cell? Did some servant sleep there? He wondered what the reasons were for this mysterious isolation in which they preferred to keep him, and why they detained him in this city, as if it hadn't already been enough years that he'd lived far from his father, or months that he'd spent traveling to get here.

He thought he heard the snores of a servant on the other side of the wall. The darkness was slightly lifted by the narrow little window. Frogs croaked near the well. The snores increased, and they were not, it turned out, from one person, but from several. The thick wall had transformed into a sheet that transmitted and magnified sound. The snores no longer sounded rhythmic or placid, but torrential. They evoked the swelling of Río del Tejar in Ibatín.

They were not snores, however, but rats. Rats running through the pipes, rafters, walls, and floor—and on Francisco's legs and neck. They unleashed avalanches of noise. They wanted to explore the territory the young man had invaded.

Francisco moved slowly. It would not serve him to declare war. He wanted to convince them to accept him as a neighbor. The rats alternated the caresses of their velvety bodies against the intruder's chest with the fleeting pinches of their nails. Every once in a while they stopped, and, turning brusquely, struck him with their long tails. Gritting his teeth, he allowed them to run over him and accept him. After hours of insomnia and resistance, he was overcome by sleep.

The following nights were more peaceful.

Brother Manuel made him confess before leaving for the port. He wanted to know what he had touched with his hands. Francisco did not understand him, and answered, "Rats."

The cadaverous monk remained silent. His long pauses were painful. Then he made a request, his voice extraordinarily kind: "Pray for our prior's health."

60

Francisco traveled through the crowds at the port of Callao without stopping, looking around anxiously; any back could be his father's. Carriages rattled by, bearing baskets overflowing with fish whose silver scales inflamed the greed of thrill seekers. Beside the docks, several galleons swayed, their sails rolled up. Squat warehouses lined the coast.

He had never been so close to the ocean. The fresh, salty air elated him. That blue surface reaching out to the straight line of the horizon possessed a startling majesty. Not far away, an island arose. Between that island and the harbor, canoes and fishermen's boats moved to and fro. He had reached the arrival and departure place for everyone and everything, from viceroys to Angolans, from tallow for candles to the precious metals from the mines. Here, riches and ambitions came and went. It was the great gate that connected the Viceroyalty of Peru to the rest of the world.

He walked southward because he wanted to touch the water. The waves unfurled like rugs over the sand that appeared beyond the docks. Flocks of birds descended toward the undertow. He stepped onto the beach and his feet sank pleasurably into the soft surface. It was an unprecedented sensation. He faced the undulating foam and put a foot into the cold water. He was touching something that had possibly kissed the coasts of Spain, China, the Holy Land, Angola. He rolled up his cotton trousers, walked in further, and wet his face and neck. He licked the salty drops. A fisherman gestured to him from his unstable boat as if greeting him in the name of fabulous underwater beings.

He turned, gaining sight of a different landscape. There was Callao, as seen from the water and the south; it was a cluster of polyhedrons attached to a vast dock at one end, and the main church on the other. This was where his father must be, because that was what the Inquisition had declared, and what Manuel Montes had confirmed. His desire to see him was so intense that he didn't dare ask for him. He feared a terrible surprise; he had become reconciled by the Holy Office, and reconciliations, though considered pardons, still carried the stigma of a crime that nothing and no one could erase. He surely wore the sanbenito, that disgraceful scapular that hung to the knees and announced the wearer's humiliated state. Those who were shamed with this piece of clothing had to wear it forever, so that the faithful might heap their contempt on them. And after the person's death, the sanbenito was hung by the door of the church with the name of the former wearer written in giant letters, so his descendants would also suffer.

He returned to the docks, walked through a kaleidoscope of cargo, and paused beside a pair of cannons. His eyes looked frenetically over the bustling crowd. Why was he looking for him on the street? His workplace was the hospital. Francisco realized that he was purposefully going in circles because he was afraid of discovering his father.

In a corner of the port, a beggar fingered scraps of food under a crown of flies. The terrible sanbenito covered his clothes. His disheveled dirty white hair fell over cheeks pocked with scars and warts. Was this what remained of his father? He approached slowly. The man was isolated by an invisible barrier that only the flies would cross. Francisco stopped a couple of paces away. The beggar looked at him indifferently. This wasn't his father—those weren't the eyes, nose, lips, ears, or cheekbones. He turned away. "I need to prepare myself," he thought. "They may have devastated him as they did this poor man."

He pulled on his mule. They turned into an alley. Excrement compelled him to cross the canals many times. He glimpsed a church and a monastery. There, behind the undulating garden wall, stood the Callao hospital. His quickened pulse made him walk faster.

He had to repeat his father's name to the servant who inexplicably stood watch at the door. The servant addressed a hunched man who came to meet the visitor. He swayed back and forth as he walked, as if his feet were failing him. As the light from outside fell on his features, Francisco recognized him. The years seemed to have compressed him, making him less tall, graying his hair and beard, wrinkling his skin, sharpening his cheekbones. They stared at each other in amazement.

The man's lips trembled as he whispered, "Francisco?" To convince himself, he had to say the name again. Francisco basked in his father's gaze but also took in the stained sanbenito that made a mockery of his dignity. They clasped each other's hands. The young man noticed that they were the same hands as before, only bony, weak. The men stood like two trees at the center of a storm howling with memories, questions, jubilation, and dread. They each felt lashed by uncontainable emotion. They stoically held back the words and sobs roiling inside them, straining to spill out. Diego Núñez da Silva finally stepped forward and embraced his son. He broke the caution he'd been keeping to avoid staining him with his sanbenito. Then he invited him to sit down on a stone bench.

They kept sneaking glances at each other. The father, dizzy with sensations, admired his son's handsomeness: his trim copper-colored beard, his deep and intelligent eyes, his virile shoulders. He was a replica of his own youth. He wanted to ask him about Francisquito, the curious, mischievous, and daring little boy who had been captivated by his stories, and who had so infuriated his teacher Isidro Miranda.

Through the refracting prism of his tears, Francisco took in the effects of his father's suffering. What remained of that powerful, cultured man? No more than scars of torment and an abject degradation.

61

The viceroy moved his head, and his barber inflicted a scratch on his cheek. He begged his pardon, full of fear, and stopped the blood with a piece of cotton. Then he cropped the sideburns with his razor and painstakingly trimmed the refined beard that fell like a ribbon from the lower lip. He used scissors, a comb, and perfumed egg whites to shape his mustache, twisting the tips into an optimistic upward curve.

The viceroy's valet presented his clothes. His Excellence glanced at them, without moving, so that the barber would not reoffend. He approved the chamois gloves, the velveteen shoes, the velvet vest, and the silk shirt. He would also wear, as he always did on these excursions, his high hat, the taffeta collar, and a gleaming jet-black cape. Then he would return to the palace to add the symbols of his investiture, as he was to welcome Inquisitor Andrés Juan Gaitán, who seemed to be in a sour mood. That man was like a splinter under one's fingernail. "I'll act with prudence," he thought.

Marquis Montesclaros, Viceroy of Peru, came from the best nobility of New Castile. He had enough titles to demolish any adversary. But, in these savage lands, there were plenty of people who hampered his management of things and tried to question the privileges that he rightfully obtained from power. When he was thirty-two, Felipe III had named him Viceroy of Mexico, a nation that he governed for four years, after which he was named Viceroy of Peru. The sovereign often fondly called him "my relative."

"The Viceroyalty of Peru is enormous," the viceroy thinks, "because it begins in the cauldrons of the equator and fades out at the southern pole, tired of mysteries." I arrived in Lima on December 21, 1607, a date that is well recorded in my memory as, the following day, I took my oath and received a shock that placed the success of my entire enterprise at risk. I had to choose the common mayors, and the feasts of welcome they honored me with concealed their desire to impede the changes I planned to make. They were accustomed to swindling viceroys, and I soured their expectations. That was the first lesson. I gave them the second one when I examined the royal coffers and found them in overwhelming disarray. Those negligent scoundrels tried to confuse me with devious explanations, but I scared them by saying that this evil had a remedy called the court of accounts. Several dignitaries whispered, "Back, Satan!" Then I became involved in the affairs of the court of the consulate, which my predecessors had not managed to set in motion. The opposition to that came from the Indian overseers, who had been bribing government officials and judges to stave off the influence of traders.

My efficiency has been attributed to my youth. A mistake. It's not about age, but about taking charge. In Peru, I represent the king; I not only have the right but the obligation to act as though I were the sovereign, as if he were here in the flesh. But I am held back by palace intrigues. I defeat them with my axiom that nobody is more essential than the storekeeper, and as such, I have resolved to be a storekeeper for the king; I cover His Majesty with large sums, to the point where his dwindling incomes depend on my deliveries more each day. In eight armadas alone I remitted ten million pesos of gold.

People also attribute my sins of the flesh to my youth. As if senile old men didn't have such sins, when in fact they not only fall prey to vice, but leave the women unsatisfied. Attractive ladies abound in Lima, and they do whatever they can to slide into my bedroom. And that stirs envy. I'm also envied for my poetic gifts. My critics are the dregs of human misery. They forgive me nothing, the rascals. I've already heard that they're working on a trial of residence for when my term is done. They hate me for my good deeds.

―――

A page helped him dress. Soldiers stood guard just outside the door, where several dignitaries were waiting. Everything was ready for another visit to the splendid stone bridge, one of his most expensive and beloved works.

Meanwhile, near the palace, the inquisitor Gaitán was putting the finishing touches on the strategy he'd use when, in a couple of hours, he would speak with the viceroy.

The official retinue, preceded by glistening guards, moved toward the bridge that spanned the Rímac, the torrent that divided Lima, the "singing river." Connecting the core of the capital with the neighborhood of San Lázaro, its waters flowed over stones and uneven beds of sand, nourishing the dry surroundings. But the river also reached the difficult terrain of the northern valleys, where important parts of the city remained relatively isolated. Marquis Montesclaros had decided to build a construction that could withstand the test of time. "Let it be an immortal stanza." He had heard of a master mason who lived in Quito and made admirable works. He was warned, however, that there were not sufficient resources to pay for a project of such magnitude. The marquis considered this and, before his interlocutors had finished enumerating the hurdles, he addressed the assistant to his right: "Have the councilmen summon the illustrious builder." He turned to the assistant to his left. "We'll obtain the resources through new taxes, and I won't touch a single coin that belongs to the king."

The bridge extended in a triumphant arch, and from its solid height one could hear the Rímac's song. The parapets on both sides were thick enough to stop the onrush of a careening carriage. On the end that let out into the neighborhood of San Lázaro, two turrets rose, bearing inscriptions that alluded to the bridge's creation. The viceroy lingered to read them closely, as if to check that no wicked hand had distorted his name or forgotten any of his sonorous titles.

His entourage believed the outing was ending, but the marquis preferred to walk on. He needed to unwind some more before his meeting with bitter Gaitán. So he continued on to the Alameda, the gorgeous promenade he had ordered to be built along with the bridge. No matter that the austere clergymen deplored the wasting of fortunes on beautifying landscapes in this part of the world. The Viceroyal court, the ministers, the officers and soldiers of the militia, and even the ladies of Lima now enjoyed the pleasures of strolling along this walkway. The rest and conversation facilitated the exchange of glances, which created subtle codes, and those codes, in turn, tended to end in unforgettable transgressions. The mean-spirited liked to say that the Alameda had been built to "count and catch" the women of Lima.

Finally, he ordered their return to the palace. He once again greeted the slender turrets at the bridge, and turned toward the river. Water carriers and black washerwomen were descending down to the shore. A few riders also led their mounts down to drink. Among them, he spied two young men, arriving from the south, one on a blond steed, the other on a mule.

62

"It's pathetic to argue with these crows," the viceroy thinks as he settles into his armchair in preparation for the inevitable fight. Nothing is enough for them. If they could, they'd seize all the power of the kingdom and the church. From the beginning they've been filled with privileges. And now they can't be stopped. What's more, they make sure that their officials, slaves, and servants respond to no one but the Holy Office. Like barbers trying to be judged by barbers, and whores by whores.

Several of my predecessors begged the king to rein in their arrogance, but it was in vain. With intrigues and terror, they got one royal document after another for their own exclusive benefit. Far from Lima, the familiars of the Inquisition are even more out of line. To the point that the archbishop asked the inquisitors for moderation in defense of its violent, imprudent officers. Useless. The Holy Office is a brotherhood where mere membership is enough to be crowned an angel.

Thence comes the need for agreements, a kind of judicial poultice to put limits on these beasts. They act superior in both civil and ecclesiastic matters, try to function like the royal court's older brothers, try to crush the viceroy under the soles of their shoes.

Through the agreement of 1610, black people under the power of the Holy Office can no longer bear arms, and the inquisitors, though they still have the right to monitor the mail that goes out, can no longer ban its *release. And they can't ban bishops from transferring priests without their consent. And they are also blocked from intervening in university affairs. It's progress.*

—∿∿—

The marquis saw the irritating figure of Inquisitor Andrés Juan Gaitán through the wrought iron door. His face resembled a skull barely wrapped in taut, pale skin, and it contrasted with the black tunic of his investiture. He approached slowly. Even his gait dripped with arrogance.

As they faced one another they spoke customary greetings. They were clear adversaries, unable to express the extent of their distrust and dislike. Their venomous hostility had to be presented in sheaths of velvet.

"You were very kind to announce the agreement with drums," the inquisitor said.

"All things concerned with the Holy Office are of first importance," the viceroy retorted cynically.

"In addition, you distributed copies to private homes—"

"The public must be informed."

"Nevertheless, the agreement has many points that need correction, Your Excellence."

"Everything has room for improvement, of course."

"That is why I have come. I presume that you recognize the Holy Office's need for the Viceroyalty's health."

"You presume correctly."

"Idolatries are continuing to trouble the souls of Indians, and heresies are doing the same to the souls of whites." Gaitán paused for a moment before continuing. "We have received word that Jews are continuing to arrive here; no Portuguese is exempt from suspicion.

There is also bigamy, and unmarried cohabitation is on the rise. Books full of filth are circulating. We've even been infiltrated by Lutherans!"

"What a catalogue! It's atrocious. And precise, as well," the viceroy conceded.

"We must discuss this."

"You have my devoted attention."

"Your Excellency, let me get to the heart of the matter: it is dangerous to erode the authority of the Holy Office."

"Oh, who would dare!"

"The most recent agreement, you know—"

"Yes, it's a tepid document."

"Do you mean to say it is less than harsh with regard to the Holy Office?"

"I did not mean to imply that, the Lord knows! I was only saying that it does not modify the previous situation in any significant way, for the good of the Holy Office as well as for the good of the Viceroyalty, of course."

"Some royal officials believe that this agreement empowers them to arrest officers of the Inquisition. Already, aberrant situations have occurred, which show signs of resentment and cruelty."

"I was not aware of this," the viceroy said.

"They forget that threatening members of the Holy Office is like threatening the Holy See! It is a sacrilege!"

"Naturally. I will punish those who have committed such an unpardonable outrage."

"I am glad to see such a strong reaction."

"It is my duty."

"Thank you, Your Excellency." Gaitán pulled at the folds of his tunic and adjusted the heavy cross on his chest. "I have another complaint, if I may."

"Go ahead, enlighten me."

"The agreement prohibits us from giving licenses for leaving Peru—it removes that privilege from us."

"Effectively so."

"It is a very grave error."

"If you say so—but, what can I do? It is the will of the king."

"The licenses we gave for travel allowed us to catch fugitive heretics. When someone requested a license from the Holy Office we could search for his name in the register of testimonies, and, if he had been denounced, that prisoner did not escape."

"You are right. And it is unfortunate that the Holy Office should be deprived of such an effective tool. I, however, cannot modify that point," the viceroy said with swift finality.

The inquisitor stared at him venomously for a long second. Then he lowered his eyes and, with forced amicability, replied, "To my judgment, you could—in any case, we will speak again. Now I would like to air another complaint: the agreement prohibits us from having armed blacks or mulattoes."

"Effectively so."

"This privilege should not be annulled. The Inquisition has been operating in Lima for forty years. What is this, a disarmament of the Holy Office?"

"You surprise me."

Gaitán's eyes were steely blades.

"You surprise me," the viceroy repeated. "And you sadden me. Who could be such a pig as to attempt to vex the Holy Office?"

"This should be corrected, then."

"But armed black people sometimes commit violent acts. They are a real danger."

"Not when they are accompanied by officials," the inquisitor replied.

"I recognize that, in such conditions, the danger lessens, yes."

"I ask you, then, for a decree of exemption."

"A decree of exemption?"

"That our blacks can bear arms when accompanying inquisitors, prosecutors, or the highest bailiffs of the Holy Office."

"I will reflect on it."

Gaitán caressed his cross. He was not satisfied by the response.

"May I ask His Excellency for a time frame?"

"I will not give you a time frame, but rather my promise to respond soon."

The inquisitor could tell that his audience was drawing to a close. "This cursed poet-turned-viceroy," he thought, "wants to have the last word and get me out of here without making a commitment. Well, I won't leave until I've thrown a reminder in his delinquent face."

The marquis of Montesclaros stood. It was the unmistakable signal. The inquisitor was to do the same and say his goodbyes, in accordance with custom and protocol. But the inquisitor seemed to have fallen prey to sudden blindness; he neither saw him, nor moved, remaining absorbed in the cross that hung against his chest. The power of Caesar and the power of God, competing. Andrés Juan Gaitán, representative of God, was almost God. With a voice that could have risen from the grave, he unleashed his speech. He spoke while seated, as if the floor were his, to a viceroy who was on his feet, tense and trapped.

"Since the founding of the church," he addressed his fingers, which were engaged in stroking the cross, "the punishment of heresy has been the domain of priests. To prevent any oversights, Pope Innocent IV created the Tribunal of the Inquisition. Great pope, great saint. And so the Inquisition might not suffer barriers in its sublime task, popes as well as kings have exempted it from civil laws, and even ordinary ecclesiastical ones. Prerogatives, privileges, and immunities, so that the task might help increase the faith. Since affairs pertaining to faith belong, at the end of the day, to the pope, the principal jurisdiction of the Holy Office is ecclesiastic. Civil jurisdiction, on the other hand—that of a viceroy, and that of a royal court, by extension—are below that. Below, well below, just as the earth is below the heavens."

He slowly lifted his gaze and feigned surprise. As if he had not realized that he was disrespecting the viceroy. He bowed, savoring his small victory. He turned and walked majestically toward the door.

The viceroy found himself chewing the aggressive phrase, "All the prerogatives . . . all the prerogatives . . ."

63

Diego's shack was around the corner from the port's hospital. Francisco struggled to hide the pity he felt for this defeated man who, incomprehensively, walked with a grotesque, swaying gait. His perpetually apologetic smile pained Francisco. It was hurtful to see this imitation of the doctor who years ago had stepped so confidently in Ibatín. His muddy hands hung at his sides like rags. He gazed at the ground, unsure of his own sight. He hesitated at his door, which was made of strips of wood held together by a couple of crossbars.

"Here it is," he murmured, ashamed.

He pushed. There was no key, no lock, no bolt, and one of the three hinges was broken. The son was embarrassed by the hole that served as his father's home. Suddenly, the orange grove of Ibatín glowed before Francisco, its pastel colors brushed with gentle lines of blue. He was dizzied by the intense hallucination. He stepped into the dark rectangle and smelled the dampness. As the light of Ibatín diminished, he made out the partially whitewashed adobe walls, the earthen floor, and the thatch roof through which he spied the eternal clouds of Callao.

"It never rains," Diego said by way of justification.

Francisco took in his father's possessions, few and shabby: a table piled with papers, books, a tin jug, and a clay pot; a bookshelf with more books, a straw mattress, and two benches—one at the table, the other against the wall. At the far end, a chest sat beside a doorless cupboard. Several nails in the wall served as hangers. Diego removed his sanbenito and hung it on one of those nails.

He opened his bony arms, as if to say, "Make yourself at home." A gloomy home, testament to his fall. He drew the second bench toward the table. Then he opened the chest; he was searching for things that might improve their surroundings and express his joy at his son's arrival. The son, for his part, found his father's search for ways to welcome him intolerable. It underscored his decline.

Francisco unloaded his baggage, which the mule, now tied to a post outside, thanked him for with a shudder. He placed his things at the center of the room. The muffled thud drew Diego's attention. "What do you have in there?" Francisco took out his clothes, the thick Bible, and a sack. He invited his father to approach. He did not understand. Francisco told him to open the sack. "A present?" he wondered, moved. Yes, Francisco would have liked to explain, but his lips could not emit a sound. "Yes," he thought, "a present from Córdoba, your faithful slave Luis gave it to me before I left and I've guarded it like a king's treasure throughout my travels."

Diego leaned forward, felt the coarse sack, and immediately his eyes shone with the intensity of the past. His fingers untied the knot and took out a scalpel; he rubbed it on his sleeve and raised it to the light. A smile that was not apologetic finally spread across his face. He placed it on the table as if it were made of glass. He found a cannula, also rubbed it, and made it sparkle in the light. He picked up, caressed, and greeted each piece, as if they were beings worthy of tenderness. He swallowed saliva mixed with silent tears. The brocade case appeared. Wearing an expression of gratitude, he shook it to hear the rattle of the Spanish key.

Then Francisco told him about Luis. It was only right to recount the miracle: how he had hidden the instruments, how he had borne the punishment of Captain Toribio Valdés and the interrogation of the commissioner. But he stopped short of describing his escapades to the slaughterhouse to soothe the family's hunger through theft. He could not yet descend into the hole of their family's tragedy; it was unbearable.

"Do you know what? I saw the viceroy. He was crossing the stone bridge. Lorenzo insisted that His Excellency saw him from above, and that his gaze was a clear invitation to join his brigade of officers."

Francisco said nothing of his fleeting sight of the Palace of the Inquisition, and he dared not mention the apparition of the inquisitor Gaitán. "Lorenzo was a good friend." He spoke of him again to differentiate him from his father, captain of the Lancers. "I think he'll have a great career. We'll hear of his exploits."

Then he recounted other adventures from the journey. He mentioned the people his father knew: Gaspar Chávez, José Ignacio Sevilla, and Diego López de Lisboa. At their names, Diego's chin trembled and he lowered his eyes. He said nothing. He said nothing about anything at all. He only listened with interest. He frequently twisted his fingers. For hours, in his damp shack, Francisco's monologue reverberated. It seemed best, seemed the tolerable thing. The son found himself talking about the Dominican monastery in Córdoba.

"I said goodbye to Brother Bartolomé," he said, "on whom I performed a bloodletting. Yes, a bloodletting—"

And he became absorbed in retelling the feat, because it was difficult to tell of other things, like the sad end of Isidro Miranda, shut up in his cell as a lunatic. He jumped around, describing his readings, his confirmation, and the appreciation he'd received from the formidable bishop Trejo y Sanabria. Then he couldn't resist, and spoke of his sisters in the shelter of a convent. "They were well," he said, repeating his mother's phrase.

Diego's eyelids began to rise more frequently. But his gaze conveyed sorrow. Intense, mysterious pain paralyzed his tongue. He could not tell. He could not ask. But he was grateful for this story, which came circuitously and in drops, like water from a bitter fountain. He wanted news of Aldonza, his eyes spoke of it. He wanted to know, because he'd already learned of her death in an abstract way, just as his family had learned of his torments and reconciliation. Francisco could not yet speak of his mother. Instead, he reconstructed the magical visit of Brother Francisco Solano.

"It was an apparition!" he exclaimed. "He was accompanied by his humpbacked assistant, he slept in a basket, and—he criticized the use of the term 'New Christian,' Papá!"

He strained to recall the brilliant argument the monk had made against that discriminatory term. Francisco declared that Solano was a saint, that he had worked miracles witnessed by thousands of people. And, in addition to the miracles, he had challenged the rabble by accompanying the family to church through a street teeming with curious onlookers. He told of the picturesque vicar in La Rioja who was accused of being Jewish.

"And the appreciation he had for your gesture, Papá, when you bought the dinnerware of the accused man, Antonio Trelles."

Again his father raised his eyes, trembling. But could not speak.

Finally, Francisco managed to tell him of the atrocities they had suffered after his arrest, and after Diego's. Then he dared to go to the core, to the painful depths. He told of the horrors. He wept, cursed, blasphemed, coughed. Until his convulsions began to calm. He dried his cheeks with his sleeve and asked the unspoken question.

"Papá, do you know anything about Diego?"

His father hung his head between his shoulders and placed a hand on his chest. This question had been stabbing at his heart. He covered his contorted face. And he began to weep, at first in isolated sobs, shamed sobs, then with moans, and finally with the roar of a flayed animal.

It was the first time Francisco had ever seen him like this, so broken, and he didn't know what to do with his words, his fingers, his legs. What could have happened to Diego? Had he died? Had he lost his reason? Had he been locked up again? The collapse of mountains could not have anguished him more than the sight of his father so shattered. Timidly, he placed his hand on his father's damp back. He was a sack filled with suffering. He calmed slightly, returning the caress.

"He left," Diego said in a coarse voice, between hiccups. "After finishing his penance in a monastery he asked for authorization to leave Peru . . . they . . . they granted it. He embarked for Panama. He avoided saying goodbye . . . who knows where he is now . . . who knows . . . what's become of his punished life? I don't know anything else . . . he never wrote . . . either that or I'm not given what he writes to me."

He leaned his fists on his knees and stood with great difficulty. He swayed toward the stove, where water was about to boil. Without looking at his son, out of shame, he asked Francisco to hand him dried meat, cabbage, and garlic.

As he cooked, he said that there were candles in the cupboard, a blanket in the chest, and some of that morning's bread in a basket by the bookshelf. Francisco did not realize, at that moment, that they had begun their dialogue. Elemental and exhausted, but a dialogue nonetheless.

64

Hypocrites! The inquisitor Gaitán devoted his sermon to condemning vanity and arrogance, staring at me. He cited Chapter 6 of Saint Matthew: "When you pray, do not be like the hypocrites, for they love to pray standing in the synagogues and on the street corners to be seen by others. Truly I tell you, they have received their reward." Who are the ones who like to show off in front of men and receive their honors, if not the inquisitors themselves?

Soon after my arrival, I had to put up with their pretensions. On the first Sunday of Lent, the Edict of Faith was to be read in the main church, as is the custom. The mayors, in a gesture of deference, went to the headquarters of the Holy Office to escort the inquisitors rather than meet them at their respective homes. What stupidity! Why did they try to innovate? The inquisitors were offended by the unexpected change in protocol, and when the entourage was arranged they did not allow the mayors to stand beside them; they ordered them to go in front like inferior officers who open the way and announce their superiors. The mayors were surprised by this harsh treatment, and, with respectful words, said they should keep the places due their station. The inquisitors answered hatefully, insulting and threatening them. The mayors were afraid, but they believed it was still possible to reach an agreement. The inquisitors revealed themselves to be even more offended, and called for them to be chained and imprisoned. In their alarm, the mayors abandoned the procession before they could be arrested, and ran to my palace. I gave them protection, of course, but, to be certain, the matter did not end there.

I wrote to the Holy Office, with flattery and courtesy in my introduction, if we're going to talk about hypocrites, telling them that, to my judgment, the mayors, in defending their jurisdiction and preeminence, had committed no act of contempt. On the other hand, I told them that they had in fact gone too far in calling for their arrest, as one of the mayors was a gentleman of Calatrava. As a solution, I proposed that the case be forgotten.

The inquisitor Verdugo, yes, as in "executioner"—a fitting surname for such a pious man—responded the next day, flashing with anger, but with a fine sense of irony, since we remain among hypocrites. He praised my efforts to strengthen the authority of the Holy Office, a task to which I was obliged as an individual, as the viceroy, and in fulfilling the will of His Majesty, reminding me in passing of my subordinate status. Verdugo deemed the fact that the mayors had not gone to meet them at their respective homes to be extremely serious, and scandalous. From his perspective, such an attitude revealed subversion against the authority of the Holy Office, the desire to obstruct their sacred work, and a poorly concealed hatred. Their behavior had had the aggravating effect of humiliating them publicly by abandoning the procession without permission. In consequence—so his letter concluded—I was to restrain myself and allow the Holy Office to jail them.

The inquisitor's insolence made my hair stand on end, and, without calculating the risk to my role or to my life, I responded without the customary, polite lies. I said that I could not consent to his meddling in my jurisdiction, because, here in Lima, the representative of His Majesty was none other than myself. I also told him, explicitly, that in this case it was difficult to separate what was essential from what was motivated by self-love. I expressed that it was possible to love and respect the Holy Office without accompanying the most illustrious inquisitors from the doors of their homes for such an ordinary act as the reading of an Edict of Faith. And that it seemed an exaggeration to call the mayors' behavior an act of *contempt, a public scandal, or an opposition or gesture of hatred toward the Holy Office. I proposed to bring the subject to His Majesty's attention.*

This time, the inquisitor was delayed in responding, and he evaluated every word. He wrote that the case of the mayors belonged to the Holy Office and that if I had permitted their arrest, everything would be resolved by now. That he would be glad to put the matter in my hands, except that he was impeded from doing so by duty.

I consulted with the Royal Court, naturally, and a few listeners opined that there was no reason to give in. That was when I received news of the charges those dogs were planning to bring against me, fabricating calumnies that would obliquely reach the Supreme of Seville. I decided to soften my stance, against my convictions and feelings, so that a foolish breach of protocol might not become my unstoppable ruin. I felt such disgust that I wrote to the king, making great effort to maintain norms. I said that those venerable fathers were very jealous of his jurisdiction; behind the criticisms of protocol lay embers of a zeal for halls of power. They were not only competing with me, but also with the church. I was relieved to learn, soon after this, that the Archbishop of Lima felt the same way. He wrote— the archbishop, not I!—that the inquisitors were trying to enjoy the same preeminence as the viceroy.

Lucky for me that the archbishop lives up to the name Lobo Guerrero! He is a wolf warrior, not a cowardly man. But, of course, one of the inquisitors is called Francisco Verdugo. What was God trying to do to me, placing me between a Lobo Guerrero and a Verdugo? It can't be a mere coincidence.

65

Francisco returned to the empty cell in the Dominican monastery of Lima. As before, Brother Manuel Montes accompanied him, entered first, and confirmed the absence of objects. He ignored the rats.

"You'll sleep here," he said coldly, as though it were the first time.

Later, the rats greeted him in a rushing torrent.

At dawn, Brother Martín passed by. The contours of the trees were just beginning to show. He did not greet Francisco, which seemed strange; something serious was happening. Francisco headed toward the hospital. He saw the pharmacy open and inhaled its piquant scent. Brother Martín came running back and collided with Brother Manuel, who was advancing with stiff steps. Martín fell to his knees and kissed his hand. The monk pulled it back brusquely. Martín kissed his feet and the monk reared back.

"Don't touch me!"

"I'm a mulatto sinner," Martín said, on the brink of tears.

"What have you done?"

"Prior Lucas is angry because I brought an Indian to the hospital."

Brother Manuel remained silent, his gaze lost in the distance. Then he leaned away so that the man's imploring fingers would not reach him, and scurried off to the chapel. Francisco approached Martín, who lay facedown.

"May I help you?"

"Thank you, my son."

He offered his hand.

"Thank you. I'm an unrepentant sinner," he scolded. "A foul sinner."

"What happened?"

"I disobeyed, that's what happened."

"The prior?"

"Yes. To save an Indian."

"I don't understand."

"An Indian covered in open wounds fainted at our door last night. I ran to him. He was alive, but exhausted. He only moaned. I went to ask permission of the prior, who was also ill. He denied it, and reminded me that this hospital is not for Indians." Martín lifted a fold of his tunic and dried his face. "I couldn't sleep, and it seemed to me that the Lord, through my dreams, was ordering me to help this poor soul. I went to the door. It was the middle of the night, and there he was, lying on the ground, covered with insects. The shadows confused me. I saw Our Lord Jesus Christ after the crucifixion." He suppressed a sob. "I carried him on my shoulder. He was so light . . . I took him to my cell, attended to him. I sinned miserably."

"What will you do now?"

"I don't know."

"You are in sin."

"Yes. I went to tell the prior, as is my duty. I just went to tell him. He became very angry. And he is very ill. The anger will damage his health. Brother Manuel does not forgive me, either."

66

The prior's illness had become a problem for the entire order. Although he took both food and drink—the servants devoted themselves to preparing nutritious stews and bringing him fresh dawn water—he grew worse with each passing day. His rapid decline was accompanied by an accelerated loss of vision.

Francisco felt uncomfortable. Specters seemed to move through the halls. Everyone was in a bad mood, and in the refectory, mealtimes were tense. Additional religious services were held and each person was to feel guilty for the illness. Francisco, too. To drive the point home, Brother Manuel told Francisco that he should perform acts of contrition and liberate himself from the ugliness that lived in his abject blood and that had surely begun to grow since he'd reunited with his father in Callao. Francisco twisted his fingers and prayed a great deal.

The monks flogged themselves to eliminate the sins that were spreading the illness through the prior's ravaged body. Nocturnal processions took place around the cloister, in tremulous candlelight. They flogged themselves in groups. The dark whips whirred over their heads and struck their shoulders and backs until they bled. Prayers rose in volume until they moved the very heavens. Some fell to the brick floor and licked up the drops of blood, symbols of what Christ had shed, until their tongues became additional sources of purifying hemorrhage.

Francisco attended one of the solemn visits of Doctor Alfonso Cuevas, physician to the viceroy and vicereine. It was his first contact with a high-ranking medical official. After the failure of treatments prescribed by several physicians, surgeons, herbalists, spice sellers, and bonesetters, the Dominican Order had decided to solicit Doctor Cuevas, with the permission of His Excellency. Viceroy Montesclaros had agreed, of course, and the physician began to attend to Prior Lucas. He would announce the hour of his arrival beforehand to give them time to prepare good lighting and a urine sample in a glass container. The monks would become excited, quibbling over which candlesticks, which containers, who would meet the doctor at the front door, who in the courtyard, who at Prior Lucas's sickbed, and who could hear the doctor's words after the fact.

When Doctor Cuevas arrived in his carriage, one servant would open the door and another would help him descend. He wore black knee-length trousers and shoes with thick bronze buckles. On his velvet vest there shone a silver chain ornamented with gold. He removed his cape and hat, which a monk would take from him with a bow. He would cross the cloister like an angel of victory. Francisco would run behind the monks, and, through the shoulders and heads, caught snippets of his intoxicating tasks.

After examining the patient's appearance and smell, the doctor studied the urine and began to formulate his impressions. This time— he conveyed with a clouded brow—he recognized that Prior Lucas's state was decidedly grave.

Alarm spread through the priests. Martín bit his lips and pressed Francisco's arm.

According to Galen's *Articella*, Avicenna's *Canon*, and the opinions of Pablo de Egina, the physician added, Prior Lucas's various symptoms called for more prayers than bloodlettings; this was an indirect allusion to a poor prognosis. He said that five disorders had accumulated, all of them beginning with the letter *P*; he had a "Penta-P." The doctor listed and translated them for his audience: *prurito*, itching; *polyuria pálida*, frequent and discolored urine; *polidipsia*, thirst; *pérdida de peso*, weight loss; and *polifagia*, outsize hunger. In addition, the pulse in his heel had disappeared. The doctor paused again, then cited Hippocrates, Albertus Magnus, and Duns Scotus, concluding that heat should be provided to his leg. If the pulse did not return soon, heroic measures would have to be taken. Then he explained, again quoting the classics, that heroic measures often resulted in a complete cure. He did not yet say what the heroic measure would be. He took out a fragrant handkerchief, elegantly wiped his mouth and nose, and made dietary recommendations: herbal infusions, vegetables, and chicken broth.

One of the monks reunited the doctor with his hat and cape, and he walked through the swarm of onlookers, more poised than when he'd arrived. He resembled a Roman general after a victory. The monks smiled happily and repeated their thanks to the Lord. They asked no questions, as that would convey insolence. Instead, they chanted the hopeful phrase, "He will heal, he will heal." With a doctor like this one, the devil must be twisting like a cockroach in a campfire.

Francisco also felt relieved. Cuevas was skilled at calming a patient's surroundings, even when the patient's actual health showed no signs of change. Soon after this, Cuevas would order the heroic measures to be taken, and Francisco would have access to the ferocity of a surgical act in the City of Kings, in the shadow of the University of San Marcos, in this same monastery of Lima.

67

I will not forget the arm-wrestling match I had with the inquisitors Verdugo and Gaitán regarding the last Act of Faith.

The resources of the tribunal and its prisoners were scarce, and insufficient to unfurl the pomp they so enjoy. Among the prisoners were wretched people of varying backgrounds and some of few assets. I recall a Portuguese doctor who had been arrested in faraway Córdoba, who used crutches and who, at my request, was sent after his reconciliation to work in the hospital of Callao to help alleviate our chronic lack of physicians.

The inquisitors had decided to carry out the Act of Faith in the cathedral. I knew that, in this manner, they were trying to gain something else, this time at the expense of Bishop Lobo Guerrero. I decided not to give them the pleasure. They, with their hypocritical mindset, wanted to twist my will. Those vile men suggested that if I felt uncomfortable in the cathedral I didn't have to bother coming, me, the viceroy. My red-hot stare ended our interview. Then they called on my confessor and urged him to persuade me. They're too much!

The Acts of Faith involve a combination of fear and entertainment. The people are summoned through proclamations and special invitations. But before it begins, civil authorities and ecclesiastics are supposed to go in search of the inquisitors—here begins the public genuflection they so adore—to then walk in a procession to the main plaza. The viceroy is supposed to walk with them, because it suggests that their power is equal to mine. In front, the standard of the faith is carried by the prosecutor of the Holy Office. These are followed by the Royal Court, the town council, and the university. Once we arrive in the plaza, we all go onstage, and there, too, a rigorous protocol is observed. The viceroy and the inquisitors sit together in the highest seats, under a canopy, once again as if equals. To our sides, and in front of us, the other authorities are arranged, in the same order they had in the procession. In the lower areas, the clergymen of the various orders sit, that is to say, far below the inquisitors and other officers of the Holy Office. Finally, in front of the official stage, the penitents are placed, as they are the morsels. The surrounding area is ringed with bleachers for the rest of the multitudinous crowd.

When this ceremony was first explained to me, and I attended one in Spain, I could not have imagined the number of conflicts of preference and etiquette plaguing each official, like welts; they were desperate to gain an inch of power. This occurs in Madrid, Mexico, Lima, and any other part of the world that celebrates Acts of Faith. Some pretentions are ridiculously over the top.

All of my predecessors suffered from the impudence of inquisitors, who have always complained that viceroys want to undermine their authority. What are the stupid issues being contested? Whether the inquisitors should be to the viceroy's left or right . . . whether their pillows should be different or the same . . . and other similar nonsense, because these things are, at their hidden root, symbols of power.

Well, since I opposed the idea of carrying out the Act of Faith in the cathedral, where it would be less expensive, those good-for-nothings asked me for monetary support. I told them that I was poorer than they were. Then, in their fury, they threatened to suspend the Act. That's fine, I said, suspend it. As if they would!

Finally, they agreed to put on a more modest Act of Faith. There were proclamations and invitations. The people poured into the streets. The prisoners were duly prepared with their shameful sanbenitos and green candles. But their officials went back and forth between my palace and the one belonging to the Inquisition, because those scoundrels feared another of my dirty tricks. They were obviously being crushed by the insolence. Finally, at midday, the procession began to make its way toward the tribunal. Before that, the prisoners had already been paraded before the palace doors so that my wife could see them through the lattice of her window. The ceremony would be carried out according to my wishes, no matter that Gaitán and Verdugo would grind their teeth. They had even accepted that only I, the viceroy, should enjoy pillows beneath my boots.

But they were false, and did not give in. My spies read the letter they wrote to His Majesty in Spain. In it, they said that they could no longer delay the Act of Faith, as some of its subjects were in poor health and could die before the celebration was carried out, which would rob the process of its exemplary powers. They wrote that I was angry and tenacious. How I would have liked to thank them for the compliment! They wrote that our confrontation was threatening to devolve into a disturbance and a scandal. They said that things were going poorly in the Viceroyalty, and that it was my fault, that remedies were urgently needed because my reach here was powerful, and the Supreme of Seville, though more powerful than me, was far away.

68

Brother Manuel announced that Francisco had been accepted to the University of San Marcos. His monotonous voice relayed no further details. It was the same voice that, in the confessional, with sporadic stabs, pulled the marrow out from sins and succeeded in making him express a desperate loyalty to the true faith. The priest added that, during Francisco's studies, he would alternate between Lima and Callao; pursuing his coursework in Lima, and training in Callao's hospital, with his father. Moved at the generosity hidden behind the monk's cadaverous appearance, Francisco imitated Martín—he fell to his knees and took Brother Manuel's hand to kiss it. His skin was cold and white, like that of a reptile. Brother Manuel pulled back in fright.

"Don't touch me!"

"I want to express my happiness."

"Then pray."

Brother Manuel wiped his nervous hand against his habit, as if to rub off the touch.

Francisco began at the university with great excitement. A dazzling world was opening. There was a library with all the books he'd read in Ibatín and Córdoba, and many he didn't know existed. Respected scholars walked the halls—experts in natural science, philosophy, algebra, drawing, history, theology, grammar. The spirits of Aristotle,

Guy de Chauliac, Thomas Aquinas, and Avenzoar floated around them. And there was a reverent nostalgia of the old universities of Bologna, Padua, and Montpellier. Scattered references connected these houses of study with the famous medical schools of Salerno, Salamanca, Córdoba, Valladolid, Alcalá de Henares, and Toledo. From the podium, for an hour and a half at a time, texts were read that the professors expounded on elegantly. Some names sounded familiar, and Francisco was elated: Pliny, Dioscorides, Galen, Avicenna, Maimonides, Albucasis, Herophilus.

He learned that Albucasis, Spain's greatest surgeon, was also Cordoban and gathered his experiences in an encyclopedia of thirty volumes that was translated from Arabic to Greek, and from Greek to Latin. He got goose bumps at being reunited with Pliny, of whose work he had only known the fantastic stories. There was so much more than that; Pliny was a fount of wisdom and his ideas had leapt over barriers; the illustrious fathers and saints of the church were intermixed with the bold ideas of Moors, Jews, and Pagans.

It wasn't only students who attended classes, but also doctors, lawyers, graduates, clerics, and noblemen. The reading of great texts was a solemn event. In silence, the students listened to sentences that dripped with the gold of truth.

69

"It's odious to admit it," huffed the irascible inquisitor Gaitán, "but to deny it would be a lie." The bishops of the Viceroyalty have no liking for the Holy Office. Since the beginning, our relations have been strained. And not through any fault of the Holy Office, which came to these savage lands to bring order to debauched customs and to defend the faith.

The Lord, who reads the depths of people's souls, knows that I was justified in my indignation with the first archbishop of Lima, Jerónimo de Loaysa, as he did not lovingly embrace us. He published an edict declaring inquisitors to be ordinary, without power. He wanted to take the war for faith back to primitive times in which the High Tribunal of the Holy Office had not yet been created and it was they, the prelates, who prosecuted heresies. With this gesture, he demonstrated that he was competing with us and wanted to push us to the margins.

I was also justified in refusing to forgive another bishop, this one in Cuzco, Sebastián de Lartaún, who publicly proclaimed the affairs of the Holy Office were under his charge—I would have liked to take a torch to his tongue. He was such a troublemaker that he called for the arrest of one of our commissioners, going so far as to lock him up in a dungeon. Can there be anything more damaging? The Holy Office needs efficient collaborators to fulfill its sacred mission. The commissioners, scattered throughout the territory, must work mercilessly to catch those demons' excrements known as heretics. But because they are clergymen, bishops claim that obedience is also owed to them, not only to the Holy Office.

As if this were not enough calamity, we must suffer hidden antipathy from the religious orders. We often assign them tasks. And what do their superiors say? That we did not consult with them, and, therefore, sowed confusion. But how can we consult them when our missions must be secret to remain efficient?

The affronts are endless. That is why we often proceed with violence. It's the only language they understand. The Holy Office is Our Lord Jesus Christ's best weapon, and we will not allow it to be ignored, marginalized, or destroyed.

70

"Is my father a sincere Christian again?" Francisco wondered. "Has he permanently abandoned his Jewish practice? Does he accept the wearing of the sanbenito as a deserved punishment?" In his prayers, he asked that it might be so. His father had suffered too much and deserved peace of mind.

Diego fasted before Mass in order to receive communion in the best possible state. At church, he knelt, made the sign of the cross, and remained alone. His sanbenito contributed to his isolation; the faithful stayed away from him, as if he reeked. It was a wickedness born from his past offenses. Perhaps, in the heights, his pain was received with sweet smiles, but on Earth the disdain of his neighbors only grew. The Roman soldiers had laughed loudly when Jesus Christ fell under the weight of His cross, and the parishioners of Callao would have laughed in the middle of the offertory if a rafter fell on Diego's neck.

He also attended processions. He was forbidden to carry effigies and did not go near the sacred images. He stayed at the edge of the multitude, always alone, lips moving. The familiars of the Holy Office, who spied on him from hidden corners, could not have found any reason to criticize his behavior.

On any given day he spent almost all of his time at the hospital. He never tired of examining patients, adjusting their medications, changing bandages, consoling the desperate, and writing down clinical observations. The sick were the only people who received him warmly. The sanbenito did not turn them against him; it was a doctor's robe. His presence gave them hope. He often sat beside a gravely ill patient to accompany his prayers.

Later, Francisco would recognize that he owed a great deal of his medical training to his father. He accompanied him, assisting in his constant rounds. Diego liked to repeat a maxim of Hippocrates that nobody obeyed: use your own eyes. And he gave a humorous example. Aristotle maintained that women had fewer teeth than men. The Bible, for its part, tells that Adam lost a rib when the Lord created Eve. By this logic, women had fewer teeth, according to Aristotle, and men had fewer ribs, according to the Bible. From this pseudo-dogma, elegant speeches had arisen on the sublime compensation of teeth by ribs— and yet, no one thought to count the ribs and teeth of healthy men and women. If they had done so they would know that Adam's defect was not hereditary, and that the mouth Aristotle examined had not belonged to an intact woman.

On the same theme, Diego told his son that sorcerers never think a wound can heal on its own. They assume that treatments must intervene and, when things go poorly, the enemy responsible for it must be found—a spirit, or another sorcerer. Those who correctly read Hippocrates and observe attentively, on the other hand, learn that for many wounds to heal in the swiftest way possible they only need to be left in peace.

Much later, Diego spoke to Francisco of the Hippocratic oath. It is the oldest oath, he said, the one that gives dignity to the profession. But it is not the most correct one. There was another one, preferred by Diego, that he recited intermittently. He assured his son that it moved him, stirred his awakening, and helped him tackle his daily tasks with strength and lucidity. He was silent for a long time. He needed to prepare his son. Francisco wondered what vow he meant. Finally, Diego raised his deep, wide eyes and solemnly said, "Maimonides."

If he was trying to make Francisco shudder, it worked. Although they were talking about medicine, he had elliptically invoked the name of a Jew.

That night, Francisco searched through a manuscript in Latin. It was the famous oath, which began, "The eternal providence has appointed me to watch over the life and health of Thy creatures." In place of the name Maimonides, which could cause problems, it said *Doctor Fidelis, Gloria Orientalis et Lux Occidentalis.*

As Francisco read, his father stared at him without breaking his gaze.

71

Diego and Francisco walked on the shore, far from Callao and its busy port. They both wanted to shake off the constant surveillance that hounded them day and night. At the hospital, they could not speak because a barber, pharmacist, monk, or servant might misinterpret them and the machine leading to a familiar of the Holy Office would be set in motion. Denunciation was a virtue, and Diego was an Inquisition prisoner, a lifelong suspect. The tribunal would appreciate anyone who came to report his having said this or that. His home was not secure, either; in the homes of prisoners of the Inquisition there lurked the invisible ears of power.

Francisco knew the southern beach; he had come here before being reunited with his father; he'd wanted to pay his respects to the ocean and suffuse himself with the infinite before testing his strength.

The waves unfolded like rugs. Their boundary was a wavy, unstable line. Another alphabet of God? Perhaps that moving line was the marvelous story of life in the watery depths. Might the vast blue slate of the sea's surface be the sky for another humanity, one that breathed water and received sunken ships like softly falling meteorites?

Diego walked with great effort. His feet were permanently damaged.

They arrived at the cliffs—a wall of cinnamon rocks carved by the tides over millennia. He removed his sanbenito and rolled it into a thin cylinder. He seemed taller without that humiliating garment. The port had become a distant crest that sometimes disappeared behind the crags. They were truly alone, and free. They heard only the roll of waves and the cries of seagulls. The eternally cloudy sky was a thick sheet of zinc. The wind opened Diego's shirt and he enjoyed its gentle caress around his neck. With this distance between them and the city, Diego was able to speak openly of his fear of physical pain. Nobody was listening except God, Francisco, and nature.

"Ever since I was a boy, I've been terrified of pain, did you know? I grew up hiding in basements and on roofs when the Jewish quarter of Lisbon was being attacked. I suffered beatings at the university, attended an Act of Faith, wrapped my head in blankets so as not to hear the clamor of those being burned alive."

They slowed their walk, as the memories were agitating his breath. He opened his mouth wide and, then, barely smiling at Francisco, forced himself to finish his story.

"I could barely comfort my friend López de Lisboa when his parents were executed. What solace was there? I had studied medicine to kill pain in others, with the secret hope that I would thereby eliminate my own, which was so intense."

He suddenly recalled the instant when the inquisitors had ordered for him to be sent to the torture chamber. It was his first direct reference to it. Francisco became tense, but Diego, as if he had succeeded in breaking the wall that had kept him from speaking, continued.

"Until that moment, life in prison had been relatively calm. But when I heard about the torture I imagined beatings, burns, cramps, and stitches. I broke into a sweat and my vision clouded over. I felt helpless and defenseless. The inquisitors demanded names, denunciations. It wasn't enough to repent, to be a good Christian again and carry forever the stigma of sin. I had to bring, as an unavoidable offering, the names of other Jews. The Inquisition does not fulfill its sacred mission by limiting itself to reforming the lost. It has to take advantage of each lost soul to trap many more. That's how it purifies the faith."

The majestic landscape stood in contrast to the gloomy tale. It was too beautiful a frame for such an oppressive painting. Nonetheless, he recounted an atrocious night.

"I tossed and turned in the cell, like a child. I moaned and trembled. Never had I descended to such indignity. I was waiting for them to come for me. Every sound made me jump. I broke these fingernails scratching the walls. I shivered from the cold. It was awful! In the morning, the bolts slid back, a sound I'd been waiting for in every passing minute. The henchmen felt my clothing, as if they'd seen when I urinated and vomited on myself. They brought me new clothes. I didn't have the strength to ask them anything. I allowed them to drag me through the sinister halls all the way to a vast room, bright with torches. The light gleamed on strange contraptions. Beside each one stood a table and a chair. There were desks, where a notary of the Inquisition would write down every word that was spoken. The cruel act was sheathed in meticulous legality and adherence to a specific protocol. Everything organized to perfection. The officials were proceeding in accordance with rules."

Francisco grasped his father's forearm to transmit his sorrow and, at the same time, encourage him to keep speaking; he had to rid himself of the shame that blocked him. Diego returned his energetic caress.

"Light shimmered in the tormentors' sweat," he recalled, head down, "while the bodies of sinners twisted like lizards. But there was a diabolical order that assigned one notary, one torturer, and a few assistants to each captive. I heard screams among the shadows. And among the screams and panic, an imperious voice rose, demanding that the victims speak, that they speak, speak, speak. Otherwise, the intensity would increase. The word 'intensity' was spoken coldly. But it referred to the intensity of the ferocious pulling of bones from their sockets, the blows, the water torture, the ropes and spikes.

"My eyes were blurred by terror and I could only catch fragments, just barely," he said. "They weren't applying any of it to me yet, though they were letting me see and hear, to break me in. Some men calmly destroying others."

He stopped to inhale a few gulps of air. Francisco stared at him like a startling marvel; the same face that in Ibatín had told edifying stories, now, here, unfurled a description of hell.

"Suddenly, I perceived a sign. My blood ran cold. I fell to my knees and prayed. They eagerly took off my clothes. My nakedness and shame increased my paralysis. They lay me on a table. Someone took my pulse, touched my wet forehead. It was the doctor. The Inquisition uses doctors to monitor torture. I looked at him, trying to transmit a plea to my colleague, to the student of medicine who had read Hippocrates and taken on the mandate *Primum non nocere*. But this doctor fulfilled the task that had been assigned to him, and was unmoved by my chattering teeth. Indifferently, he said, 'You may begin.'"

Diego coughed.

"They put me in the rack, tying my wrists and ankles to ropes connected to a turning wheel. The notary, a Dominican monk, dipped his quill in the inkwell and waited for the names I was to provide. The torturer grasped the turning wheel and began to tighten the rope. I felt the murderous pull. I howled; they were pulling out my arms and tearing at my hips. The traction slowed, but did not stop. My chest was blazing. They wanted names. But I could not speak. Another turn of the wheel and I fainted.

"In my cell, I was attended to by a barber, who placed damp cloths on the torn joints and performed a bloodletting. Vast bruises formed. The Inquisition was patient and waited for me to recover before resuming with other torments.

"I thought they would subject me to the pulley, because it's worse than the rack. They tie your arms behind your back and hook your wrists to the pulley, and then hoist the whole body from the tied wrists.

Men break, and their tendons snap quickly, one after another. If the body holds up, they weight your ankles. And if the captive still persists, they let him fall with a thud. I doubted I could survive that trial. But the torturer had a different torment in store for me."

Francisco asked whether he wanted to stop.

"No, I'll go on," Diego said, pausing for a moment to look at the sea and gather his thoughts. "They returned me to that loathsome table, tied my limbs and neck with rough cords, and put a funnel and rags in my mouth, which made me retch. I retched more, couldn't breathe. But that was just the beginning. The notary dipped his quill and waited. It was exceptional for a person not to confess under such circumstances. This method was affectionately known as 'singing out of longing.' The torturer began to pour a barrel of water into the funnel. I swallowed, drowned, coughed, swallowed again, felt that death was finally at hand. The doctor ordered a pause in the proceedings. He took the large cloth from my mouth, turned me around, and brutally slapped my back. The ensuing pulmonary congestion lasted for weeks. I tried to find a poison with which to kill myself—"

Again, Francisco touched his father.

"The day of opprobrium arrived, my son." He lifted his head toward the bed of clouds as if asking God to listen to him, too. "I shivered all night. There was no mercy. I was a sheep in the slaughterhouse. At dawn the henchmen slid the bolts back and offered me a clean robe. Again, I'd urinated and vomited on myself. What awaited me now? Clamps? Blows? Ropes? The spiked belt? More of the rack, the pulley, water torture? They lay me down on another table. They tied my limbs in the shape of a cross: arms open, legs together. 'This is how they killed Jesus Christ,' I thought, 'only He was placed vertically while I am lying down.' My legs were raised into the air, though I didn't yet know why. The Dominican dipped his quill and reiterated that he was waiting for names. My head spun with the people whom I could not turn in. I wanted to frighten them so they wouldn't ring the bell that unhooked my tongue. To mention a name was to condemn that person forever. I thought of animals. I said to myself: 'puma, snake, bird, blackbird, chicken, vicuna, lamb,' so as not to leave any space for the name of a future victim. But I became terrified. There was a man in Potosí by the name of Cordero, or 'lamb,' who might not even be a New Christian. I might commit a crime. So I began, in my exasperation, to call the names of the great ones who were long deceased: 'Celsus, Pythagoras, Herophilus, Ptolemy, Virgil, Demosthenes, Philo, Marcus Aurelius, Zeno, Vesalius, Euclid, Horace.' As that torrent flowed, the Dominican leaned in to catch the valuable denunciation. They greased my feet with pig fat. Then, below them, almost touching my heels, they placed an overflowing brazier. The heat seared into my skin, sharpened by the grease. I tried to pull my legs back, but I couldn't. This was the torment that would make me speak: a slow burning, penetrating, unbearable.

"'Names,' the inquisitor demanded.

"'Homer, Suetonius, Lucanor, Euripides,' I answered in despair. The torturer fanned the embers. The grease burned my feet and dripped noisily.

"'Names.'

"'David, Matthew, Solomon, Luke, John, Marcus, Saint Augustine, Saint Paul,' and my unsettled mind filled with the animals I preferred to avoid: 'ant, rat, frog, firefly, partridge, armadillo.'

"'Names—'

"The pain pierced my bones. The searing was worse than the rack, pulley, clamps, or water. 'You have walked the path of sin,' a monk said. 'If you do not speak, you won't ever be able to walk in virtue.' I fainted, and they gave me a few weeks to recover. The Inquisition has time; it is the esteemed child of the church and shares its immortality. But the healing was not satisfactory. The fire had produced irreversible lesions. You can see it; I walk like a duck." He pointed at his boots. "As they applied salves, they kept on pressing me for names, day and night. I hoped that my wounds would become infected and put an end to the nightmare. I didn't expect the cunning blow that would change the course of events."

Diego unrolled his sanbenito and spread it like a rug over the sand. He sat down with his legs pulled in, and Francisco followed suit. After a pause, he broached the most painful part of his memories.

"I was visited by a defense attorney who worked for the Holy Office and whose job it was to convince prisoners that there was only one way to become free: submission. Until that moment I'd been able to keep my lips from betraying me. Despite the terror and helplessness, I hadn't mentioned the names that passed through my restless sleep: Gaspar Chávez, José Ignacio Sevilla, Diego López de Lisboa, Juan José Brizuela. The lawyer told me that Brizuela had been arrested in Chile, and that he had behaved more virtuously—he revealed names. And one of those names belonged to Diego, your brother. I can assure you, Francisco, that I've never felt a more horrific blow. I was stunned."

His brow furrowed and his bent back shook. Francisco stood, took off his cloak, and draped it over his father's wide shoulders. How he loved him! How it hurt him to learn of this suffering! His father thanked him with a few light pats on his hand, then rubbed his damp eyes.

"In the next session, I was newly accosted by the fire torture," he continued in a low voice, almost inaudibly. "The grease on my feet made me convulse. I thought I was going mad. This time, the inquisitor was precise.

"'Your son Diego has practiced Judaism, we know this. Testify to it,' he whispered in my ear.

"'The poor boy is retarded!' I lied. 'He's an innocent.'

"'Has he practiced as a Jew?'

"'He doesn't even know how to, he's an idiot,' I said, lying again, as in that instant I couldn't think of any other way to respond.

"'Has he practiced as a Jew? Testify to this with a yes.' His mouth was burning my ear.

"'He knows nothing,' I sobbed.

"'Has he practiced Judaism?'

"'It's as if he hadn't, because—he's an idiot!' I shouted. 'He's innocent! He's a fool!'

"'Then he has practiced Judaism. Take the brazier away.'

"The notary's quill scratched the sentences of confirmation onto paper. The inquisitor knew that one crack was enough for the torrent to pour out. I had testified against my own son. I would try to save him, of course, but my clumsy speech included facts that transformed suspicion into certainty.

"I could not have felt more destroyed. The brusque suspension of the torture did not induce relief, but rather terror. It was proof that they had gotten what they'd wanted, and that I had condemned poor Diego. That's when I lost my last moorings and became a piece of trash floating in the abyss. There was nothing more to do, or to defend, or rescue. Nothing. The Holy Office, on the other hand, seized their infinite advantage; the trash that I was would gain the mercy of something real and powerful if I surrendered. I had to obliterate all resistance and discretion; I'd have to confess down to the dregs."

"Did you?" Francisco ventured.

Diego was stiff for a few seconds and then nodded, full of shame.

"I did it." He inhaled deeply. "I was a corpse. My soul had come untethered, driven past madness, and who knew where it roamed. I confessed that I had taught Diego Judaism. I confessed the truth—that he had hurt his ankle and I took advantage of the intimacy of those moments to explain who we were. I told them that Diego was surprised, and afraid, as it was not easy to accept that one is descended from Jews.

"'What else?' they asked me.

"'I promised to teach him our history, our traditions and celebrations. I did this in Ibatín, and kept on doing so in Córdoba.'

"'What else?'"

Don Diego leaned forward and, with his hand, erased the drawings he'd made in the sand as he recounted his journey through hell.

"What I can't erase now"—his tone changed, and he shook his pale head—"is that distant moment when, in that dim room in Ibatín, I explained to Diego for the first time that we had Jewish blood. What a face he made! I think he may have been assaulted by a premonition of the coming tragedy. It was so many years ago—we were alone in his room—"

Francisco's gaze roved over the folds of that wrinkled face, full of pity.

"No, Papá. You were not alone."

His father startled. "What are you saying?"

"I was a witness."

"But," he stammered, "you were so little!"

"And so curious. I spied on you from the shadows."

"Francisquito!" His throat tightened as he remembered the small boy his son had been. "You used to bring me the bronze tray with figs and pomegranates. You'd beg me for tales and stories—" He removed the cloak Francisco had draped over his shoulders and returned it. "Here—you're not warm enough."

"You keep it on—please, Papá."

They recalled the afternoon on which Diego had opened the velvet case and explained the wondrous significance of the Spanish key. They recalled the classes in the orange grove. The journey to Córdoba, and when the trunk of books was stolen in the middle of the salt flats. They recalled the brief period in which they'd lived together in Córdoba, in the house left to them by Juan José Brizuela and his family. And then, together, they recalled the brutal arrests.

"I was too hopeful, Francisco. Despair makes us lie to ourselves," his father lamented. "In the dungeon, after confessing, that is to say after surrendering into the 'merciful' arms of the Holy Office, I thought that poor Diego and I might regain our freedom. I behaved the way my so-called defense attorney told me to. I begged for mercy with abundant tears, just as the inquisitors like it. I expressed my repentance in every possible way. I abjured my filthy sin, over and over. I insisted that I wanted to live and die in the Catholic faith, for good. I begged to be granted reconciliation. And, every once in a while, I begged for my son, whom I had led down the wrong path, taking advantage of his young age. I wanted to live to reform him, to teach him to behave like a good Catholic and be worthy of divine grace. I said and did all these things, Francisco. Never had I been so broken."

He began to draw in the sand again.

"Finally, they informed me that my son had also abjured. But both of us had to wait for the Act of Faith to regain our freedom. Maintaining us in jail was not a problem for them, as it was paid for with the possessions they had confiscated from us. I walked with crutches. They would not let me see Diego. Despite my docility, they often hurt my wrists and ankles again with iron shackles, to remind me that I was still a prisoner and that my offense had been very serious."

Francisco rose, walked to the edge of the water, and rolled up his trousers. He waded in to his knees. He splashed his face, then stood absorbed in the straightness of the horizon. Cold saline drops slid down his skin. He had not only heard his father, which he had so deeply longed for, he had suffered through it as if he had been torn by instruments of torture. He returned slowly to the aged doctor's side, adjusted his cloak on his shoulders, and sat back down.

"What was the Act of Faith like, Papá?"

Diego threw a piece of seashell toward the foam and gathered his concentration. He had yet to dislodge that bone from his throat.

"The day before the Act of Faith they come and read your sentence to you. I was visited in my dungeon by the inquisitor and an entourage of officers and clerics. The inquisitor was carrying large documents. The lawyer elbowed me to remind me to fall to my knees and thank the mercy of the just tribunal. The remaining hours before the Act were to be devoted to prayer, for which I was accompanied by a pious and vigilant Dominican. It resembled a wake. Before dawn the sounds of iron, shouts, steps, and swords echoed down the hall. They put me in this sanbenito." He stroked it. "Look, such an ordinary garment that draws so much contempt! Nothing more than a wool scapular, as wide as the body, that reaches to the knees, its length no different from what monks wear. Its yellow color is supposed to invoke something ugly and dirty, as it evokes the Jewish condition. Luckily, it isn't painted with flames, meaning that I had not been condemned to be burned. When the prisoners were gathered to be taken to the Act of Faith I saw your brother in a sanbenito just like mine. Can you imagine my inner tumult? I stared at him, longing to embrace him, kiss him, and ask his forgiveness. I had to beg his forgiveness! But Diego did not want my forgiveness. He looked away from me. Imprisonment and torture had distanced him from me forever. They put a green candle in his hand and did the same to me. They ordered us to advance along the macabre corridors. The Dominican monk walked right at my shoulder, praying insistently. I did not stop staring at Diego, who avoided me with rage, fear, and shame."

He broke off. The embers of memory were drying out his lungs, and he needed to inhale great gulps of air.

"We walked out through the tall doors of the Holy Office, toward the plaza of the Inquisition. We were received in the street with brutal celebration. We were monsters, adding color to people's routines. Around us marched gentlemen and religious orders, with great showiness. The armed militia of the viceroy was there. The gunmen shot into the air, the club-bearing soldiers of the crown were before the Royal Court, and pages walked among the high officials. They made us walk in front of the palace, like exotic animals, so that the vicereine might enjoy the sight of us from behind her latticed windows. I don't know why the Act took a long time. Some of the condemned fainted. It seemed that there had been a problem with regard to protocol. Finally, we were taken to the scaffold. We were pitiable creatures, atrociously comical. On our heads we wore painted cardboard cones, and in our hands we carried green candles. Standing, under the contemptuous stares of the crowd, we had to listen to long sermons. And after the sermons, the detailed sentences. Each prisoner was addressed separately. Some were relieved to the secular branch, where they would be given death by hanging and then fire, or death directly by fire. The rest of us were all publicly punished, some with whips, others with a range of sentences; we had saved our lives through repentance. I was sentenced to the confiscation of my possessions, the wearing of a sanbenito, spiritual punishments, and six years of prison. Your brother's sentence was lesser: the confiscation of possessions, the sanbenito for one year, spiritual acts of penitence, and six months of absolute isolation in a monastery for reeducation. Then they told me that, at the request of Viceroy Montesclaros and the kindness of the most illustrious inquisitors, I should remain in Callao and work in the hospital. In this manner, my dearest Francisco"—he made an ironic face—"I recovered my freedom and they made me return to the religion of love."

72

At the monastery in Lima, the sepulchral atmosphere grew. Prior Lucas Albarracín's maladies had changed all routines and activities. Doctor Alfonso Cuevas, after another florid preamble, had spoken the terrible word "gangrene." The moment was approaching for those heroic measures that he had referenced in earlier visits. The monks increased the honors, litanies, masses, and flagellations so that heaven might restore their leader's health.

Brother Martín looked haggard and thinner than before. He took personal responsibility for the prior's suffering. He visited his room frequently, changing water that had just been changed, and refreshing herbs that had only just begun to boil in their aromatic pots. He came and went in hopes that his exhaustion might be looked on kindly by the Lord, that he might then concede the awaited miracle. He fasted. He then attended to each patient and locked himself into his cell to flog himself with the intensity of a torture device. He placed rough cloth over his wounds and ran back to Prior Lucas's bedside.

Doctor Cuevas asked for the order to call a meeting, as an urgent decision had to be made. The leg had to be amputated before the gangrene spread to the thigh and ended the man's life. The monks sobbed and beat their chests with heartfelt mea culpas. The doctor brought another colleague, who examined the patient and agreed that the surgical procedure was absolutely urgent. He promised to arrange for skilled surgeons to come and perform the amputation.

Brother Martín offered his services throughout and was on the alert for the slightest request to send him off like a lightning bolt. The superior's cell—where the treatment would be performed—was supplied with washbasins, wide braziers, bandages, salves, oil, mallow leaves, ground garlic, and pitchers full of liquor. Francisco helped Martín, eager to be present for the procedure.

On a small table covered in white cloth they arranged the instruments: scalpel, saw, chisel, hammer, tongs, and needles. To one side, they placed half a dozen cauterizers, which were long steel spatulas with wooden handles.

Doctor Cuevas excused himself from attending the operation because as a doctor he did not wish to interfere with the skilled surgeon, who ordered that, from the evening before, the patient should be made to drink a glass of liquor every half hour. Several monks offered to keep vigil beside the prior through the night, and they faithfully administered the drink with the help of an hourglass.

Never had the priest had so much to drink. At first, it made his throat burn and he protested weakly. Then he began to realize that he liked it, and he smiled. The monks recognized, in this smile, a sign from the Lord, and they gave thanks for the imminent miracle. Father Lucas asked for more liquor before the allotted half hour had passed. They reminded him of the surgeon's instructions. The superior said, "I shit on the surgeon," and demanded to be satisfied. The monks feared this ominous choice between committing a sin of disobedience or a sin of negligence. One upheld, logically, that disobedience was worse, because it defied the superior of their order, while the negligence only involved a surgeon. He was so satisfied by his own reasoning that he walked toward the pitcher to indulge the patient's growing vice. Another monk held him back by the sleeve. He said that, in this case, the sin of negligence was worse because it could cost a man's life. Prior Lucas sat up in his bed as if he'd suddenly grown ten years younger; his nose red, eyes glittering, he shouted at them to stop saying stupid things and fill his glass once and for all. A struggle broke out among the monks and, while one pointed desperately at the clock, another handed over the liquor. The prior took the glass with trembling hands, gulped down the drink, burped, and let out a terrible blasphemy. In their shock, the priests crossed themselves, beat their chests, and called on the devil to leave the monastery.

In the morning, the surgeons arrived with a retinue of minor barbers. Prior Lucas could barely open his eyes. They lifted his light body, a fragile casing containing two liters of liquor. They placed him on the short operation table; his legs hung off. The main surgeon told them to bring a chair over so he could rest his heel on its high back. In this manner, the gangrenous leg extended into the air, well exposed.

The monks prayed more loudly than ever. Their pleas had to reach heaven before the scalpel reached the bone. A miracle was still possible. Martín and Francisco saw to the cauterizing tools, immersed in embers.

The infected leg was washed and dried. That was the last friendly gesture. The main surgeon authorized the start of the operation. The other surgeons flanked their patient, one on each side. They glanced at the instruments and crossed themselves. The one on the right wound a tourniquet around the knee and tightened it until the patient moaned through his drunken haze. The barbers focused on clamping down his other leg, along with his arms, head, and chest.

The gleaming scalpel sliced the flesh and circled the leg. The cut was clean and decisive. A few muscular fibers, however, refused to separate. The blade had to be moved back and forth as if working at a tough piece of meat. Prior Lucas shouted, "Son of a whore!" The surgeon continued his work as the prayers rose to swallow the vulgarities. Blood flowed heavily into the washbowl below the leg, which a barber monitored.

"Cauterizers!" the surgeon to the left commanded.

Martín took out the red, almost white steel, and handed it to the surgeon, who inserted it into the wound. The fire's contact with the blood produced smoke and crackling sounds. Prior Lucas jumped, almost pushing off the assistant, and hurled out blasphemies.

"Saw!"

The surgeon on the left now carried out the work. He inserted the blade in the wound and made energetic movements back and forth. In four strokes, he sawed through the aged bone. Another surgeon was left holding the lower part of the now severed leg, pouring out blood.

"Cauterizer!"

Francisco handed it over and it was applied to the wound. The prior brayed a thundering "Damn it to hell!" and lost consciousness.

Martín passed over the next cauterizer, while Francisco stirred the embers where the rest of them remained. The cell was like a smoke-filled cooking pit. The main surgeon raised a candelabra and studied the cauterized stump between the clouds. He declared it ready to be bandaged.

A chorus of prayers gave thanks for the surgery's happy result, which had been achieved in just six minutes. The black-and-red wound was covered with oil, while one of the barbers made the patient inhale garlic powder so he might recover consciousness.

In the afternoon, Doctor Cuevas arrived in his carriage. He advanced with great solemnity, as if grave problems geometrically increased his importance. He examined the patient, who was not yet awake. The prior's breath exuded clouds of alcohol. His pulse was quick and labored. A sweet, cold sweat covered his body, which suggested that he would not have the fever that often followed such an operation. The wound did not stain the bandage, which proved that the cauterization had been successful. The doctor asked to see the man's urine. "He has not urinated," the monks responded. Doctor Cuevas stood up, gave the patient a last glance, and said that the sickness remained in the prior's body.

Exclamations of surprise filled the room.

Martín, kneeling, asked what would be done with the amputated leg. The physician took out his perfumed handkerchief, grazed his nose, and said with displeasure, "It is to be buried, of course. What else could be done with it?" Then he spoke of post-operational complications and recommended various concoctions that should be administered carefully by the teaspoon, taking care to prevent choking.

Martín was suffering greatly. Where would he bury the piece of leg? He had wrapped it as if it were a precious relic. If the superior was a saint, then that foot would have miraculous powers. But he was a living saint; he could not attribute more powers to a portion of the man than to the man himself. He pressed the amputated foot against his chest as if it were a baby and placed it beside the image of Lord Jesus Christ in his cell, with the hope of receiving some form of guidance.

Then the three surgeons arrived. They examined the bandage and exchanged satisfied glances. The surgical intervention had been quick and perfect. They had done good work. They had only to wait for the patient to recover consciousness and begin to eat. The main surgeon asked about the amputated leg. Martín trembled, clasped his hands, and fell to his knees.

"I've put it away, as a relic," he said.

The surgeons exchanged glances again. They understood that, in the face of such a destiny, it would look bad to take the limb home and use it to practice anatomical dissection, as they had hoped to do. The church did not appreciate their macabre arts. The councils of Rheims, London, Letrán, Montpellier, and Tours decisively forbade the practice of medicine and surgery by priests, as well as the dissection of cadavers under any circumstances because *Ecclesia abhorret a sanguine.*

Lucas Albarracín did not return to consciousness. He went from drunkenness to death. His face bore the smile that had first broken through on the eve of his operation, as he'd enjoyed the liquor.

73

Back in Callao, Francisco opened the door of his father's home—which had no lock, no bolt—and placed the saddlebag on the mattress. It contained a change of clothes and the *Aphorisms of Hippocrates*. The room was in order, as he had left it days before. The rusted nail where his father hung his sanbenito was glaringly bare.

"I'll find him at the hospital," he thought.

The death of Prior Lucas had stirred his fear over his own father's health. He could not tolerate the stiffening of his skin, the ugly hunch in his back, the weakness of his voice, and the shaky gait with which his torturers had left him. He wanted to tell his father about the prior's sad end and, above all, to talk about the brutal operation. Would he have recommended it? Would he have used the same technique?

He did indeed find Diego at the hospital. It was a relief to see him examining a patient's chest. He had become an old man before his time, bent by suffering. Francisco wanted to embrace him, tell him that he loved him, and longed to absorb all his wisdom, all his kindness. He stayed by his side until his father became aware of his presence. They smiled at each other, exchanged pats on the arm, and moved out of earshot together. Francisco told him of his recent experience.

"Would you have called for the amputation?"

"I don't know." He scratched his head. "Doesn't Hippocrates say *Primum non nocere?*"

"Wouldn't he have been killed by the spreading gangrene, in any case?"

"*Primum non nocere*—from your description, Francisco, it seems that the superior was already very weak. He couldn't endure the consumption of liquor, much less the amputation of a leg."

He observed that his father, too, was weak. Was his sickly appearance comparable to the superior's dying days?

"But he had to be helped," the young man insisted. "Something had to be done."

The corners of Diego's eyelids creased. "A good doctor must recognize his limitations. Be wary of impossible successes, for they are paid for by the patient. Sometimes the only thing that can be done, since something must be done, is to help the patient to die well."

"That doesn't seem like good advice, Papá."

"I thought the same at your age."

The hospital was a dark building, with narrow, dusty windows and walls of adobe and stone. Its roof was little more than a lattice of long cane joined together by palm fronds. It consisted of three rooms lined with mats and mattresses. It could house many sick people. Callao was the main port of the Viceroyalty, and received exhausted crews. There were also many victims of fights. When survivors of a shipwreck came to port, not even the vestibule was free; two or three patients piled onto each mattress, and the hall was lined with straw for the rest. Those were exhausting days that demanded visits from monks and nuns to offer solace, hand out rations, and carry out the corpses. This was where Francisco received his practical training.

Diego squatted at the side of a middle-aged man whose face was disfigured by burns. He examined him carefully.

"You are better."

The man smiled with gratitude.

"I'll apply another layer of salve." Diego glanced at his tray, which held several pots full of green, yellow, red, and ivory substances. He chose the last one. It looked like onion. He placed it gently on the damp sores.

"Is that onion?" Francisco whispered.

"Aha!"

"Wouldn't he heal faster spontaneously?" Francisco said with a wink.

"In this case, onion wins. Shall I tell you?" He stood, with his son's help, and walked toward another patient. "Ambroise Paré was a war surgeon. He was called on to attend to a gravely burned man and ran to fetch his usual salves. On the way, he ran into one of the prostitutes that accompanied the troop. She said that burns healed better with finely chopped onion. Paré, open to any kind of advice, tried out the method—"

He cut himself off, agitated. He breathed deeply four or five times and went on.

"The result was satisfactory. But, here's the interesting part for you"—he raised his index finger—"another man would have said, 'onion heals all burns.' He, on the other hand, before claiming such a thing, asked himself, as you do now, 'Might the wound not have healed faster without the onion?' There you have a true doctor: he asks himself questions, always investigates. So what did he do? He tried again. How? Well, when he encountered a soldier with his face burned on both sides he applied onion to one cheek and nothing to the other. He proved that the side with the treatment healed faster."

Diego sat down beside another wounded man. He had to rest. As he recovered his breath, he gazed at the patient, who had a high fever. A cross-eyed, disheveled barber was applying damp cloths to the patient's head, chest, and thighs. A nut-sized bullet had torn into his left arm, causing large, tattered wounds. Don Diego removed the cloth. A vermilion crater appeared, edged with blue, golden blisters about to burst, and small worms dancing inside. With tweezers, he pulled them out one by one and threw them into the fire. The patient emitted incoherent sounds, his feverish delirium on the rise.

"You should cauterize that with boiling elderberry oil," the barber reproached him.

Don Diego shook his head. He examined the pots on his tray and chose dry egg yolk, which he dusted into the opening. Then he grazed it with rose oil and turpentine.

"This is better."

The barber frowned in disagreement.

"Keep on with the fresh cloth. And try to make him drink a lot of water. In a while I'll return with silver nitrate."

They went to the pharmacy in search of the substance. When they were far from the barber, Diego acknowledged that the wounded man was doing poorly. But he would not use the hot elderberry oil. They entered the pharmacy and he requested silver nitrate. The pharmacist was a bald man with a wide beard, who wore an ironsmith's apron. He gestured for them to sit and wait.

Francisco settled onto a bench and relaxed his back. He inhaled the riot of scents that shouted through the pharmacy, and he felt suddenly happy. His father seemed to have recovered a modicum of strength and humor. It shone through when he worked as a doctor.

After some time the pharmacist filled a metal bowl with the silver nitrate. "Here, take this and go."

They returned to the man with the gunshot wound. The coarse, cross-eyed barber was still applying damp cloths. The fever persisted. Don Diego lifted the bandage.

"I'll apply this. It's very effective."

"He won't get any better without cauterization," the barber muttered in disgust.

Diego picked up the shaving brush as if it were a quill and dipped it in the bowl. He painted the wound from its damp center to the inflamed, uneven borders. The patient kept emitting hoarse groans, without seeming to notice the treatment he was receiving. Pleas for help rose around them. As soon as one patient received attentive care the others began to grow desperate. The doctor spoke to his son as he skillfully moved the brush. It was no sin to recognize that this procedure was invented by the Moors, who also discovered the beneficial properties of alcohol and mercury chloride.

"Did you know that?" Diego asked the barber.

"I'm no man of letters," the barber said testily before leaving the room.

74

"Sin covers the world as mist covered the abyss before creation," Inquisitor Gaitán murmured furiously. "The men who should fight it most energetically are the very ones who most irresponsibly surrender into its arms."

The viceroy, for example, representative of the monarch that God anointed, is a disaster. He didn't even send me a letter of thanks when I agreed—reluctantly—to shortening Diego Núñez da Silva's prison sentence so he could be assigned to the hospital in Callao. And, what's more, he is a sordid, hedonistic poet who doesn't let a day pass without provoking our displeasure. What moral authority does he have? He's already stained the virtue of many ladies and offended the dignity of several gentlemen. He favors his relatives and protégés too much. It's true that he isn't original in this regard. All the viceroys have been corrupt. All of them. Therefore, my hand will not shake when I sign my denunciation. I have well-documented proof.

This untamable sinner has named several of his ridiculous servants to high posts in the armada of the southern seas. He made his favorite, Luis Simón de Llorca, the captain of the galleon Santa María, head of the armada, and that Llorca is a thief who kept nine hundred pieces of merchandise off the books, in complicity with his benefactor. Something even more serious took place with his servant Martín de Santjust, who brought 1,900 bars of silver and a great deal of unregistered merchandise, and took years to pay for the cargo, which was less than it should have been. In that same line of corruption, another of his servants, Luis Antonio Valdivieso, hid fabulous illegal shipments under stores of gunpowder.

In addition, he handed the street fairs and mule markets over to his nephew, who returns the favor with a percentage of his gains. He has donated fertile land so that his relatives can enjoy income from it. There is no limit!

These iniquities could be stamped out by the Holy Office. But we are blocked on the civil side as well as on the ecclesiastical side. We are blocked out of fear. Why the fear? Because the sword strikes at the center of sin.

If at least the men of the church would not interfere with their sabotaging scruples. If they, who have been trained in the faith, would only help facilitate our task. Oh, Sacred Virgin, how many sins your supposed servants commit, and what resistance they put up to our just activities!

75

The mourning over the prior's death deepened Francisco's insecurity. Refuge in his rat-ridden cell and his ability to continue at the University of San Marcos depended on Brother Manuel Montes, who only acted under the consent of obscure superiors who never showed their faces. When Francisco crossed the threshold of the monastery—he no longer had to use the church's side entrance—he braced himself for a monk to stop him with disdainful eyes and inform him that the hospitality was over. Nevertheless, he kept going to class, learning alongside Brother Martín in the monastery, and practicing with his father in the hospital.

Martín treated him with esteem. Once, as they were healing the insect bites that had almost paralyzed a monk, the mulatto pointed out that Francisco had never complained about his cell. It was usually used for penance; garbage was often buried behind its back wall.

"I have black blood, and you, Jewish," he explained in resignation.

Francisco could not muster a response to this grim observation. He couldn't think of anything relevant. Martín caressed him with his gentle gaze.

"It is a burden the Lord placed on us to test our virtue."

On another occasion, they attended to an Indian overseer who'd been struck by the mysterious illness that had felled the conquistador Pizarro. His face and body were deformed by tumors that appeared out of nowhere, as large as figs. Although they broke out in all places, whether visible or private, most of them were on the face. The growths hung from his nose, forehead, chin, and ears. Some grew more than others and reached the size of an egg. They hurt, bled, and became infected.

"This Indian overseer realizes his evil treatment of the Indians," Martín whispered. "Now he's promising to be good to them and not hold back their pay."

Francisco helped him pinch the abscesses, appease the infected edges, and cover them with pigeon droppings.

"Some doctors believe that these would heal faster if left alone," Francisco offered, without mentioning his father.

"I have heard that," Martín admitted. "But here they order us to use powders, salves, and poultices. I have no authority to challenge that."

"We could try."

"That would be disobeying."

"But the patients would benefit—I don't think it would be disobedience."

"What else could it be?"

Martín placed his thumbs in his mouth, licked them, and then slid them along the Indian overseer's pustules. Saliva was a liquid full of healing properties that Jesus himself had used in his miracles.

"Saliva should be enough," Francisco insisted.

Martín stared at him. "You're tempted by disobedience, eh?"

Later, pausing near the pharmacy, Martín said, "Careful! Don't spoil your merits. The Lord might be more troubled by your disobedience than by the Indian overseer's laments. Perhaps He wants him to have the salves and suffer a few more days, so that his heart may soften."

"Sometimes I wonder whether the Lord likes for me to be silent all the time, for me to be humiliated and afraid."

"Your modesty is pleasing, do not doubt that. The Lord made you be born with wretched blood so that you might recall this. He did the same with me, and it's a privilege, if you examine it carefully. We have a mark on us that unequivocally shows the way—to be inferior, to submit. That is how He wants us to be."

Francisco stroked his short beard. The ways of the Lord were so very complex.

"You have been loved by your earthly father. You have him here, close, in Callao, and you can speak with him," Martín said. "I, on the other hand, received my father's just contempt at an early age. He was a Spanish gentleman to whom my mother, a black African, bore two mulattoes. He did not want to recognize us, of course, and he abandoned us. His contempt made me pour my love toward the Eternal Father. From another perspective, Francisco, I have an advantage over you. Because the gentleman returned when I was eight years old, as it seemed that I'd been spoken highly of to him, and he resolved to send me to school. But then he abandoned me again. The Lord helped me, as always. I ended up becoming a barber. When I reached adulthood I felt called to the cloister, and was accepted to this order." He placed his hand on his knee. "My destiny is straight and clear. Do I have the right to demand new signs? I'm a mulatto dog, a horrible being, and yet I have the great privilege of living in a house of God, serving His ministers, and treating His patients. I believe that the Lord has favored me more than He has you because my lowliness is recognized immediately from the color of my skin. But you also have advantages. You should learn to discover them."

"I'd never thought about it that way."

"It moves me to hear you say that. I am happy to help you."

"You're a very good man, Martín."

"Only for the glory of the Lord."

"And you are pious."

"For the glory of the Lord."

76

Potatoes, corn, cabbage, dried beef, garlic, onion, and beans boiled in the sooty cooking pot. Father and son gazed at the concoction in the relative intimacy of that home, where the walls had ears.

Diego had had an exhausting day of work due to the arrival of a galleon whose crew had been accosted by an illness marked by hemorrhaging in the digestive system, gums, and even respiratory tracts. He was able to get dried fox lungs, considered ideal for combatting such symptoms, and had called for spiderwebs to be placed over the gums to stop the bleeding. He also ordered something even more important: a good diet, as they were consumed by starvation.

Francisco, on the other hand, bore more unsettling news. The viceroy had visited the university, accompanied by his retinue and guards. He wanted to be informed regarding the progress of that house of study, and to pay it tribute. This last part was emphasized because the University of San Marcos was already "a jewel of the West Indies," and "gave wings to the learned soul."

Joaquín del Pilar was a friendly classmate who had witnessed a past visit.

"He warned me that I'd see the light of fireworks in broad daylight," Francisco recounted. "According to him, this was not a threatening inspection by civil authorities, or a report on academic authorities. The main concern was not knowledge or how it is taught. There was no genuine interest in professional training or the richness of the library. It was a visit to the university that had nothing to do with the university. 'With what, then?' I asked. My colleague answered: 'With putting on a spectacle.'"

Don Diego dipped his ladle into the pot and filled two bowls with flavorful stew.

Joaquín del Pilar was older than Francisco, and was about to undergo the tests that would earn him his degree in medicine. The theoretical exam had to be preceded by another in natural philosophy, which he had already passed. The ceremony would take place in church, in great solemnity, before the altar of Our Lady of La Antigua, patroness of academic degrees. Francisco gathered this information with a mix of hope and fear; could he—an Inquisition prisoner's son—complete his studies, testify to the practical knowledge he was truly gaining, succeed at the test in natural philosophy, a subject he loved, and, finally, command the attention of the academic body in his graduation exam?

"It's another spectacle," Joaquín assured him. "I approach it that way to keep calm about it, and also because it's true. Listen." He counted on his fingers. "The Acts of Faith are a spectacle, processions are another spectacle, the inauguration of the viceroy, the same, the inauguration of the archbishop, and so on. They're all spectacles. So is the election of the university rector. As you've seen, that's pure spectacle, too, because the election is followed by a speech lasting several hours, plagued by repetitions, exaggerations, strikes of the fist for effect, promises, threats, and boundless praise.

"I will be the protagonist of my graduation," Joaquín added, "just as you, Francisco, will be of yours. But in reality, we are puppets of a spectacle that would have gone on without us. I've already told you the sequence of events. You'll take vows before the altar of Our Lady of La Antigua. There will be a high canopy bearing the insignia of the university and the crown. The rector will sit in a high-backed, ornamented chair before the altar. You will have to call on the dean and accompany him to church, just as the mayors call on the inquisitors for the Edict of Faith. When everything is ready, the ceremony . . . sorry, I mean spectacle, the spectacle begins. They will open texts at random for you, especially those by Galen and Avicenna. You will have to read a paragraph aloud and comment on it. Demonstrate in beautiful Latin that you know it, accept it, and love it, before a public that will spend hours listening to you or waiting for you to be tricked."

"Spectacle—" Diego mused.

"Didn't you have to do the same, Papá?"

"Yes, of course. That's the model for graduation that is replicated everywhere. I believe it comes from Salamanca. Perhaps it would be more apt to call it representation, or"—he searched for the right word—"appearance."

"Why?"

"Well, because it's like a game of cards. Some cheat others."

"I don't understand."

"Pomp, lectures, ceremony—to win. To win spaces of power, Francisco. Each of those spectacles, from graduation to an Act of Faith, is the sand where the bullfighters flaunt what they have to differentiate themselves from the bulls."

"But in graduation, the purpose is to evaluate the future graduate."

"Graduation is performed to give a title, it's true, and the Act of Faith to punish sinners. There is always a stated objective." He refilled Francisco's bowl. "But, as it happens, that objective is used to set paraphernalia in motion for a different, hidden end—the power of those who are, or aspire to be, on top. Not a recent graduate or a sinner. They're hypocrites."

"Do they publicly adhere to Galen and accept Vesalius?"

"For example."

"Or they express their nonexistent love for the viceroy, Papá. I heard that. It was incredible."

"Tell me."

"Joaquín confided in me, before the Act began, that the rector despises the viceroy."

"There has always been tension between viceroys and clergymen."

"Nevertheless, Papá, the viceroy gave a lecture full of grandiose, ridiculous poetry."

"They say the marquis is a poet."

"If he's any good at writing verses he must have been bored."

"Were the viceroy's poems so poor?"

"Nothing but foam."

"A spectacle, you might wish to say."

Francisco frowned before saying, "Do you know who was part of the Marquis Montesclaros's personal guard?"

"No."

"Lorenzo Valdés."

"Your traveling companion?"

"And the ambitious son of the captain. Amazing. We exchanged glances the whole time. He climbed the ranks fast."

"He must be good with weapons."

"The uniform suited him."

"Who else spoke?" Diego asked a while later, as he took the pot from the embers.

"The master of arts, the head doctor, and Inquisitor Gaitán."

A shadow crossed his father's face. "What did Gaitán say?"

"He was brief. He exalted ethical and creative virtues."

"Aha! Ethical and creative virtues," Diego said, dragging himself toward the mattress.

His son helped him lie down. The day had depleted him.

"Do you know what? I met your classmate's father," he murmured as he opened a book to settle into his bedtime reading.

"Joaquín's father?"

"We prayed together, at a height of four thousand feet, in Potosí."

"What a surprise I'm going to give him! Is he also—was he also—Jewish?"

"He died when Joaquín was small."

77

The afternoon turned tempestuous. Father and son sought privacy on the beach. The sea was choppy, sending crests into the dark distance. Seagulls circled, indifferent to the autumn weather. It was an ideal place for confessions, as they had painfully proven a few days earlier. Both of them felt the urgent need to communicate on subjects they could not broach under the threat of denunciation.

"The sea, nevertheless," Diego said, "is not a favorable place for revelation. Not even when it opened before the staff of Moses."

Francisco listened tensely as that reference brought back memories of Ibatín.

"Moses parted the Red Sea and the people witnessed an incredible miracle," he added, "but the revelation took place later, in the desert and on a mountain."

"Deserts inspire spirituality," Francisco noted, looking at his father. "Jesus went there, too, after His baptism."

"I also went to the desert," Diego confessed.

The young man paused in his walk. They took stock of each other, beside the sea, where revelations didn't usually occur, and yet one was about to unfold.

"Which desert?"

"I mentioned it the other night. It's at an altitude of four thousand feet. It's a replica of Sinai." He covered his head with his cloak, giving him the look of a prophet. "Do you know who was guiding us?"

His son put two and two together.

"You imagine correctly," Diego said. "But you should know the whole history so you can understand that decisive pilgrimage." He reached a hand out toward the horizon. "I came from Portugal, a country that could have been a pious refuge, but was instead turned into a battlefield by fanatics. I even witnessed, at an Act of Faith, the sentencing of the father of a friend, someone you know."

"Diego López de Lisboa?"

His father's face contorted. The memory still hurt like a knife in the throat.

"We fled to Brazil. This wasn't original on our part," he said, forcing a smile, "because we were forbidden to travel to any destination not governed by the crown. They hated us and—a curious thing!—insisted on retaining us."

"To exterminate them!" Francisco deduced, using the third person to convey that he did not include himself among the Jews.

His father raised his eyebrows. "That's right—so you know, too. Exterminate us, as if we were insects." He coughed. "They were drunk with hate."

"López de Lisboa dared tell me of his trip to Brazil, and of the disappointment you experienced when you arrived."

"You say it well, my son—'he dared.' When fear enters us, it puts down roots."

"He abhors his past."

"It's terrible—he wants to forget."

"He wants to be a good Catholic."

His father's brow furrowed. Was Francisco reproaching him?

The drizzle had ceased. Light that could not fully express itself struggled through the thick, dark clouds. Brushstrokes of ochre appeared across the cinnamon-colored cliffs. They pulled their cloaks around themselves tightly.

"I was telling you," he said, inhaling briny air, "that I walked toward the peaks, toward proximity to God. I had powerful sensations. As I rose, my strength grew. The hard blue sky made me smile for the first time in years. I had stopped smiling in Lisbon."

"Were you alone?"

"No. We were in a group. There were several whom I . . . remembered . . . in the torture chamber."

Francisco gulped.

His father broke off. A wide stone beckoned him to sit. He picked up an oyster and drew something on the sand that he immediately erased with his foot. Then he drew the letter *shin*, the same one that gleamed on the handle of that venerated Spanish key.

"We took the pilgrimage to the desert to read the Bible," he went on, "because it was in the desert that the word of God was received. We went there to understand that word. To study it. Love it. We were a dozen people who had been converted by force. The idea was conceived by Carlos del Pilar, your classmate's father. You know several of my daring companions: Juan José Brizuela, José Ignacio Sevilla, Gaspar Chávez, and also Antonio Trelles, who settled in La Rioja."

"Most of them ended up in prison."

Don Diego's brow furrowed again. Another reproach?

"Trelles," he said, clearing his throat, "was arrested in La Rioja, Juan José Brizuela in Chile, Gaspar Chávez you saw—he runs a prosperous business in Cuzco—and José Ignacio Sevilla has settled in Buenos Aires, or, perhaps, as he hinted during your journey, he might decide to settle in Cuzco."

"Papá, why did you all go to the desert? Is there something you haven't told me yet?"

Diego erased the letter *shin* and threw the oyster into a crowd of birds. Francisco feared that he might go mute again.

"We were crushed with pain, my son." He loosened the cloak around his neck. "Each of us carried baggage of the dead and of humiliations. The New World had not brought peace, as we had hoped it would; there were intermittent clashes with converts, with Indians, with black people, with the Dutch. In addition, the Indians clashed with each other, Catholics with each other, mestizos with Indians, and mulattoes with mestizos. The authorities executed and transgressed on the one hand and, on the other hand, acted with too much leniency. Nothing was stable. Carlos del Pilar incited us to search in the silence of the highest peaks for the light of the Lord."

"That was not sinful."

"Sinful, you say? Of course not, but some denounced it as a sign of heresy to read the sacred texts without the guidance of the church."

"Did you confess this to the Inquisition?"

"Yes. But they were not satisfied. I already told you that they demanded the names of everyone who took that journey with me."

After a heavy silence, Diego stared directly into his son's eyes and gave voice to a hard question. "Let's go to the heart of things. What does 'practicing Judaism' mean to you, Francisco?"

After an instant of reflection, the young man responded without sugarcoating. "It means offending Our Lord and the Catholic Church. It's a crime."

"Your accusation seems . . . vague," his father responded calmly.

"Vague? To practice Judaism is to perform filthy rites."

"What rites?"

"Ones that are offensive to Our Lord."

"That is what is said, yes. But—what are those rites? Describe them."

"It's already been explained to me that they don't involve worshipping a pig's head."

"You're nervous," Diego said, taking his son's hand. "But when I was practicing Judaism I never offended Jesus Christ or the church."

"That comforts me."

"Do you know what those abominable rites consist of? Respecting Saturdays by dressing in a clean shirt, lighting candles, and dedicating the day to study. Another rite is the celebration of liberation from Egypt under Moses. Fasting in September so that God might forgive our sins. Reading the Bible. Also, Judaism is a religion that exalts the importance of one's fellow man, which is why people gather to pray, study, think. For this reason, we went to the desert as a group."

"Did you also confess to all of that?"

"Somewhat. Each word was dangerous. But when I learned that Diego had been arrested, my precaution collapsed and I broke open like a watermelon. I spoke with the hope that they would reward my honesty, my transparency. The notary broke quills in his hurry to record my words without letting a single one escape him."

He looked into the distance, overwhelmed.

"Do you know how my confession ended?"

"Giving names—"

His father's skin turned cadaverous. "Yes. The inquisitors did not soften. My companions and I had practiced Judaism. And my despair didn't reach even the wax of their ears. In tears, I confessed that I later read the edifying works of Denis the Carthusian, that I trained myself with that text and, thanks to it, returned to the Catholic faith. I assured them that I would never practice Judaism again."

Francisco watched him in silence. His eyes asked the question: "Were you telling the truth?"

From behind the curtain of clouds, a semicircle of quicksilver reached down toward the ocean. The tenuous wind pushed their hair over their noses and urged them to leave the beach.

"Sevilla, Chávez, and López de Lisboa feel great gratitude toward you," Francisco remarked as they headed back toward the harbor.

"I didn't denounce them, happily," he sighed.

The brushstrokes of evening gave a spectral quality to their path.

"I am at the end of my life, and I want to offer you some advice." Diego placed his hand on his son's shoulder. "Don't repeat my trajectory!"

Then he added more words. The wind pulled at them as if they were elastic.

"My ending is even worse. You are watching it. May it not be yours."

Francisco pushed back a fold of his cloak that the wind had draped over his mouth.

"You don't want me to practice Judaism. Is that it?"

"I don't want you to suffer."

He noticed his father's ambivalence. What was it he really wanted to say?

They reached the alleys of Callao. At Diego's door, a black man with a lantern awaited them. A galleon had arrived from Valparaíso with sick crew members, he said. The doctor needed to report to the hospital immediately. Among the travelers was a commissioner from Córdoba: Brother Bartolomé Delgado.

78

In distant Córdoba, the delirium of Isidro Miranda had been hidden for years in La Merced monastery, where the old priest with bulging eyes had been locked up. But shards of that delirium escaped like lizards. His mad ravings about Jews infiltrating the clergy frightened all the religious orders. The denunciations were at first considered false, though dangerous.

The local commissioner, Brother Bartolomé Delgado, had called for an exorcism. The devil had to be removed from his body. Brother Isidro was no longer the submissive man of past days, and had become a blazing eccentric spouting barbarities. The commissioner summoned a Dominican of great reputation and asked him to act immediately and tear Satan from Brother Isidro's innards. It was determined that, if necessary, tearing out his tongue and even his useless testicles would be condoned.

The exorcist had a hefty build and a potent voice. He locked himself into a cell with the toothless Isidro, and brandished a cross before his bulging eyes as though it were the sword of El Cid. He intoned formulas and ordered the devil to abandon the man's body. Satan must have felt the blow because Brother Isidro began to run in circles. His legs became incredibly agile, like those of the Evil One. He was trying to flee from the thundering voice. The two men's shouts competed in volume and velocity. The exorcist's cross pursued the back of Isidro's thin neck as if with the blows of an ax. The devil took advantage of the old man's last reserves of energy, forcing him to resist. But, in the end, he collapsed. Then the herculean exorcist squeezed, pulled, urged, and tore the tenacious demon from the punished body. He pressed him onto a table sprinkled with holy water and blinded him with the shining cross.

Brother Bartolomé received a meticulous report of the operation. "The nightmare has ended," he sighed in relief.

Nevertheless, the poison that the sickly Isidro had spilled was captured by the antennae of the High Tribunal of the Holy Office. In Lima, the situation was not considered simple, and the demonization of the old monk was in doubt.

At that point, the whole story took a turn.

One of the inquisitors—it is believed to be Andrés Juan Gaitán— interpreted the emaciated monk's denunciations as true. It seemed absurd that a man as perceptive as Brother Bartolomé would have wasted time silencing the man with an exorcism, rather than summoning a notary and recording the information.

The order was issued immediately. Both monks—the destroyed Isidro and the stunned Bartolomé—were to travel to Lima and submit to trial. One would testify to the practitioners of Judaism he claimed to know of, and the other to his extremely grave acts of concealment.

Brother Bartolomé suffered several dizzy spells on his journey to the Chilean port of Valparaíso, where he was to embark. He could not reconcile his new circumstance as an arrestee with his role as an official with the Holy Office. He struggled to recognize, in the officials who guarded him day and night, an authority superior to his own. He was assaulted by stabs of cold on hot days. His formerly ample double chin became a rag. When they crossed the Andes, his sheep-like cat died of cold. He buried it in the snow and, on tear-streaked days, hallucinated its golden eyes between the ice-capped peaks.

Brother Isidro arrived at the port of Valparaíso hanging from his mule, as if the beast were dragging a skeleton. When the galleon was on the high seas, he asked his companion in misfortune to give him his last rites. The former commissioner shivered and, retching with tremulous vision, put on his stole, prepared the sacred oil, and said the sacramental words. The frail teacher and informer felt the cross on his forehead and flew to the next world. But his eyes could not be closed; they kept on emitting flames, like flashes of color.

The captain of the ship ordered the corpse to be thrown into the sea. Brother Bartolomé then came to his senses and foresaw that the Holy Office would not tolerate a second wasteful act. The first one had been failing to further investigate the practitioners of Judaism named in Isidro's delirium; the second would be the loss of Isidro's body. If the Inquisition decided that the deceased should be burned at the stake, they would never forgive his body going to the fish; his corpse had to suffer the purging fires of an Act of Faith. To that end, the commissioner confronted the captain and succeeded in having a trunk emptied and then filled with the remains of the deceased.

A few days later, the feared biological process began. An unbearable fetid odor leaked through the trunk's seams. They wrapped it in blankets. The captain insisted that the body could not be kept until the end of the voyage. They covered it with onions. Useless. The smell spread everywhere. They decided to put it in a corner of the hold, by the porthole through which chamber pots were emptied, so the excrement might cover up the corpse's stink.

One night, the crew was awoken by an explosion. Wood creaked, as if the ship had run aground. The trunk was cracking under the pressure of the decomposing corpse. The furious captain ordered it to be thrown overboard at once. The commissioner grabbed it with both hands, racked by nausea, and threatened to send anyone who dared commit such a crime to the flames. They agreed to put it out on deck, tied to the main mast. Its putrefaction would be relieved by the wind.

The blankets covering the coffin opened like flags. The lid flew off. The body of the once-frail priest rose like the stomach of a giant. His enormous eyes were braziers that terrorized the clouds. The ship glided over the Pacific as if sustained by an unlikely monster glued to the mast. At the port of Callao it took fifty dockworkers to pull him down.

Brother Bartolomé left immediately for Lima, escorted by officers of the Inquisition. Several oxen, in turn, dragged the pestilent mountain into which Isidro Miranda had been transformed.

79

At the monastery, consternation reigned. Not only was the death of the prior being mourned, but now there was also talk of the unexpected arrest of Bartolomé Delgado and the inexplicable postmortem growth of Isidro Miranda. This event was particularly disturbing for Manuel Montes, who became like a figure made of wax. He stood paralyzed in the tiled gallery, and his absent eyes and strangely unmoving lips repeated an enigmatic phrase: "They have touched evil." Francisco asked him whether he could help. He received no answer. Not even an acknowledgment. Francisco then learned that Brother Manuel was Brother Bartolomé's half brother.

Isidro Miranda's corpse was buried in a gigantic grave. The Holy Office appreciated the efforts made to deliver the body so they could dispose of it on their terms. If heresy had been committed, the bones could be opportunely exhumed and punished by fire. It was their almost-certain destiny; that monstrous deformation could not be anything but the devil's work. Although in life he had been a small, fragile being, Brother Isidro had been plagued with disproportionate eyes—a disturbing sign. According to some versions, Satan had tricked the exorcist, and never came out of the old body. The Evil One had remained in the monk's blood. For this reason, when he died on the high seas, the whole body became a cauldron of pestilence, Beelzebub's den. His swollen entrails sheltered a stove of sin. His flesh did not submit to the laws of death, but rather to the whims of beasts.

Francisco was surprised to learn of the blood ties between the obese commissioner of Córdoba and Brother Manuel. Now he could understand the delegation of that harsh paternal role: Brother Bartolomé had wanted him to be guarded up close, and, at the same time, assisted. Brother Manuel had accepted this request and conscientiously fulfilled it. One of them was not as evil as Francisco had thought, the other not so cold.

The prior's death had filled every corner of the monastery with bitterness. Feelings of guilt arose, and the lash of flagellations could be heard at all hours. Brother Martín was haggard and more jumpy than he'd been two weeks before.

Brother Manuel wandered around like Lazarus after wiping off the cobwebs of the beyond. He kept saying, "They have touched evil."

"What could it mean?" Francisco wondered. At the library, he found Joaquín del Pilar. He was reading and taking notes, accompanied by thick volumes of Galen and Avicenna. It was not a place for talking, and much less for telling him that their fathers knew each other. He waved in greeting and headed toward the crammed shelves in search of *Summa Theologica*.

As he glanced across the gold-lettered spines with an increasing desire to dive into their contents, he read "Pablo de Santamaría, of Burgos." He gasped. Was this the famous work of Rabbi Solomon ha-Levi, who was baptized during the massacres of 1391, changed his name, donned the habit, and rose to the role of Archbishop of Burgos? Was this the text that served as his invincible sword? The scribes of Spain had copied it with great effort and distributed it throughout the city to break the spines of the few Jews who remained. The intellect that had been at the service of the synagogue became an intellect in service of the church. Francisco reread the title. It was the famous book, without a doubt: *Scrutinium Scripturarum*. He glanced at Joaquín. He felt a pang of shame. He took out the volume, leaned it on the table, and began to read the "Examination of the Writings." It was written in an elegant Latin. Two figures debated: Saulo and Pablo. One, Jewish, represented the synagogue, while the other, a Christian, stood for the church. One defended the Law of Moses, the other that of Jesus Christ. Each argued with erudition. Saulo was an old man refusing to see the light of the Gospel, and Pablo a young man pouring that light in streams.

Francisco lost track of time. He did not stop reading until a hand touched his shoulder. It was Joaquín, gesturing that the library was about to close. He picked up the book and returned it to the shelf it shared with Saint Augustine, Saint Thomas, Duns Scotus, and Albertus Magnus. The dense text had dizzied him. Each page was a torrent of references and quotations. Only a man who had studied the sacred writings with utter devotion could achieve such acrobatics with his prose. The author had studied deeply as a rabbi, and then, once again, as a priest and bishop. Nobody could be more of an expert. The arguments and refutations were brilliant. Francisco would have to keep on to the end. Something was rearranging inside him. In the *Scrutinium*, young Pablo always triumphed. His reasons were stronger. But his success over the browbeaten Saulo did not give the young man any peace.

He accompanied Joaquín to the tavern around the corner, where students gathered. Noise echoed from walls covered in caricatures and inscriptions. Pots steamed in one corner. Black and mulatto waiters and waitresses made rounds bearing trays. They distributed jugs of wine, bottles of liquor, and bowls of stew. Around the table, patrons shouted and sang. A few reached out to pinch the women and make them spill their jugs or bowls. The ruddy, sweaty innkeeper gave orders from the counter. On recognizing Francisco and Joaquín, the other students made room for them to sit. They nudged and jostled each other on the narrow bench like children. They needed to loosen up after so much studying.

Francisco grabbed a piece of bread and devoured it before the stew arrived. A classmate mocked his hunger, and another elbowed him in the stomach. He drank wine and elbowed back. They sang. He hurt his mouth in the middle of a drink when a classmate shoved a waitress, causing her to fall on the group. The innkeeper approached, fists up. The woman struggled to get back up while several young men groped her breasts. Joaquín ordered another round of drinks.

An hour later, Francisco headed back toward the monastery, tipsy and alone. The tavern's noise and the effects of alcohol made his head spin, as did the grotesque end of Isidro Miranda, the arrest of Bartolomé Delgado, and the ardent dispute between Saulo the Jew and Pablo the Catholic. A dirty drainage canal streamed down the center of the street, shining like a broken mirror. It exuded an unmistakable odor, almost the defining feature of the proud City of Kings. To keep the thick shadows from playing tricks on him, Francisco walked close to the plastered adobe walls. He arrived at the monastery and leaned against the doorjamb. The sky was still covered by its eternal sheath of clouds.

He walked down a corridor. A few moments later, he was struck by fear.

80

Brother Manuel Montes, racked with guilt over his compulsive masturbation, dragged the brazier that heated surgical cauterizers into his cell. He filled it with incandescent embers until it transformed into a fantastic bowl of rubies. They emitted a magical, bloody light. He prayed to a sacred image that hung on his wall. He raised his hands and showed his palms to the Virgin. He was not thinking of Bartolomé, his half brother arrested by the Holy Office; he was thinking of his own horrible sins. He said, again, looking at his raised hands, "They have touched evil."

He stood, swallowed his tears, and took three steps to reach the brazier. He kneeled again. Purple light washed across his bony face. The light fascinated him, and dizzied him. Ashes coated the coals like velvet, and the coals, in turn, were slowly breaking down into pebbles like living eyes. Once again he raised his hands and, with violent decision, crushed them against the embers.

Snakes of flesh-burned smoke rose between his open fingers and filled the room. Brother Manuel trembled. "They have touched evil." Unbearable pain made him sink his fingers in farther and destroy them with the blades of burning coals. He was pouring sweat. A grimace of pleasure deformed his dry face. He began to spasm uncontrollably. He was able to submerge his hands even deeper into the merciless rubies before letting out a scream of victory and fainting.

The burns had reached his bones, consuming joints, nerves, and veins. Two uneven stumps remained. The alarm sounded. He was moved to the hospital. Martín was woken, as were the pharmacist, the servants, and all the monks. Figures rushed and collided in the shadows. Some searched for others, muttering prayers and mea culpas. Martín applied the first treatment. Brother Manuel's heart beat weakly; the monk could die.

Francisco was immediately taken to his benefactor's side. The scene was horrifying. His thin forearms ended in two black, mica-flecked balls. Martín insisted that the man was a saint.

"What a shame that he won't be able to use his hands for any more acts of charity," Francisco replied in repugnance.

"He's a saint, he's a saint!" Martín repeated as he strained to keep the stumps in the air and cover them in emollient substances.

"A madman," Francisco said, unsettled.

"No," Martín insisted. "This is an offering from the body to purify the soul."

"If he hadn't fainted, he would have kept on to his forearms, his shoulders, his head. Absurd."

Martín stared at him in shock. "What are you saying, idiot Jew! This saintly monk might hear you!"

"He's half dead."

"God blessed him by making him faint just in time, don't you see?" Anger blazed in Martín's eyes. "Be quiet, now. Help me bandage him."

Francisco unwound cloth and wrapped it around the burned hands. They worked in a tense silence. Afterward, they adjusted the body so that his head would be somewhat elevated.

Martín stared hard at Francisco. He was tearing up. His sweat glimmered in the trembling light.

"What's the matter?"

Martín bit his lips. "I beg your forgiveness. I have no right to offend you."

"It's all right."

"Forgive me."

"I forgive you."

"Thank you. I'm a mulatto dog. An irredeemable sinner—" He held back an imminent sob. "Your Jewish blood is not your fault. Not even the proximity of a saint like Brother Manuel keeps my tendency toward wrongdoing at bay."

"Don't be so harsh to yourself."

Martín pressed Francisco's wrist. His face became impassioned. "Come and whip me," he proposed.

"What?"

"Come. I beg you! You should punish my intemperance. Father Albarracín died because of my sins. Brother Manuel burned himself because of my sins."

Francisco pulled his wrist back. His head was full of the cacophony of the tavern's wine, the *Scrutinium Scripturarum*, the metamorphosis of Isidro Miranda, and Brother Manuel's self-punishment. Now Martín was asking him to become a tormentor. He wiped his forehead with his sleeve and walked out to the dim courtyard. A multitude of eyes stopped him; the monks had gathered to pray before Brother Manuel's cell. He tried to go past them, but they would not let him through.

Suddenly, pincers bit his stomach. A ribbon of fire rose in his throat and his vomit landed on the habits closest to him.

81

The rats in the cell had grown accustomed to Francisco. They ran through the beams and walls to mark their territory. They swung from the cane roof or bolted across the dirt floor with no concern for the student's body. They had even stopped running over his legs and face.

It was not the rodents, therefore, that impeded his sleep that night. The recent cataclysms seeped through the tangle of his fatigue. Manuel Montes's charred hands had still emitted smoke; his fingers were black claws encrusted with blood and ivory attached to a lifeless body surrounded by a chorus of weeping monks. Between the cassocks, two artificial figures appeared, wearing ancient mantles, with mouths like those of marionettes; they were expounding on the sacred writings with great knowledge but little logic. They debated. Better said, they dramatized a debate: Saulo—old and antiquated—said exactly the things that Pablo—young and intelligent—could refute. And whenever Pablo became distracted in a weak argument, his senile adversary helped him with a new one so he would receive more blows to the head. The decrepit Saulo strove to lose with the same effort that the brilliant Pablo put into winning. From *Scrutinium Scripturarum*, Francisco returned to poor Brother Manuel. What if he died? Who would be his guardian before the university authorities?

As his body turned on a spool of evasive sleep, an opaque radiance grew in the narrow window. It was the middle of the night and Francisco stared at the opening as Moses had at the burning bush. A revelation surely had to come through there. Then he heard the whir of a whip, and ensuing moans. There were no words, as Moses had heard, but rather the cries of a flagellation. The blows came in a steady rhythm.

The good Martín was delivering his third round of lashes near Francisco, to leave no room for doubt as to the sin he was trying to purge. Francisco, trapped, covered his ears to escape.

Francisco knew that Martín engaged in regular, biweekly flagellations, in addition to the ones he undertook as called for. When he finished those sessions and the monastery grew quiet, he shut himself in to pray. His body and soul progressively divided into many pieces, all of them burning and alive. The man's reddened eyes became buttons of ecstasy, his muscles tense as rope. He stripped his torso, pulled the stretcher that served as his bed, which was also used in the monastery to carry corpses, against the wall, and took down a chain with steel hooks on it. His mind imagined becoming many people. The dimness, isolation, and inner turmoil created a fantastical state of fragmentation. His arm grasped the chain, and he became his father. The arm poured rage onto the offspring who tried to be a son. He shouted, "Mulatto dog!" He unleashed deep disappointment and fury onto his shoulders. Instead of a white descendant, this cockroach had come to him. "Ridiculous black man! Idiot! Disgusting!" The insults gave strength to his arm. Martín was Martín, doubled over and suffering, but he was also his father, marvelous and resentful. His shoulders belonged to a condemned man, his arm to a nobleman. His mouth hurled insults and smiled with power. The blood of a despicable black man flowed from his back. For several minutes, his brain and arm functioned as those of the gentleman Juan de Porres, whom the king of Spain had distinguished with a mission to the New World.

He also became the harsh slave trader who hunted human beings in Africa and prevented their escape through beatings. Like this one. He had to destroy his own dangerous love of liberty and stomp on the urge to rebel. Martín saw those embers within himself. They had to be put out in a clean blow. "Take this, disobedient black crook!" He was a monster who should lick the sandals of those above him. His skin slashed open and drops of blood flecked the walls.

When felled by the strong arms of his father and the slave traders, the beating ceased. Martín lay gasping on the ground. The savage residents of his body were wounded. And his soul would be relieved. After recovering his breath he would grasp the table or stretcher and clamber to his knees, then to standing. He would hang up the chain and cover his wounded shoulders with cloth. He would go out to the courtyard where the cool night air gifted him with a caress. By the well, frogs sounded their guttural castanets. Martín dragged himself through the shadows toward the chapel. He could have gotten there with his eyes closed. He opened the door quietly—he would not wake the monks, who were far away. He kneeled before the image of Christ, and rested.

In his mind, ignited fragments painfully rearranged themselves. His arm could also belong to the soldiers who had whipped divine skin. It was good and purifying to imitate Christ. *Imitatio Christi*—to act impotent, to allow oneself to be mistreated. He filled his soul with the supreme example of Our Lord and returned to his cell. His eyes, in a state of trance, would begin to glow again. He would pull the cloth from his shoulders, making the blood clots jump. He would grasp the chain and resume the discipline. To the prior insults he often added, with intense pain, "You bastard son of a bitch!" Suddenly Martín was his own mother. He'd fall to his knees. The chain would wind around his neck, then spin in the air and lacerate his shoulders again. The Panamanian woman who was taken by the gentleman and gave birth to a mulatto shouted, out of breath, "Mercy, Lord! Mercy!" She had

had the privilege of being impregnated by one chosen by the king, and brought an inky fetus into the world. Martín was also of her race: black, hunted in remote lands, tied like animals, subjected to hunger and thirst, then buried in the airless holds of ships. They would die there, surrounded by excrement, worms hatching in their festering wounds. And then they were thrown to the sea. Their corpses formed an underwater tapestry between Africa and the New World. Martín would shout, "Mercy, Lord! Mercy!" from his abysmal helplessness. There was no Brother Bartolomé de las Casas to advocate for them. Not even a miraculous man like Francisco Solano to offer them a sermon. As the lashes rained down, he was Christ, and Christ was a multitude of defenseless black people, and the black multitude spun through the cell, crying out for mercy. That much pain had to graze—even if just graze—the foot of that sky-blue throne.

The harsh arm grew weak. Without air or strength he fell facedown on the stretcher, a cadaver like the ones those hard crossbars transported. He would doze for a few hours.

Routine flagellation, the horrified Francisco knew, occasionally has a third phase.

When mysterious light filled his narrow window, a needle would pierce Martín between the eyebrows. He rose, gathered a few quince tree branches, and peered outside his door to ensure no one was there. It was cold, and the edges of things seemed gilded in a lining of frost. He moved through the familiar, narrow paths of the monastery, hewing close to the walls. He found himself before the Indian he had hired. He was a short man with a wide back and a taciturn face. He belonged to another scorned multitude. Martín, a servant of the Lord, offered him a symbolic revenge. He who represented the foreigners, the king, and Jesus Christ would allow himself to be punished by one who represented the natives, the dethroned Incan, and the idolatry that had been eradicated. An inferior Indian would remind the superior clergyman not to succumb to vanity, and show him that those who are offended can also offend. They glanced at each other fleetingly through the film of aluminum light shed by the moon. In a ceremony charged with terrible meaning, Martín handed over the quince tree branches the way a general surrenders his sword. The Indian received the weapon in silence, rigid as a statue in a church. Martín bared his torso and raised an arm. That was the sign. Then the Indian turned into a representative of millions.

That was happening now. Francisco tossed and turned on the floor, irritated by the torture happening so close to him. His nerves twisted at the sound of moans. He stood, paced between the damp walls, and kicked a rat with such anger that it squashed against the cane roofing. Its shriek wrought havoc among the other rats, and Francisco ran from the room. The black shapes of plants and walls did not stop him from instantly reaching the improvised gallows. Martín lay facedown on the earth, the Indian still lashing at a steady pace.

"Stop!" Francisco shouted.

The frightened Indian backed away. Francisco made him drop the branches and ordered him to leave. After a moment of hesitation he disappeared through a crack in the wall. Martín, in a semiconscious haze, mumbled, "More, more—"

"It's me, Francisco."

Martín broke off his mutterings. He did not connect him with the Indian. He struggled to do so. He shook his head and became ashamed.

"Cover me."

Francisco placed Martín's dirty habit over the man's back, which was covered in flowering blood.

Then Martín asked for help getting to his feet. His limbs buckled like leaves of lettuce. Francisco carried him on his back. As they approached Martín's cell, he began to recover his strength. He started to walk. He opened the door, climbed onto his morbid bed, and lay facedown.

"Thank you."

Francisco handed him a jug of water.

"Forgive me," he added, in a barely audible voice. "I had no right to offend you."

"I've already forgiven you."

"I . . . truly deserved . . . this."

In the morning, Brother Martín arrived at the hospital full of enthusiasm. His face showed no sign of his nocturnal activities. He was a lily stripped of stains.

82

"Have you realized, Francisco," his father said, "that I've been spending less time at the hospital?"

"Only when I'm there, I suppose."

He nodded and adjusted his sanbenito, which the ocean wind had pushed toward one shoulder.

"These walks are beneficial to your health."

Diego smiled melancholically. "A reminder of health, you mean to say."

"You're better than you were when I arrived."

"Only in appearances. There's no use fooling ourselves. My bronchial tubes have aged too much."

"As long as I'm in Callao we'll take this stroll on the beach every day. You'll get stronger, Papá."

When they were far from spies, Francisco cut to the heart of things. "I found an important book at the university." He'd been burning to share his discovery and bewilderment for some time now.

"Yes?" His father's indigo eyes lit up. "Which one?"

"*Scrutinium Scripturarum.*"

"Ah." Shadows returned to his face.

"You know it?"

"Of course!"

"Do you know what seems false to me?" He dared venture the phrase.

His father closed his eyes. Had sand gotten in them? He began to rub them.

"Let's sit down here."

"Did you hear me?" Francisco demanded.

"That it seemed false to you—" He lay the sanbenito down like a rug. His joints hurt.

"Saulo, the Jew defending the Law of Moses," Francisco said, "lets himself be defeated like an idiot. From the first page he's doomed to lose the fight. He only speaks so that the young Catholic, Pablo, can jump on his words and refute them."

"Perhaps Pablo is the one who's right."

"Pablo doesn't convince me either. He doesn't listen." Francisco was getting heated. "It's not really a dialogue. All of it is written to show that the church is glorious and the synagogue an anachronism."

"The church greatly values that text. It's been distributed all over the place."

"Because it honors it, flatters it. It doesn't defend it with the weapons of truth, Papá."

Don Diego sensed that his son was edging toward a steep slope. "What are the weapons of truth?"

Francisco glanced at the ochre cliffs with their green manes to the north, and the empty beach to the south. Nobody was listening; he could keep airing his doubts, frustration, and rebellion.

"Truth?" His eyes shone. "To answer as to whether, since the time of Jesus Christ, we truly live in the messianic times foreseen by the prophets. The Bible proclaims that Jews would no longer suffer persecution after the Messiah's arrival, and now they not only suffer it, but even lack the right to exist."

His father stared at him in fear.

Francisco clasped his father's wrinkled hand. "Papá. Tell me, once and for all—"

The waves crashed the sand with a mighty sound.

"I don't want you to suffer what I have suffered," he answered quietly.

"You've said that before. But suffering is mysterious. It depends on what you make of it."

"I don't believe in the Law of Moses," Diego suddenly said.

Francisco's eyes opened wide, in shock. "It's not true—"

His father bit his lips, chewing on words and thoughts. "I don't believe in what does not exist."

"Are you saying that the Law of Moses doesn't exist?"

"It's an invention of the Christians," he went on. "From their Christ-centric worldview they have fashioned something equivalent for Jews. But for Jews, only the Law of God exists. Moses transmitted it, but he is not the author. That is why Jews neither worship Moses nor consider him infallible, nor absolutely saintly. They love and respect him as a great leader, they call him *Moshe Rabbeinu*, "our teacher." But he also was punished when he disobeyed. On the "Jewish Easter," or Pesach, when the story of liberation from Egypt is retold, Moses is never mentioned. The one who frees the people is God."

"You believe in that law, then," Francisco said, in an effort to clear his doubts once and for all.

"In the Law of God."

"Is that the horrible filth that they call practicing Judaism?"

He faced him directly. "Yes, my son, to respect the Law of God as it is written in the sacred texts."

The roar of the sea underscored their solitude on the beach. Francisco studied his father's face, reminiscent of wood, and his wizened fingers as they played with a white mound of sand. They were the face and hands of a just man. Emotion surged through him.

"I want you to teach me, Papá. I want to turn my spirit into a fortress. I want to be who I am, in the image and likeness of the Omnipotent One."

The old man half smiled. "Read the Bible."

"You know I've been doing that since childhood."

"And that's why you immediately understand me."

Francisco sat beside his father, also facing the ocean. Their shoulders touched. They felt an intimate delight at their formalized alliance. The father glowed with an ineffable pride: the quality of his seed. The son was overcome by an intense emotion: the integrity of his ancestry. At last, they had been able to transmit the tenacious secret. At last they trusted each other completely.

"Now I'm not alone anymore, Papá." He reached out his hands toward the dark blue that glittered with shards of silver, then up, toward the seagulls as they rode invisible currents. "I belong to a family full of poets, princes, and saints. My family is innumerable."

"You belong to the ancient House of Israel, to the long-suffering House of Israel, which is also the House of Jesus, of Paul, of the apostles."

"My wretched blood is the same as theirs. As worthy as theirs."

"The same blood as Jesus, as Paul, as the apostles. They cannot digest that. They don't want to see it. They draw a hallucinated line between the Jews whom they venerate and the Jews whom they scorn and exterminate."

"The *Scrutinium* tries to expand that border." Francisco could not shake off the shoddiness of the libel. "Saulo and Pablo are portrayed as close, yet very different. The apostle Saint Paul would have been Rabbi Saulo before conversion, as Pablo de Santamaría had been the Jew Solomon ha-Levi. Ha-Levi forgot his origins. His ambition drove him to indignities, Papá."

"His fear, my son," his father corrected him. "Fear is worse than death. I have felt that fear."

His son nodded sorrowfully. That was the most painful of subjects.

"Out of fear, I abjured, wept, lied, confessed," his father murmured. "My being disintegrated. I said what they ordered me to say."

"Papá, please tell me, at what moment did you return to the Catholic faith?"

He opened his hands, suddenly surprised, and then stroked his beard. "You ask if I returned—but was there ever a time when I was part of it? For Catholics, it's enough to receive baptism. That's why they do it by force. That kind of proselytizing is easy. But those who are baptized against their will do not believe in their hearts. It's as if someone asked you to swear your loyalty to someone but someone else does it for you, then they call you a traitor for not being loyal to the person you never swore to be loyal to—an incongruence that might make one smile, were it not so tragic."

"Baptism doesn't bestow grace?"

"Grace comes with faith. My son, I have often wished to have faith in the dogma of the church, so as to no longer be persecuted. You have seen me in services and processions. It isn't always only to pretend. I concentrate, listen, pray, try to feel. But I only see a ceremony that is not my own."

"Would you stop being Jewish, Papá?"

"Of course I would! Like so many. Like millions, sick and tired of being the outcasts of the world. But I would also have to stop being who I am. Forget my parents, my past, the iron key."

"It's not only religion, then."

"It is something deeper."

"What?"

"I'm not able to capture it. History, perhaps. Or a common destiny."

"Jews are the people of the sacred texts, of the book," Francisco mused. "History is a book, is the written word—what a paradox, no? Who else other than Jews has cultivated so much history, and, at the same time, been so stubbornly punished for it?"

After a while, Diego murmured, "It is not easy to be Jewish, just as it isn't easy to walk the path of virtue. Not only that, it is not permitted to be Jewish."

"And so?"

"So you either convert, in your heart—"

"The heart won't respond to will," Francisco broke in, "you just finished saying that."

"—or you pretend. That is what I do."

"Representation, appearance. We are the same as them, or worse." He shook his head in sorrow. "How sad, how unworthy of us, Papá."

"They force us to be false."

"We accept being false."

"Yes."

"Is there no other possibility?"

"There is not. We are captives in an indestructible prison. There is no alternative."

The time had come to leave. A gray curtain of clouds swelled over the horizon. The air had grown cool and the waves were advancing on the shore.

"It's hard for me to resign myself," Francisco thought. "I sense that another path exists, and that it's very narrow, very difficult. I sense that I will break the prison walls."

83

"*A new adversary of the Holy Office is rising cautiously,*" thinks Inquisitor Andrés Juan Gaitán in his austere room. *It is more dangerous because it links its vigor to a devastating political capacity. It was born to defend the true religion from Protestant assault, but it is maneuvering to hold all the power of the church. This is the Society of Jesus.*

They bring a subtle ambivalence: aggression and piety. The Jesuits, in the brief period of their existence, have already gained the stature of other religious orders. Not satisfied with such success, they often shamelessly report on the weaknesses and incompetence of Dominicans, Franciscans, Mercedarians, and Augustinians, to indirectly demonstrate their own superiority. Their lack of modesty has allowed them to advance on all fronts. They have dazzled Rome and Madrid. Their next target, which they will approach with twisted strategies, is the Holy Office. I must discuss this point with my colleagues. But even with them, I must be prudent. I can't let them think that I'm driven by spurious interests.

One example of the twisted method they use to gain ground is their approach to Indians. They insist on pious techniques and claim to convert more swiftly and effectively. They're rascals. First of all, they lack originality, because since the time of Bartolomé de las Casas, many priests have advocated for the natives. Secondly, their objective isn't limited to conversion, but, rather, leveraging it to build power. The settlement of Indians that they're building proves it; they want to form actual republics under their exclusive jurisdiction. With the reasoning that the Indian overseers are cruel and greedy, they've excluded the presence of others. They're Indian overseers in monks' robes! And very ambitious.

Now they're closing in on Lima; the viceroy, the archbishop, and the Inquisition are supposed to bow to them. I say this because, on one side, the Jesuit republic grows in Paraguay, with thousands of Guaraní Indians at their service. On the other side, the Jesuit republic of Chile includes thousands of Arauco Indians. Those two blocks will suffocate us. This is as obvious as the sun, impossible to see due to its own intensity. The Jesuits are sanctimonious enough to present the successes of their enterprise as victories for the faith. And they are believed.

It goes without saying that they seek to undermine the authority of the Holy Office. They deny the importance of surveilling New Christians, claim that Jewish practices won't unsettle the church, and insist on prioritizing indigenous conversions.

But the Holy Office's job is not to evangelize, but to prevent poisons from entering the faith. They place no importance in that. They are demons.

84

Who didn't know that the cynical war between various jurisdictions of the Viceroyalty—civil power, ecclesiastic power, the Holy Office, religious orders—also included battles within the jurisdictions themselves? The rule—a healthy but impotent one—was to unite all these varying tendencies under the authority of the king, and faith in Christ. But the archbishop stuck his nose into everything, and Lima's councilmen, whose charge was strictly municipal, tried to sniff around the privacy of monasteries, Inquisition prisons, and the business of the viceroy. The Royal Court, tasked with justice, saw itself as interfered with, bought off, and mocked, and, as a result, was spurred to return those attentions with interferences, bribes, and mockery of its own. Even the University of San Marcos, the pride of the Viceroyalty, was a prisoner of conflicts and a provoker of the same.

This constant battle was suddenly interrupted. The author of the unexpected miracle was not a local figure, but, rather, a Dutch Protestant, Joris van Spilbergen. He was about to invade Peru and set off an apocalypse.

Francisco could not believe the legend being spread about his intelligence and cruelty. He was described as a herald of the devil.

His father received instructions to evacuate the chronically ill from the hospital, to make room for those who would soon be wounded in battle. Francisco, Joaquín del Pilar, and other students, graduates, and doctors of Lima were summoned to Callao to support the cause. Joris van Spilbergen was a pirate ready to turn the City of Kings into ash.

A sudden solidarity swept through Lima like a new wind. Spaniards, Creoles, Indians, mestizos, mulattoes, black people, laypeople, noblemen, artisans, farmers, merchants, and clergymen put aside their quarrels to unite against the common enemy.

Holland, after having battled for more than forty years to gain its independence, had not ended its conflict with Spain. The terms of their treaty were only honored in Europe, not on the high seas, where the Dutch attempted to gain territories and fortunes. The war continued in the nearby islands called the Moluccas, and now seemed to be spreading.

In effect, the Dutch had decided to exploit the route to Asia through the Strait of Magellan. So they formed a squadron with plentiful troops and placed Joris van Spilbergen at the helm. Their ships crossed the Atlantic without troubles, arrived at the Brazilian coast, and then went south; they had to cross the strait before the winter winds arrived. The adventure was extremely dangerous, and one of the ships deserted. The admiral said, "We have orders to cross the Strait of Magellan and I have no other path. Our ships may not separate." The squadron entered the labyrinth of ice. The canals were white tombs, whistling with wind that presaged death. Waves broke against the ivory walls and avalanches of foam obscured the zigzagging path. The ships could break against the blocks of ice or run aground against the rocks. The route was deceiving; one day they thought they were back at the entrance of the strait. Finally, the five abused ships reunited in the bay on the other side, after escaping rough waters and currents that could have sunk them.

Meanwhile, Spanish spies in Holland had learned of this intrusive mission and reported it to Madrid. The marquis of Montesclaros placed his nephew Rodrigo de Mendoza at the helm of the Viceroyal fleet. He was a young, brave man, though inexperienced. The viceroy's nepotism did not cede even in the face of such a significant threat.

The Dutch headed north, keeping the Chilean coast in sight. They arrived in Valparaíso and panic ensued. Spilbergen disembarked with two hundred men and a piece of artillery. The Spanish set fire to their own homes as the Dutch torched them from another direction. There was more damage and screaming than killing. In the mist of twilight, after provisioning themselves to their satisfaction, the invaders embarked to charge against the fortifications of Callao as soon as possible in order to reach Lima and the coveted gold shipped to Spanish ports.

The viceroy's nephew decided to confront the Protestant pirates on the high seas. He would surprise them; he had reasons not to trust the army, whose soldiers were better prepared for a carnival parade than for an actual battle.

As the confrontation was imminent, the night in Callao was sleepless and tense. More than two thousand men were assigned to posts armed with guns, swords, and knives to fend off the intruders.

Francisco was given a spear and a leather shield. He grasped one in each hand, feeling ridiculous. Like him, the majority of his neighbors had no real knowledge of how to wield such weapons. The officials in charge of artillery were even worse, as they had just learned of the deterioration of their cannons. Despair stirred so much rage that some men took it out on the cannons, kicking them to pieces.

Servants placed torches in even the most remote posts, to make the pirates think there were more people than there actually were. The clergymen, in their extreme nervousness, moved through the groups giving blessings; they had slandered the Protestants so much that the least they now expected was to be eaten alive as soon as the enemy took hold of the port. The soldiers were to spread out along the coast and monitor neighbors to prevent desertions. One high-ranking officer on horseback issued curt orders; it was Lorenzo Valdés.

The cold soaked into people's bones. Soup cooked in pots over scattered fires. The inexperienced defenders approached the warmth, discussing the news. The viceroy's nephew was an irresponsible lad to some, and an implacable force to others.

"The Dutch will devour him," one man proclaimed, as he noisily sipped broth from a mug.

"That's not true. He'll capture the Dutchman and shove his balls into his mouth!" another man answered.

"I agree," a third man said, extending his mug toward an enslaved man ladling out broth. "The pirates won't dare set foot on this land. Look at all these burning torches. They know that we're thousands of soldiers."

The skeptical neighbor laughed loudly. "Thousands of soldiers? A few, no more. We're thousands of neighbors without any training. That's what we are."

"Might you be Portuguese?" the young man said angrily.

"No. Why would you accuse me of that? Is there something wrong with my pronunciation of Spanish?"

Francisco felt uncomfortable. His father, the Portuguese doctor, was right at this moment a selfless guard who would attend to these sons of bitches if they needed it.

"The Portuguese are happy to see these provocations from Holland."

"I'm not happy about this, young man!" he reproached emphatically. "And I'm not Portuguese. Also, I beg you not to be stupid or confuse things."

"I won't permit you to—"

"You're too young to give me permission. I'm telling you not to confuse matters." He pointed at him with his mug, eyes flashing. "The Portuguese are one thing, and Portuguese Jews are another." He emphasized the word "Jews."

The chorus went silent before the man's authority. Only distant voices and the neighs of horses could be heard.

"Portuguese Jews are the ones who would be happy," he said after a while. "Protestants are their allies in hating our faith."

Francisco couldn't keep drinking his ration. He wanted to hurl it in the man's face.

"All Portuguese people are Jews," someone said.

"Not all."

"I don't know a single one who isn't."

Francisco turned toward the sound of approaching hoofs. It was Lorenzo. He waved at him.

"None of this loitering! Let's go!" the handsome rider scolded. "Each man to his place!"

The men had their mugs refilled and scattered along the walls.

"How are you?" Lorenzo said, happy to see his old friend's spear and shield in the dim firelight.

"Bad." Francisco forced a smile.

"Are you afraid, then?"

"I'd do better in the hospital, preparing instruments. I don't know what to do with these weapons."

"It's true that they don't look natural on you," Lorenzo said, laughing.

"But orders are orders."

"That's right," he said, stroking his horse's neck. "A doctor should wield weapons, too. Didn't your father take part in security back in Ibatín?"

"That's true."

"You're security in Callao." He adjusted his helmet. "Speaking of which, how is he?"

Francisco hung his head. Lorenzo regretted the question.

"Forgive me."

"Nothing to forgive. He's sick and depressed. He's at the hospital. That's his post. He's going to attend to the wounded."

"If there are any."

"You don't think there will be?"

"Look at this row of torches. Do you think a few pirates are going to disembark to be slaughtered by thousands of soldiers?"

"They aren't all soldiers."

"The Dutch don't know that." He pulled on his reins. "Goodbye, Francisco!"

"Goodbye."

Francisco walked toward the rampart and sat down. He put down his weapons, loosened his belt, and curled up under his hat and cloak.

He needed to get some sleep. A new accusation fluttered inside him: "Portuguese." Until this night, he'd had to prove a lack of wretched Jewish blood; now he also had to avoid being suspected of Portuguese nationality. A story without end.

—✻—

The wait stretched on.

The following afternoon, the feared sails appeared on the horizon, resembling fangs. They were harnessing a good wind and were approaching Callao. Spilbergen, with the devil's help, knew the port's defenders were tired and inexperienced. And he believed that his four hundred privateers would be enough to break the barriers, defeat the few good soldiers, and take unprecedented spoils.

Rodrigo de Mendoza leapt to his ship and ordered an attack at sea. He rushed toward the intruders. Meanwhile, on land, terror prevailed. Officers galloped between posts, pushing the reluctant to their stations. The artillerymen sweat in fruitless attempts to repair the cannons. Slaves were forced to the beach so that their chests might be the first in the line of fire. Francisco stood beside other defenders armed with shields and knives.

The first bombardment erupted near Cerro Azul. The responding barrage unleashed enormous clouds of smoke. Between spheres of ash, fire flashed and cannonballs flew. Many men fell to the sea. From land, it was impossible to help, or even differentiate between flags amid the sooty foam. Nevertheless, as the afternoon deepened into twilight, the battle was clearly closing in on the port. The explosions were becoming louder, and the smell of gunpowder sharpened.

Mendoza, dirtied by soot and blood, thought he understood Spilbergen's ploy: to leverage oncoming darkness to reach the shore. He ordered his troops to pursue him relentlessly. They fired several cannonballs, but the growing dark kept him from seeing his own tragic error. He was not attacking a Dutch ship, but one of his own, which was sinking in the midst of a horrific uproar.

The more experienced Spilbergen devoted himself to gathering his men and pointing his prow toward a refuge he'd already set up in a rocky area of San Lorenzo Island, where he could heal the wounded and repair his squadron.

The Dutch ships disturbed the peace again three days later. Their fast advance caused a harried commotion. Several clergymen held up images of saints, carrying them on platforms to the shore so they might better intervene on behalf of mortals. The last weapons were distributed; this time Francisco was given a gun.

"I had a spear and leather shield," he said.

"Take this and don't complain, damn it!" The angry officer pushed him toward the rampart as he handed another gun to the next citizen.

The soldiers used their swords to strike black people and Indians who resisted lining up on the shore to offer their lives. The admiral of the fleet had not even reached the dock when a cannon thundered and a projectile flew over the gathered people, destroying a few outlying huts. Panic broke out. It was too late to keep them out at sea. Prayers, blessings, and confessions rose with more strength than the clouds of gunpowder.

Spilbergen, however, had not planned to fight a war on land; he was outnumbered. So he bid them farewell with a burst of laughter, like a good offspring of Satan.

Equal parts defeat and victory, the viceroy drew lessons from these events; he went about perfecting his absurd fleet and fixing the artillery; war should not only be fought against internal competitors, but also against enemies in Spain who now revealed their true ambitions.

Gaitán went even further. He opined that the Dutch incursion not only came from his own greed or hatred of the church, but also from the role of Portuguese Jews, or Marranos. Hadn't the Dutch attacked in Brazil and, after a few successes, allowed the Jews to reopen their synagogues? It was, obviously, a conspiracy. Therefore, it was not enough to repel sporadic attacks or—as the inefficient viceroy was doing—improve fleets and artillery, it was urgent to uncover, persecute, and exterminate the internal enemy.

"The internal enemy's name is Marrano," Gaitán said.

85

"A fine thing they've done to me!" Montesclaros reflected months later, on the galleon taking him back to Spain. While I was fending off Spilbergen, Felipe III was designating my successor. What an injustice! That's how loyal functionaries are rewarded. I owe this to the Holy Office, which has been sabotaging me from day one.

My successor is called Francisco de Borja y Aragón, Count of Mayalde. He comes from a family plagued by scandals and illicit unions, including with Moors and Jews. That family had the good fortune to produce a man like San Francisco Borja, whose saintliness disguised the stains. My successor sold his testicles to marry the daughter of the fourth prince of Squillace and take on that undeserved title. Now that good-for-nothing makes people call him "the Prince of Squillace."

My sense is that this so-called prince arranged this post so he could come have fun in Peru, and to fill his coffers, without considering the conflicts that reign over here. A shining ceremonial sword hangs from his belt, but his hand must tremble before touching any weapon. I knew that when Spilbergen and his ships were far away, he and his entourage of eighty-four servants were hidden in Guayaquil, awaiting more security. He didn't want to enter Lima until the defenses I'd been preparing were ready.

Those who accuse me of nepotism should watch this one, too. They say that he even imitates me: that he's a poet. He boasts of mastering the art of *humor. He's one of those men who thinks that making a man laugh is the same as disarming him, and making a woman laugh is like getting her to the bedroom. Idiot.*

As soon as he disembarked in Callao, an imaginative and obsequious local author wanted to gain favor by praising his lineage. His name is Pedro Mejía de Ovando and the work is called La Ovandina. *As the new viceroy showed no interest in offering any compensation, the poet in question exacted revenge by including, in his written lineage, the names of Moors and Jews. This denunciation upset the inquisitors Francisco Verdugo and Andrés Juan Gaitán, who immediately prohibited the text. It was the first stumble, and surely there will be more, and even better ones.*

The defenses I had worked on seemed adequate to him, but he disliked their cost. He wanted to please Madrid by sending more funds than the ample amount I'd been sending, keeping a fat portion for himself. But the maintenance of troops and squadrons demands many pesos, because the sails and hulls of ships deteriorate in the damp air and briny waters. The panic set off by the Dutch attack has translated into an emigration to towns further from the coast.

Why bother thinking about this Prince of Squillace, who will soon be drowning in problems? The Holy Office will make his life impossible, as they did mine. I need to turn my mind to the trial of residence awaiting me in Madrid. They're ungrateful shitheads—my favors were never enough for them. Luckily, trials of residence cause little more than the anxiety of the trial itself. The verdict and sentence are delayed, diluted, and forgotten. It's enough to have good friends in the corrupt court.

86

The tavern near the university shook with laughter, liquor, and tangy stews. Lorenzo Valdés, Joaquín del Pilar, and Francisco had begun meeting up there. Lorenzo liked to pinch the serving women's bottoms as they moved between tables with steaming bowls, asking his friends not to be effeminate, to do something risky. Then he pushed Francisco to a dark corner where they could talk alone. They were both holding mugs of liquor.

"I'm warning you"—he stared at him in distress—"that bad times are coming for the Portuguese."

Francisco held his gaze. His pupils shone between the smoke and shadows.

"I'm a Creole. I was born in Tucumán."

"Don't play games, not now!" Lorenzo suddenly grew sad. "Something ugly is happening."

"I'm willing to hear you out."

"I think, Francisco"—he swallowed—"here, in Lima, doors will be closed to you. Your father—"

"I know," he broke in.

"Soon you'll graduate and have your degree. That's what you wanted to achieve here. After that—"

"What?"

"You go where they won't bother you! That's what you should do."

"Does such a place exist?"

"Lima is a whorehouse. No?"

"You don't like it anymore?"

Lorenzo grasped his arm even harder. "When Spilbergen attacked, you felt uncomfortable holding a spear. Are you going to feel comfortable under suspicion and slander? Here, intrigue is people's daily bread."

"I have no stains. And I am not involved in intrigues."

"You're trying to convince me? I'm not your enemy." His accusatory index finger pointed around the room. "On the other hand, many of those who are now drinking with us, tomorrow would celebrate your sentencing."

"Should I leave this city?" Rage rose inside him. "Should I flee tonight?"

"I'm worried about everything being said about the Portuguese: that they called on Spilbergen to come here, that they're traitors and betrayers, that they're all Marranos."

Francisco drained his cup. "Where can I go? To Córdoba?"

"Would you return to Córdoba?"

"No."

"I agree with you."

"Panama? Mexico? Havana? Cartagena? Madrid?"

"You don't have to decide right this moment."

"Is there a favorable place? Do you know of any remote arcadias?"

Lorenzo pressed his lips together and patted his friend's back affectionately. "It must exist."

"In Pliny—"

"Where?"

"In the books written by Pliny. There are monsters with backward feet and teeth in their abdomens."

"They say they've been seen in the south," Lorenzo said, laughing, "in the land of the Arauco Indians."

"Talk about imagination!"

"Seriously. The Jesuit Luis de Valdivia has dazzled the new viceroy with tales of Chile." Lorenzo raised his own mug of liquor. "You see? There you have an excellent place."

Francisco felt something important taking shape in his spirit. Might Chile be where he reached his zenith?

BOOK FOUR

NUMBERS

CHILE, BRIEF ARCADIA

87

Papá taught me more medicine than those stuck-up university professors. We reread the classics and experimented with indigenous recipes, which often led to surprising results. He engaged me with the discoveries of an attentive clinical exam and demonstrated the importance of carefully documenting the developments of each person's illness. I'll never forget his analogy between the human body and a temple. He said that professionals should approach the human body with devotion. So many enigmas dwell in its compressed space that all the wise men in the universe are not enough to decipher them. That machine composed of bones, nerves, muscles, and humors is the visible seat of the spirit, with which it is mysteriously interwoven. The machine's imbalances alter the spirit, and vice versa. Just as a temple is constructed from materials found in all buildings, the body is made of elements that also give life to animals or plants. But it contains something that doesn't exist in animals or plants. To harm it is to profane it. The body is, and at the same time reflects, an unfathomable mystery. No two bodies are identical, just as there are no identical people. Though people's similarities are infinite, so, too, are their differences. A good doctor sees similarities between one body and what he's learned from another, but he should never forget that each human being has a quota of singularity that must be recognized and respected. Each individual is unique. To care for a person's integrity is a hymn of gratitude. To torture or kill someone is blasphemy. It is to barge into a temple, knock down the altar, dirty the floor, break the walls, and let scoundrels ransack what's left. It mocks God.

Our discussions of medicine frequently ended on topics involving Judaism. He acquainted me with the opinions of Philo of Alexandria and Maimonides regarding the dietary rules observed by Jews when not suffering persecution. He taught me the Hebrew alphabet on paper that he later burned. He also taught me about the feast days and their meanings.

From Friday afternoon on, we'd prepare to welcome Saturday; it was a secret we shared in jubilant complicity. For us, it was a celebration. In the trunk, we kept clean clothes that we wrinkled as a form of disguise, in case an informer intruded on us, and a white tablecloth with an old stain. We prepared different dishes using quail, duck, or chicken, always well seasoned, with side dishes of fava beans, cooked onion, olives, and squash, and dried fruit or a sweet pudding for dessert. The hut was no different in appearance, but it bore an air of dignity. Saturday, my father always said, is a queen who visits the home of every Jew; she enters with her tulle, invisible gems, perfume of flowering valleys, and harp's melodies. The candelabra exudes energy as its arms transform into tall torches. For six days, one is a scorned Jew who has to flee, hide, or disguise himself to survive. On Saturdays, one rises to the heights of a prince. A man can rest as God rested, and celebrate as God celebrated.

If a familiar of the Inquisition had broken down the door, his eyes would have seen nothing different: father and son ate at a table with the same dinnerware as always, a few books open around them, as was also their custom. These everyday appearances glossed over the reality that father and son were enjoying a feast because they had spoken the blessing in a low voice—so that the ears in the walls might not hear—and they ate with the elegance of a banquet, hearts happy, conversing about the sacred texts the Lord had placed at the feet of Sinai.

Saturday night was glorious. Intimate, secret, calm, and brilliant. Before we got up, Papá would suggest that I not ignore my circumstances. We were Marranos, that is to say, flesh for tormentors. The following day we'd have to don our disguises again. I therefore had the obligation to take care of myself, so that the temple of my body might not be profaned.

On those nights of tranquil joy, we studied the strange privilege—and obligations—involved in directly receiving the infallible *word*. We reflected on envy, and specifically on the enormous fear produced by the possession of that *word*. It was like holding dominion over lightning. That *word* had been taught to Jews in a systematic matter since the ancient times of Ezra the Scribe. Each week, an excerpt was read so that in the turn of the year, the whole text would be perused. But the rabbi was not the only one who read it: the faithful themselves rose in the synagogue and took out the sacred rolls, opened them, studied the tidy Hebrew characters, and enunciated the resonant words.

"That's why I created the academy in the orange grove. Study is our obsession."

We had fun together, doing acrobatics with the texts; one of us said a few lines from memory, and the other found them in the appropriate book. My father liked to recite the psalms. I preferred the prophets, because those pages catalogue the virtues and miseries of humanity.

"Francisco, do not repeat my horrible path," he often insisted.

In the final weeks of his life he stayed in bed. His feet hurt, and his lung condition worsened; he had never completely recovered from the water torture. His life was slowly coming to an end.

One afternoon, his trembling hand stroked the brocaded case and he said, "This key symbolizes the hope of return—perhaps it also symbolizes something even stronger: hope. Simply that."

He kissed the case and gave it to me. Then his index finger ran over the shelves, indistinct in the dim light. With his savings he had kept on endlessly buying books. He had formed another respectable library, with a scope not inferior to the one confiscated in Córdoba. He had recovered several of his most beloved authors. There were Hippocrates, Galen, Horace, Pliny, Vesalius, Cicero. He had also included *Treasury of True Surgery, General Antidotes, Treatise of the Drugs and Medicine of the East Indies, Ten Privileges for Pregnant Women*, and a medical dictionary. Along with these stood treatises on laws, the qualities of stones, history, and Christian theology. One long stretch was occupied by works of literature, among them Lope de Vega's comedies.

"They're yours," he said.

Finally, he pointed at the *Scrutinium Scripturarum* by Pablo de Santamaría.

"I bought that for you, so you may have the pleasure of refuting it. But do it mentally—don't write it down. That could get you burned alive."

His breathing worsened. I adjusted his pillows and added mine to his bed. This did not bring relief. His skin became discolored; his lips and tongue were dry. I offered him a spoonful of water. Even the whites of his eyes darkened.

He was dying. He pressed my hand, clearly tormented by suffocation. He wanted to tell me something. I brought my ear to his indigo lips. He mentioned Diego, Felipa, Isabel. And I promised to search for them; my sisters were still in the convent in Córdoba and were surely all right.

I went to refresh the herbs boiling in the pot. In truth, I did so to dry my tears, so he would not see my devastation.

With the little breath he had left, he managed to smile. It was a strange, profound smile. He inhaled for every word, solemnly uttering, "You remember?—*Shema Israel . . . Adonai . . . Eloheinu . . . Adonai Echad.*"

He gave up, the effort too great. He closed his eyes. I dampened his lips and tongue. I fanned him. His pain agonized me.

He felt around the edge of his bed until he found my hand, and stroked it.

"Take care of yourself—my son."

Those were his last words. His head was blue, his eyelids swollen. His accelerated breathing ceased. His gaze was immobile, seeming startled by an object hanging by the door. The shameful sanbenito.

I closed his eyes and removed a few pillows. His skin began to thin and he seemed to sleep. I let out sobs. In absolute privacy, without restraint of any kind, I could shake, gasp, let out moans, and bathe in a river of tears. Later, relieved by the release, I whispered, "Now you can relax, Papá. Spies and tormentors won't persecute you anymore. God knows you were good. God knows that Diego Núñez da Silva has been one of the righteous of Israel."

I washed my face and paced the room. Papá had died as a Jew, but he'd had to pretend otherwise. His wake and burial would have to follow the norms of his disguise. It would be very suspicious that he had not confessed before dying, or received the oil of last rites. He had died, but the farce to which he was condemned had not.

I left his head uncovered, arranged his blankets as if he were asleep, and went in search of a priest. My pain, on the other hand, required no impossible containment; the tears that fall for a dead father are no different than the ones that fall for a dying one. The priest was impressed by my face. I said that my father was suffering intense cardiac pain and implored him to hurry. I made him run through the black streets. The priest, in his agitation, shouted words of comfort.

When he faced the corpse, he looked at me, bewildered, and I cried again, this time with no reservation at all. The ceremonies that followed went well, under the attentive gaze of witnesses: a couple of barbers, the inflexible pharmacist from the hospital, the frustrated priest, and two gravediggers.

—◆◆◆—

The assistant to Sergeant Jerónimo Espinosa receives an order in Concepción when charged with the prisoner: he should enter Santiago de Chile under the cover of night so that the presence of the captive—a famous man in that city—does not generate turmoil.

And so he waits for the shadows to gather. In an hour, he'll be free of this complicated mission.

Francisco Maldonado da Silva rides at his side. He is an unusual prisoner. His incredible elegance unsettles those around him.

88

My father appeared in my dreams, wearing his denigrating sanbenito. He walked jerkily and dragged his burned feet. Fragments of Ibatín and Córdoba floated by, and his brutal arrest occurred again, along with Brother Bartolomé's condoned looting of our home, escorted by the sheep-like cat, and the whipping of heroic Luis.

The only person in whom I could confide, in those days, was Joaquín del Pilar. He listened patiently. A few weeks later, he proposed to relieve my pain with a visit to people whose suffering exceeded mine.

"The pain of others will calm your own. Also, a good doctor should see, up close, the most punished people of the world."

Then he told me that his family had also had the help of a black couple. Joaquín loved them dearly because they had played with him, and cared for him when his father died suddenly. One day, the woman cut her finger deeply while cooking, but felt no pain. That privilege was her doom—she was diagnosed with leprosy. The medical council sent a team to investigate and discovered that her husband had already contracted the disease, though he had been keeping it secret. Both were immediately exiled. They were not considered bearers of a pestilence, but rather as living pestilence. They were pushed at spear point toward the neighborhood of outcasts. Lepers had to stay isolated in one section of Lima, the most miserable part, until they died. Even their corpses would never leave.

Joaquín suggested I help him with amputations and treatments.

"Hippocrates lives in that neighborhood," he assured me. "Not in boring readings."

My grief was so intense that I didn't have the energy to either accept or reject the offer. I let myself be pulled along.

We crossed the stone bridge with its proud turrets. Instead of heading in the direction of the fragrant Alameda, we turned toward the lepers' enclosure in the neighborhood of San Lázaro. From afar, I could smell the anguished odor. As we entered, I saw that all the lepers were black. They were suffering from the oldest of illnesses; they were morbid proof of divine rage.

"Do you know why they are the castigated ones?" asked Joaquín.

"Bishop Trejo y Sanabria explained to me, a long time ago, that Noah cursed the descendants of his insolent son, Ham."

"Ham the black man," Joaquín mused. "'May his seed serve the seed of Shem and Japheth.' From there comes the rationale for justifying slavery, of course. I've heard that in several sermons."

"That's the explanation that eases the conscience of slave traders."

"You don't consider it valid, then?"

"The Bible is full of curses and blessings," I stammered. "Sometimes they contradict each other."

"Sometimes they're used to support whatever is convenient. But wasn't slavery enough of a plague, to then impose leprosy on top of that? I'm asking you this without ulterior motives. I don't have the answer."

"I don't either, Joaquín. God is omnipotent and our small brains barely register the experiences of a brief life."

"Do you smell the stink?" He inhaled deeply. "It's like hell. Are you willing to keep going?"

"I am willing," I said, indifferently. "We might even be infected."

"It's been half a century since lepers appeared and were piled into this pigsty. It's strange that in all that time not a single white person has contracted the disease."

"It could still happen."

The crowding of huts barely left room for narrow alleys through which dirty drainage ditches ran. A few healthy-seeming children rushed toward us. We were a rare visit. From peripheral corners, men and women poked their heads out, wearing once-white tunics that announced their status as lepers, as law required. A woman ran after a boy who was trying to grab my doublet. She reached out her hand and seized him by the neck; she was missing two fingers and had calcareous stains on her skin. She caught my look of surprise and immediately disappeared. Then we were passed by a man without a nose.

Spectral figures rose out of the walls. A few columns of smoke conveyed the nearby presence of cooking fires and ovens for bread.

We continued toward the chapel. My depression began to mix with consternation. There were limbs reduced to stumps, wounds infected with lice, rotted flesh that left bones exposed to the air. I pushed Joaquín to prevent him from colliding with a legless dwarf approaching quickly on a wheeled plank. From this side and that, people emerged, barely disguising their loss of eyes, fingers, ears, or chin. Their forearms had been subject to spontaneous amputations that belied the body's supposed unity.

Those bodies, like dolls that could be dismantled, also formed families and had children who were healthy, for a while. Their souls needed sustenance, just as all souls did. Priests, however, found no way of offering them the necessary attention. Every once in a while the bravest ones, protected by crosses and rosaries, dared venture to the chapel while a few altar boys, wielding sticks, beat back the scoundrels who tried to touch their habits.

"Brother Martín de Porres has also come," Joaquín remarked.

"He's been reprimanded for it every time. They told him that he could infect the hospital."

"He's kept coming anyway. Wherever there is suffering, he appears."

"He is an exceptional soul," I said.

Joaquín found the man who had brought joy to his childhood. He was seated on a rock beside his shack. He seemed anchored in putrefaction. He had neither hands nor feet. His face had a terrible hole where his nose should have been. He raised his eyes at the sound of his name, and smiled a bright, toothless smile. He reached his stumps out toward Joaquín. My classmate clasped the left one, which had a greenish wound.

"It's infected you again," he lamented.

Around the wound, the skin was hard and cracked, like wood. Joaquín opened his case of instruments to begin the medical treatment.

Shouting arose at the far end of the alley. Suddenly, a torrent of lepers, waving their dirty tunics, lunged toward us, pursued by officers on horseback. Cripples and blind men and women toppled onto us like split trees. The dust cloud barely hid the officers' arms as they ruthlessly beat the lepers they were trampling.

We pressed against the uneven wall of the shack. Two black men without tunics leapt on the terrified lepers. The police were clearly trying to capture them. The agile fugitives saw us and exchanged a glance. Suddenly, I felt the breath of one of them on my cheek and his blade at my throat. We became hostages. The riders stopped, intensely irritated. They were all yelling. The officers' curses blended with the threats of our captors. The blade was hurting me.

"Drop the knives, murderers," a soldier commanded.

"Go away! Go away!" the black men replied, gasping.

One of the officials was Lorenzo Valdés. I later learned that they'd been pursuing the two men all the way from the bridge, where they had stabbed a gentleman. They had tried to disappear among the lepers. Both were strong. In his panic, my captor did not notice that the tip of his blade was cutting my skin. Everything was happening at vertiginous speed, something nicked my ear, and an instant later I felt a dull blow. My captor loosened his grip. I turned, and my ear knocked against the spear that had penetrated his skull. He collapsed, slowly. From his curly hair blood flowed, along with cerebral matter. Joaquín's captor, paralyzed with terror, surrendered.

Lorenzo dismounted.

"Are you all right?" he asked, running a finger over the drops of blood on my neck.

"Yes, thank you."

The uniform gave him an impressive bearing. Even the wine-colored stain on his face seemed to have faded.

"What are you doing here?"

"I'm a doctor now, don't forget that," I explained, making a face.

He clapped my back affectionately. "These murderers were trying to hide among the lepers." He gestured toward the soldiers to remove the corpse.

"It wasn't such a bad idea."

"They thought we wouldn't dare enter—"

"They didn't know you."

He clapped my back again. "Francisco"—he leaned in close to my ear—"I know you're leaving for Santiago de Chile."

"No lack of spies, not for you, eh?"

"Thank God—and my own scruples."

"You think it's a good place for me?"

He smiled. "As long as you don't venture among the Arauco Indians. The Calchaquí Indians who terrorized Ibatín are angels in comparison."

"I'm talking about the city of Santiago."

"They say it's beautiful. And that its women are beautiful."

"Thanks for the information."

"But seriously, now, Francisco." He placed his hand on my shoulder. "You're doing the right thing in leaving. The new viceroy, who demands to be called 'Prince,' gets along famously with the Holy Office. That wonderful relationship will mean—well, you know."

He mounted. His svelte horse pirouetted down the dirty alley and almost knocked down the wall of a shack.

"Be careful!" he exclaimed, trotting into the distance.

———

They take him to the Monastery of San Agustín. They've already reserved a cell equipped with shackles. Francisco offers no resistance. He gives the impression of being in some kind of hurry. He tells the monk who shackles his hands and feet that he is ready to address the authorities.

Jerónimo Espinosa is received in the room by Brother Alonso de Almeida, examiner of the Holy Office, tasked to judge a prisoner's condition and evaluate the theological implications of the circumstances. The notary, who was dragged from his bed, can't stop yawning. The examiner orders the sergeant to turn over the confiscated possessions. The notary scratches his quill against the long parchment; the inventory raises no objections whatsoever. There are two hundred pesos, two shirts, two short trousers, a pillow, a mattress, two sheets, a pincushion, a blanket, quilting, and the monkish robe with no buttons or buttonholes that Francisco will wear in prison.

Jerónimo Espinosa obtains a receipt bearing an official seal, and can return to Concepción. He feels relieved. He has not, of course, imagined that he is on the verge of losing his captive.

89

The day after my arrival in Santiago de Chile, I went to visit its only hospital. It had twelve beds, a few sheets, and no more than five chamber pots for the patients to share among them. The supply of surgical instruments was reduced to three syringes and two thin, sharp knives. I spoke to the barber Juan Flamenco Rodríguez, who encouraged me to present myself for the open position of senior surgeon. He said that there was a great deal of work and a need for a trained professional with university credentials. Juan Flamenco guided me through the dirty nooks and crannies of the building, lamenting as we passed the empty pharmacy, "We don't even have a decent supply of herbs."

I interviewed with the authorities, showed them my diploma from the University of San Marcos, told them of my experiences in the hospitals of Callao and Lima, and even offered to use my own instrument case. They received me with relief and never tired of repeating how fortuitous my arrival had been. Since the governor had founded this hospital, and another to the south in Concepción, they'd never been able to secure a university-trained professional. I would be the first legitimate doctor in Chile. This warm reception gave me strength to bear the discouragements of bureaucracy, which were part and parcel of life throughout the Viceroyalty.

In mid-1618, a special session of the local municipal council took place, during which it was officially stated in writing that the Santiago hospital needed a doctor. An attorney was tasked with gathering the funds for my salary. But I had to wait eight months before the "urgent matter" was discussed again and the plan finally approved for me to serve alongside the barber Juan Flamenco Rodríguez. And even then, the bureaucratic proceedings weren't over; the governor's signature was still needed. The governor spent most of his time combating the Arauco Indians in the south.

Juan Flamenco shrugged. "All we can do is wait." Then he winked at me. "You can't attend to patients in the hospital until the decree is signed, but you can give me advice on difficult cases."

I began to offer my services to the city's residents, backed by a dazzling diploma, replete with seals and signatures. The good women of the city spread word of my merits.

I had the prudence to silence my criticism of any witch doctors, quacks, or enema providers who prospered by promising miraculous cures. My circumstance as a Marrano taught me silence as an essential tactic.

In August of 1619—more than a year had passed!—Governor Lope de Ulloa signed the decree of my appointment. Could I now take charge of the hospital? The unbelievable answer: no. It was necessary for the document to arrive in Santiago, as it had been signed in Concepción. Once received, the bureaucracy then had to create an act of appointment. For this to be completed, the file circulated to several desks over the course of five additional months. I thought it best to forget the decree, the hospital, and my early enthusiasm.

In mid-December, I received, at last, word that the act of my swearing-in was being organized. A special act? Yes, special. A flamboyant affair. A show, as Joaquín del Pilar would have put it. The town council, judiciary branch, and a military regiment were all summoned to appear in full regalia. Officials sat in high-backed chairs beneath the standards of the king. A haughty official read the decree, which ordered, on my behalf, "all the honors, graces, favors, preeminence, liberties, prerogatives, and immunities that should by reason of this office be enjoyed, with no lack of anything whatsoever."

Juan Flamenco smoothed his mustache, smiled mischievously, and said that he'd already reserved a few difficult cases for me.

90

The loud, insistent knocks threatened to beat down the door. I sprang from the bed and approached it, hands extended. The thick night disoriented my steps. I opened, a barely visible hooded figure filled the frame.

"The bishop is in grave condition," he said, gasping.

"I'm coming," I answered.

I dressed rapidly and collected my instrument case. I followed him with long strides. The streets of Santiago were deserted, weakly silvered by the moon. Before we caught sight of the bishop's residence, two more men came out to meet us.

"Faster!" they urged.

We broke into a run. A small group holding lanterns stood guard at the door. They guided me quickly to the prelate's bedroom. Every ten yards there was a monk bearing a lit candle.

"Give him a bloodletting, Doctor! It's urgent. He's dying," his bedside assistant begged.

I sat by the bed and asked for more light. I was before the feared blind bishop of Santiago de Chile, the former inquisitor of Cartagena. His skin was as white as his pillowcase. His sparse ash-colored hair stuck to his sweaty face. I took his pulse, which was weak. I touched his wet forehead. His eyes were half open; in place of pupils, I saw a limestone-colored stain. This helpless man had been a whirl of fury two days earlier, Sunday, hurling lightning bolts at a congregation crouched in fear. During that tempest nobody would have imagined him in bed, anemic, almost felled by his own threats.

"He's already bled a great deal," I said, gesturing with my chin toward the chamber pot on the floor.

"That's not blood from his veins," the assistant ventured. "It's shit."

"Yes, but it's shit with blood in it. Black blood. He's shitting blood, you understand? His pulse is weak and this bodes poorly for another extraction."

"What will you do, then?"

"We'll give him milk to calm his stomach. And we'll place cold cloths on his abdomen."

The assistant did not understand, so I added, "At the same time, we'll warm his chest, arms, and legs."

"It's too cautious a remedy for such serious symptoms," he grumbled.

"That's true," I answered, "but my orders shall be carried out."

The man bowed at the firmness in my voice and left to relay the order. The old prelate began to search for my hand between the folds of the sheet.

"Well done, my son," he whispered. "They do not yet know how to obey."

"They are very worried about your health, Your Eminence."

"As am I . . . I am sick of bloodlettings." He could barely speak.

"You've had a severe intestinal hemorrhage. It's not possible to justify removing more of your blood now."

"What is a . . . severe . . . intestinal hemorrhage like?" he asked, with great effort.

"Black, very black."

"I eliminated black blood, very black? Then I have been purified. Black blood . . . bad blood." He sighed.

"I advise you not to tire yourself, Your Eminence."

"They tire me more, those imbeciles."

His face was that of a man subjected to perpetual tests. His warped forehead was creased at the center, his hirsute eyebrows furrowed. I had heard him preach, red with rage. He had demanded humility and alms at the top of his lungs. He threatened the congregation with illness, drought, and catastrophes. He declared that he'd called for a list to be drawn up of those who had not tithed, to curse them in his prayers. He was a pestle, turning the paralyzed multitude into something worse than powder.

A bedbug bit my wrist. I pulled it off and crushed it against the floor. The prelate interpreted the sounds.

"You just killed a friend," he said.

"A bedbug."

"A saintly friend."

"If Your Eminence will not take offense," I stammered, "I will tell you something."

"Speak."

"I see too many bedbugs in these sheets. They do not help your convalescence. You need repose, relaxation."

His opalescent eyes blinked. His thin lips moved without making a sound as they searched for an adequate response.

"I won't allow them to be removed," he said at last, voice gravelly. "They bite my flesh to clean my soul—and, also—they are God's creatures."

"They do not let you rest."

"They break . . . my dreams. You understand?" he added angrily.

I did not understand. I helped him drink the milk and showed his assistant how to apply the cold cloths on his abdomen as I warmed the rest of his body.

His progress was good. The hemorrhaging ceased. In my subsequent visits, I observed that the austere bishop appreciated my professional authority. One afternoon, out of the blue, he asked whether I would consider getting married. I gave a start; this man saw everything. After my surprise over his untimely curiosity, I confessed that something agitated me: I felt very attracted to the governor's daughter. He studied me for a long time.

"I appreciate your sincerity, Doctor. But I already knew that."

"You were testing me, then?" I smiled uncomfortably.

"We are always being tested before the Lord."

"I still have not had any response from her father, however," I remarked, not measuring my words.

"The governor is her adoptive father."

"But he acts as though he were her real father."

"Yes. I infer that there will be no objections. Even more, he would like for you to join his family—once, of course, you can agree on the dowry."

"I don't have much to offer."

"Don't be stingy! You are a good professional and will earn a great deal. From this, I say your donations to the church will be steady, as for everyone else! I want your hand to be as generous with money as it is skilled with disease."

"I will try, Your Eminence, I will try." Another bedbug bit me and I crushed it with a loud slap.

"Do not murder a saint!" he protested angrily.

"They are virulent."

"Marvelous! They break my dreams."

"I am sorry, but I do not understand, Your Eminence."

His mouth twisted. "They break my dreams. Dreams are like a shell inside of which we are Lucifer's victims. We roll within that deceitful concavity, with nowhere to land. Our voice has nobody to hear it and our strength is less than a gust of air. Inside that shell the devil does whatever he wants to us, according to his whim."

"Not all dreams are nightmares."

"Do you speak of pleasurable dreams? Those are the worst ones!" His white eyes shone like metal spears.

I held my silence.

"Those are the worst. The devil tricks us and makes us fall into sin. Inside that shell we become slaves of temptation—and so, these friends intervene, my only friends, the only ones who know nothing of lust: bedbugs. They bite my flesh and break the shell, break my sleep. They return me to armed vigilance."

"They might wake you in a moment when you're not dreaming," I heard myself venture.

He moved his lips irritably, searching for a response. "We are always dreaming! The devil takes advantage of our rest. When we loosen our muscles and exchange the tension of defense for relaxation, then we are trapped in that impermeable shell and corrupted. In addition, he makes us forget many of our dreams so that we won't be able to clean off their grime. We are hurled into lust, and then wake up believing ourselves clean. When in reality, we are dirtier than pigs."

"Are we guilty of a sin when what happened was against our will?"

His bony hands folded the edge of the blanket. The vertical crease between his brows deepened. "We are guilty of allowing temptation to survive in our spirit. And the devil takes advantage of this. Our fault lies in not combating it with the constancy required. We are sinners, my son. The flesh is weak." He pressed my hand. "For this reason, you should marry soon."

"Thank you, Your Eminence."

"Priests, on the other hand, must persist in our solitary battle. The vow of chastity is not only fulfilled by abstinence, but also in forbidding women from invading our senses."

"Is that possible?"

"The Lord has blessed me with blindness; at least I can no longer see them. But the devil carries them into my dreams. It's horrible." He broke off, frowned, and felt for my hand. "I wish to get up, Doctor. I feel ready."

Before I could respond, he burst out, "Women are worse than Jews and heretics!" He made a sound with his lips, and went still, wanting to hear my response.

"Do you wish to exclude them from the world, Your Eminence?" I finished his thought with sudden unease. This man was subjecting me to a skillful investigation. Did he suspect my origins? Had he sensed my Judaism? His abrupt question about my marriage and his no-less-sudden reference to Jews had me worried.

91

I had seen the beautiful Isabel Otáñez at Sunday Mass. She was in the front row, beside her adoptive parents. I watched her take communion with great devotion. After the service I stood in the center aisle, where dignitaries exited with slow and solemn steps. They wore their best clothes, and their faces combined sanctified nobility with the demonic impulses of exhibitionism. She passed near me and our eyes met. Hers were the nostalgic color of honey. I followed her without realizing that I was mingling with officials. The delicacy of her figure seemed extraordinary to me. A councilman's elbow pushed me out of the regal line so I walked toward the side chapel and tried to reach her in the street. She was surrounded by her family and several arrogant courtiers. To me, she was the most beautiful woman in Chile. I wanted to gaze into her sweet eyes again. I was as maddened as a bee near nectar, not responsible for my actions. I adjusted my shirt, cape, and hat, and smoothed my trim beard and hair. I kept fragments of her body in sight as they flashed in and out of the crowd around her, and approached decisively. Sunlight embellished the embroidery and jewels of the colorful group of women around her. A soldier barred my way so firmly that several heads turned. But fortune wished for her to look at me one more time. Her gaze was brief, but intense. Swollen with absurd hope, I walked slowly away.

Two weeks later an armed messenger appeared at the hospital. He bore a note from Don Cristóbal de la Cerda y Sotomayor, interim governor of Chile, who had recently become my patient. He was inviting me to his residence for a social gathering. I turned the paper between my fingers incredulously. My name was clearly written, and the bulky seal identified the highest authority in the country. Even though I had begun to attend to his ailments, I intuited that this invitation was not professional in nature, but rather implied something with regard to his daughter, Isabel.

The governor had been in the position for a few months. He had ten years of experience in government service, and his ancestors had been part of the glorious legions that had conquered the New World. He had studied jurisprudence at the University of Salamanca, where he was honored with a doctorate. Despite scarce resources, he had advanced public works—buildings for the town hall and the Royal Court, a prison, and an ample stone levee on the Mapocho River.

I arrived at his official residence in the midafternoon. At the door, I presented the note to a group of armed soldiers, two of whom led me inside. I thought of my distant ancestors, who fearfully entered the castle of kings and caliphs only to later be elevated to the status of magnificent princes. They were tormented by fear of illegitimacy. They were commoners; they were Jews. But they offered great services; they had education and good intentions. Some, nevertheless, stirred envy and came to bad ends.

I was guided to the parlor, in which quite a few people were gathered. As I grew accustomed to the dimness I saw a group of women at the far end.

The governor received me with exaggerated gestures of affection, but he did not rise from his armchair, in accordance with his status or comfort. One leg rested on a flat cushion, and his fingers caressed the ends of his armrests as if they were fruits. He had recently been shaved around his fine mustache and small triangular beard. His eyes pierced like needles and missed nothing. I could feel him examining me from head to toe, calculating my assets from my style of dress and my temperament from my bearing. Then he paid attention to my words. The accounts of his wisdom were not false.

Don Cristóbal introduced me to other guests: a toothless theologian, an infantry captain, a cross-eyed mathematician, a fat notary, and a young merchant whose face gave me chills. At the far end of the room were his wife, his radiant daughter Isabel, and a few more ladies. I focused my eyes to devour the image of Isabel and take in the melody of her eyes. The governor asked me to tell him of my studies in San Marcos. I began to speak. A servant approached with a tray of chocolate and assorted sweets. The men standing there, listening to me, concentrated their gazes on my mouth. I thought they made a grotesque ensemble, so I sipped the thick chocolate to stall and consider what to say next.

"The University of San Marcos hierarchically organizes the queen of sciences," I said, addressing the monstrous theologian. "The knowledge that flows from other sources must be reconciled in the great central river, which is knowledge of God. In all the years one is there, those studies are deepened and expanded."

The theologian moved his tongue around his empty mouth; his flaccid cheeks stretched, first one side, then the other. He spoke a few concepts in Latin, with errors in his declensions and terrible pronunciation, to show that he was not surprised. He, too, had studied at a university.

Then I referred to the courses in mathematics. The cross-eyed man seemed enthused. He wanted to know whether emphasis was placed on algebra or on trigonometry. He had studied in Alcalá de Henares.

"Tell us something, too, about the art of notaries. We have an illustrious figure here with us." The governor gestured courteously at the stiff gentleman, who, on hearing himself mentioned, forced a smile and raised up his nose.

"I have no words for that profession."

An uncomfortable silence followed. Don Cristóbal moved his hands in a request for help. A muffled laugh rose from the group of women. The notary squirmed in his chair and adjusted the footstool in front of him. He seemed to be preparing for a violent physical reaction.

"What are you insinuating, Doctor!" he exclaimed in the tone of a challenge.

"That my studies did not include a notary's matters, nothing more."

The hidden laughter rose again. Then I added, "We studied theology, mathematics, anatomy, astrology, chemistry, grammar, logic, herbalism. But not notary, I am sorry to say."

"In Santiago we still have very few professionals," the governor said, to change the subject. "We don't even have a library."

"I brought many books," I remarked.

They stared at me in surprise.

"Approved by the Holy Office?" the theologian asked, in a low, confidential voice.

"Of course," I answered sonorously. "I bought them in Lima." I did not say that I had inherited most of them from my father.

"Many?" The mathematician grew even more cross-eyed.

"Two trunks full—almost two hundred volumes."

"Have they been duly registered?" The notary turned up his nose even further.

"What do you mean?" The question unsettled me.

"I am referring to your passing through customs."

"All of my belongings have been monitored by customs."

"Of course!" the governor intervened, slapping his thigh. "And I celebrate that this city has been enriched by its first library! I am a man who loves and values culture."

"If Your Excellence will permit me," the notary said, coughing, "I would like to note that this is not the first library. I have quite a few books. There are also books in the Dominican, Franciscan, and Jesuit monasteries."

"I have about forty," the theologian remarked.

"I have filled a shelf with twenty-five tomes," the mathematician pointed out.

"How wonderful!" the governor applauded. "In my study, I've only cobbled together ten or fifteen. But those are—how to put it? Collections. A library, my dear friends, consists of at least two trunks." He winked at me.

But his complicity made me uncomfortable. It was too much praise for someone he'd just met. It provoked envy, and I had no need to compete for this title. My books were intimate friends, not some sort of entourage to be put on display for reasons of vanity.

The infantry captain's name was Pedro de Valdivia.

"The same name as the conquistador and founder," I said in amazement.

"I am his son."

I looked at him sympathetically, thinking of Lorenzo Valdés, who would surely come to resemble this man over the years.

On the other hand, who was the merchant? I had seen him somewhere. He said that we would see each other often.

"Why is that?"

"I supply the hospital pharmacy."

"Ah!" I exclaimed in relief. "Then you must bear with my requests; the pharmacy is a desert."

The governor clapped again. "That's what I like! For order and virtue to come to this mad kingdom!"

"I am not responsible for the pharmacy, Your Excellency." The merchant placed his hand on his chest. "I am only its supplier."

"I know that," said the governor, making a calming gesture. "I only wanted to praise the attitude of Doctor Maldonado da Silva."

"Thank you, Your Excellency." I glanced at the corner where the women sat. Were my possibilities with Isabel improving?

"He has demonstrated energy, resolution! We need more of that."

"Your Excellency is a decisive, valiant man," remarked Captain Pedro de Valdivia. "This is why you also value energy in others. You demonstrate this daily. Ever since you arrived among us, it is as if we have been infected with your strength."

"Not everybody thinks this way, my friend."

"There are those who think with meanness."

"That is true," the theologian broke in. His toothless elocution made it difficult to understand him, as did his habit of interspersing his speech with short Latin phrases. "I praise Your Excellency's recent ordinance as the justice of God."

"I admire Your Excellency," the notary put in, "but your justice is not of God. It is secular."

"Of God!" the old man shouted. "The ordinance against the servitude of Indians is like a jubilee."

"Explain yourself," the mathematician said. "I do not connect the ordinance with God, and it doesn't sound like a jubilee to me. Is it correct to use the word 'jubilee' to understand this ordinance?"

An irrepressible impulse set my tongue in motion. "Let us recall what a jubilee is," I said. "It is the divine mandate to reestablish the original conditions of the universe. Leviticus says, 'You will count seven weeks of years, a length of time equivalent to forty-nine years. You will declare the fiftieth year sacred and proclaim freedom for all the residents of Earth. That will be, for you, the year of jubilee. Each will reclaim his property, each will rejoin his clan.'"

The theologian shivered.

"A powerful memory!" Don Cristóbal reveled.

"It is the jubilee of indigenous people! Do you realize?" the theologian crowed. "I am right."

I regretted having spoken more than necessary. A reputation for carrying the Bible in my head would not keep me safe. Excess love for the Bible raised suspicion. Other virtues sufficed to be considered a good Catholic. My father had insisted that I be careful.

"My ordinance regarding the servitude of Indians is not exactly a jubilee," the governor clarified. "It attempts to abolish the personal service that has so often been condemned by the kings of Spain and by the church. But I will be honest with you, do not be afraid. I sense that it will fail. I am a man of the law, and I recognize that an abyss exists between word and deed."

"Why so much pessimism?"

"We wipe our asses with the law here—begging the pardon of the ladies present."

The theologian tried to soften the harsh remark by citing, incorrectly, a maxim against the skeptical philosophy of Zeno.

In the shadowy corner, Isabel Otáñez held a sewing basket as her eyes flowed toward me. I wanted to commit the mad act of going right to her side, to bow deeply and kiss her hand. God restrained me.

When we rose, the silent merchant sidled up to my ear and whispered his name. I was paralyzed. I stared at his severe face, known and unknown at the same time. Almost twenty years had passed.

"I am Marcos Brizuela, of Córdoba," he had said.

Francisco is almost asleep with the heavy shackles on his wrists and ankles when he is startled by the sudden clash of iron. A key turns, the outer bolt slides back, and the door creaks. A hooded figure appears. It is a well-known examiner of the Holy Office, Alonso de Almeida, illuminating himself with a three-pronged candelabra. Francisco knows this man. He is about forty years old, intelligent, and energetic.

At last, the awaited combat will begin.

92

It was still light when we went out to the spacious Plaza de Armas. In front of it loomed the Cathedral of Three Naves. The crests of Santa Lucía Hill grazed the garnet clouds. A couple of nuns hurried past, headed back to their convent. Marcos Brizuela was sullen; almost nothing remained of the tender, expressive boy I had met in Córdoba. We touched on that brief and long-past encounter, and he asked, disinterestedly, as if for the sake of having something to say, about the hiding place behind the house that he had bequeathed to me. I recalled its entrance hidden by thick roots, the warm darkness, and the many hours of solace and fantasy it had provided me. I said that I could never thank him enough for it. He made no comment. Clearly, he was bitter about something.

"We could have run into each other earlier," I lamented. "Santiago is a small city."

"I knew of your arrival," he answered, to my surprise. "I'm on the town council."

"They made you a councilman?"

He raised the brim of his hat and looked at me coldly. "I bought the position."

"Is that better than being elected?"

"Neither better, nor worse. If you buy it, you have money. If you have money, you're respectable."

"What merchandise do you work with, Marcos?"

"All kinds."

I glanced at him questioningly.

"Food, furniture, animals, slaves, belongings."

"Are you doing well?"

"I can't complain."

We walked. When we were boys we had gotten along. Now we were separated by suspicions. I could not recall having inflicted any damage on him, but he behaved as if I were guilty of something. At the corner, I told him that I needed to make my last rounds with patients for the evening.

"I voted for the endowment of your hospital to be improved," he remarked. Was that a reproach?

"Thank you. We lack many things. It's difficult to work without minimal resources."

"I also called for the general attorney to be sanctioned over the matter of your salary," he added, in the same cold tone.

"I don't know what you mean."

"The council placed him in charge of negotiating with citizens regarding their contributions to your salary. That scoundrel made two accounts: a tidy one to show, and a second one to keep hidden. He meant to keep two thirds of your pay."

"What did he say when you uncovered the scheme?"

"What did he say? He offered me half."

"Thief!"

"A functionary, nothing more."

We arrived at the place where we were to separate, only steps away from the rustic door of the hospital, a lamp already lit just beside it. Our faces blurred in the sooty darkness.

"I'd like to see you again," I said. "We have things to talk about."

His jaw clenched.

"I only just learned that you live in Santiago," I added.

"I have to confess, Francisco, that I'd rather avoid you."

I was going to ask him why, though I already suspected the reason. It was horrible.

I turned to the left and bypassed the hospital door, to give myself time to digest the blow. I passed the church of Santo Domingo, then La Merced, and the Jesuit college. The twilight rebuilt the shadows of that marvelous hiding place Marcos had given me.

I returned to the hospital half an hour later, tired and nauseated. Juan Flamenco was waiting for me. We checked the twenty-five patients filling the only room, twelve of them in beds, the rest of them on mats on the floor. When we finished, he invited me to his home for dinner. I accepted, reluctantly.

93

We sat at the table as his wife put their second child, who was two years old, to bed. A servant brought us cheese, bread, radishes, olives, wine, and raisins.

"So the governor invited you to a gathering?" Juan Flamenco tested the blade of his knife with a fingernail. "He's a grateful patient, but be careful."

"Why?"

"He's ambitious. He won't hesitate to use any resource he can to elevate him higher."

"He's already high up."

"He's only interim governor. He wants to be governor. And then something more: viceroy, for example."

"He's a cultured man who likes to gather with illustrious people. He hasn't been sparing." I picked up a slice of cheese. "I'd say that his excessive frankness exempts him from your disqualification."

"Frankness? About what?" He poured wine into both our cups.

"He spoke of his ordinance on the servitude of indigenous people, and predicted that it would fail. He seemed sincere to me."

"He didn't say anything different from what's already known. I assure you that, on the other hand, he'd never let a word escape him about matters that yield him benefits."

"He's that avaricious?"

"Oh! You can't imagine. He is only lavish with public funds. He has an enormous levee built, and buildings, but not a peso leaves his pocket. The bishop can't get him to tithe what he considers an appropriate amount. He's even insinuated threats from the pulpit against 'the sinners who govern us.'"

"How did Don Cristóbal react?"

"He didn't acknowledge the reference. But he started arriving late to functions. A governor can always find excuses, especially when annoyed. The bishop, for his part, was not so much bothered by the stinginess as, I think, by Don Cristóbal's ability to garner gifts, which, to add insult, are never channeled to the church."

"I'm surprised."

"It's all an art. Ever since his time as a judge for the Royal Court he's been deploying methods that, in exchange for his favors, draw off-the-record gifts to his coin purse."

"But he enforced steep penalties on people who attempted to bribe authorities."

"That's exactly it. He's a genius. He enforces the exact opposite of what he does himself. Opposed to all kinds of favors, he's succeeded in getting residents to buy him favors of all kinds."

"What else have you heard?"

"Don Cristóbal never 'finds out' about the bribe; he doesn't see it, smell it, or hear it. It takes place purely between the weeping petitioner and Don Cristóbal's deep purse. Not a word, not a gesture. If the gift was sufficiently generous, the donor will learn of it through the result of his request."

"What a shame," I said.

"You're disappointed?" he asked, pouring more wine.

"Of course."

"Don't exaggerate, Francisco. Isn't it worse in Lima?"

"Perhaps. But I never had access to power there."

"Well, here it's the governor who stands out, there it's the viceroy. They do whatever they like. The man who doesn't take advantage of these privileges isn't seen as honest, but as an idiot. In a society riddled with vice, the honest man isn't seen as a guardian of virtue, but as bothersome, like that story of the annoying garden dog who neither eats nor lets others eat."

"Beautiful world we find ourselves in."

"Let's turn to more interesting matters. Have you seen the governor's daughter again?" Juan Flamenco rubbed his hands together in a conspiratorial gesture.

"Sort of."

"Sort of? You should get married. Marriage will make you smile more often."

"You're a gossip, and hear all kinds of information." I leaned toward him. "Tell me whether she'd accept me as her husband."

"Of course she'd accept you!" He covered a burp with his fist. "Well, I don't know whether she—but her father would."

"Why?"

"Let's see." He pulled the candelabra closer. "First of all, Isabel Otáñez isn't Don Cristóbal's daughter, but his goddaughter. This has points both for and against. For: she doesn't inherit his greed. Against: she doesn't inherit his fortune. You'd be marrying a poor woman."

"That doesn't factor into my decision."

"How selfless of you! But Don Cristóbal would accept you. Why? He's your patient, and he values your culture. A good doctor in his family would bring benefits."

"I can't think of them."

"I, for example, would have been an ideal son-in-law." His lips stretched. "I would have supplied him with all the city gossip, all the underground news. Through me he could have channeled advice to people as to what to give in return for his favor. I also would have served to persuade royal officials and clergymen to grant him more power."

"That isn't even false, but grotesque."

"I'll add a prophecy: he'll skimp on his goddaughter's dowry and make you give more than you have."

"First I have to gain permission for her hand."

"You can take that for granted."

―∞―

Alonso de Almeida stares at the prisoner for several minutes. It's difficult for him to recognize, in this dirty man with long disheveled hair, the doctor who was honored by the nation's authorities. He received praise for his fine manners and knowledge of matters both sacred and profane. But, surely, the excess of profane reading, including heretical texts, has distorted his reason. It is necessary—and possible—to pull him out of his sophisms and make him see the obvious.

This examiner of the Holy Office has plenty of experience; when he faces a sinner, nothing is more effective than an extremely severe rebuke. And so, he prepares to unleash a deafening discourse. He orders the cell door closed, looks Francisco in the eyes, and lets out the first reproach.

94

After the first time I examined Don Cristóbal, a routine clinical exam for his chest pains, he invited me to his study to sample the wine he'd recently received as a gift from an Indian overseer. We sat on low chairs, facing each other. An enslaved woman placed two thick wineglasses and a ceramic bottle on the small walnut table.

"I've been betrayed, Doctor," he said out of the blue.

I stared at him in surprise.

"Would you do me the favor of filling the glasses?" he added. "This blow is the reason for my relapse, I just know it."

I uncorked the slender bottle, releasing the wine's pleasant aroma.

"The viceroy, spurred on by the Jesuits, has appointed a ridiculous old octogenarian to be governor."

"But there was strong support here in Chile for you to continue in the role."

"Yes." He took the glass, gazed at the glimmering wine, and inhaled its scent. "Everyone supports me: the municipalities of Santiago, Concepción, and Chillán; the army generals; the priors of the Franciscan, Mercedarian, Dominican, and Augustinian orders; even our own angry bishop. But it was all useless."

"I don't understand it, then."

"It's easy, my friend—Luis de Valdivia and his Society of Jesus are stronger than the honorable authorities, and stronger than reason."

We sipped for a while. It was a noble product from an excellent vine.

"This Indian overseer, he gave me a very good gift," Don Cristóbal said, smiling. "He's a rascal. Now he'll come asking for favors in exchange."

I held his gaze, and he returned to his earlier subject.

"Do you know what matters to the viceroy?" Don Cristóbal rubbed his nose. "That the defensive war with the Indians continue. Why, when that war is so disastrous? Because it's cheap. I've transmitted the truth, and that was my error. The truth doesn't matter, only people's interests. My failing was one of political perceptiveness. The viceroy doesn't want to put funds into an offensive strike that could control the Arauco Indians once and for all. What's more, the viceroy knows that the Jesuit Luis de Valdivia has ardent protectors in Madrid."

"And they'll replace you with an octogenarian?"

"That's right. He's an old curmudgeon who's been sleeping in Lima for half a century and whom the marquis of Montesclaros often discredited. But since he agrees with the defensive war, the new, irresponsible viceroy has entrusted him with nothing less than the oversight of this godforsaken kingdom."

"What will happen to you, Don Cristóbal?"

"I'll continue in my role in the Royal Court. And I'll laugh at the new governor. We'll see how long his enthusiasm for the defensive war can last. I'll advise him to pop down to the south, to see the devastated forts and chat with the residents of Concepción, La Imperial, Villarrica. He'll piss on himself with fright. The Arauco Indians will only bow before the sword. The Jesuits preach to them in their tongue, but they won't convince them to be subdued or to retreat to reservations. They're not like the Guaraní of Paraguay."

"The focus of the Jesuits, nevertheless, seems praiseworthy," I opined.

The governor raised his eyebrows.

I added, "Indigenous people have been subjected to innumerable abuses, and anyone can understand that they're bitter and furious. A conversion that doesn't rob them of their land or reduce them to servility could change the way they perceive Spaniards."

"I'm surprised that you would think this way."

"Why?"

"Because you're an erudite man, not a naïve one. The Indians are savages, and they don't want us around, not even in their memories. They don't want us. We're intruders. They disdain our order and prefer to keep turning in their own shit."

"They don't see their own reality as shit, Don Cristóbal. That is our opinion."

"Yours as well?"

"In any case, it isn't theirs. There are different points of view."

"But there is only one truth, no?"

"There might be more than one—" As soon as the words had left my mouth, I regretted saying them and wanted to fix my dangerous statement. "They don't recognize our point of view as the true one."

"Ah!" He scratched his double chin. "Then they must learn."

"That's why I was saying that the Jesuits, by preaching in their language, suppressing forced servitude, and blocking military offensives might be able to create a change of heart. If they can show that the king of Spain wants peace, they will end up accepting it. It would be better for them. But until now, the Indians have only received hatred and exploitation."

"You speak like Father Valdivia. It sounds persuasive, but it's false. It's been a decade since this infantile strategy began. There have been parliaments, the release of prisoners, pacts, the dismantling of our advancing positions. And what's happened? They burst into our cities and set fire to several forts. They're cunning! They don't want peace. They want to expel us from Chile. They want to make us disappear."

That was exactly what the Inquisition wanted of Jews. I asked, "Isn't there some point of encounter, of harmony?"

"Either we triumph, or we keep enduring this conflict."

"But they can't make us disappear," I said.

"Of course. And so they choose to bleed us. They trust that, in the long run, they will triumph. That's why they must be subdued, like wild animals being broken in."

"Isn't it possible to convert without humiliating?"

"Look, Francisco, sensible men like you tend toward confusion. The sooner the Indians are crushed the better it will be for everyone." He raised his glass so I could pour him wine. "Do you know what some Indian overseers do to keep their Araucos from escaping? They hold them down, put a clamp on their ankles, and cut off all their toes with an ax."

"That's horrific!"

"The bleeding is stopped with a red-hot iron, you know, an excellent coup de grâce. These actions wouldn't be necessary if the Arauco people were simply defeated as a whole."

I lowered my eyes. Don Cristóbal patted my knee.

"Keep practicing medicine. Never try to be governor."

"Don't worry about that. Not even in my dreams!"

He stood. I followed suit.

"One more thing," he said, smiling indulgently. "I have the vague impression that you've sometimes wished to strike up conversation with my goddaughter, Isabel."

I was disturbed by the abruptness of the suggestion. His head-on approach left no room for an evasive response.

"Yes, Your Excellency." I took a deep breath. "She is a person with whom I'd be pleased to converse."

"Very well. I wanted to tell you that you may count on my permission. At the end of the day you are my doctor, no?"

—⁓—

Francisco listens, mouth agape. The Inquisitorial examiner Alonso de Almeida is vehement. His words punish like whips attacking a disobedient child. He rebukes him for exchanging gold for dross, for producing disappointment and mourning. God, the Virgin, the saints, and the sacred church poured blessings upon him, but instead of thanking them, he disdained them. He urges the prisoner to bow down and repent, urges him to hang his arrogant head, to weep, to tremble.

95

I strolled with Isabel Otáñez in the broad light of afternoon, as befitted the goddaughter of a decent family. Two servants followed us, as a guarantee of modesty. We passed, at a prudent distance, part of Santa Lucía Hill. Along paths dotted with grazing goats were detours to hidden forest alcoves, which were not discussed in honorable conversations as they shrouded the adulterous embraces of harsh Santiago de Chile. The green labyrinth of those slopes brilliantly hid those ardent bodies. The pulpits denounced those sins, so frequent in the mazes of the hill.

She had been born in Seville. She became an orphan at the age of seven, and was adopted by Don Cristóbal and Doña Sebastiana. She told me that they were generous and deserved her unconditional gratitude. Then a shadow passed over her as she told me of the brutal assault to which they fell victim in the Caribbean, attacked by English pirates. The retelling made her shiver, but her emotion only made her more fascinating.

I told her about my childhood in Ibatín, my adolescence in Córdoba, and my younger years in Lima. Our journeys seemed like rivers flowing in search of each other. Hers had begun in Spain, and mine in the Americas. Mine, in reality, had also begun in Spain, generations before, and then made its way to Portugal and, later, Brazil.

Our rivers had wound through rough terrain and traversed many miles to come together in this city.

More strolls followed this one, and they gradually became more frequent. Her soft cheeks made me think of porcelain, and her eyes were always tender, lighting up like stars when she became enthused. I could not let twenty-four hours pass without seeing her, and had to make great efforts to avoid becoming a tiring presence. I'd make excuses to appear at her residence and invite her out for another stroll.

Sometimes we arrived at the shore of the Mapocho River; its waters came from the snow that whitened the nearby mountain range. The wooden barriers built during the thaw had not always been effective, hence the costly levee Don Cristóbal had constructed. From its banks, canals slid out to irrigate the nearby farmhouses. Sometimes we walked all the way to the placid meadow where the Franciscans had built their large monastery. We passed orchards full of fruit trees and cypress. In the adjacent countryside, lilies and Madonna lilies spread out in blankets. Strawberries also abounded. If it wasn't yet too late, Isabel would invite me in to drink chocolate in the parlor, accompanied by her godmother and, sometimes, Don Cristóbal. My encounters with that beautiful woman became an unwavering routine. I started to feel happy in an unprecedented way.

96

A servant ran into the hospital and handed me the note. It was written in a hurried hand, and signed by Marcos Brizuela. He was asking me to come quickly to his home, as his mother had suffered a stroke.

I was welcomed in by two servants who seemed to be keeping watch, and who showed me the way. A frightened woman appeared, with a child in her arms, perhaps his wife. She greeted me with a timid wave and left for a nearby room. I made out a bed in the shadows. The man sitting beside it rose to meet me.

"Mamá just got worse," Marcos said in a low voice. "Maybe you can do something."

I took up a candle and brought it near the bed. In the light I saw the cadaverous body of an old woman. Her eyelids were darkened, her skin was waxy, and her breathing was ragged. I took her pulse and examined her pupils. The symptoms seemed terminal. Her right arm was contracted from a long-ago stroke. Very gently, I tried to extend it, but it was no use. The air leaving her mouth raised her right cheek. This woman's current episode was taking place on an already fragile foundation.

I began to inquire about medical history. Marcos stood behind me. His demure wife stood near us.

"A long time ago she became paralyzed and nearly mute," he said with great effort.

"How many years has it been?"

I heard him take a deep breath. He began to pace the bedroom.

"Eighteen," his wife responded.

I calculated that it had been just before they settled in Chile. I said this aloud.

Marcos paused, blurred by shadows. His chest swelled again. "It was a while after that."

I tried to open the deformed hand. Then I kept on with more medical gestures and thought. I rubbed her temples, felt her carotid arteries, gently moved her head, gauged her temperature.

Marcos's slow pace resembled that of a caged tiger. I suddenly thought he might pounce on my neck. His mother's illness wasn't only stirring sorrow, but his bitterness. Why had he called me? He could have summoned Juan Flamenco. Or one of the doctors without titles. His hostile voice came out full of spines.

"I wanted you to see her," he muttered in a hoarse voice.

I turned in my chair. He was standing behind me again. He placed his hands on my shoulders, hard, leaning his weight on me. This was the puma's pounce—I grew alarmed. His fingers pressed into my flesh.

"That's what happened to her when my father was arrested."

I tried to stand up, but he was stronger than me.

"That's what happened," he said again, jaws tense, forcing me to look at her again.

With my right hand I patted his left arm, which had become a claw biting my shoulder.

"And it was all because of the denunciation your bastard of a father made, Francisco—" He suddenly released me and took a few steps back.

"Marcos!" his wife exclaimed.

My head trembled at the accusation. I turned to stare at them.

"After his horrific arrest, she suffered a stroke," Marcos said. "Apoplexy. Or a seizure. As you like to say, you doctors—words, words!" He waved his hands as if to scare away flies. "She lost consciousness for a week. Several bloodlettings were performed. But she still became a cripple. Paralyzed and mute. Eighteen years! Yes, she managed to move with help, to talk like a baby. My father imprisoned in Lima, and us, here, with Mamá destroyed."

His wife approached in an effort to calm him, but he kept her at bay with a wave of his hand.

"I truly feel what you are saying, Marcos," I murmured, mouth dry, confused, ashamed. "My mother was also destroyed by the brutal arrest. Hers was a sadness that took her life, swiftly, in three years."

Marcos raised the candle and illumined our faces. His eyes were bloodshot. The firelight spilled flickers of black and gold across his skin.

"I've cursed you, Francisco!" He bared his teeth. "You and your traitor of a father. We welcomed you in Córdoba with open arms, we left you our home—but your father, your miserable father—"

"Marcos!" I grasped his wrists. "They were both victims!"

"He denounced my father."

"He never told me that." I shook his wrists, at the verge of sobbing, because he had told me but I had not wanted to register it.

"You think he'd confess to such a crime? The facts are eloquent enough; a short time after they arrested your father, the order for my father's arrest was signed. Who, if not he, had given his name?"

"My father is dead now. The torture left him broken."

"Let me go." He freed himself from my grip and went to the far end of the bedroom. "Let's see if now you can do something for my mother."

I asked his wife to help me adjust the patient's position. Turning an unconscious patient on her side can help with breathing. I cleaned her mouth with a damp cloth. I felt a thick, devastating tumult inside me.

Marcos summoned the slave who had brought me from the hospital and handed him a scroll.

"Take this to Brother Juan Bautista Ureta. In the La Merced monastery. Tell him to come immediately to give my mother her last rites."

I opened a vein in the patient's foot and let out dark blood. Then I covered the incision with a bandage. I washed the scalpel and cannula and closed my instrument case. I cleaned the patient's mouth again. Her breathing had become regular.

A few minutes later, Marcos welcomed Brother Ureta. He thanked him for having come so quickly. He was a hardy priest with deep bags under his eyes. A few neighbors also entered the bedroom. The priest put down a small case and leaned in close to the patient. Then he looked at Marcos, his wife, and me. His sinister gaze lingered on me.

"I'm the doctor," I explained.

"She's not dead, but—is she conscious?" he asked.

Marcos and his wife lowered their gazes. The priest's criticism was clear and serious. A terrible negligence had been committed, because this old woman's soul could no longer give a confession, could not take communion, could not receive adequate preparation for the eternal voyage. She would be defenseless.

I had to solve the problem, and not admit that I had found her unconscious and they had requested religious assistance too late. I decided to lie to protect Marcos.

"She fainted during my bloodletting. When they called for you, Father, she was still speaking lucidly."

"She was speaking?"

"She babbled sounds, Father, as she has in recent years," I said, realizing my error. "She was conscious."

He took out his sacred paraphernalia and arranged them on a chair beside the bed. He placed the stole around his neck, opened his prayer book, and began to pray. The neighbors followed suit.

The prayers resounded from the walls.

"I absolve you of your sins." He dipped his thumb in the oil and traced a cross on the pale forehead. "In the name of the Father, the Son, and the Holy Spirit. Amen."

"Amen," we repeated.

He gathered his sacred items, closed the case, and stared at me again. His attitude was a mix of curiosity and doubt.

"Aren't you Doctor Francisco Maldonado da Silva?"

"Yes, Father."

His face softened somewhat.

"Do you know me?" I asked.

"Now I know you personally. Before, I knew you by reputation."

I shivered. Reputation? What did that mean? Marcos accompanied him to the front door with a couple of neighbors. Then he returned to the bedroom and thanked me.

"It's fine, Marcos. I've been through similar situations myself. It's very painful."

"Tell me how much you charge."

"Let's not talk about that now."

"As you like." He sat down near the bed. "What more can we do?" He gazed at his mother, biting his lips.

"Keep her company."

"I understand. Thank you again." He covered his face with his hands. "How much she's suffered, my poor mother!"

I approached and put my hand on his shoulder. He stiffened. Then he backed away. "You can go, Francisco. You've fulfilled your role."

I searched for another chair and brought it to his side. He seemed startled, but said nothing. The servants refreshed the candles. A few neighbors left, others came, always silent. When night fell, they brought us pots of hot stew. We only exchanged words in relation to the patient, her change of position, the wiping of phlegm from her mouth, replacing the cold cloths on her forehead. We dozed. I was woken by a hoarse snore. The bedroom was darker; a few hours had passed. The patient was sliding onto her back and choking. She had suffered a lapse in respiration. I adjusted her head to the side and pressed her chest until the rhythm of her breath became steady. Then I again turned her on her side. The servants refreshed the candles again. I slept sitting up for an uncertain amount of time, until someone shook my arm. I saw Marcos. I became alert and went to her. Once again she was on her back, but silent. I felt for her pulse and looked into her pupils. It was over. I reached out my left arm, respectfully. Before me, confused, Marcos had risen to his feet. Our fingers and lips moved, hesitantly. And we embraced.

Only then could he weep.

He says, finally, that the Holy Office of the Inquisition is benign. That he should ask for mercy because it will be granted.

Alonso de Almeida wipes the foam from his lips without taking his eyes off the prisoner, who remains immobile, seated on his narrow bed, against the wall. He believes that his sharp words have cut into the man's heart.

Francisco swallows and blinks. Now, it is his turn.

97

Marcos's revelation moved me deeply. It had been inevitable that my father, broken by torture, would cede to the demand for names. The inquisitors weren't naïve. But it was acutely painful to me that he had denounced his friend Juan José Brizuela when he had heroically kept his silence about Gaspar Chávez, Diego López de Lisboa, José Ignacio Sevilla, and so many others. Papá had been a noble man, but he was no saint, and he didn't become a martyr. Above all, at the end of the day, he was a selfless teacher.

I owed him my identity as a Jew. He knew how to fill it with dignity; he knew how to show me its values.

He had loved the Sabbath feast. And he'd loved it especially because its observance was forbidden. It was a form of rebellion against oppressors. With the Sabbath, since ancient times, the importance of time was marked, as well as the right of human beings, animals, and even the earth to rest. Saturdays gave order and shape to progress. Papá had explained that, in Hebrew, the days of the week had numbers for names: Sunday was day one, Monday was two, and so forth, and, after the sixth day, the culmination arrived—a different kind of atmosphere, *Shabbat*. This enshrined a binary system of tension-relaxation, struggle-rest. Like life—inhale-exhale, systole-diastole.

To help enjoy this contrast I often took long walks along the outskirts of Santiago. I put on clean but wrinkled clothes to evade the suspicion of the Holy Office's alert tentacles. I carried a small emergency instrument case, though without the heavy tools inside. If several people claimed to have seen me loafing about on a Saturday, it could send me to jail, and, after that, perhaps, to be burned alive. For that reason, I also varied my path.

Sometimes I walked toward the east, murmuring the psalms that describe the wonders of creation because the mountain range stood before me with its ermine cape draped over its peaks. Other times I walked toward the north, crossed the cold waters of the Mapocho River and entered the walnut copses, where I'd sit on a fallen trunk and read the sacred word. Occasionally I chose the path to the west, which led to the sea. I also walked toward the unsettling south, where the Arauco Indians questioned the rights of conquest. It was a good opportunity to meditate on the many wars against Jews by so many peoples who did not accept our right to exist.

Some Saturdays I did not go out on these walks—it could draw attention that I walked so far every seven days. I decided to explore Santa Lucía Hill. Ancient Greece would have exalted it, as it was an ideal place for nymphs to be chased by the god Pan and his entourage of ardent fauns. The dense glades offered certain hiding places in which the kisses, caresses, and promises of sinful Santiago freely roamed. In its hidden corners there vibrated a joy as invisible as it was ineradicable. The advantage of being seen there lay in the fact that nobody could accuse me without admitting his own guilt. No one wandered through those verdant spaces without the spur of lust. But it was better to be caught out being lustful than to be suspected of heresy.

I climbed the gradual slope. Nobody appeared between the bushes or beneath the dark trees. It was possible to believe that the place was enchanted and that its erotic visitors had been transformed into foliage. I ascended the rough path all the way to the top of the hill. The city of

Santiago and its cultivated fields spread out before my eyes. The pure air filled me with a sense of well-being. I recognized the spacious central plaza, with its government buildings and stone cathedral. I located churches, monasteries, convents, the Jesuit college, the hospital where I was supposed to be working at that very moment, Marcos Brizuela's house, Pedro de Valdivia's house, and the place where Isabel lived. I stayed there for a long time, thinking optimistically and thanking God for smoothing out my complicated life.

My bond with Isabel kept growing. I truly loved her, and she was beginning to show signs of affection. Every time I went to visit her, I not only heard bells in my chest, but also saw happiness in her eyes, joy in her hands, and sun in her smiling lips.

I had also achieved a long-held dream to reestablish contact with my sisters in Córdoba. They had at last responded to my letters. Their status as orphans had instilled them with so much fear that they were ashamed of my letters and felt obliged to show them to their confessor. And the confessor took a few years to give them permission to respond. Felipa, who had been rebellious and daring like Papá, had become involved with the Society of Jesus. For her part, Isabel, who more closely resembled our mother, had left the convent and married Captain Fabián del Espino, an Indian overseer and local councilman, to whom she bore a daughter named Ana. But the poor woman had just become a widow. This sad news was accompanied with guilt; she said that she had not known how to attend to her husband as his fragile health had required. They were alone, and in a state of constant distress. It did not escape my attention that both of my sisters signed with the single last name "Maldonado," with its Old Christian sound. "Silva" was excluded—it was associated with my father, his Jewish lineage, and the mythical polemicist Haséfer. It was clear that these poor women had not recovered from the stigma that had killed our family. In my most recent letter, I had invited them to be reunited with me in Santiago. I told them that this was a treasured goal I had kept with me since the very night of our last separation. I also asked about Luis and Catalina, and begged them to find out whom they belonged to and how much it would cost to buy them back.

That day, I inhaled the pollen of the Sabbath and retraced my steps toward home with the hope of soon having a family again. Still hidden behind the trees, and before appearing in one of the hill's sinful regions, I took the precaution of glancing in both directions. I saw only a couple of black people pushing a cart. I walked directly toward them, at a rapid pace, to better evade being seen. But before I reached them I felt a corpulent presence that stopped me in my tracks. I recognized his eyes of coal.

"Good afternoon, Brother Ureta," I said, greeting him and trying to seem indifferent.

The inspector monk took a few seconds to reflect before responding. If he'd seen me coming from the hill, I thought, he would not connect a sanctified Saturday with the sin of fornication. He would of course suppose that I'd been rolling around with a whore. That was better than him suspecting my Judaism. But I was wrong.

98

Among the groups that formed in the cathedral's atrium after leaving Mass, I once again discovered the imposing Juan Bautista Ureta. It would have been too much to think that he'd been looking for me. Nevertheless, to my surprise, the monk zigzagged between the faithful and ended up right in front of me. I felt a chill.

"I need to speak with you," he said coldly.

I stiffened my back. At the prospect of attack it was best to bring one's bones into solid balance.

"Whenever you like." I made myself sound cold.

"Could it be now?"

"With pleasure."

"Let's go outside to walk, then." He gestured with his head toward Isabel's family. "Is there anyone you need to greet first?"

"Yes, thank you. I will say my goodbyes to Don Cristóbal de la Cerda." Too much docility or obsequiousness would only raise suspicions.

I paid my respects to Doña Sebastiana, her husband, and the enchanting Isabel. I excused myself for leaving immediately, as Brother Ureta had need of me. Doña Sebastiana invited me to come by her residence during the afternoon to sample the sweets she had prepared with fruits from the south. Isabel sensed my hidden nervousness and stopped smiling, but she didn't ask any questions. In the middle of that frustrating moment, I realized that we had already begun to share invisible forms of communication. I looked at her gratefully, thinking, "This must be the woman of my life."

Brother Ureta knew of the process my father had endured, and of my good behavior in the Dominican monasteries of Córdoba and Lima. He was aware of my light and my shadow.

"Your father was granted reconciliation by the Holy Office," he spat out first. "He was a fortunate man."

What was he getting at?

"Your father abandoned his Jewish deviations," he added, staring at me with dark eyes that seemed to be devouring me.

I realized that he was taking me to Santa Lucía Hill, to the same part where he'd run into me the previous day.

"The information gathered leads one to think that your deceased father and you have behaved with devotion."

"Thank you."

He forced a cough. "When you attended to Marcos Brizuela's mother—"

I tilted my head. "What?"

"When you performed that bloodletting on Brizuela's mother"—he emphasized the word "bloodletting"—"you forgot that it was more urgent to save her soul."

"Why would you accuse me so unjustly?"

"With that bloodletting you made her lose consciousness and deprived her of her last confession."

The accusation was so serious that I was on the verge of dissolving into explanations, but I would only have become tangled in them. And I couldn't put Marcos and his wife in a risky position, because they were the ones who'd decided to summon a doctor before summoning a priest.

"I didn't suspect that my treatment would produce such a lamentable effect," I lied.

"Our holy mother church is wise," he exclaimed. "*Ecclesia abhorret a sanguine.* In a series of councils it prohibited priests from practicing medicine, to protect us from clumsiness like yours."

"I realize that mine is a sad profession," I replied humbly. "Every shortcoming fills us with guilt, Father. Please, do not discredit us. We work with an object that is extremely difficult and sensitive—the human body."

"The body! Doctors live obsessed with the body! They even grope cadavers to reveal its mysteries. It's a vile profession, loved by Moors and Jews for good reason. They neglect the soul and forget that illness is the direct consequence of sin. Sometimes they try to persuade us that they come from a purely physical disturbance, as if we were machines."

"I don't simplify things so much."

"But when it comes to the facts, you bear the guilt for Brizuela's mother having died without confession," he blurted harshly. "Do you admit to your horrifying error, or not?"

"I've already told you that it wasn't intentional."

He stopped walking for a moment, turned his hulking body toward me, grabbed the edge of his cloak, and folded it. He showed it to me.

"How many folds are there?"

"Three."

"Spread them out."

I shrugged and did as he asked.

"Now what do you see?"

"No folds—just the cloak."

"So what do you think, then?"

"I don't understand."

"No?" He invited me to keep walking. "A few years ago, in the city of Concepción, the sublieutenant Juan de Balmaceda was arrested. You haven't heard anyone speak of him? Then I'll tell you. Finding himself one night in the presence of other soldiers, having had a few too many drinks of wine, he claimed that God had no son. A barbarity, an extreme

435

heresy! The soldiers warned him that this was absurd. And to prove it to him, one of them folded his cloak as I just did—made three folds, and tried to illustrate the idea. The three folds are the three beings of the Holy Trinity—one God alone, the cloak, and three, the beings. But the sublieutenant tugged at the cloak, undid the folds, and replied through his laughter, 'Can't you see that the folds are an illusion? Only the cloak exists.'"

I walked at his side with my head down, searching furiously for the comment that would free me from the labyrinth in which he was trying to trap me. But before I could speak he changed topics. He was destabilizing me.

"You wish to marry Isabel Otáñez." The directness of these words was an unusual strategy. It hit me like a club over the head.

"I have not yet asked for her hand. 'There is a time to be born, and a time to die,'" I answered, with the support of Ecclesiastes. "'A time to plant and a time to harvest.'"

He smiled slightly. "'A time for silence, and a time to speak,'" he added. "So you know the scripture as well as a theologian."

"I began studying it when I was still a youth, in the monastery in Córdoba."

"Shall we return to the subject of your marriage?"

"It is hasty to speak of marriage, as I have not yet spoken to her father."

"And negotiated the dowry," he added.

I was silent.

"Negotiating the dowry," he insisted. "As well as obtaining his consent, of course."

I was enraged by this intrusion, but had to restrain myself.

"I would like you to know," he said, "in case you are not aware, that I am bound to Don Cristóbal by an old friendship from when we were students back in Salamanca. That friendship has been strengthened by the mercy of my enthusiastic work among religious orders to raise support for keeping him in his role. It's no secret, and, in fact, he himself has told you of this."

"No, he never spoke to me of you. I am sorry."

"In that case, I praise Don Cristóbal's discretion. Excellent!" He lowered his voice to whisper an intimate matter. "We are united by our criticism of the defensive war."

"It's a delicate issue."

"It's not supported by the bishop, by the orders, or the captains."

"But it is supported by the Society of Jesus."

"Only the Society. Even the commissioner of the Holy Office has stopped hearing reproaches. The new governor already knows it's a useless strategy. You'll see, Don Cristóbal will be duly vindicated."

"Let's hope so."

"He deserves it. He is a great man and has accomplished admirable things, but do you know which is the most transcendent of them all?"

I blinked. I thought of all his construction projects, campaigns, and decrees. I couldn't decide.

"His struggle against corruption."

I stared at him in surprise. Where was this man leading me?

"Don't you think so, too?" He grunted in annoyance.

"Y-yes. It could be—" Was he being sarcastic? Or setting a trap?

"As soon as he arrived he proclaimed with kettledrums that he would ferociously punish any attempt to bribe servants or relatives. Nobody was ever so energetic."

I felt a profound unease. Brother Ureta was turning my ideas the way wind turns a weather vane.

"There are slanderous versions of this that have spread in the city," he added. "Do you know who feeds them? Those miserable people who don't make good on their taxes. They neglect their legal duties and then respond with absurd fabrications. These lands are plagued with men who enrich themselves on the one hand, and then skimp on their contributions and alms on the other. Doesn't our bishop denounce this every week?"

We were very close to Santa Lucía Hill. A few of its paths were already in sight. People moved at a prudent distance, as if the mountain could emit hooks and ensnare them.

"I sense that you will have difficulties in negotiating the dowry."

Once again, he was meddling in my private affairs. I pretended not to feel the impact.

"Don Cristóbal," he added, "lost almost all his wealth to English pirates. He cannot give what he would like to. He loves his goddaughter, and, therefore, he will tell her that he is in no state to agree to her marriage because you, Doctor, are a person who also lacks sufficient means to maintain a family."

"That isn't quite true, Father. I have a salary and charge fees for my home visits."

"Ah, yes?"

"Do you doubt my words?"

"No. Only that your words are contradicted by the amount of your alms to the church."

"I am impartial."

"Subjectively. The objectivity I have, on the other hand, disagrees. Don Cristóbal will not evaluate his goddaughter's economic security based only on what you say, but, rather, on what you demonstrate."

"Demonstrations can be false."

"I, as a church inspector, need you to lend me money now, for example," he burst out point-blank. "My order can't provide funds, neither can the bishop. Understand that I am not asking for sacred alms, but for a loan."

I bit my lips. "I would like to reflect on this."

"All right."

We returned to the city center. He made no references to Santa Lucía Hill, and did not accuse me of fornicating with prostitutes, but—why that route? Why had he taken me to the same place where he had found me yesterday? As we approached the Mercedarian church, he asked questions about Bishop Trejo y Sanabria, Francisco Solano, and the University of Lima. He calibrated the effects. Suddenly, he stroked his cheeks, and, looking up into the clouds, asked, with an affected innocence, "Yesterday was Saturday, no?"

—∿∿—

Francisco knows that to ask for mercy does not mean absolution. In any case, it would be an indirect gesture of submission. But he has not arrived at this point in his life to retreat. He is in the middle of a war from which he did not want to flee; he knows that, on occasion, he spoke lightly, and at other times he moved with little speed. He is no stranger to the reasons for his imprisonment.

The examiner Alonso de Almeida is probably sincere. The whips of his words are soaked in anguish, and he wants to save Francisco, but—save him from what? That good man is sure of having made an impression, and of being able to straighten out the main distortions in his spirit. But he will be disappointed.

99

In the calendar of festivities that my father taught me, the fast of September is meaningful. In that month, the Hebrew year is renewed, and then comes Yom Kippur, the Day of Atonement. The contrition of fasting detoxifies the body and soul. Through this privation, we strengthen our will and show God and our own selves that we have reserves of energy. Fasting is also a form of penitence. We Marranos need it to relieve our hearts of that horrible fault into which we are forced: lying to our fellow man, and denying God. The prophet Jeremiah, facing the catastrophe that took down Jerusalem, preached, "Hang your heads, but live!" This coincides with animal instinct because any strategy that allows us to keep breathing counts. But it shatters our ethical principles. Every minute of life is contaminated with betrayal. And so fasting helps us restore our balance. Joaquín del Pilar showed me that, in Lima during Yom Kippur, some Marranos would stroll along the Alameda after lunch with toothpicks in their mouths. In reality, they were fasting, but the toothpick quelled suspicion, since inquisitors were always on the hunt for clues.

I intentionally chose to visit Marcos on Yom Kippur. We still had not established trust, as Jews had to be extremely careful. I didn't know whether or not his conversion was sincere, and, therefore, how he related to things having to do with his old faith. Our fathers were judged and then reconciled by the Holy Office, forced to wear the despicable sanbenito until they died. In Santiago, Marcos had prospered as a good Catholic. He had married Dolores Segovia, had two children, and had bought a position on the local town council. Did he still have any reason to consider himself Jewish? Did he have any desire to maintain that scorned identity with study, prayer, and the cultivation of traditions?

I tried to find traces of Judaism in the handling of his mother's corpse. The physical hygiene outlined by the sacred texts—seen by the Inquisition as a "filthy rite"—extends to the dead: Jews wash their bodies with warm water and wrap them, when possible, in a pure linen shroud. After the burial the living wash their hands and eat hard-boiled eggs without salt, because eggs are symbols of life. The mourning of relatives dignifies the deceased and their loved ones and helps channel feelings of loss into the furthering of love, easing the burden. Close relatives sit on the floor for seven days, praying, talking, and eating fish, eggs, and vegetables. It's a funeral rite full of wisdom. But I didn't see any of this in Marcos's home. However, my not having seen it could point to the success of the act, and not to the lack of apostasy.

And so I visited him on the Day of Atonement, still unsure of his deepest sentiments. The fact that he was home, and not working, didn't prove anything either; the hours of his labors were irregular and depended on the arrival or dispatch of merchandise.

"Work is a curse, Francisco," Marcos said to excuse himself. "It's one of the first punishments. It says so, outright, in Genesis."

"Do you know where the Spanish word for 'to work,' comes from?" I recalled a linguistic discovery I'd made. "From the Latin word *trepaliare*. It means 'to torture.'"

"It's perfectly clear, then!"

"But we belong to the laboring class, Marcos."

"I'm no farm laborer."

"Laborers, in the sense of workers," I clarified. "You as a merchant, and me as a doctor. Though we may not like it, we are closer to the artisans, metalsmiths, and carpenters than to orators and noblemen."

"The choice was not up to us."

"We could have become orators if we'd wanted to. The priest, who is an orator, has sacramental power as intermediary between Christ and man." I looked deeply into his eyes.

"I didn't have the necessary upbringing to become a priest. You, on the other hand, lived in monasteries."

"It's not so much a matter of upbringing as a matter of vocation, Marcos. In any case, you don't have a priest's vocation."

"Though I do have the vocation of intermediary! Priests are intermediaries, too," he said, laughing.

"Your intermediary work is not as appreciated as that of priests."

"That's true. I don't do commerce between Christ and men, but only between men." He was still smiling. "And I charge for it."

"Everybody charges." I was pushing things further.

"Priests don't charge; they receive alms."

"What about tithes?" I corrected him. "When alms seem insufficient, they make demands and even threats."

"Just like merchants?"

"Shhhh!" I placed my index finger over my lips. "Don't blaspheme."

Marcos pulled his stool closer to mine.

"I'd like to have the eloquence of our bishop," he whispered. "I'd do much better collecting from delinquent clients."

"Don't blaspheme," I warned again.

"You know who's behaved worse? The town halls that sent letters to the viceroy and the Archbishop of Lima requesting the creation of an ecclesiastical court of appeals to defend themselves from the judgments hurled so violently by our bishop. Did you know about that?"

"He's a passionate man."

"Passionate and blind. Blind with fury."

"Don't make fun of his illness." I restrained my smile. "Also, may I confess a speculation? I have my doubts as to whether he really is blind. I have the sense that he uses his supposed blindness to throw people off course and see selectively—to see only what he wants to."

He became serious at the sound of steps.

A servant offered me a tray of sweets, and a piece of cake, and a bronze pitcher of liquid chocolate. I thanked her but declined. She tried to leave the tray at my side, as she had been taught to do for guests, but I insisted that she take it with her. Marcos observed me closely. He was testing me. After the servant left I begged Marcos, with a wink, not to be troubled by my choice. I added that the episode put me in mind of the fourth psalm.

"Do you recall it?" he asked.

"'You have put gladness in my heart, more than in the season when the grain and wine increased,'" I recited.

The house filled with light.

"'I will lie down in peace,'" he added, "'and immediately I will sleep; for you alone, O God, make me dwell in safety.'"

We stared at each other.

"The fourth psalm," I repeated. "The most beautiful prayer a just man surrounded by unbelievers can invoke."

"Are you saying that we are two just men surrounded by unbelievers?"

Our eyes shone. We were both aware that we had recited a psalm and omitted the phrase *Gloria patri,* which all Catholics intoned at the end. That absence was irrefutable, moving proof. We had revealed our intimate worlds to each other.

We studied each other for a long time, as if we had found each other after a long and arduous journey.

—m—

"You just finished telling me," Francisco responds, measuring each word, *"that we should fear the devil and his tricks because they lead to our downfall. That we must fear heretics and the filthy rites of Judaism. You have said all this with deep certainty.*

"Nevertheless, Brother Alonso, believe me that, because of your work and that of many men like you, we Jews now fear something much closer and more evident than the devil: you, the Christians."

100

"'Kiss me with the kisses of your mouth! For your love is sweeter than wine, gentle is the scent of your perfume, your name is a salve that spilleth over.'"

"Francisco, you're so courteous, such a poet!"

"It's the Song of Songs, of Solomon, beloved."

"How beautiful!" Isabel exclaimed. "Go on, go on."

"'Your cheeks are lovely with ornaments, your neck with strings of jewels.'" I caressed her.

"I don't know how to respond." She shivered.

"Say, 'A bag of myrrh is my beloved to me, which lieth between my breasts.'"

"Francisco—"

"You didn't like it? I'll give you another verse, just for you: 'Like a lily among thistles, so is my beloved among the virgins.'"

"Tell me a verse that I can repeat."

"'Like an apple tree among the trees of the forest, so is my beloved among the young men.'"

"I like that. 'Like an apple tree among the trees of the forest, so is Francisco, my beloved'"—Isabel smiled—"'among the young men.'"

"Add this: 'His left hand is under my head, and his right hand embraces me.'"

"I love you very much."

"Say, 'Francisco, my husband.'"

"Francisco, my husband."

"'How beautiful you are, my beloved, how beautiful! Your eyes are like those of a dove, behind your veil. Your hair reminds me of a herd of goats descending the slopes of Gilead. Your lips are like scarlet ribbon. Your cheeks are like halves of a pomegranate. Like the tower of David is your neck, built with rows of stones.'"

"How excited you've become! I'm trembling all over!"

"'Your breasts are two fawns, twins born from a gazelle, grazing among the lilies.'"

"Oh, my love."

"'How beautiful you are, how enchanting, oh my love, in your delicacies! Your stature is like a palm tree, your breasts the clustered fruit.'"

Isabel caressed my forehead, chin, and neck. We held each other in the magical atmosphere of Solomon's verses. A flowering laurel branch moved against the wall, greeting the night of love.

I had improved my home before the wedding. I had expanded the parlor, plastered the bedroom walls, and built servants' quarters. I had bought chairs, two rugs, and a wide armoire. I'd hung an impressive candelabra in the dining room and added candleholders along the wall that could give off plenty of light. In the back courtyard, piles of adobe and stone awaited future expansions.

My request to Don Cristóbal for his daughter's hand had not been trying after all because he parted the waters. He told me that he valued me as a person, but that he needed to be assured that his beloved Isabel would not suffer privations after marriage. Therefore, he would not object to the union as long as I could guarantee that my current assets and future income would be sufficient. I sensed the shadow of Juan Bautista Ureta circling around us like a vulture. Although Don Cristóbal knew my salary consisted of 150 pesos, a respectable sum, as well as income from additional private services, he delayed his consent because of the inspector priest's interference. My status as a New Christian was a difficult obstacle to remove. Finally, we reached an agreement, and he summoned a notary to formalize it. We needed two witnesses; he proposed that we invite Captain Pedro de Valdivia, the inspector Juan Bautista Ureta, and Captain Juan Avendaño, a relative of Doña Sebastiana.

The notary wrote up a long document and read it in a loud voice. People assented and we signed it with the same quill, which the notary extended to us with a sure hand and arrogant nose. The text began as follows: "I, Doctor Francisco Maldonado da Silva, resident of this city of Santiago de Chile, by the grace and blessing of the Lord Our God and His blessed and glorious Mother, am arranged to be married to Doña Isabel Otáñez." It went on: "In support of the dowry, the esteemed Don Cristóbal de la Cerda y Sotomayor, judge in this our Royal Court, has promised me the sum of five hundred and sixty-six pesos and eight reales." Of that sum, only 250 pesos were given to me in cash, and the remainder in the form of clothes, fabric, and a few minor objects that the notary itemized in morbid detail: "one woman's dress, with lace, valued at forty-four pesos"; "six lady's blouses, ornamented along the chest, valued at forty-four pesos"; "petticoats from Rouen, France, embroidered, eight pesos"; "four new sheets from Rouen, France, valued at twenty-four pesos"; "an underskirt, used, eight pesos"; "four handkerchiefs, one peso"; and so forth. Don Cristóbal had triumphed in the negotiations. That same document stipulated that I would pay a compensation of 300 pesos, and it committed me to increase that sum with another 1,800 pesos such that, if the marriage should be dissolved by death or any other reason, that money would remain in Isabel's hands. It was also added that "I recognize said donation to be accepted and legitimately declared," and that I did so with all that was required to provide for my wife.

In our home, after reciting the Songs, I gazed at my beloved's profile in the twilight. She had fallen asleep, and a strand of hair rose and fell rhythmically on her breath. Her tender body stirred me. Her mere presence spilled optimism into my life. Thinking of her, of us, I went back through the books of Ruth, Judith, and Esther. "With her, I'll build the family that, in time, will repair what I've lost," I thought to myself. "I'll have children, and enjoy unconditional surroundings."

The wedding ceremony had taken place with the austerity demanded by our circumstances. Isabel was a devoted Christian, and I duly respected her sentiments. She knew nothing of my Judaism, and it was essential that she never find out. There was not the slightest option of burdening her with my secret identity. This asymmetry was, of course, ethically objectionable.

But, as Marcos put it, the alternative had not arrived. To maintain a certain amount of freedom—how ironic!—I had to chain my freedom; I had to concede to Don Cristóbal, be wary of Brother Ureta, and hide from my own wife.

I was following in my father's footsteps, but I was determined not to be defeated as he had been. It was a challenge worthy of a cyclops. Or of a reckless man.

101

Felipa and Isabel wrote to me again. They had considered my proposal regarding coming to Chile, and, after seeking advice, they had agreed to travel. And they allowed a heartrending phrase to leak onto the page: they missed me! They expressed their congratulations for my marriage and sent their affection to my splendid wife.

In another letter, which arrived shortly thereafter, they told me that they'd begun to plan their departure. Isabel had to settle some debts and sell a few possessions that had belonged to her deceased husband. Her young daughter, Ana, was leaping with joy at the thought of crossing the highest mountains in the world and meeting her Uncle Francisco.

Toward the end of the letter they added that they had succeeded in purchasing Catalina, who, using her one healthy eye, still made clothes very white when she cleaned them and prepared stew just as she had in their youth. They would bring her to Chile. Luis, on the other hand, had passed away after being arrested for another escape attempt; he'd been accused of witchcraft and sentenced to two hundred lashes. He died in a pool of blood.

I put down the letter on the table and sank my head into my hands. That noble, magnificent man had never resigned himself to enslavement. I wept for him, for his repressed grandeur. I recalled his swaying gait, his ivory laugh, his courage, his suffering. They had killed him as though he were a mangy dog, when in fact he was the son of a tribal doctor, and himself a marvelous being. Those tormentors considered themselves guardians of the law and made out their poor victims as dangers to society. The prevailing order was in fact a disorder that roared with immorality. The death of Luis, relayed by my sisters as a humdrum fact, made me tremble. It inflamed me. But—against what? Against whom?

I said the Hebrew prayer for the dead. The sonorous cadences of the Kaddish could represent the forest winds of his childhood. He had not been a Christian, or a Jew. He had believed in gods who would not be irritated by my Kaddish. It was true to his roots.

—

"Be careful what you say!" Alonso de Almeida exclaims in horror. "You are speaking to an examiner from the Holy Office. In the name of God and the Virgin! I am obliged to repeat everything you tell me, word for word. Snap out of your diabolical trance! Put an end to this madness, for your own good!"

"I am not mad."

"Listen." His voice grows tender. "The Holy Office is waiting for you to repent and ask for mercy, and will be lenient with you. It will grant you clemency, I assure you, because you are in a place of God."

"Of God?" Francisco leans his head against the wall. "There is only one God, and He is merciful, to be sure. But I cannot accept the idea that He has delegated His place, or His power. It makes no sense whatsoever. Now that is what I call madness!"

102

Marcos Brizuela appeared at the hospital. He was checking on a silversmith who'd been injured in a quarrel. The smith was a highly skilled mestizo who had made him beautiful items. Marcos told me that it would be a shame for him to become disabled, as the city would be deprived of a great artist. I heard out this story and guided my friend to the nurse, who was moved to tears; his visit was an honor, a form of recognition. Marcos gave the nurse a bulky pouch.

"Let him want for no food or medicine," he said.

"Thank you, sir, thank you."

Afterward, we walked as I escorted him out.

"The stitches are progressing well, for now," I remarked. "There are no signs of infection."

"I'm relieved to hear it. The man has a good soul, and exceptional talent."

"I'd like to see the wonders he creates."

He drew me to a solitary corner and glanced around him. "I'll show them to you the day after tomorrow, in the evening, Francisco," he whispered. "In fact, I came to invite you."

"The day after tomorrow?"

"You'll come alone, Francisco. And you'll enter as discreetly as possible."

"To see the silver—"

"To do something more important."

I stared at him.

"To celebrate Pesach."

I pressed his hands, a shudder running from my body to his. We were bound by fraternal emotion and knowledge that we could share in the celebration known as *pascua judía*, or "Jewish Easter."

"Pesach," I murmured.

That night, I opened the Book of Exodus and read it from beginning to end. It was not spring, as it was in the northern hemisphere, but fall. The placid air bore the scent of ripe fruit. A cautious coolness flowed in through the open window.

On the night of Pesach I put on clean clothes, without taking the precaution of wrinkling them as it was not Saturday, and I took my black cloak out of its trunk. I told Isabel that my obligations would delay my return. I kissed her mouth, and her carmine-flushed cheeks. How I longed to share this old, ever-relevant festivity with her!

On the street, fallen leaves crackled under my cautious steps. I wrapped myself in my silky cloak and took the necessary detours. I approached Marcos's house on the sidewalk across the street. When I was absolutely sure that no one could see me, I crossed the road. I did not use the knocker, only grazed my knuckles against the wood. The shutter over the peephole opened slightly. I recognized the slave who served as messenger.

I spoke the password: "Sauté."

The door opened just enough to let me slide inside. The courtyard was dark, barely lit by a lamp that hung among the colonnades. The parlor was also dim; one candelabra bearing three candles allowed me to make out the furniture. It gave the impression of a house whose residents had gone to bed. The enslaved man offered me a chair and disappeared, leaving me alone. The music of cicadas ebbed in from the courtyard. I waited anxiously. The mother-of-pearl inlay in dozens of small bureau drawers glimmered tenderly. Beside my oak chair I made out a lectern with an open book on it, surely brought in from a Spanish monastery. I stretched out my legs over the ceramic floor.

After some time the dining room door opened. Marcos's head seemed to float over the lights of the candelabra and he asked me to follow him. We entered a solitary enclosure in which I could just barely see tall chairs around a table. We moved through a double door—was this his deceased mother's bedroom? I was disoriented.

No sign of people. Then he illuminated the ground, and, with the tip of his shoe, lifted the edge of a black wool rug, which had, sewn to its underside, a cord whose other end disappeared between the floorboards. An iron ring appeared. Marcos handed me the candlestick, pulled hard on the ring, and uncovered a narrow stone staircase that led into the dark depths. He gestured for me to descend. He followed behind me, closed the trapdoor, and pulled on the cord that would pull the rug back over us. The candlelight gleamed on the bottles and pitchers in the wine cellar around us. The place was cool and welcoming. I was intoxicated by the scent of wine. He leaned his hands on a shelf and pressed until it emitted a creak, then he pushed with his left hand and a row of bottles began to turn. Light poured out of the hidden alcove. I was stunned.

On a table draped with a tablecloth, a large bronze candelabra burned. Around it, a few people stood, among them Dolores Segovia, Marcos's wife.

I took them all in with a glance. My heart raced. Next to Dolores stood the cross-eyed mathematician whom I'd met at Don Cristóbal's house. He was speaking to a man with an ash-colored beard, dressed in a white tunic and gray belt. He held a tall staff and had the look of a hermit. I'd never seen him before. The last member of this clandestine gathering forced me to rub my eyes. He was watching me from his inscrutable corpulence with a soft, friendly smile: it was the ecclesiastical inspector Juan Bautista Ureta. My brain exploded; so he was a Jew, too!

Marcos closed the secret door. The hermit extended his arm around the circle; he was at the head of the table, and was inviting us to take our seats. The chairs were supplied with thick cushions.

Marcos placed a deck of cards on the table, saying, "We can begin."

"The cards will remain here all night," the stranger explained. "Better for us to be accused of playing illegally than of celebrating the Easter of Unleavened Bread."

"They won't discover us," Ureta reassured him. "This place is impregnable."

Dolores reached under the table and pulled out a silver platter. It was heavy, both because of its metal and the various items carefully arranged on its surface. She raised it to eye level and then placed it reverently at the head of the table. It bore slices of unleavened bread, a piece of roasted lamb from which bone protruded, various herbs, a hard-boiled egg, and a tiny bowl of cinnamon-colored puree.

Marcos took out clay pots and cups and distributed them to his guests.

"I received them yesterday," he said. "They are completely new, as it should be."

"And they will be duly broken for our next Easter," Dolores laughed.

"As it should be," the stranger murmured, adjusting the flat bread on its platter.

Marcos leaned his hands against the edge of the table and faced each person solemnly.

"My brothers, we are reunited this evening by a Seder for Pesach. 'We were slaves in Egypt, and the Lord, with His strong hand, guided us to freedom.' The centuries of despotism were redeemed by the renewal of the Pact, the gift of the Law, and the journey to the Promised Land. Today"—he paused, and his tone became grave—"we are slaves of the Holy Office and the new pharaoh is embodied in inquisitors. We are oppressed by something worse than the building of the pyramids: we are oppressed by their hatred and contempt. Our ancestors suffered abuse and punishments but they could be open about what they were. We, on the other hand, have to hide everything, even our sentiments."

He reached his hands toward the hermit.

"Our celebration is gladdened by the rabbi Gonzalo de Rivas. He is a learned man who has made the pilgrimage to the Holy Land and visited the scattered people of Israel. Welcome to our home and to our city, Rabbi! You honor us, and you lift us."

I stared obsessively at Juan Bautista Ureta; it seemed unreal to have him here in his Mercedarian robes, participating in a Jewish ceremony.

The stranger caressed his curly beard and gazed around at our faces with damp eyes.

"All parties require time to prepare," he said. "Marcos took care of the new clay dishes, and Dolores baked the matzo, lit the candles, and blessed them. Each and every one of you made arrangements to be able to attend, and I was able to adjust my travel so that the two weeks of my stay in Santiago could coincide with the Seder."

He opened the bottle of wine and poured it into the cups.

"I believe that everything is now ready for us to begin." He raised his gentle gaze and seemed to understand that we needed more clarification. He stroked his beard again and then said, "Brothers, this is the oldest living festivity of humanity. Many other festivities have disappeared, while others still have emerged more recently. The celebration of Pesach and the traditions of the Seder are three thousand years old. It is notable that such a distant, long-ago event should deal with an aspiration as desired as it is difficult: freedom. Difficult, desired, and never forgotten—freedom. Because today, in 1626, we do not say that, millennia ago, some unknown ancestors, whose remains are no more than dust, suffered slavery in a distant land called Egypt. We say that we were slaves and that we experienced the turbulent passage from oppression to freedom. The experience is not over, rather, it is renewed, because, now, under new guises, slavery continues and we must dream of our freedom with renewed hope. These extraordinary facts invigorate us, and show that, in the most desperate circumstances, the prospect of a solution ever dwells."

He looked at the tray.

"Here, symbols are placed: The matzo recalls the bread of misery that our ancestors prepared on the scorching stones of the desert. The lamb represents the animal that was sacrificed for the last, decisive plague, and whose blood saved the lives of our ancestors. The bitter herbs make us taste the anguish of life for the oppressed. The puree, made with apples, wine, nuts, and cinnamon, recalls the clay our grandfathers kneaded in Egypt." He raised his index finger. "Finally, the egg: it symbolizes the cycle of life, and the resistance of the Jewish people, because the more you boil it the harder it gets. But the egg is also an object of mourning; we eat eggs after burying a loved one, and now we do so for the Egyptians who drowned in the Red Sea and who indirectly played a role in our epic story. In this manner, Jews remember that we must not hate our enemies because all men are made in the image of God."

He pointed at the central cup, a chalice brimming with wine.

"From that cup, the prophet Elijah will drink. He is our symbolic guest. A carriage of fire bore him to heaven, and now, in a carriage of mist, he goes to the caves and cellars where we Jews celebrate the Seder."

He settled into the cushions on his chair.

"We sit like princes. On this special night, we are free men." He smiled and reached out his arms. "The table is white and glowing like an altar. We shall drink wine and share unleavened bread. Then we will enjoy the food Dolores has prepared for us."

The rabbi Gonzalo de Rivas stood, and we respectfully followed suit. He raised his cup of wine and blessed it. He took a sip and then offered us the cup. Each of us accepted it with both hands. Then he picked up a fistful of vegetables, sprinkled them with salty water in a bowl, and distributed them. He broke a piece of matzo in two, returned one half to the tray, and placed the other half among the cushions.

"This gesture of hiding one portion recalls the anguish of the oppressed, who must deprive themselves of food and save it for later. It is also the sublime teaching that bread must be shared."

He placed both hands under the tray of matzo and other symbols, raised it to eye level, and said in a sonorous voice, "Behold the bread of misery eaten by our ancestors in Egypt! May he who hungers come and eat, whoever is in need, may he come and celebrate Pesach. Now we are here, next year may we celebrate in the land of Israel. Now we are slaves, next year may we be free."

He put down the tray and turned to Dolores and Marcos, who were staring at him, spellbound.

"I know that children cannot participate. It's dangerous. In Rome and Amsterdam, where Jewish communities enjoy a few rights, children are central players. The ceremony begins with the youngest person present asking four questions. This leads to the reading of the Haggadah, the story of Exodus. Tonight, the four questions can be spoken by Dolores. I invite you to say them, my daughter."

Dolores blushed and read, with emotion, "Why is this night different from all other nights? One: on all other nights we eat leavened or unleavened bread, but on this night we only eat unleavened. Two: on all other nights we eat many different vegetables, but on this night we only eat bitter herbs. Three: on other nights, we do not season our food even once, and on this night we do so two times. Four: on other nights, we eat seated or reclined, but on this night we all eat reclining."

"These innocent questions," the rabbi said, smiling, "based on the novelty a child sees, invite us to answer transparently. It could be said that we exercise our memories so that the grand events that marked the birth of our people may bring their strength to bear on our current times. We were and are slaves; we won and will win our freedom. For three thousand years, on this night, the formidable epic has been told and embraced."

He opened a Bible.

"We have no Haggadah. We will replace it with excerpts from Exodus."

His voice vaulted, shimmering with emotion, tracing those heroic times back into being. The known sequence of events became palpable, and we shivered at hearing the tale of the pharaoh's harshness, the terrifying plagues, the sacrifice of the lamb, and, finally, the departure of multitudes.

He sipped wine and sent the cup around again. Then he raised up another piece of matzo, broke it, and passed it around. The solemn part was coming to an end.

"We have shared bread and wine," he explained. "This is what our ancestors did in the land of Israel, and what all Jewish communities do on this night, all over the world. This is what Jesus and his disciples did during their Seder, as we do now. The Last Supper was an intimate Seder, just like ours. Jesus presided over a table transformed into an altar, just as I am doing. Just like me, he passed wine to drink, and unleavened bread to eat. But this cannot be said, or even insinuated, before the new pharaohs."

He stood up.

"I invite you to stand. Let us taste the lamb in the same way our ancestors did in the desert: on our feet."

"At some point they sat," joked Juan Bautista Ureta.

"And at some point they also obtained yeast for their bread," the rabbi replied. "But we use symbolism to recall significant moments."

"Forgive me, Rabbi," Ureta apologized.

"Judaism accepts joking—don't worry. Insolence is part of our dynamic."

The atmosphere aligned with the description Papá had given me. The tone was not overly ceremonious. There were no ornaments, and the senses weren't bewildered by a spectacle of colors, sounds, and smells. Instead, there was the atmosphere of a warm home, human contact, conversation, a feast. The person presiding over the traditions was no fearsome pontiff hurling lightning bolts from the heights, but, rather, an affectionate father, or perhaps an older brother, someone whose knowledge transformed into a generous fountain. The charm of this celebration resided in its potent simplicity.

"I never would have suspected that you are Jewish," I said to Ureta as I chewed the roasted meat. "I was frightened to see you."

"Being a disagreeable monk lets me hide all the better. Also, I can enjoy reading the Bible without generating any suspicion."

"It must be difficult to be a monk and a Jew, eh?"

His large, jet-black eyes became clear.

"My status as a monk gives me no burden, but rather advantages."

"But—to be a minister of a religion in which you don't believe."

"I'm not the only one. You are forced to disguise yourself, just like I am. Some Jews managed to join the order of Santo Domingo, which is like joining a branch of the Inquisition. And they became bishops."

Marcos placed his hand on my shoulder, becoming part of the exchange, saying, "I owe you an apology for the surprise."

"And what a surprise it was!"

"You know what? You can never be too cautious. When you attended to my mother, I didn't know whether you were the Catholic you seemed to be or the Jew I now see before me. I called Juan Bautista, a severe ecclesiastical inspector, so that my lateness in calling for last rites wouldn't get me in trouble. And so the neighbors would see that I was not depriving her of the sacred oils. Later, Juan Bautista put you under pressure to test your integrity, even, I believe"—he smiled—"going too far! After you visited me on the day of the Jewish fast and did not eat, we recited a psalm and you did not seal it with the words *Gloria patri*. These elements would have been enough for me to invite you to participate in the study sessions we occasionally hold in this cellar. But we've learned to be cautious. The Holy Office doesn't only work with visible functionaries—anyone can submit a denunciation. I decided to wait a few more months, and now, with frank joy, we welcome you to our miniscule community."

"An ecclesiastic inspector like Juan Bautista serves as the screen," I said ironically. "But, please, it's too much!"

"As a Mercedarian monk," Ureta said, "I have vast experience. My order has been responsible for getting hostages back from Moors by good, bad, or bribery. Today, though, that task is useless. The most important wars are not being waged against Muslims, but against heretics. And here, in the New World, our order seems drunk, unsure of how to distinguish itself. My work as an inspector comforts it, because I help support conversions. Meanwhile, I help Jews."

"Admirable."

Rabbi Gonzalo de Rivas raised his staff.

"I'm not going to hit you with this," he laughed. "Only remind you that now, after dinner, we are to read a few psalms and sing songs. This is a party!"

We returned to our places. Dolores handed out nuts and raisins. Marcos refreshed the candles and gave out palm fronds.

Exhaustion wears at de Almeida's patience. This prisoner has turned out to be harder than quartz. The rebukes have not pierced him, neither have pleas moved him. His mouth is dry and sour at the thought of his unbelievable failure. He stares at the prisoner one last time with pity and rancor. He thinks that only very deep suffering will succeed in clearing his soul.

He beats on the door, for the soldiers to open it. Then he drags himself, aggrieved, toward the fulfillment of his duty: to inform the inquisitors of the atrocities he has heard during this long hour, word for word.

103

I accompanied Isabel to the Holy Week services. I had to participate visibly, as there was methodical vigilance in the atriums, naves, and pulpits. The few Marranos in the city had impeccable attendance. This was one of the most ruthless tests to which we were subjected. We had to carry out the farce of a false devotion, which gnawed at the soul like an acid, and to endure accusations of having killed Jesus.

Every time a priest referred to the Passion and death during Holy Week, my heart raced.

Palm Sunday celebrates the entry of Jesus into Jerusalem and his welcome with olive, laurel, and palm fronds. Who gave him such a warm, affectionate welcome? I waited for it to be said: "Jews!" Because they were women, children, and men of his own blood, of his own people, who embraced him joyfully and with love. But Jews were never associated with positive events, never with anything good.

On Holy Thursday I waited to hear the sermon of the divine mandate. I recalled the faraway Santiago de La Cruz and his moving words on the teaching to "love each other." But the kindness of Christ did not inspire as much as his physical pain. They spoke of the Last Supper without mentioning—not even with the slightest allusion—its link to the Seder and to "Jewish Easter." They repeated ad nauseam that Jesus had passed around the wine and said, "This is my blood," and that he had passed around the bread, saying, "This is my body." He gave his chalice to drink from just as Rabbi Gonzalo had done with his cup, and shared bread that was none other than matzo. On Holy Thursday, they also gloated over the betrayal of Judas Iscariot. How they gloated! They told the story, filling it with unparalleled foulness. He was the most disgusting person in creation, the recipient of torrential hatred. This was not only about a single individual who sold out his teacher for thirty coins, but, rather, about "the Jew." His disloyalty was that of a Jew. His greed was Jewish. His hypocrisy, Jewish. To say "Judas" was to say "Jewish." Even the first three letters of "Judas" and "*judío*" were the same. The connection was unstoppable. Each time a priest giving a sermon uttered the syllable "jud," my ear filled with the ending "ío." The fact that, instead of "ío," we sometimes heard "as," did nothing to lessen the pain.

Friday was an even more crushing day. From "cursed race" to "murderers," all manner of disdain was heard. And this was taught for generation after generation, like an incessant hail—centuries long— that penetrated people to the marrow. The Jews are the judges, torturers, slanderers, and tormentors of God. They are a lawless people, without light or mercy. They preferred a murderer like Barabbas and ordered the crucifixion of Jesus because they like to watch suffering. If the Romans were the ones who carried out the torture and cut his divine forehead with a crown of thorns, it was because the Jews made them do it. "The Jews killed Christ!" Not Veronica, not the three Marias, not little John, not the two thieves, not kind Joseph of Arimathea—none of them were mentioned as Jews. And neither Holy Saturday nor Easter Sunday offer any mercy. Except for a few occasions, the priests pontificated in such a manner that Jesus did not seem to have sacrificed himself for men's salvation, but due to the imposition of those vultures, the Jews. And his resurrection was no triumph over death, but a triumph over Jews. The more blows struck against that breed of snakes, the more glory one offered the throne of God.

And to think that Jesus was as Jewish as I am. What am I saying? Much more Jewish than me! Son of a Jewish mother, descendant of dozens of generations of pure Jewish lineage, circumcised as a Jew, educated as a Jew, living among Jews, preaching to Jews, and choosing only Jews for his apostles. Even in the gallows he was elevated to the highest level that a true Jew can reach, no less than King of the Jews. Only this much evidence can generate so much blindness.

104

My sisters finally arrived in Santiago. Isabel brought her little daughter, Ana, and Felipa wore the habit of the Society of Jesus. They were accompanied by Catalina, whose curly hair had gone completely gray.

They were very tired when they arrived at our house, and I noticed that their baggage was scant. I assumed that Isabel had kept the proceeds from her sales in the form of cash.

I had used the adobe and stones behind my house to build an additional room. So I was able to offer them a comfortable bedroom, in which I placed beds, rugs, a desk with many small drawers, trunks, and chairs. My wife helped enthusiastically, because she'd lost her family as a child, in far-off Spain, and it gave her intimate joy to partake in this reunion. It also made her happy to see me so elated.

Felipa had transformed into a placid nun. Her teenage insolence had been diluted under the black tunics of the Society. She told me that, on the day she took her vows, she was accompanied by Brother Santiago de La Cruz. The ceremony was unforgettable, with music, flowers, and a moving procession. There were many guests, because the Society had grown throughout the Viceroyalty of Peru and included many neighbors. The captain of the Lancers, Toribio Valdés, was in attendance, as was a generous Portuguese councilman, Diego López de Lisboa.

I listened without comment. I would not say a word about López de Lisboa until my sisters proved their ability to keep a secret. Her reference to that man stirred dread in me, and in them it must have set off an earthquake of suspicion about what I might know.

Isabel had sweetened. Now a mother and a premature widow, she revived the tenderness of our own mother. Her eyes—which also resembled those of my wife—were damp and seemed to caress with their gaze. Little Ana clung continuously to her mother.

"I'll present myself to the local branch of the Society," Felipa declared. "It's the correct thing to do."

"You can stay with us," my wife offered.

"Thank you. You are truly generous. But I belong there."

My wife nodded.

A loud noise interrupted our conversation: the falling of tin pitchers and the shattering of ceramic plates crashed in from the kitchen. Two cats had sidled in among the vessels, climbed a barrel, leapt onto the stove, been scalded, and were twisting around on a table laden with dinnerware.

My wife was concerned by the copious amount of salt that had spilled onto the floor.

"This bodes misfortune!"

My sister started and stared at me with her large, tender eyes.

—⁓—

The testimonies gathered in Concepción and Santiago are quite damning to the prisoner. The meticulous Inquisitorial process, nevertheless, demands that there be no hasty actions, no skipping of bureaucratic steps. All that material, along with the confiscated assets and the prisoner himself, are to be dispatched as soon as possible to Lima, where the High Tribunal will carry out its inexorable sentence.

Almeida hears the decision and begins to carry it out.

105

The loud knocks penetrated my sleep, like bells. Isabel shook me by the shoulder.

"Francisco, Francisco, someone's calling."

"Calling, yes—" I got up and wrapped myself in a cloak I'd left over a chair. The knocks did not stop.

"Coming!" I felt for a match, grabbed a candle, and lit it.

"Quickly," a voice implored from the other side of the door.

I opened to find a hooded, impatient figure.

"The bishop—" he began.

"Another hemorrhage?"

I raised the candle and revealed the monk's anguished face. He blinked and grasped my arm.

"Come immediately, please. He's dying!"

I dressed in a flash.

"What's happening?" Isabel asked, sitting up.

"The bishop is hemorrhaging again."

Little Alba Elena began to cry.

"We startled her, poor thing!"

Isabel picked up our daughter and tenderly sang a lullaby. I kissed Alba Elena, caressed my wife's soft cheek, and shot out to the street.

"When did the bleeding begin?" I asked without slowing my pace.

"Just now. He'd been complaining of stomach pains all night."

"Why did you wait so long to get me?"

He didn't answer, short of breath as he was.

"What were you waiting for?" I reproached him again.

"He didn't want to—"

"He never wants to! And then he calls for me after the fire."

When we arrived, a pair of lanterns trembled at the ancient gate. I strode fast through the familiar halls. In the bedroom, a small candelabra burned. I caught the smell of diarrhea between the medicinal vapors rising from a metal bowl.

"More light," I ordered.

I dragged a chair to the edge of the bed. The prelate was massaging his stomach and emitting weak moans.

"Good evening."

He didn't hear me.

"Good evening," I repeated.

He startled. "Oh, it's you."

I took his pulse; he'd lost too much blood. When more candelabras were brought into the room I was able to verify the acute anemia in his skin.

"The heavens have sent me sanctifying pain," he insinuated with an ironic smile.

"Bring me a cup of warm milk," I ordered the assistant.

"Milk? That will make me vomit. I do not want it, absolutely not. Soon I'll be reunited with the Lord. I am purging my sins with His help. The enemas of heaven are more effective than those you doctors give." He laughed maliciously, but he broke off suddenly and his hands flew to his abdomen. "Ay!"

"I'll put cold cloths on you."

"There's no need," he moaned, twisting back and forth.

The assistant extended a small copper tray toward me, bearing the cup of milk.

"Drink this."

"Yuck!"

He was pressing at his stomach. We helped him sit up. He took two sips, with great repugnance. The third sip he spat out on my shoes.

"I want to receive the last rites again."

He lay back down in defeat and his assistant began to sob.

"Quickly," he muttered, feeling with his right hand until it reached my knee.

I offered him my hand.

"You, don't go," he said. "You have the privilege of watching the transit to the next world of a sinner who did not want to sin."

"A sad privilege."

"Sad? Transit is sad? Only for sinners. The virtuous, they enjoy this moment. I've already lived enough, now I can enjoy the arrival of death."

The wavering candlelight emphasized the vertical crease on his brow. This man still exuded authority. Not long ago he'd made the faithful shiver with another sermon. "What had he been like years ago," I wondered, "when he worked as an inquisitor at the tribunal in Cartagena?" My thoughts mysteriously connected with his. A chill ran down my spine. I told him that I admired his courage. And he sank into a horrific memory.

"Sinners, the more they sin, the more they suffer—how they cried, the Marranos of Cartagena!"

I could not believe my ears. This man had a demonic perception.

"Ay!" He sighed, and massaged his abdomen again. "How those cursed people wept!"

"How many did you send to their deaths?" I heard myself ask, despite the danger of approaching the subject.

He opened his blind eyes, then slowly moved his head.

"I don't remember. Did I send any?"

I felt his pulse again. It was still thin, perilously weak.

He grasped my hand.

"Did I send any to their deaths?" he asked anxiously.

"Please be calm, Your Eminence."

"I was weak with the Jews—" He was becoming agitated. "That's where my sin lies. I was weak."

"Merciful?"

He shook his head.

"Mercy is sometimes betrayal, in matters of faith. I recall that a Jew was weeping. Abjure, then! I implored him. But the poor wretch could not abjure because his sobs were too intense—"

Drops began to roll down my forehead.

"I was a bad inquisitor. I condemned very little. Ay!"

The assistant entered with the bishop's confessor. I rose.

"Don't go!" he said, still gripping my hand.

I nodded and backed against the wall of the ample bedroom.

The priest kissed the crosses embroidered on his stole and hung it around his neck. He mumbled a few words and kneeled beside his superior, kissing his ecclesiastical ring. For a few minutes, my ears were privy to the murmur of swelling waves plagued with monsters. This man, aggressive, dissatisfied with his long-ago task of inquisitor and with his pastoral actions, was asking for forgiveness before God, like a warrior before his captain. There was no reckoning with gestures of love, only with the lack of cruelty. The terrible destiny of a man who had chosen the wrong career. He would have liked to be a Moor killer and an Indian killer; instead, he was a mediocre Jew killer.

The priest's thumb dipped into the oil and traced a cross on the bishop's forehead.

A sepulchral silence followed. I approached the patient. His eyes were closed. His breathing was rapid. I sat back down at his side.

"How is he faring, Doctor?" his assistant asked in my ear.

I turned, whispering into the assistant's ear, "Badly."

The man covered his face with his hands and left to pass on the prognosis. After a few moments I heard the lashes of flagellation.

The bishop stirred from his drowsy state.

"Ah, you . . ."

"Yes."

"Heaven is sending me new cramps—ay!" He contracted violently. "Ay!"

"Drink a little more milk."

"No—" His body relaxed, though he was paler than before, and more agitated. "Milk is for children. It does nothing for me. In any case, I want to purify myself."

"You've already done plenty," I said, trying to console him, and rising to call for his assistant.

"Don't go!" He held on to my clothes. "Please."

I sat back down.

"You, you doctors, you only think about the body." The reproach reinvigorated him for an instant. A curious temperament, his; he'd cling to me like an orphan, then immediately attack me like a gladiator.

"We don't only think about the body," I replied.

"And Jews—"

Again with the Jews! I bit my lips. What an obsession! I burst out from deep inside myself: "Why do Jews matter to you so much?"

His chalky face filled with surprise. "My son—that's like asking why sin matters."

"You associate them with sin," I heard myself say.

He nodded, stroking his stomach.

"Some Jews can be virtuous," I added insolently, unable to restrain myself.

He drew back suddenly. Another cramp accompanied his shock.

"What are you saying? Ay! Virtuous?" He raised his head, his blind and sinister pupils searching for me. "The murderers of Christ, virtuous?" His head fell in fatigue.

"Calm down, Your Eminence." I stroked his arm. "Some Jews are bad, but others are good people."

"Poisoning our faith?"

The sweat from my forehead had reached my lips. I glanced around me, happy to see that there was no one else in the bedroom.

"You are the ones who poison the faith!" I said, driven to madness. "Jews only want for you to leave us in peace."

The bishop made a face and immediately released it, as if he were about to vanish. His white lips strained to speak. "Circumcised man! You cursed circumcised man!"

"I am not that," I said, adding in a low voice, "yet—"

"Get back, Satan!" he whispered, shaking his head in desperation. "Get back—"

I dried my face. I had just committed suicide. I had denounced myself before the bishop of Santiago. Had I lost all reason?

I took his pulse again: more tenuous still. From through the walls and windows I could hear the prayers of those who had gathered to pay their respects. I stood up, just as several clergymen burst in. Now dozens of religious men would be witnesses to my self-betrayal. The bishop could sentence me to death in a matter of seconds.

"How is he doing?" his assistant asked.

I looked at the bishop one more time. He probably would not return to consciousness. My life now depended on his death.

They push him into the galleon's hold. The briny dampness of the wood recalls the trip he took so many years before, from Callao to Chile. In those days, he was fleeing the hunt for Portuguese people and their descendants, his baggage consisted of two trunks full of books and a diploma, and his heart beat with the prospect of freedom. Now he is returning with shackled wrists and ankles, his baggage contains his confiscated assets, and, in his breast, there beats the prospect of a war.

106

I took a long walk toward the east, admiring the wondrous mountain range. It was Shabbat, I was wearing clean clothes, and I was alternating moments of reflection with stirring recitation of the psalms. "The bishop had been buried with great pomp but," I wondered, "had he said anything before dying? Might his old role of inquisitor been potent enough to shake him out of paralysis and make him mutter the terrible denunciation?"

My spirit lacked the peace of prior years. I suffered a conflict that didn't come from outside myself, but from within. I now had more clarity on many subjects that made my outlook more definitive. Before, I floated among the clouds; now I walked under the sun. I had to recognize that I was a soldier who didn't want to fight, and as such, I didn't wear my armor well, and I didn't have a firm grip on my sword. But was it true that I didn't want to fight? Or had I not yet found the mission that would give meaning to my whole existence? Just as a good Catholic is energized by confirmation, because he fully embraces his identity, a Jew should be energized by the full ownership of who he is. My condition as a Marrano was devastating. How could I bear to continue denying my own self? For how long would Marranos keep being Marranos? My doubts were proof of my fragility, and my fragility, in turn, was a punishment I deserved for not daring to battle on behalf of my convictions. I couldn't stay like this forever—it was dissolving my spirit's peace.

I sat down on a few stones. An idea returned to my mind that often frightened me with its risk and near absurdity. Around me, the countryside spread out, scattered with clusters of cypress trees. In the distance, the branches of olive trees rippled in the breeze. The fragrant atmosphere brought to mind the exalting joys of creation celebrated in the virile poetry of the psalms. If I bled a great deal, I said to myself, I could resort to ligation. Abraham was circumcised when he was a grown man. It had been practiced for so many generations, and there were never any problems. Did I dare carry it out myself, on my own body? I thought through the technical steps as if I had to perform them on someone else. I calculated the time I'd need to section the foreskin, cut the frenulum, and free the glans of membranous remains.

Then I asked myself, again, whether my judgment was perhaps impaired. Marranos avoid circumcision for obvious reasons. Still, it had become known that in secret prisons, some Jews had been revealed because they had been circumcised. The bishop had synthesized his horror and scorn with the phrase "circumcised man," perhaps because he had discovered a few in Cartagena. I, however, did not feel diminished by this insult because it sounded like the opposite: a recognition of an ancient pact with God. Perhaps I even felt remiss because I wasn't circumcised, making me only somewhat Jewish. Perhaps he had made me see, as no one else had, my essential lack.

If I circumcise myself, I thought, I mark my body indelibly. Any future hesitations would have a reference point that couldn't be ignored. There would be no doubt as to my deepest, inalienable identity. I'd have the same body that Abraham had, and which was then borne by Isaac, Jacob, Joseph, Saul, David, and Jesus. I'd be irreversibly joining the great family of my glorious ancestors. I'd be one of them, not someone who only says he is.

———ᴍᴍ———

The trip from the southern port of Valparaíso to Callao is shorter than the same trajectory in the opposite direction, because the ocean currents from the icy southern seas push ships northward as if their sails were perpetually full of wind.

Francisco overheard that they would arrive in thirty days. They don't undo his shackles, and don't let him out to the deck. Are they scared that he might escape? Or that he might leap overboard into the waves, taking refuge in the belly of a marine monster like the prophet Jonah?

107

As our family expanded, the flavor of home life became intense. My wife appeared before my eyes with growing beauty; I had desired and waited for her all my life with such precise patience that it seemed unreal to have found her. It moved me to see her with our little daughter, Alba Elena, in her arms, tickling her nose. The baby's small fingers would grasp my short beard or manage to get into my mouth, and she squinted her little black eyes and closed her lips in the shape of a heart. Catalina, ever attentive, would come in with a tray, and my daughter and I would share some blackberry water. Her tiny teeth not only bit my fingers, but relished tearing crumbs from bread fresh from the oven. Isabel and Felipa also played with her, as did her cousin Ana. When she took her first steps, we all wanted her to do it again and again, until she was exhausted. I had chosen her name: Alba means dawn, a luminous beginning, purity, optimism. I had married a beautiful, intelligent woman, was gaining prestige in Santiago, had brought my two sisters and young niece over from Córdoba, and had even been reunited with old Catalina, which was like the preservation of a relic. Harmony reigned, but not all harmony is eternal.

My sister Isabel looked so much like my mother that her delicacy and self-denial made a great impression on me. I felt closer to her than ever. It also felt easier for me to talk with her than with Felipa, whose habit formed a barrier between us. And I saw Isabel every day. We shared food and even games with her daughter Ana and with Alba Elena. Once, I sat staring at her for so long that it startled her.

"What is it, Francisco?"

"Nothing. I was thinking."

"While looking at me?" She smiled. "Now you have to tell me what you were thinking."

I struck the arm of my chair.

"Córdoba, Ibatín. That's what I was thinking about."

She looked down. Memories disturbed her. She had never inquired after my father, or about our disappeared brother Diego. The little she knew was because I had told her almost by force.

"Now we are fine," she said gravely. "You are generous, we are an exemplary family, you're appreciated. There is no point in looking back on a time full of misfortune."

I pressed my lips together. Marcos Brizuela and his wife Dolores sprang to mind. They, too, were a beautiful family, only they were grounded in the truth of their own history. This was forbidden to me. I would never try to question the faith of my beloved Christian wife. But my two sisters were daughters of a Marrano, and their grandparents and great-grandparents had lived and died as Jews, so they did have a commitment to something greater than all of us, as did I.

A sudden storm rattles the ship. The hull and masts shriek with pain, and a lashing wind tears off a sail. Francisco falls into the growing puddle in the hold. The crew runs back and forth as waves toss the galleon as though it were made of paper. Watery mountains spill onto the deck, sweeping it with savage force.

"Could it be God's will for us not to reach Lima?" wondered Francisco. *He thinks again of Jonah, the prophet, his adventures and grandiose mission before the powerful men of Nineveh.*

For a few hours nobody pays him any mind; that is exactly why he's kept in chains.

108

Don Cristóbal de la Cerda decided to travel to Valparaíso to await the arrival of a brig bearing officials from Peru. He would spend a few weeks in that beautiful bay as a well-deserved break from his judicial endeavors. He would be accompanied by his wife and a good assortment of servants. He looked forward to gorging on the coast's extraordinary seafood and enjoying the incomparable landscape, far away from files and stress. He had earned a lot of money and needed to win over the people coming from Lima.

In a burst of affection, he made an invitation to my wife as we all sat together one evening.

"Would you come with us, Isabel?"

"But—what about Alba Elena?"

"Bring her with you."

"And Francisco?"

"Oh, that's up to him."

"I can't abandon the hospital for so many days. Thank you, Don Cristóbal."

"Would it bother you for Isabel to join us?"

"Not at all. Isabel deserves such a gift, and Alba Elena will enjoy the sea."

"It's only a few weeks," Don Cristóbal assured.

It was our first separation: a prelude.

The former interim governor, now a respected judge, charged a gentleman with searching for a large house for them in the port city of Valparaíso. Then he dispatched a caravan with rugs, beds, blankets, tables, chairs, cushions, dishware, candelabras, and even sacks of flour, corn, potatoes, sugar, and salt, determined not to suffer any privations while also being able to offer a lavish welcome to the officials who'd be arriving from an exhausting journey by ship.

They left on the western route.

Our house echoed with emptiness, reminding me of the echo that had terrorized me when we left Ibatín. Here, though, there was furniture. But absence settled in. Absence has its own voice; it can breathe, and frighten. The departure of my beloved Isabel and Alba Elena stirred thoughts of other departures that had not exactly been joyous. I shut myself into my bedroom to read. But my thoughts wouldn't let me concentrate, flowing swiftly toward an inevitable resolution. A fierce energy impelled me to press on, to correct my body in order to harmonize it with my soul, to cut my flesh so as to unify my spirit. I would divide myself, as Brother Martín had done with his flagellations. My hand would be the surgeon and my member the patient. I'd lock my jaw to drown the pain, and so the scalpel could stay steady. Perhaps a part of me might faint, but the other part would keep working to the end. Circumcision is a rite that draws accusations of barbarism, linking it to a Jewish taste for blood: first the foreskin's blood, then that of one's fellow man. Circumcision, one clergyman had said, stirs cruelty. Christians are not circumcised and for this reason they are stirred by love. "Of course," I thought ironically, "that's exactly why they persecute us, slander us, and burn us at the stake—to duly punish our cruelty." But this line of thinking, I realized later, was not a good one to follow, as it expresses resentment and is fed by the attitudes of those who hate us. What really matters and counts was a full connection to my roots.

After a while, I told myself that if I was still hesitating, it was because I had doubts. I recalled that a passage in the Book of Kings insinuated that the Jews had wanted to abandon circumcision long before Christ and the prophets condemned this renunciation as a betrayal of the pact. The Books of the Maccabees mentioned the tyrant Antiochus Epiphanes's order forbidding the circumcision of boys, but the people's rebellion defeated the tyrant. Long after that, Emperor Hadrian also tried to prohibit the procedure and suffered, as a response, the Bar Kokhba revolt. Centuries later, Emperor Justinian tried again, but various communities responded with systematic insubordination. Each of these decrees had a deeper, unspoken goal: to erase Jewish difference. They were not based on a sincere horror of blood; their armies spilled rivers of blood. Rather, they were based on a horror of Jews.

Why, after dozens and dozens of generations, were Jews still born with foreskins? The heroism of the patriarchs was enough to make us emerge circumcised from the womb. I sought out new answers that afternoon, and I liked one that took the shape of a question: Who says that circumcision, the pact, and choice are a pure privilege? All privilege, if it is not spurious, demands an exchange. God chooses Israel, and Israel sacrifices itself for God. Commitment on both sides: a pact. Also, I had learned something at the Seder of Pesach: each generation had to commit itself. It was necessary to be and act like them, to reprise the epic: "We are slaves in Egypt," and "We are free men," "We cross the Red Sea," "We receive the Law." Abraham began the pact, and celebrated it. We renewed it, gave it currency and momentum. My circumcision, then, meant as much as that of Isaac, Solomon, or Isaiah.

I opened my clothes and pulled at my foreskin, which had come as part of me so I could amputate it in a painful gesture of commitment. I gauged its sensitivity, going over the surgical techniques in my mind; I'd sit on a thick cloth bunched between my legs, ready to catch any dripping blood and, in arm's reach, I'd have my instruments ready, along with gauze, scarring powder, thread for a possible ligation, and bandages.

I would do it this very night.

I gathered all the necessary items in my bedroom, placed fresh candles in the candelabra, filled a bottle with blackberry water, and gulped down a glass of pisco liquor. I bolted the door closed, noisily, to convey that I did not wish to be disturbed. I arranged my instruments on the table and made sure they met the specifications described in the Book of Leviticus. I then removed my clothes. I placed a thick cloth over the chair. I brought the candelabra close. Everything was ready for me to begin.

"My God, God of Abraham, Isaac, and Jacob," I murmured, "I do this to renew our pact, to seal my loyalty to You and to Your people."

With my left hand I pulled back the foreskin. The thumb of that hand could feel the glans. I held the instrument tightly and carefully cut, like a scribe taking great pains to trace a perfect line. The blade descended into the red wound at the edge of the thumb; in this way, I avoided damaging the glans. I felt very sharp pain, but my attention remained focused on the surgical task. My fingers held on to the separated foreskin. I placed it on a small plate and applied warm, wet gauze to my bleeding penis. A few hemorrhaging spots emerged from the vermilion ring, but they were all weak. No ligation would be needed. I pressed my penis so the glans would surface, but it did not. As I had predicted, there was a piece of frenulum and transparent membrane in the way. I chose a pointed pair of scissors and completed the resection.

I was perfectly unfolded; the complaints of a patient don't make a doctor panic, they only make him long for excellence. The more it hurt, the more I applied myself to do my job well. I held the membrane with tongs as the scissors worked at it gently. I cleaned it again with damp gauze. There was very little blood. I dusted it with scarring powder and wrapped myself with a bandage.

"My God, God of Abraham, Isaac, and Jacob!" I murmured again. "With this Brit Milah I am an inseparable member of Israel. Accept me in your flock. And protect me."

I drank another glass of pisco.

That night, I woke frequently. But there was little pain, which proved what was essential lived in my spirit.

<center>~~~</center>

It was the only storm on the journey. There was no shipwreck, or loss of human life, or pirate attacks.

On July 22, 1627, Francisco disembarks in the port of Callao. He glances around him and the familiar landscape pinches at his entrails. He wears a rough, stained tunic and imagines that he must look as miserable as that beggar crowned with flies whom he'd confused with his father near this very place, on the esplanade, when he first set foot here.

A few yards away the captain of the galleon formally turns over the prisoner and his belongings to a few officials. Now he is only separated from Lima by the path he took so many times when he was a student.

109

I could urinate without any trouble and was only bothered by tension and a light itch. I changed the bandage on my penis, which was no longer bleeding. I had my customary breakfast and left for the hospital. At noon, I felt fatigued, and returned home to lie down for a few hours.

My sister's voice in the courtyard gave me the idea. That night, the one following my circumcision, I convinced her to accompany me for a few days to the baths that lay six leagues from Santiago. Both of us needed relaxation.

She looked at me in surprise and praised me yet again for my generosity.

There was no need to take much clothing, I explained. I had no wish to compete with my father-in-law's fortunes. I was inviting her to a simple getaway, wanting to enjoy some time with her. The baths were not like the famous ones at Chuquisaca. They were not in a remote plateau, but in green plains with the blue mountains behind them. The waters were hot springs, and a Spanish family lodged visitors in their modest farmhouse. A small legion of servants cleaned the pools, saw to the rooms, and served food.

Things I brought with me: books, paper, ink, and the decision to speak frankly to Isabel. I wanted our bond to stop relying on fragile threads and uncomfortable silences. The circumcision had thrown my excess caution to the wind, as I had imagined it would. Now I felt strong and resolved. But I had to act intelligently.

One afternoon, as we strolled through the shaded surroundings of the farmhouse, I decided to broach the subject that gave my life meaning.

"Isabel. Our father—"

She kept on walking without paying attention.

"Do you hear me? Our father—"

She grazed my arm. "I don't want to know. Don't speak to me about him, Francisco."

"You have to know!"

She shook her head energetically.

"In Lima, I was with him for several years," I pressed on. "He told me important things."

Her eyes took on a tragic luminescence. They were terribly similar to my mother's eyes at the end of her life.

"Did he tell you that he denounced Juan José Brizuela?" she blurted out.

"You know that, too?"

"Who doesn't?" she said angrily.

"Yes, he did that, but under torture. They burned his feet—he was almost paralyzed."

"His sin was great."

"Don't talk that way. You're not a familiar of the Holy Office."

"It's because of his sin that he had to abandon us, and because of it we lost our brother." She began to cry. "Because of his sin our mother died."

"It wasn't his fault. He suffered enormously."

"Then whose fault is it? Ours?" The edges of her lips were trembling, and her cheeks were wet.

I offered her my handkerchief. "I want to explain."

She blew her nose. She shook her head again. "Don't explain."

"Isabel, I need your help!" The child in me burst out, the one who longed for his mother's warmth, and I heard myself saying dramatic words. "Isabel, my future depends on you."

She raised her glassy gaze.

"I'm so alone," I added.

"Alone?" Her hand brushed against me. "I can't imagine—" she stammered, confused. "Are you having marital troubles?"

"No, it's not that. Since I married and our daughter was born, and then you all came, it seemed that my dreams were coming true. But in my spirit there is something deeper, something that goes beyond family—a fire."

"God has been merciful with us. Stop, Francisco!" Tears streamed down her face. "Don't ruin what is going fine."

I kissed her hand. "My sister. Things are not fine."

"What's the matter, then? Are you sick?"

"Ah, if only it were that—"

We walked in silence along the winding path. We were both tense now, like strings on a lute. I had to open her mind, remove her fear, and show her what belonged to us. I had to pull out the prejudice that poisoned her soul. But she had hardened her ears against me.

"Our father was reconciled, but—" I pressed on.

"You're back to that again? I don't want to know!"

"Our father did not betray his true faith. He deserves admiration."

"Be quiet, for God's sake, be quiet." She put her hands up to defend herself from my assault.

"He was always Jewish!"

She covered her ears.

I embraced her.

"Isabel, my dearest. Don't flee."

She shrank into herself.

"What are you afraid of?" I caressed her head, leaned it against my chest. "You already know."

"No!" She shook herself in fright.

"Our father was a just man," I said. "He was the victim of fanatics."

She stared at me reproachfully and hissed, "Why are you speaking to me this way? We're brother and sister!"

I was surprised.

"You're trying to drag me to hell!"

She backed away from me as if I were her enemy.

"Isabel, what are you saying?"

"You're ignited by the devil, Francisco."

I grabbed her wrist. "Listen to me. There's no devil here except the inquisitors. I believe in God. And our father died speaking his unshakable loyalty to God."

"Leave me alone! You've gone mad."

"I'm not mad," I insisted. "I'm Jewish."

She stuffed a fist into her mouth and let out a suffocated scream. Then she covered her ears again.

"I want to share it with you, with someone from my own family," I said, shaking her by the shoulders.

"Leave me alone, please!" Her cries were draining her of strength.

I embraced her again.

"Don't be afraid. God sees us, and is protecting us."

"It's horrible!" Her words were broken up by sobs. "The Holy Office persecutes Jews—takes all their belongings away. It burns them!" She beat her fists against my chest. "You're not thinking of us, of your wife, your daughter!"

"I don't want to involve them, I have no right."

"Then why me?"

"Because you belong to the people of Israel. You have the blood of Deborah, Judith, Esther, Mary in your veins."

"No, no."

"I've read the Bible several times. Listen to me, please. It says, clearly, insistently, that idols should not be made or worshipped. That anyone who proceeds that way is offending God."

"That's not true."

"It also says in the Bible that God is one, one only, and they want to impose the notion on us that God is three."

"That is what the Gospel says. And the Gospel is truth."

"It doesn't even say that in the Gospel, Isabel. If only they would comply with the Gospel!"

She broke away from me and ran toward the farmhouse. Her skirt snagged in the bushes along the way.

"Would you say that blessed are the meek because they shall inherit the earth?" I shouted, pursuing her. "Are the afflicted blessed, the merciful, those pure of heart, those who hunger and thirst for justice? Listen to me!" I was gasping. "What about the peacemakers, are they blessed? Can you say the same about the persecuted—like our father? They deny Jesus himself, Isabel!" I followed her, index finger held high. "Jesus said, 'Do not think that I have come to abolish the law and the prophets, for I have not come to abolish them, but to perfect them.' And now they say the law is dead."

She stopped, suddenly. Her face was devastated by tears, burning with reproach.

"You want to confuse me—" She was gasping, too. "You're inspired by the devil. I want to know nothing, absolutely nothing about the dead Law of Moses."

"The law of God, you mean to say. Is the law of God dead?"

"I believe in the law of Jesus Christ."

"Which one? The one they say belongs to Jesus Christ? The one of the jails? Denunciations of friends? Torture? Fires for burning people alive?"

She resumed her flight.

"Don't you realize that the inquisitors are like pagans?"

She was tripping. She couldn't stop crying. I kept calling after her, reciting verses, comparing prophecies with reality. My words fell on her like whips. She'd contract a shoulder, lower her head, wave me away with her hands. And she kept running. She was a terrified creature striving to protect itself from my implacable hailstorm.

She shut herself into her room.

I stayed outside her door, recovering my breath. I heard her sobbing. I waited for her to calm down before calling to her. But in the end I did not call. I went out for a walk. I'd been harsh, I thought, and emphatic. I hadn't taken into account her delicate nature, her fears, or the strength of the teachings with which she'd been inculcated. She'd been subjected to a spiritual cleansing that had washed away her love for her father, or had changed that love into its opposite. In my passion I'd taken the wrong path. I had to act more prudently, to speak of these matters in a long, tranquil way, to give her time. I was making her swallow stones, and this required patience.

I walked, burdened, until wrapped by night. The starry sky awoke the fireflies of the plains; they winked far and wide, beckoning seductively. Were they an alphabet? I'd been obsessed with this idea since childhood. I caught an insect in my hand. Its green glow pushed between my fingers, and its tiny, desperate legs scratched at my skin. I let it go so it could be reunited with its multitudinous family and the party could continue. It was unconcerned with my despair.

The following day, Isabel stubbornly avoided me, and would not even greet me. She was yellow, gaunt. Later, I found a note under the door of my room that said, "I want to return to Santiago."

—⁂—

The officials wait until night falls and the city streets empty of people to take the prisoner to Lima. Francisco recognizes his surroundings despite the darkness. He immediately identifies the fearful plaza of the Inquisition, and the imposing building with the engraved words Exurge Domine et Judica Causam Tuam.

They advance toward a sinister wall and stop before the door, which is guarded by soldiers. This is the mayor's residence, and its depths—this is well known—lead directly into the secret prisons. He is ordered to dismount. Then he is ordered to cross the threshold.

110

I made the mistake of attributing feelings to my sister that, in fact, only beat in my own chest. She was not ready, and even the longest, most tranquil talk in the world would not change this fact. What I'd expressed had struck her brutally, and I had hurt her deeply. Despite the years that had passed, she had not overcome the blows our family had received. Nobody had helped her see, in our misfortune, anything other than a punishment, and she could not stand the thought of being punished again. To practice or believe in Judaism, for her, was ridiculous and bad. It was to make a pact with the devil. In this light, my mouth was no longer mine, and the words I spoke did not come from my heart. She began staring at me as if I were a stranger. When my gaze caught hers, she'd avert her eyes and she could not bring herself to speak to me again.

Back in Santiago, I found a piece of paper under my bedroom door. I recognized her handwriting and leapt to the joyous conclusion that she had understood me a little and wished to talk more. But no, she was begging me to abandon my madness, that for the love of God I must disavow the ruinous thoughts that had made my head sick. Under no circumstances would she believe what I had said to her.

I tried to see her resistance in a positive light. What if it hinted at a struggle that had begun to take place in her heart? She was a sensitive, affectionate woman, and she had suffered terrible losses. It was logical for her to start with a rejection, but perhaps that rejection soon would transform into slight understanding and then into complete understanding. I preferred to suppose that she would not have written to me if my words had not had an impact on her. Something had clearly broken inside her. Our conversation at the baths, though rushed, had functioned like the trumpets of Jericho. Sounding them one more time, I thought enthusiastically, would be enough to make the walls collapse.

So I dipped my quill and began to write. I had to be lucid and precise, illuminating each concept with plenty of candles. I had to show her that the devil actually dwelled in the Inquisition, not in the persecuted—in those who silence and asphyxiate others, not in those who think. I spoke of histories, martyrs, wise men, beautiful works. And the burning need to connect with our roots. I told her that I was trying to become more consistent every day; I fasted, honored the Sabbath, and prayed to God. That a year ago, I'd stopped confessing at the Society of Jesus, the most intellectual of Catholic orders, because it was enough for me to tell my sins directly to the Lord.

I reread my letter, corrected a few phrases, and folded the pages. I was satisfied. I was like a man in love who'd succeeded in pouring the fever of his passion into a poem. I left my bedroom in search of my sister. I found her in the courtyard.

"Here." I extended the folded sheets toward her. "Read these carefully."

She raised her eyes, which were red from crying. She didn't dare take my letter.

"It's a well-thought-out response."

I raised her reticent hand, opened her fingers, and pressed them around the pages.

"Please, reflect on what I've written. And answer me thoughtfully. Take three days."

Her eyes remained anguished. I pitied her. She was suffering. And she seemed very afraid. She moved away from me, head bent, elbows glued to her body, smaller somehow. She was like my mother when the avalanche of misfortune had rained on her. I followed her for a few paces, hands in the air, wanting to offer her a caress. But she broke into a run toward the refuge of her room.

"Hopefully, she'll find serenity," I prayed, "and read my frank thoughts again and again. Hopefully she'll find the courage to talk more with me."

Again, I was wrong. Isabel was in no state to reason calmly. The mere thought of calling into question what had been consecrated by years of indoctrination horrified her. It didn't matter what I said because any hint of rebellion against the power that had lashed at our family made her suffocate in panic.

She shut herself in—I found this out later, when it was too late—and began to cry. She cried and cried without solace. Between hiccups, snot dripping, she opened my letter. She read the first few sentences and abruptly balled it up. She could not tolerate expressions that sounded like outright blasphemy. She kept on crying until dinnertime. She washed her face, took a walk around the garden, and tried to hide her anguish. She entered the kitchen, ordered the servants to go find fresh vegetables and, when she was alone, took my long, unread letter from her clothes and threw it in the fire. The flames twisted the folds like edges of an effigy, blackening them and making them glimmer with drops of blood. Isabel had the intense impression that she'd just burned one of Beelzebub's hoofs.

It wasn't enough. She was disturbed. Sorrow bit at her heart. I had told her that my future depended on her. It was a real warning, because I had put my fate in her hands, in her weak hands, without registering the consequences that step would have. Why did I do it? A vast question. It was the same as wondering, why did Jesus enter Jerusalem and show himself in public when he knew the Romans wanted to seize him?

Why did he let Judas Iscariot leave the Seder to fetch the soldiers? Had I spoken with my sister to indirectly make the Inquisition arrest me? Was I pushing her to become my own Judas Iscariot, that tragic link who spurs on the decisive battle? Had I done this so I could be brought before the present-day Herod, Caiaphas, and Pilate to show them that an oppressed Jew mirrors Jesus better than all the inquisitors put together?

In her torment, Isabel prayed. Her knowledge was a burning coal. She urgently needed to expel it, or share it with someone. She recalled my warning: "My future depends on you." I was already in the arms of death—to her mind—and I would drag along others with me. She went out in search of Felipa. Halfway there she stopped, wrung her hands, sighed, and turned back. But before she arrived home, she turned again. She walked back and forth so many times that she felt on the verge of fainting. Hours later, my two sisters sobbed together because once again misfortune had befallen our condemned family.

"What will we do?" Isabel pleaded.

Felipa paced her cell, worrying her rosary beads. In a hoarse voice suffocated by tears, she finally said, "There is one thing I cannot avoid."

Isabel stared at her, trembling.

"I must tell my confessor."

Francisco casts a last glance at the black street of the powerful City of Kings, which represents a false, elusive freedom. He crosses the threshold, and, with his head held high, descends into hell.

BOOK FIVE

Deuteronomy

Depths and Heights

111

A damp stench creeps through the thick wall. They cross a desolate room, enter a hall, and cautiously descend several uneven stairs. The lantern draws out the creases in the plaster walls and ceiling, which resemble the skin of an endless monster, breathing, waiting to devour its prey. Francisco trips, and almost falls, tangled in the chain that connects the shackles to his blistered limbs. The black man carrying the lantern guides him into the depths. They are lost in a gloomy labyrinth. Where are they going? The man stops in front of a wooden-slatted door, opens a lock, lifts the bolt. An official grasps the prisoner's arm and forces him through. The door closes and the last tremors of lantern light slip through the slats. Francisco is left in darkness. He feels through the emptiness until he reaches the adobe walls and discovers a stone bench. Now that nobody can see him, he collapses in exhaustion.

He is alone again, but in the true, chilling jail of the Holy Office, in its entrails. He knows they will make him wait—as they did in Concepción, and in Santiago—to soften his resistance. He turns to the psalms for strength.

He knows a great deal about the Holy Office, but not about its surprising irregularities—no one has ever spoken to him in sufficient detail. For this reason, he is surprised when, at the end of a mere hour, the bolt is pulled back again and a bronze face appears with a lit candle.

Are they already taking him to the torture chamber? So soon? It's not the same man as before, but, rather—a woman! She approaches him cautiously and sheds light on his head, wrists, and ankles, without saying a word. She places the candle on the floor, exits into the hall, and returns with a pot of warm milk. Francisco studies her face, so similar to Catalina's years ago, and tries to understand this extraordinary gesture.

He drinks, and is comforted. The woman sits at his side. She exudes the scents of a kitchen, of fried things.

"Thank you," the prisoner whispers.

She watches him in silence. Francisco points his chin toward the open door.

"What about it?" the woman says with a shrug. "You want to escape?"

Francisco nods.

"You wouldn't be able to." She lets out a long sigh. "Nobody escapes from this place."

Who is she? Why is she helping him? It all seems like an absurd apparition, a trick of dreams. He asks questions, and she is not stingy with her answers. She has no power at all. Her name is María Martínez. She was arrested for witchcraft; to alleviate the sentence that has not yet been handed down by the tribunal, she fulfills certain tasks in the warden's house.

What kind of tasks? Bringing warm milk to arriving prisoners? Showing them that it's not worthwhile to attempt to flee even though the doors are open? Coaxing information out of them?

She smiles sadly and unfurls her story: The commissioner of La Plata ordered her arrest for falling in love with a young widow whom she regularly visited. (Francisco wonders if she tells everyone the same story.) The commissioner admitted that he himself would have stabbed her to death because it was intolerable for a woman to bed another woman, and that this was worse than the denunciations for reading prophesies in wine, or for having stuck seven pins into a dead pigeon so that the young widow would never stop loving her. Her arrest took place under the charge of witchcraft, which was a less serious offense. The inquisitors preferred to interrogate her over the rites she performed to obtain the devil's help. The woman speaks in a slow, confused manner, but as she speaks, she sticks a toothpick in her nose to release drops of blood. She does this to keep the blood in a handkerchief that she gives the Virgin so that she may exempt her from further torture. Each person does what they must to ease their own suffering. Finally, she tells Francisco that the warden has left for a few hours and told her to serve him a bit of milk. He is not a bad man, she says.

"Serve milk to me?"

"Aren't you the doctor who was just brought from Chile?"

Francisco tries to decipher the jumble of it; after being arrested in Concepción and enduring an exhausting series of rebukes, interrogations, and transfers, they send a prisoner to him? Had the Holy Office gone mad?

The woman asks what crime he has committed.

"Crime? None."

Her toothless mouth laughs, and she remarks that everyone always denies having committed a crime.

"I don't deny the cause of my arrest," he responds. "I'm only saying that it is not a crime."

"Bigamy? Homicide? False titles?"

"None of those. I'm a Jew."

The woman stands up and shakes out her coarse dress.

"Yes, a Jew," he repeats, more loudly. "Like my father and my grandfather."

"Them, too? All of them?"

"All of them."

She crosses herself, invokes Saint Martha, and stares at him, stunned. "Aren't you afraid?"

"Yes, I'm afraid, of course I'm afraid."

"Then why do you say it in such an unabashed way?"

"Because that's what I am. And because I believe in the God of Israel."

She stares at him, frightened, full of pity. She whispers, "Don't say it that way to the warden. They'll burn you alive."

"You know what, María, I've come all this way precisely to say it to him. I need to say it."

"Shhh!" She covers his mouth with her plump hand. "The warden is merciful, but he can turn violent. If you say that you're—that—he'll condemn you!"

She picks up the empty pot and the candle.

"If he comes back in a calm mood," she says, "and you tell him— please! Don't tell him!"

Francisco shakes his head, moves his shackled hands, and realizes that this poor woman will never understand. Nevertheless, she deserves an explanation. It's been a long time since he's been able to share his ideas with anyone, and soon he will have to describe them to the inquisitors. Sooner or later they will call him and will want to hear from him, directly, about what is already recorded in his documents. Why not practice with this woman?

Francisco begs her not to go and begins to explain, but he's interrupted by the bracing sound of a closing door. María looks out into the hall and returns to warn him.

"It's the warden! Stand up, quickly!" She helps him rise, arranges his hair, and adjusts his dirty shirt.

A short, burly man enters, followed by a servant carrying a lamp. He approaches Francisco and examines him from head to toe as if wanting to suggest that their difference in height will give him no advantage. His gaze is full of scorn. He snaps his fingers and María leaves with the pot and candle. The warden disappears, too. Suddenly, Francisco is alone again, in the dark. The abrupt changes dizzy him.

Before his eyes can adjust to the dark, the servant with the lamp returns and orders him to follow. He knows that, sooner or later, his body will be subjected to abuses in attempts to make him surrender, but his crazy longing is to achieve a triumph of the soul. And so, let them take him here and there, let them expose him to cold or heat. He wants to arrive once and for all at the moment when he can assert his defense. He is naïve; he's idealistic; he is all the things that are not taken into account during a trial. But he can no longer withdraw; he himself closed the easier routes. The shackles drag down on him, making it difficult to remain upright. He follows the servant through a hall that vibrates when touched by the light. The guide turns to the right, and, after another stretch, turns again, and stops in front of a sturdy door. He raises the lamp and knocks. A voice orders him to enter. Behind a desk, in the light of a candelabra, sits the warden.

Francisco remains on his feet and waits, bent with fatigue.

The official reads the papers piled on his desk and doesn't say a word. They must be the documents of his denunciation, drawn up in Chile. He lingers over each page; he is a responsible official who reads with difficulty. The pain in Francisco's ankles sharpens, and a mist invades his eyes. Intermittently, the warden peers over his papers to confirm that he is still in the same place.

After some time, his neutral voice orders, "Identify yourself."

"Francisco Maldonado da Silva."

The official takes a while to ask the next question. "Do you know the reason for your arrest?"

Francisco rests his weight on one leg; he can't stay standing for much longer, as the fatigue of two horrific months is overcoming him. "I suppose, for being a Jew."

"You suppose?"

A grimace pulls the edges of his lips, and he answers, "I am not the author of my arrest, and I cannot know its cause."

The warden's hand moves to his sword; such insolence is unacceptable.

"You're crazy, too?" he scolds, face red.

Francisco leans his weight on his other leg. A heavy mass is crushing his shoulders, the back of his neck. The objects around him move and blur.

"I urge you to tell the truth," the man says in a bureaucratic tone.

Francisco stammers his response: "That's why I'm here."

The mist thickens and he can't keep his knees from buckling. He faints.

The warden rises slowly, walks around the desk, and stands next to the prisoner. With the tip of his shoe, he kicks Francisco's shoulder. He's accustomed to receiving cowards and liars. He digs his shoe into Francisco's ribs and tells the servant to throw water over his face.

"Weakling!" he says scornfully, returning to his chair. He strokes his chin and thinks. "Take him back to his cell and make him eat."

112

A couple of slaves dress Francisco in a monk's habit. Then they offer him milk and a piece of freshly baked bread. Eating causes pain in his jaw, throat, and sternum.

"Let's go," they order.

"Where are you taking me now?" Pain radiates through his whole body.

With conspiratorial laughs they push him into the hall. Is it the same hall as hours before? They've succeeded in disorienting him. Will they start with the rack, as they did with his father? He notices that the warden is walking at his side, hardy and severe. When did he show up? Francisco's hands rise to his chest. His perception has become distorted; fatigue strains his lucidity. The chain tangles around his ankles.

"What's the matter?" the warden says.

"Where are you taking me?"

"To a hearing with the tribunal."

Francisco trips again and the warden holds his arm and breaks his fall. Not in his most naïve imaginings would he have guessed such a rapid process. Were supernatural powers at work? For months, they had excluded him, the commissioners had made him feel abandoned, impotent. Now, in the belly of the Holy Office, its central authorities were rushing to see his face and hear his voice. Could it be true? He had the impression of passing through doors that opened before his arrival, and of being observed by silent men. They brought him into a sumptuous room, lit up by high lanterns.

Someone pulls a stool toward him, and the warden grasps his arm again to make him sit. He has to hold the stool tightly with his hands. Is this where the tribunal carries out its function? He retches.

In front of him, on a platform, three plush ecclesiastical chairs upholstered with green velvet stand behind a long mahogany table with six legs carved in the shape of sea monsters. At the ends of the wide table, candelabras glow, like bodyguards for the crucifix that glints at the center. Francisco sees, to one side of the platform, an almost life-sized Christ, solemn, eyes gazing at the prisoner's ankles; his father had told him that it was miraculous, as its head moved to refute the captives' lies or support the prosecutors' accusations. A shudder runs through him. On the right-hand side wall, there are two closed doors, and he supposes that the judges will emerge from there or, if not, that the doors lead to secret rooms, or the torture chamber.

Tension keeps his eyelids up. He means to recognize the objects in order to establish a sense of context and manage his fear. What's hidden behind the black curtains in front of him? Black represents the church's mourning for the persecutions it suffers due to cursed heresies, and green symbolizes the hope that sinners may repent. The objects are weapons wielded at his head. He shrinks back on seeing the Holy Office's coat of arms on a defiant flag that proclaims the owner of this place and reminds prisoners of their abominable condition. He stares at it, spellbound. It consists of a green cross on a black background, and to the right of the cross, an olive branch promises mercy to those who repent; the left side is embroidered with the thick sword that administers justice to the stubborn. Under those symbols a spiny bramble glows, proof of the inextinguishable wisdom of the church, as is the fire that will consume anyone who persists in rebellion. All of this is surrounded by words in Latin, taken from Psalm 73: *Exurge Domine et Judica Causam*

Tuam—the same words he read apprehensively the first time he saw the Inquisitorial palace upon arriving in Lima at the age of eighteen, his soul a knot of conflicts. He can't take his eyes off the flag; it is the monstrous ear that listens to the innumerable accused and then goes out to the plaza to preside over the Acts of Faith. Finally, Francisco increases his own vertigo on discovering the famous ceiling, talked about throughout the Viceroyalty. It is a colorful arrangement of thirty-three thousand pieces, assembled without a single nail, carved from noble Nicaraguan wood brought over the sea especially for this purpose.

From a corner of the room, a court clerk watches him and verifies that the shackles are keeping his limbs immobile.

The first door on the right creaks, and a pale man with glasses walks in. He is a morose apparition; he doesn't speak, look up, or seem to register Francisco's presence. He moves like a marionette: slowly, stiffly. He stops at the bare table and, with the calm of a priest at the altar, arranges a quill, inkwell, sheets of paper, blotting paper, and a large book bound in leather. Then he sits, hands in prayer, and stares at the green-and-black coat of arms of the Holy Office, still as a corpse.

After a while, the door creaks again and three solemn judges file in. The air grows tense and acquires the scent of death. They glide majestically, with short steps. They walk to the platform, where the high-backed chairs have been moved to ease their entry. This is a procession without images or multitudes of the faithful, with no more than three figures shrouded in black tunics.

The notary stands and cocks his head. The warden's firm hand presses Francisco's arm, forcing him to rise. The sound of his chains profanes the macabre pomp. The judges stand beside their chairs, cross themselves, and pray. Then, in unison, they sit down. The warden pulls on Francisco's arm again. The notary turns his head to the left for the first time, signaling for the warden to leave. The court clerks leave, too. In the courtroom, only the three inquisitors, the secretary, and the prisoner remain. The trial is about to begin.

113

The prisoner has thought of this moment, imagined questions, and practiced answers, but his mind has now gone blank. He can only assume that they will treat him with the same contempt they expressed toward his father. They will ask him to tell the truth, and every word will be neatly registered to be used against him every time he makes a mistake until he breaks. Suddenly, he recalls that his father asked him not to repeat his own trajectory. It's an inopportune thought; he shouldn't think of his father, but of how to perform before the icy inquisitors. The unwanted reproach grows inside him; he has disobeyed his father's advice, and now he has to settle accounts with the tribunal. Unlike his father, however, Francisco recognizes that the denunciation was made against him because he himself sought it out when he decided to shed his double life. It remains to be seen whether he'll be able to withstand the severity of the Holy Office, showing them that he has no reason to repent for being who he is, and defending the beliefs that sustain him. He knows, of course, that he is a mere mortal, and that the Holy Office brims with experiences and methodologies for destroying the strong of will.

One of the judges places his glasses on the bridge of his nose, smooths the fine ribbons of his mustache, and orders the secretary to announce the beginning of the hearing. Francisco hears that this day is

Friday, the twenty-third of July, in the year 1627. And that the tribunal consists of the extremely illustrious doctors Juan de Mañozca, Andrés Juan Gaitán, and Antonio Castro del Castillo.

Andrés Juan Gaitán—that same one who praised Viceroy Montesclaros on his visit to the university—fixes his stare on Francisco and says, monotonously, "Francisco Maldonado da Silva, you will solemnly swear to tell the truth."

Francisco returns his gaze. The priest's brilliant pupils and those of the helpless offender touch, like the fleeting strike of steel blades. Two opposing ideologies take each other's measure. The recalcitrant supporter of unblemished uniformity, and the weak, but also obstinate, defender of freedom of conscience. The inquisitor hates the offender; the prisoner fears the inquisitor. Both will battle in the ambiguous stadium of truth.

"Place your hand on this crucifix," he orders.

The inquisitors' heads, through Francisco's eyes, seem to rise out of the table, and the tops of their green velvet chair backs resemble crowns. They are three disembodied heads, gray and sullen. Francisco makes no visible move, but the disturbing, subtle shudder is torturing his every finger.

"Sir," he says after a deep breath. "I am a Jew."

"That is the charge for which you are on trial."

"I therefore cannot swear in the name of the cross."

The notary snaps his head up and breaks his quill.

"That is the procedure!" the inquisitor replies in frustration. "You must conform to the procedure."

"I know."

"Then do it."

"It makes no sense. I ask you to understand me."

"You teach us what does or does not make sense?" His face winced at the prisoner's brazenness. "Are you trying to persuade us that you're insane?"

"No, sir. But my vow of truth will only have value if I do it in accordance with my beliefs, with my laws."

"For us, your law does not apply, neither do your beliefs."

"But they do apply for me. I am Jewish and I can only swear by God, by the living God who made heaven and Earth."

The secretary writes rapidly, his handwriting growing larger and more uneven. The finely wrought ceiling creaks; its thousands of pieces, so masterfully carved, have never heard such a reply. The inquisitors' hearts beat hard in their chests, but they feign serenity. They reflexively decide that this miserable man cannot imagine for one moment that he has gotten under their skin.

"You mean to impose your law on us?" Gaitán's voice strains to maintain its dry monotonousness. "This attitude will be prejudicial to you."

"If I swear on the cross, I will have committed my first lie."

Gaitán turns to his colleagues. They speak quietly, clearly struggling to arrive at an agreement. The prisoner watches them while they take their time, assuring they don't make a mistake in response to this unexpected insult. Finally, Juan de Mañozca addresses the secretary.

"The prisoner may swear in his own manner, but let his accursed obstinacy be recorded."

For the first time, a strange vow resounds in that room, and the Nicaraguan wood groans.

Then Francisco responds to the interrogation. He has endured too much falsehood and is eager to reveal himself without the mask of shame, cowardice, and betrayal. Betrayal of God, of others, of himself.

The inquisitors find themselves faced with an unprecedented problem, a mix of insult and frankness. A case that doesn't evade the gravity of the questions or the threat of the charges. A man who doesn't hide his sins, doesn't deny his condition as a Jew or his abominable practices, who doesn't try to confuse the judges. Worst of all, he seems sincere. He repeats that he is a Jew, as if he took morbid pleasure in uttering that word full of evil resonance. He insists that he is Jewish, as was his father—who had a penance imposed on him by this very tribunal—and his grandfather and his descendants in a long, dirty genealogy of wretched blood. He informs them that his mother, however, was an Old Christian and died in the Catholic faith. He tells them that he was baptized in remote Ibatín and confirmed in Córdoba by Bishop Fernando Trejo y Sanabria. He has a solid religious education, which started in childhood; he was Catholic until the age of eighteen, when he came to Callao to reunite with his father. Although doubts riddled his soul due to the mistreatment his family had suffered, he confessed, took communion, attended Mass, and was obedient to all the acts a good Catholic should observe. But the moment came in which a powerful turbulence blossomed in him, and this happened when he read the *Scrutinium Scripturarum*, written by the convert Pablo de Santamaría. That deceitful book nauseated him; the argument between young Pablo and the old, senile Jew Saulo was artificial, mendacious, and did not demonstrate the triumph of the church, but, rather, its acts of abuse. That was when he asked his now-deceased father for intensive teachings in Judaism.

Behind the imposing desk, Andrés Juan Gaitán and Antonio Castro del Castillo shift in their chairs. The torrent of blasphemies is more hurtful than a spear, and they struggle to maintain their composure. Juan de Mañozca decides to interrupt him and orders him to demonstrate his Catholic education by crossing himself and uttering the prayers of the law of Our Lord Jesus Christ.

Francisco suddenly goes mute. What kind of idiotic test are they asking of him? The quality of his studies is now reduced to an exam for illiterates? Are they mocking him? Do they not believe in the veracity of his tale? And then something else springs to mind: they want to find out whether an outright Jew is capable of carrying out a Catholic rite without repugnance.

"It does not harm the law of God for me to cross myself or to utter Catholic prayers."

He crosses himself, says the prayers, and recites the Ten Commandments.

The inquisitors watch and listen with forced neutrality on their faces. The secretary continues to write quickly. He has already broken his third quill.

"Continue," orders Mañozca.

Francisco is left without knowing the reason for such an elemental test; he passes his tongue over his lips, and completes the story of his life. He offers it to them generously. While he was hiding his identity, he was amputated as a man, and now that he exhibits it, he holds himself upright. A healing lightness has filled the interstices of his body and soul. He tells them that he married Isabel Otáñez, a native of Seville, an Old Christian—he emphasizes this, so that they will not dare bother her. He adds that they have a daughter and await their second child. He describes the suffering this separation has caused, and begs the most illustrious inquisitors to let news of him reach her, and to not confiscate all their belongings. She is a devoted Christian and should not suffer due to a faith of which she knows nothing.

"With whom did you share the secret of your Judaism?" Gaitán asks.

This is the unfailing question, as his father had told him so many times before: "They ask for names, they demand names, it's not enough for them to see their captive bathed in tears and full of repentance." He is not surprised by the question, or by the tone. They will ask it again with zeal and draw on all the power of their voices. But he has already prepared and planned the answer he will always use, whether awake or asleep, in the courtroom or in the torture chamber: that he only spoke of Judaism with his father and with his sister Isabel. His father is already dead and his sister has denounced him through Felipa's confessor.

"With who else?" the inquisitor insists.

"No one else. If I hadn't talked about it with my sister, I wouldn't be here today."

114

They transfer him to another hole. Although inside he is still battling a diffuse fear that comes and goes, he is satisfied with his defiant conduct during his first hearing with the tribunal. His body is like that of a crushed mule suddenly freed of its burden: he has shown who he is to the most feared men in all the Viceroyalty. In that august hall, he has made the name of the only God resound, and he has faced—from his own physically weak state—the tribunal's arrogance. It has surely been rare for anyone to show them that they do not hold all the power. This should not turn into hubris— he corrects the possible slippage—because "I am no more than a miniscule man, unworthy servant of the Eternal." But it is obvious that the inquisitors, accustomed to receiving frightened prisoners who defend themselves with lies, who throw themselves on the floor and dissolve into tears, must study his case and, perhaps, approach it with a certain understanding. Perhaps the angelic radiance that exists in each human being will make them see the inalienable right that belongs to Francisco.

As his head spins, he doesn't notice where they're taking him. Does it matter? His gaze has withdrawn and he barely registers that the tiles have now become adobe and, in the end, a packed dirt floor. The corridors echo with steps, iron, and moans, and the darkness increases. The court clerks have received the order to abandon the arrival cell and bury him in a dungeon. He has already passed through the verifications demanded by the legality of the Holy Office; he is not an unclassified prisoner but an accursed Jew whose blood and spirit are infected. He belongs in a small, damp space, a suffocating trap in which his bad thoughts can be softened. Although they cannot change his blood, they can at least try to wash his spirit.

They lock him in and reinforce the door with crossbars, a bolt, and locks. Everything has been arranged to convey that his insubordination is useless and that, in the prisons, he does not possess even the most basic rights.

～

The inquisitors pass around the pages the secretary wrote during the hearing. They are a synthesis that neither reproduces all the despicable sentences, nor the fiery tone in which the prisoner uttered them. But it provides enough evidence to give him an extremely severe sentence. They coincide with the documents written up in Chile after each interrogation. They are also consistent with the denunciation brought by the commissioner of Santiago de Chile when the captive's sisters— Isabel and Felipa Maldonado—testified in their confessions. This situation, however, gives no clues as to his path toward repentance. His history and evident courage could serve for light as much as for shadows, could help him recover the true faith or lead him further astray with his sophisms. Perhaps he would be voluntarily reconciled, with sincere tears. Or perhaps he can only be persuaded by forced reconciliation, under the light shed by torture, as was the case with his father. The crime of Judaism has four exits but only two are compatible with life: voluntary or forced reconciliation. The other two end in death and differ in that the Jew who repents before being devoured by flames can take refuge in a faster death through hanging or the garrote.

Gaitán places a paperweight on the pages and rests his head against the high back of his chair. He is irritated at Mañozca and Castro del Castillo for letting the prisoner swear in his own way. They have, indirectly, let him offend the cross, and they have conceded a right to him that will only augment his confusion. He does not agree, not remotely. These people have to be reminded that the Omnipotent One is only on one side and that the truth is incompatible with substitutes. Who is this insolent physician to impose his wishes on the tribunal? The tribunal, on satisfying them, has given away a shred of its own strength, has unnecessarily conceded power. Why? What for? Mañozca and Castro del Castillo have fewer years of experience in the Inquisitorial office than he does, and they have not yet learned to recognize the trash that comes here as flies in human form. Like flies, they only deserve to be crushed. They are unworthy, ungrateful, and irrational. This doctor has been baptized and confirmed, has been housed in monasteries, instructed at the university, and has taken an Old Christian to his bed, only to throw all this away like so much waste and proclaim his wretched blood with raging pride. It is the height of deviation. What's more, he has the impertinence to consider himself solely responsible for his actions. Gaitán believes this to be true, that the man is solitary, that he has not cultivated his Judaism with anyone save his dead father and the attempt in talking with his devout sister. But the intolerable thing is that, instead of accepting his extreme smallness and scalding at the majesty of the Holy Office, instead of trembling, sweating, and falling to his knees, he has the nerve to refute the true faith with his oath on the God of Israel. He has shown them irrefutable proof of his subversive nature and his venomous will to erode the order of the universe.

Gaitán is tired. He is the one who most carefully reads the reports, compares testimonies, evaluates confessions. For the past two years he has been requesting permission to return to Spain. He is sick of the Viceroyalty of Peru and its miseries. But his application has not been accepted quickly. The authorities in Spain appreciate his services, his unyielding harshness, and prefer him to stay in his role for a few more years.

115

His wrists and ankles have been freed because he is imprisoned in a dungeon from which not even a spider could escape. The cell is narrow, equipped with a stone bench with a mattress, and a chest in which they've placed the belongings that accompanied him from Chile. Francisco spends hours staring at the high window, small and inaccessible, through which the cloudy light of an inner courtyard leaks in. He is bored by the slow unfurling of hours, and wonders whether he'll overcome the tests to which the Holy Office will submit him. One of those tests consists precisely of this, keeping him inactive for days and weeks. The black servants who bring him his rations throw him a phrase here or there, like crumbs. Francisco wants to strike up a conversation, but they are spurned people who relieve their suffering by spurning those who are worse off than they are. Among the incoherent words they have for him are admonitions that he may not read or write, or communicate with other prisoners, much less with the outside world. He may, on the other hand, request a few comforts that are sometimes granted: a warm coat, food, furniture, more candles. These benefits are paid for with the confiscated money. But if his money runs out, the benefits are gone.

How long will they keep him cut off like this? Isolation is arduous. His anxiety grows and unleashes an avalanche of despair. He talks aloud to himself, at the edge of madness, because his heart longs to connect, to express ideas and feelings. This had already happened to him before, in the cells of Chile and in the stinking hold of the ship: he reached a point at which he couldn't take it anymore, and hope dissolved. It's what the Inquisition wants.

Four days after his first hearing, he is ordered to put on his coarse wool clothing and prepare for a second one. He receives these orders with ambivalence. The shackles close around his blistered limbs, as if he were in any physical condition to escape. He is guided to the august courtroom. Just as before, he is accompanied by the hardy warden and two armed men. He realizes that his current prison is in the depths of the gloomy fortress, as he must go through tunnels, up and down steps, and across many thresholds before entering the space where that beautiful textured wooden ceiling offers its sarcastic dissonance. It's all the same as before: the three tall chairs upholstered in green, the six-legged desk, two candelabras, and the crucifix on which he'd refused take an oath.

The cadaverous notary enters, his glassy eyes glued to the small desk onto which he places his writing materials. Then he sits, clasps his hands in prayer, and gazes at the black-and-green flag of the Holy Office.

One of the side doors opens, and the three inquisitors emerge. A hearing is a ceremonious event, and there can be no changes to the script. The sequence is rigid, always the same. The judges ascend to the platform with short steps, the ecclesiastical chairs are drawn back, and they remain standing like spears, cross themselves, and pray in low voices.

Mañozca orders Francisco to confess what he kept quiet in the last hearing. Does this turn of events mean that his previous testimony was accepted as true? Does it mean that they might be more disposed to listen? Could the angelic radiance that exists in each being make them see that his identity as a Jew gives no offense to God? Francisco's spirits rise, and he decides that he'll go further now to show them that his behavior is not arbitrary, but rather obedient to the sacred commandments, as the Bible instructs.

He confesses that he has observed Saturdays as holy days, as called for by the Book of Exodus, reciting the relevant verses from memory. He confesses that he has often invoked, for courage, the song in Chapter 30 of Deuteronomy, also reciting it from memory. The inquisitors' fingers fidget on their armrests, as they are amazed by both this man's unabashed recognition of his crime and his mastery of Latin and the Scriptures.

Francisco reads astonishment on their cold faces, bare hints of it, but enough to know he's gotten under their hard skin.

The notary writes anxiously, resigned to his own inability to record so many words in both Spanish and Latin. He limits himself to mentioning that the prisoner fluidly uttered the psalm "that begins *ut quid Deus requilisti in finem* and another very long prayer that begins *Domine Deus omnipotens, Deus patrum nostrorum Abraham, Isaac, et Jacob*," and that he recited "many other prayers spoken with a Jewish intent."

The hearing stretches on until the inquisitors decide that the prisoner is no longer offering anything new. The session is closed, and the warden accompanies Francisco back to his narrow cave.

Locked up and alone, he waits for days, then weeks, then months to be summoned again. The door only opens to give him tasteless food or remove the chamber pot. The Holy Office is patient, and knows how to break the stubborn. It will let immobility and the void do their part.

116

Francisco struggles not to lose his reason. He knows that everything they do with him, including cutting off communication, is part of a strategy. His battle will have surprising aspects, but will always be a battle. He must fight. Now his life has no other goal but this prolonged, cruel combat.

He decides to organize his days of compact boredom. There is one healthful activity they can't take from him: thought. But thought is not just an activity; it's his only weapon. He must protect and cultivate it. He will exercise his memory, his logic, and his rhetoric. He will fill his long vigil methodically, from the break of dawn to sundown. He'll utter prayers and recite his beloved one hundred and fifty psalms. He'll keep many Biblical texts fresh in his mind, along with Greek and Latin scholarship. He'll practice answers for difficult questions, and plan provocative inquiries that he can use to shake up dogmatic assertions. He will let their grudging dialogues flow through his mind. He will ask himself questions, respond, refute, and ask again. For each hearing he might have with the inquisitors, his spirit will endure one hundred.

The inquisitors, meanwhile, attend to other matters. Francisco Maldonado da Silva has filled them with rage and a sense of impotence. They need a break from an individual who tears them from their usual lifelines. His tongue is nourished by the devil, and they should listen to him as little as possible. They'd like to see him dead, but if they kill him without breaking him first, the devil will have won. They must tighten their fists and work hard to bring him to his knees. Only then can they kill him with triumphant joy.

In any case, they do not want for work. They must judge cases of idolatry, problems with civil authority, and angry conflicts over jurisdiction among ecclesiastical powers. Every day they face financial complications or abuses of protocol. Blasphemies pile up before them, as do heretical visionaries, bigamy, vulgar superstitions, and, as the height of sin, crimes within the clergy itself: seductions in the confessional, celebration of Mass by those who aren't ordained priests, cases of monks who have married or who engage in a shameful cohabitation. Sin floods the countryside and the city, like a swollen river.

Gaitán cannot find peace. This Jewish doctor—he mutters—who boasts of his infected blood, is a powerful opponent. It won't be easy to make him beg for mercy, because he doesn't see himself as guilty. He has presented his offense as a merit. And he has done so with an abundance of citations that favor his mistaken belief. He is physically chained, cannot leave or communicate with anyone, and is half dead. Yet, he expresses himself as though he doesn't know he is facing the tribunal that could quickly sentence him to be burned. Doesn't he realize that the Holy Office has the power to make stones weep? Didn't his father tell him that? Because his father broke, talked, and denounced. He offered signs of repentance, was accepted into reconciliation, and received a light sentence, too light a sentence, clearly, since he then returned to his disgusting rites. A curse! The tribunal was naïve, then. It forgot that, in order to completely fulfill its mission, it had to be more exacting than what balanced logic might suggest. For there to be order and for Christ and the church to reign, victory was more important than justice, power more important than truth.

Now, Gaitán would not modify his position, not even if the Supreme of Seville himself begged him to do so. History proves the need to harden ever further against the devil's aggression. Recently, in fact, he'd discussed the matter with Castro del Castillo, who still dreams of achieving results through a soft hand. It's true that the first laws against heretics did not include capital punishment, but one had to remember that back then no one knew how persistent and evil they were. The church let a thousand years pass without duly punishing heretics, and has thus shown itself to have a patience proportional to its vast stature. But it has also shown that tolerance does not lead people to the right track—in fact, just the opposite: it increases the advantages of the Antichrist.

Gaitán reminded his merciful colleague that Pope Gregory IX created the Papal Inquisition, which would become the Holy Office of the Inquisition, and put forward the principle of violent repression for dealing with heretics. The papal edict *Ad extirpanda* of Pope Innocent IV, published in 1252, overcame unfounded fears, and unequivocally established the legality of torture. This disposition was not easily adopted, to the harm of the church. Even now, with heretics burning across Europe and the Americas, enemies were not beaten with enough severity. This was why a man like Diego Núñez da Silva—Gaitán mutters on—returned to the dead law of Moses and confused his son. If he'd been punished better, if, for example, he'd been burned at the stake, they could have kept him from leading other souls astray.

117

The servants who bring the prisoner his food are struck by his gaze, which stays fixed on the wall, as if he were reading a text. When he senses their presence, he turns his head and accepts the steaming bowl.

"Reading is forbidden," they remind him, even though no books or notebooks have been allowed into his cell.

Francisco nods as he brings the spoon to his mouth. A slave approaches the wall where he imagines prayers to be engraved. He finds no signs of them and traces the wall with his fingers to ensure that his eyes have not deceived him. Then he stares at the prisoner, who is slowly sipping the stew and has the magical ability to capture the invisible.

"Reading is forbidden," he repeats, "but you can request other things." There is a new tone of respect in the slave's voice.

Francisco raises his eyebrows.

"Other foods, another blanket, another chair," the man says, opening his hands.

Francisco drains the bowl. This is the first time they haven't left immediately, which shows their fascination.

"What's your name?" Francisco asks one of them.

"Pablo."

"And you?"

"Simón."

"Pablo and Simón," he says. "I'd like to request something."

"Ask."

"To see the warden."

"You may," they say, smiling enigmatically.

Francisco watches their speedy departure, though they do not forget to lock and bolt the door.

That afternoon, the door creaks and the warden enters with an armed guard.

"What's going on?"

Francisco is surprised, and holds back from making his request point-blank. Days of heavy silence have passed, during which he's been completely ignored. In these interminable times he's recited entire books of the Bible from memory, and has recalled a good part of his library with the exacting rhythm that would have been demanded at the university. The warden stands with his legs apart, staring at him reproachfully. His job as a jailor obliges him to respond to calls, and he does so in a rough manner for the sake of internal discipline. He seems shorter and pudgier than when Francisco last saw him.

"I need to speak with the inquisitors," Francisco says.

"Another hearing?" he says, startled.

———

He can scarcely believe that he's achieved it. Three days later he is ordered to put on the monkish woolen robe, his limbs are shackled, and he is brought to the feared room. One of the inquisitors tells the notary to record the voluntary nature of this hearing. Then they fix their gazes on Francisco, who has practiced his speech. He wants to move their souls and shake them out of their granite-hard hostility. He is less than David, and they are greater than Goliath; he is not trying to defeat them, but to humanize them.

"Today, I am Jewish, inside and out," he tells them with a suicidal transparency, "while before I was only a Jew inside. Surely you can appreciate my decision not to hide behind a mask." He is silent for a few seconds as he calibrates the words he will utter next. "I know that, in speaking the truth, I am placing my life at risk. I may already be condemned, yet I am filled with profound inner peace. Only someone who has had to bear a double identity, spending years in fear and shame while hiding what he knows to be his authentic self, can know the depth of such suffering. Believe me that it is not only a burden, but a blade that stabs you even in your dreams."

"It is bad to lie, certainly," Juan de Mañozca says coldly. "And even worse when one is lying to hide apostasy."

Francisco's eyes shine as if the inquisitor's harshness had brought tears to them.

"I have not lied to hide apostasy, but to hide my faith." He raises his voice, involuntarily. "To hide my ancestors, to hide my very self, as if my feelings and convictions and preferences were worth nothing."

"They are not worthy to the extent that they oppose the truth."

"The truth?" Francisco repeats.

A light echo moves through the room. The prisoner presses his lips to avoid breaking into arguments that would only bounce off the tribunal's ears. Despite his expectations, this battle is even harder than he thought.

"Why did you request this hearing?" demands the angry Gaitán. "You haven't confessed to anything new."

"I wanted to make you record that I have not embraced my Jewish identity lightly, but, rather, out of deep conviction. For years I've searched my conscience, and I haven't found any other path that is compatible with morality."

Francisco takes a long pause and the inquisitors show signs of impatience.

"To fully be a Jew," he continues, in the calmest tone his heart will allow, "it is necessary to endure a very painful test that God and Abraham determined in their pact. Chapter seventeen of Genesis establishes it. Do you recall it, Illustrious Ones?" Francisco half closes his eyelids, and recites from memory: "'You and your descendants will honor my covenant throughout the generations, all the males among you will be circumcised, and this will be a sign of the covenant between us. Thus my covenant shall be marked on your flesh, like an eternal covenant.'" He opens his eyes. "I tell you this with all due respect, so that you may abandon the notion that I betrayed, out of caprice or irresponsibility, a faith in which I no longer believe, however hard I've tried to do so, and that I am now only toying with a different faith. Believe me that in order to take such a risky step I've had to bear the fires of doubt, disregard dangers, and sacrifice endless advantages. I've had to harm my own flesh, sink the scalpel in, and finish the task with scissors. I have fulfilled God's task from the depths of my soul. My ancestors' faith is no less demanding than that of Christ; it also calls for fasts and afflictions. But it puts me in vibrant contact with the Eternal and with my own dignity. That is why I spoke to my sister Isabel, only with my sister Isabel, sweet and understanding Isabel, as sweet as our poor mother, that she might join the family we are part of, a family that dates back to the prodigious Biblical times. But my sister's judgment was overcome by panic, and she couldn't comprehend that when one embraces the deep mandates, one also reaches the peace of God." He pauses again, and gazes directly at them. "That is all I wished to communicate."

He lowers his head in exhaustion.

Antonio Castro del Castillo entwines his fingers over his abdomen to keep himself still, as a sharp ache bites his intestines. This doctor defends his errors in such a manner as to move him. He glances sidelong at Gaitán the imperturbable, Gaitán the uncompromising. Just a few days ago, he reminded him again that a good inquisitor never regrets having been overly harsh but will regret being overly soft. He massages himself surreptitiously and prays a Hail Mary.

The session is concluded.

As the warden escorts Francisco, he focuses on the chain tangled around the prisoner's ankles and, all of a sudden, decides to help him, lifting the chain. The servants are surprised. Never before has the warden offered such a courtesy to a captive. Francisco is also surprised, but he says nothing. They continue down the damp corridors, bathed in the torch's morbid red glow.

"I was able to hear part of your declarations," says the warden, quite unexpectedly. "I still can't believe it."

Francisco notices that the man has gone pale.

"What part do you not believe?"

The warden, like a boy who can't break his fascination with a gruesome story, asks, "Is it true that you cut your own foreskin?"

"Yes, it's true."

He lets out a whistle full of incredulity and fright. "You Jews, you're bloodthirsty all right!"

118

After enduring such a barrage of projectiles, the inquisitors concur that Francisco Maldonado da Silva is a skilled man, whose audacity suggests that his stubbornness will be lasting. Not only does he confess haughtily, but he tries to persuade the judges, that is to say, to corrupt them. He shapes arguments with a demonic intelligence and presents them with a deceitful innocence.

He must be crushed as soon as possible, just like an ant, Gaitán declares, and his colleagues assent. This is not just a case of someone who changed his faith for another, the way he might change his shirt, but someone who spits atrocities. He has been doing so since the beginning of his anti-crusade, since Chile, perhaps even before then. Francisco doesn't know, of course, that the tribunal has already interrogated María Martínez. That woman, accused of witchcraft, serves them well, as she likes to tell of her abominations and, in this manner, stir the captives to a sincerity that has them spewing out confessions at her first question. The aberrations that Francisco confided in her on his first night in Lima's jail already thicken his awful file.

Forty days later, he is again brought before the judges to round out the accusatory information. They are ready to dispense with his unacceptable insolence.

Francisco, on the other hand, is enlivened by the hearing. What do they want now? He's already told them his life story, and has repeatedly explained the strength of his identity. Perhaps they've begun to glimpse that his Judaism is not a form of aggression. Is it possible? No—he answers himself, so as not to sink into naïve enthusiasm.

The inquisitors are saying that they want to know more. Francisco thinks that the mysterious condition of being a Jew must both fascinate and frighten them. Then he explains to them that, between Judaism and Christianity, there are more parallels than differences, and that the recognition of those parallels could create more tolerance of the minor differences. But the tribunal interrupts him to state that only the differences are of interest, in particular those aspects of Christianity that bother a Jew.

How strange! Do the inquisitors wish to be enlightened? Do they want to slide into the skin of a Jew in order to reflect on their own dogma from a new angle? It sounds incredible. But it could be an ambush.

He responds that Jews are not bothered by the precepts of Christianity. He simply doesn't accept them because they violate a few commandments: the worship of idols, not respecting the Sabbath. From the Jewish point of view, Christianity has fulfilled a commendable task in bringing millions of souls closer to the One and Only God and has spread His word throughout the globe. This is a thought sustained by many wise men and, especially, by the distinguished Spanish doctor Maimonides.

The judges confirm that the notary is transcribing wildly. The prisoner has, unfortunately, avoided the trap; they need to make him blaspheme. Then they ask him about the crucial issue of the Messiah. Francisco remains candid.

"We Jews are still waiting for him," he confesses outright, "because the prophesies described for Messianic times have not yet come to pass. In Christianity, something similar is accepted, because it's obvious that the prophecy of universal peace has not yet been fulfilled. So Christ will have a second coming, which, all told, will be the first one for the Jews. You see that, even in such a decisive subject, there are parallels."

"Aren't the miracles of Our Lord sufficient proof that he is the prophesied Messiah?"

The prisoner prepares to respond sincerely, not noticing that the notary has become tense, as he is about to hear the blasphemy the tribunal needs to unleash its accusatory cannons.

"Miracles are not enough, or even necessary, to demonstrate the presence of God," Francisco responds, as if he were musing on some trivial theme. "Let us recall that a miracle implies the violation of the universe's laws. Miracles refute and break the natural order."

"Weren't there miracles in the Old Testament?" Castro del Castillo says, with irony.

"Yes, there were, of course there were—only not to prove the existence of God, but to address extreme needs. The Red Sea parted to save Israel from the Egyptian army, manna fell from the sky and water sprang from rock so that those who'd just been freed wouldn't die of hunger or thirst. None of these miracles were about making people believe. Those who are experts at magic can also perform miracles. The prophets, for example, talked, persuaded, and recriminated using words alone. Those who demand miracles in order to believe"—he is silent for an instant, stunned by the incredible metamorphosis that's taken place, because all of a sudden he, an accused wretch, is in the role of accuser—"those who demand miracles to believe indirectly undermine the laws of the Lord, the laws with which He created the world and set it in motion."

The edges of Gaitán's lips stretch into a horrible grimace. Still, he is pleased; the captive has said enough to deserve a thunderous punishment.

Mañozca adds a biting detail. "We have found, among your clothes, a notebook containing the feast days of Moses and a few prayers."

"Yes," Francisco admits. "My father taught them to me."

"That is enough. The hearing is over."

As the prisoner is taken away to endure weeks of isolation, Mañozca thinks: Is it not a sign of madness for an isolated, helpless, unprotected man to try to resist the formidable machine of the Holy Office? How can he keep holding his head so high before an institution brimming with jails, torture devices, officials, money, prestige, and impenetrable secrets? It is the most feared organization in all the Viceroyalty, in all the empire, in all the Christian world. Its goal is to stamp out insubordination, and it does so without hesitation. It spares no resources of any kind, be they material or spiritual, using any and all instruments of intrigue, slander, and panic. The Holy Office mobilizes hundreds of feet and thousands of arms, but has only one brain, armored to the point where it feels nothing. It is not moved by people's despair because it is not with the people, but with God. It works only for Him. Anyone who faces the Holy Office is facing the Almighty. This prisoner, therefore, seems unreal, seems a nightmarish hallucination. He is a being who must be thoroughly humiliated. He must be brought down, shaken, until he accepts the purification that will save his soul.

The inquisitors and their helpers draft an extremely detailed accusation against Francisco. It is fifty-five chapters long, and includes ample outside input. They presume that isolation, darkness, and meager rations will have softened his hard-headedness. And so they summon him again. He is brought to the room with the ornate ceiling. They make him stay on his feet so that exhaustion can add another dose of suffering.

He is ordered, again, as is the custom, to swear on the cross, which may seem like a useless repetition. But the tribunal wants to know whether the prisoner has abandoned his stubbornness in the meditative capsule of his cell. Lamentably, the prisoner is a reptile who still insists on swearing on the God of Israel. Then the notary conducts a monotonous reading of the accusation. After each point he interrogates the captive with his gaze, to confirm his agreement with the contents.

The judges shiver—with indignation, with surprise—when this monstrous being does not consider these fifty-five roars of thunder enough, but, rather, adds another insolence: he informs them that, during his quiet days in jail, he composed, in his mind, several prayers in Latin verse and a story in honor of the Eternal One's law. He also tells them that, last September, he fulfilled the fast of Yom Kippur so that his errors may be forgiven.

This fly, this piece of trash they will send to twist and turn in the flames, shows no signs whatsoever of remorse! Nevertheless, it is announced that the laws governing such proceedings require them to offer him lawyers to work on his defense.

"Who assigns them?" Francisco allows himself to say, with irony.

They do not answer. The hearing is over. The prisoner is still speaking: let them be erudite people, and attentive.

Castro del Castillo, standing before his ecclesiastical chair, notices that the notary is writing down this request.

The prisoner adds, "So they can know how to clarify my doubts."

Gaitán and Mañozca exchange a glance. Is this statement the first sign of good sense from this prisoner? Has he begun to change? Is he starting to bend to their will?

They almost smile.

119

But the deep repentance the inquisitors demand is not yet emerging. Francisco's resistance is exceptional. He knows that he is a particle that can barely be distinguished from nothingness; his mouth can be muzzled, his hands paralyzed, his body destroyed, his remains buried in that very cell, and his name forgotten forever. And yet, he retains a flame that cannot be extinguished. A force that sustains him, and nourishes him, like the energy that seethes in lunatics and saints. It is a mysterious flame, ungraspable. What does that flame dream? Does it dream, perhaps, of overcoming the inquisitors' intransigence? Or of obtaining acceptance of his rights?

Recently, the rats had been making familiar noises as they approached along the ceiling beams in his cell, as they had at the monastery in Lima. But in that stampede, he also heard blows of another kind, which had not caught his attention before. He wondered what those dry, rhythmic impacts might be. They resembled African music. Was someone amusing himself by scraping a jawbone's teeth, as the good Luis used to do as Catalina undulated her hips and shoulders? One night, as the guards departed and the rodents whirled into motion, those rhythms began again. This time, he listened very closely, and realized that they weren't rhythms but rather clusters of impacts, separated by a brief silence: tock-tock-tock. Fists and palms, or a piece of rubble against the wall. Were they the calls of other prisoners? Were they trying to communicate with him? He responded, once, twice, a third time. The other sounds ceased and even the rats seemed to prick their ears to listen. He waited for responses, and received a torrent of knocks separated by surprising pauses. What did the pauses mean? And the sequences?

"They're messages in code!" he said to himself.

In remote Ibatín as a boy, he had played with his brother Diego, gently knocking on walls, imitating words and songs. What did these groupings in this labyrinthine jail symbolize? What did one blow mean, or two, or five?

"For years I tried to decipher the alphabet in the stars and fireflies," Francisco marvels. "I never would have imagined, then, that the Lord had allowed me a premonition of another system, not composed of the light in open spaces, but of vibrations sent through walls."

The knocks were an alphabet, then, and he had to learn to read and write in its code, as he had done with Latin and Spanish. Francisco surmised that one blow must mean the letter *A*, two the letter *B*, and so forth. He lit a wick and paid attention. He picked up a small chicken bone, sat down on the floor, and began to trace short lines at each series of knocks. Then he counted them and translated them into their corresponding letters to form words. It was difficult: some letters, like *S*, *T*, and *U*, required many knocks and he lost count. He had to practice. After all, he didn't learn to read and write Spanish in a single day. He attempted to answer. He converted his name into the code and, slowly, transmitted his first message. The walls disseminated three words: Francisco—Maldonado—Silva. That night, dozens of men and women took note of his captivity.

120

Each prisoner was assigned a "defense attorney," an employee of the Inquisition who pretends to take the victim's side after some minor error in the legal proceedings is discovered. His real goal is to convince the prisoner to submit as soon as possible. Nevertheless, his presence brings a fistful of hope.

Eight long sessions take place in Francisco's cell. His defense attorney is a strapping monk, better suited to physical warfare than the intricacies of jurisprudence. He makes a good impression on victims, because he looks like a potent and affectionate ally. Francisco is not immune to these hopes; he gives the monk his story, shares his fears and desires. In reality, this is no different than what he's done since he was arrested; he is always repeating his naked, bothersome truth. In addition, he speaks with emotion of his innocent, beloved wife Isabel, of his little daughter Alba Elena, and of the baby who must have been born by now, a baby who had not once been held in its father's arms. The lawyer seems understanding and promises to improve the situation. He says that he could quickly lessen the sentence if he, Francisco, were to abjure his mistaken beliefs. Francisco, in turn, asks many questions that the lawyer prefers to leave aside, as they involve theological and moral issues. His mission, the lawyer insists, is confined to offering concrete help.

"But it depends on you," he concludes. "It depends on your agreeing to abjure."

On one occasion, Francisco confides that the idea of betraying his conscience for his own benefit seems like a bribe. In another session, he says, "If I abjure, I'll stop being myself."

The lawyer informs the judges, loyally and punctually. Mañozca and Castro del Castillo think that Francisco is an insane yet erudite man who should be forced to debate learned people so his theories can be undone.

"The prisoner has no wish to reform himself because he commits the sin of pride," Gaitán replies.

Mañozca allows a few seconds to pass, then says, "We must preach to the level of each person's soul, and this man's soul demands strong ideas, developed by learned men."

"Not even the most learned man," Gaitán says, staring hard at him, "could break this man, much less in a debate. He's a good polemicist, like Lucifer. It'll only complicate things for us."

"Do you," Castro del Castillo says, with unrestrained irony, "consider him as keen as Lucifer, so as to assign him victory in a debate that hasn't even begun?"

Gaitán glares at him, irritated. "It's not a matter of keenness, but of talent and caprice."

"Demonic talent and caprice are broken by the light of the Lord," Mañozca insists.

"Don't be naïve, for God's sake. Don't submit to the devil." Gaitán's words drip like molten lead. "Giving him concessions—"

Mañozca and Castro del Castillo shift uncomfortably.

"It is not a concession to let him swear on the God of Israel, or bring in learned men as examiners," Mañozca says, justifying himself and his colleague.

The discussion has nowhere to go and is finished in absolute secrecy. The tribunal must not allow any fractures to be seen.

Days later, people renowned for their theological training are summoned to evaluate the prisoner's doubts in the inquisitors' presence. Four eminent figures are chosen: Luis de Bilbao, Alonso Briceño, Andrés Hernández, and Pedro Ortega, all of them considered jewels of the Viceroyalty.

The session is prepared with painstaking care. It must end with an exemplary victory, one that will be hailed far and wide for many years.

Francisco is brought into the hallowed room by the warden and two armed guards, as always. They place a stool behind his knees, and the notary repeats his ceremony of arranging his writing implements. The four learned men enter, wearing the habits of their respective orders, and they stand before the chairs that await them, two to the prisoner's right, two to the left. After another minute's wait, the side door creaks, and the air grows tense with the arrival of the inquisitors, who march with characteristic majesty toward the high platform, make the sign of the cross, and pray in a low voice. The learned men follow suit, and then the warden pulls on the prisoner's arm to make him sit.

Mañozca begins by explaining the generosity of the Holy Office: it has provided the opportunity to express doubts, so that these distinguished theologians may address them. As the prisoner has insisted that his errant conduct is based on the Bible, the tribunal is offering a copy of the sacred text so that he may cite passages without distortion.

They invite him to speak.

Francisco stares at the heavy copy of the Bible, which rests on a lectern, and he raises his shackled hands toward the pages. This reunion with the familiar text sparks his first words. He says that the love Jews have for books—and for this book in particular—is love of the word, the word of God. God built the universe with His word, and in Sinai, He revealed Himself with words, too. Words are more valuable than weapons or gold. God cannot be seen, but can and should be listened to. This is why He forbade idols and ordered the fulfillment of His law, which He transmitted through words. Those who obey Him implicitly become part of the moral order. "Those who, on the other hand," he went on provocatively, "only claim to adore Him and even shout their faith, but do not fulfill the commandments, repudiate God with their actions."

One of the learned men interrupts this daring lecture to remind Francisco that they've come to resolve his doubts, not to hear a dissertation. Then Francisco pages through the Bible and indicates the verses that express commands, reiterations of commands, and rebukes for the violation of those commands. He cites Genesis, Leviticus, Deuteronomy, Samuel, Isaiah, Jeremiah, Amos, and Psalms. He reads aloud in fluent Latin, and provides a brief commentary on each excerpt. He maintains that he has been arrested, not for wrongdoing, but for fulfilling the law of God.

The theologians listen, tense as warriors on the battlefield, and plot their responses. The majority of the prisoner's observations are part of the known repertoire of arguments held in Spain between rabbis and brilliant orators from the church. When Francisco stops, the theologians deliver their replies.

The Jesuit Andrés Hernández stands and says, "My son, you cannot have any difficulty in recognizing the mercy of the church and the Holy Office. Now they are offering you the privilege of obtaining illumination from four figures who have put aside other obligations to come to your aid. Contrary to the lies hurled by heretics, you can prove that the Inquisition was not established to do harm, but to reconcile sinners with the true faith. Each of the theologians you see before you is anxious to see you abandon wrongdoing."

"The fourth council of Toledo, presided over by San Isidro," Alonso Briceño recalls when his time comes to speak, "established that nobody should be made to believe by force. But what are we to do with those who have received the indelible sacrament of baptism, as is your case? A baptized person who practices Judaism is not a Jew, but, rather, a bad

Christian—an apostate. You, therefore, though it may sound harsh, have committed an act of betrayal, and you are judged for this reason."

"The commandments that you claim to obey," Pedro Ortega explains, in the best tone of voice his ferocious appearance can allow for, "are the repertory of a dead law, an anachronistic law. Instead of seeking out the path of virtue in the Old Testament, which is called 'old' for a reason, study the New, and the teachings of the fathers and doctors of the church."

Luis de Bilbao then takes his turn, and responds in minute detail to the verses Francisco cited as proof of his reason and innocence, to make him see that he was interpreting them in the outmoded manner of the sophists of Athens. "You see," he concludes, "the majority of these do not support your right to keep being a Jew, but, rather, announce and prefigure the birth of Christ, the erection of the church, and the advent of the new law."

The inquisitor Juan de Mañozca thanks the examiners for their outstanding work and asks the prisoner whether his doubts have been resolved. The notary takes advantage of the brief pause to wipe sweat from his face. Francisco rises to his feet.

A sepulchral silence reigns, and a light, expectant breeze passes through the room.

"No," he replies calmly.

121

Two days later, Francisco is summoned to another hearing. Castro del Castillo interrogates him in the sweetest tone his obese throat will allow.

"What motives prevent you from accepting the errors of a dead law? Four extraordinary figures of the Viceroyalty have listened to your torrent of questions, and they have answered with the patience of angels. They answered your Biblical references with Biblical references of their own, and replied to your every query. Why is your obstinacy so great?"

"I am sorry that the theologians did not understand me," he responds. "Perhaps I was not able to express myself clearly enough due to the anxiety this room causes."

Hours after he was returned to his dungeon, the servants Simón and Pablo gave him a heavy Bible, four sealed pages of parchment, a quill, ink, and blotting paper.

Then the warden enters to tell him that the tribunal, as additional proof of their mercy, has offered Francisco the opportunity to write down his difficulties, without the pressure of gazes on him or the stress of the courtroom. Francisco stares, dazzled, at the precious volume on his beat-up table, and recalls once again the scene of the donkey bitten by the puma. "I have to resist like that heroic animal." It is the inquisitors who are now softening, because they can't stand the firmness of his convictions and need him to repent because his firmness challenges their power. This hurts them more than the church itself.

That night, when vaulted correspondence begins to run through the walls, Francisco strokes his copy of the Bible and communicates with his invisible companions, telling them that he is no longer alone, but accompanied by the word of God.

He can't sleep. The pages of the sacred text fill him with energy. He reads until his candles run out. Then he calls the guards, and a servant brings him a couple more.

"That's it?" he says, aghast. "They've asked me to write. I need light."

After a while, a box full of candles arrives. He reads until dawn, until his reddened eyes are a feast of words. He lies down to sleep a few hours while his mind spins with excerpts, ideas, commentaries, questions. The treasure trove of images and answers is infinite; it will be difficult to compress them into the four sealed pages, even writing in his smallest hand.

In the days that follow, he surrenders to the pleasure of constant reading, and writes very little. When he decides to do it systematically, he closes the book and addresses the learned men in a new way. "Instead of posing dry questions," he says, as if to a multitudinous audience, "that would be answered in one way or another, instead of staying in my place as a perplexed man begging for clarity, I'll ask them questions that unsettle them, not for their ideas, but for their conduct. I will rub their noses in their own incoherence and immorality."

The closed door, the four walls around him, and the thick silence turn his dungeon into a marvelous bell. He sits still before the table and papers and enters the trance of creation. His stillness is a sheath around fermenting thoughts. His bright gaze falls on the blank pages, and his thin, delicate hand grasps the quill. His mouth tightens slightly, and he starts to form small letters. As the lines emerge, a vein protrudes between his eyebrows. He addresses the four learned men, but not only them, also the monster that is the Inquisition. Incredibly, God has given him the privilege of writing down His words, which can therefore penetrate more deeply, perhaps be reread, put away, then read again.

His statement begins with a question to make a person's hair stand on end: "Do you want to save my soul, or do you want to oppress it? Saving my soul would call for study, and affection. For oppressing it, you have prisons, the cutting off of communication, torture, contempt, and the threat of death." Further on, he skewers them with another question: "Why do you claim to imitate Christ when, in reality, you're imitating the ancient Romans? Just like the Romans, you privilege power, use weapons, and crush the rights of those who think differently from you. Jesus, on the other hand, was physically weak, never took up arms, never called for anyone to be tortured or murdered. Wouldn't an imitation of Christ begin with the elimination of weapons, torture, and the hatred you are using against me?"

Francisco reminds them that the one and only God is also referred to as Father by Jews. "Jesus prayed to the Father, only to the Father, and taught the Our Father." But bad Christians pray the Our Father and simultaneously offend the Father, because they persecute those who worship Him exclusively. "If this is a matter of imitating Christ, I imitate him much more than you, because I pray to the same Father who was the recipient of Christ's prayers," he writes in thick lines.

Francisco's entire head throbs now. He puts the quill beside the inkwell and rereads what he's written. In his tone he recognizes the insolence of the prophets. He hasn't weighed the serious consequences of certain words, because they were dictated to him from within. He has sworn to tell the truth, and they have demanded truth from him. Here it is, then.

He adjusts the lights and resumes his work. Brow furrowed, lips slightly open, breath quickened. "The Holy Office, with its investiture as Exterminating Angel, likes to affirm that it represents God. I ask: Does it replace God? In that case: Does it consider itself God? A monstrous mistake; there is no room for two Almighty Ones." His cheeks burn.

He draws a comparison between the weakness of Jesus and the power of the Holy Office. The lie of imitating Christ appears once again, and Francisco dangerously adds, "Christ is portrayed as a suffering, mocked man, victim of the Jews. He is not portrayed this way so we may be meek like him, but, rather, to avenge him. Do the eminent theologians wonder why the Holy Office is trying to avenge and save the Savior? I offer my modest opinion: because, sacrilegiously, it places itself over him."

His breath is agitated, forcing him to lie down. The small David, in venting his thoughts, has just hurled his worst insult at the imposing Goliath.

122

On the fifteenth of November, 1627, Francisco hands over the four pages of parchment, which the tribunal has copied and read with indignation. They summon the theologians and order them to prepare a crushing response. The theologians request more time. The questions and reflections were inspired by the devil, and they won't have their rebuttal ready until mid-January.

"Fine," the disappointed tribunal concedes.

Francisco, meanwhile, is now without a Bible, paper, ink, or quill. Isolation, which was fecund as he wrote, reveals its horrors again, its lifeless hole. He struggles to maintain the order of his days through prayer and by recalling his beloved books, as he had in the first days after his arrest. At night, he communicates with his brothers in misfortune through their noisy code; he has mastered it now, and no longer needs to count to recognize five, eight, ten, or fifteen knocks in a row— the corresponding letters come to him immediately. They exchange names, crimes, and questions about each other's families. Each message is painstakingly constructed, as if their correct emission could set them free.

He can tell when the suffocating routine is going to change by the subtle variations in how the jailors open the door. Or the amount of food they bring. Then come the shackles, the long chain, and orders to put on the habit worn for hearings. Once again they move through tunnels, stairs, doors, halls, and into the dim courtroom with its unvarying décor. The four learned men are present. One of them, the Jesuit Andrés Hernández, doesn't take his eyes off Francisco; they are tender eyes. The three judges also march onto the platform, make the sign of the cross, pray, and sit down. The theologians pass Francisco's writings around among themselves—writings they've already reread to the point of nausea—and ask questions in turn, rising to their feet. They do it with friendly voices and appeal constantly to supporting excerpts from the sacred text. The audacity of many paragraphs has convulsed their intellects, and the four of them have invested more hours than expected into building the arsenal needed for victory. The pages of parchment emit a fearful glow; the ideas expressed there must be demolished like the bricks of an enchanted fortress.

The notary writes down everything, for hours, dripping with sweat. Francisco listens, thinks, and skillfully responds.

Soon thereafter, at another hearing, they let out an avalanche of arguments. On that occasion, the prisoner is forbidden to respond. The four theologians cite the Bible abundantly, leaving even the judges astonished.

At the end, when Francisco seems to be collapsing from exhaustion, the tribunal thanks the learned men for the light they have so plentifully poured out. Not even rocks could fail to soften before such a prodigious accumulation of proof. Then Mañozca asks the prisoner whether his doubts have been addressed.

Francisco pulls at the folds of his habit and, raising his gaze, says no.

They send him back to the dungeon, wishing they could just send him right to the flames. The room bristles with rage. On the gloomy path back, the warden also scolds him, pulling at his chain and shaking his arm.

"You're an idiot! All those arguments aren't enough for you? The most illustrious men of the Viceroyalty have worked—for you!"

Francisco keeps his eyes on the clean bricks of the ground so he doesn't trip over his long chain.

"It's time to ask for mercy!" the warden continues. "Do you want to be burned alive?"

Francisco doesn't answer.

"I assure you"—the warden's voice breaks—"I assure you that you have made quite an impression on me. That's why, for your own good, I advise you—stop being so stubborn, my dear man! Ask for mercy, weep, repent. There's still time."

Francisco stops and turns to the burly warden. His swollen eyes blink; it's been a long time since he's received a show of high esteem.

He murmurs, "Thank you."

123

The inquisitors are so disturbed that they dispute the best course of action to take after this fiasco. Gaitán rebukes his colleagues for the grave error into which they forced the tribunal. For some prisoners, he insists, benevolence is counterproductive; haughty men like Francisco only reason when their joints are torn or their feet are burned.

The theologians, for their part, wonder whether their polemics failed, whether perhaps they hadn't shaped their arguments well enough, whether perhaps they'd confused the man by speaking to him in a cacophony of four voices. The Jesuit Andrés Hernández, who devotes many hours a day to his interminable *Treatise of Theology*, suggests holding another personal conversation with the prisoner, but in the intimacy of his cell.

"He is visited by the sin of pride," he explains, "and it's hard for him to repent in public. A more informal conversation would break his stubbornness."

The inquisitors take weeks to grant this request, which smacks of an excess of piety. They allow it, but only on the condition that Hernández takes with him another father from the Society, who should act as witness and, if needed, come to his aid to counter any unexpected sophisms.

The servants illuminate the cell, refresh all the candles, and fill mugs with water. They remove the chamber pot and ask Francisco to sit up. The priests enter.

"I am Andrés Hernández."

"I am Diego Santisteban," the second priest says.

Francisco smiles sadly and says, "I suppose that I need no introduction."

Hernández invites Francisco to take a chair beside the rickety table. His kind gaze initiates a less harsh conversation.

"I haven't come to argue," he declares, "but rather to bring you relief. Perhaps you saw me in Córdoba, decades ago, because I went to that city to help Bishop Trejo y Sanabria in his great endeavors."

A chill runs through Francisco. "What happened to that selfless bishop?"

Hernández tells him that the tireless Trejo y Sanabria was already feeling old back then. At the age of fifty, he launched his final pastoral journey and returned with his health definitively broken. But he managed to lay the foundations of the University of Córdoba. He would never be forgotten. Hernández knows that this saintly prelate had administered the sacrament of confirmation to Francisco.

"You gave that good bishop reason to rejoice," he says.

Hernández pours water into the mugs and offers one to the prisoner. Little by little, he goes over the solid education that Francisco has received.

"Your wealth of knowledge and the grace of the sacraments must have formed a rich inner garden. A garden"—the Jesuit gestures with his hands—"enclosed by impassable rivers, like those that surround Eden."

He insists that, in Francisco's soul, there flourishes a garden that pleases the Lord. It is necessary to return to it, to inhale its perfume, to caress its fruits. And, for this, the rivers must be crossed, painful as such an endeavor might be. "When you do this, the walls of this cell will also fall. Light, liberty, and joy will flood around you." His impassioned face glistens.

Francisco thanks him for all the praise and considers his response.

"Inside me, in truth, there exists a garden that pleases the Eternal One, but it is nourished by other sources. It would be useless to open and reveal it, because, despite your goodwill, Father, blindness can exist for the understanding as well as for the eyes. Only God knows my garden, and He will care for it until I die."

Hernández does not give in. He wants to help. He has been impressed by the prisoner's culture, as well as by his courage.

"This is not false praise," he says, eyes misty, "but your serene firmness, Doctor, reminds me of the martyrs."

"Why not recognize me as a martyr of Israel?" Francisco says, his face lighting up.

Diego Santisteban grazes Hernández's shoulder and whispers that he has strayed from the right path. Hernández realizes his own bewilderment, and tries to correct his own words. "Sometimes, the devil creates confusion. How can I call you a martyr if you reject the cross? How can he who commits crimes be a martyr?"

"All the Christian martyrs were criminals in the eyes of pagans," Francisco remarks.

"They were pagans," the Jesuit replies. "They couldn't see the truth."

"Protestants are heretics, and therefore criminals to Catholics, while the converse is also true. All the heretics persecuted by the Inquisition believe in Christ and swear by the cross, and yet—"

"Heresy was born to undermine the church, and the church was created by Our Lord, through the work of Peter. And so, the converse has no meaning."

"That is what Catholics say. But religious wars demonstrate that this argument doesn't work the same way across the border. Why do some wish to impose themselves on others? Don't they trust the power of the truth? Must they always resort to the act of murder? Does light need the shadows to support it?"

Hernández rises to his feet, perturbed. He isn't angered by Francisco's response, but rather by his own incapacity to keep the dialogue focused in a way that will allow him to get under his interlocutor's skin. The thing he'd been trying to avoid from the beginning is unfolding: a confrontation. The confrontation will be futile. It will only replicate the useless arguments from before.

He sits, sips some more water, dries his mouth with the back of his hand, and says that he senses in Francisco a very sensitive nature. Therefore, he would like to reflect together on the marvelous sacrifice Our Lord Jesus Christ made to save humanity, as well as on the marvelous Eucharist, which renews this sacrifice in all times and places. This incomparable sacrifice has definitively eliminated the sacrifice of human beings, which, for example, was practiced by the indigenous people of this continent. Also, that of animals, which took place under the Law of Moses. How could such a delicate spirit fail to recognize and appreciate this extraordinary advance? Hernández demonstrates that, as a fruit is first green and then ripe, or as the day breaks with tepid rays and only later reveals its fullest light, so the revelation has occurred in two phases: the Old Testament announced and prepared for the New, as dawn prepares for midday.

Francisco meditates. The man speaks well and deserves a cordial response. But he should not be deprived of his rebuttal. So he responds that, in effect, he has listened on other occasions—including sermons— to descriptions of these differences with the old Hebrew people and with savages. Christ no longer allows human sacrifice because he sacrificed himself on everyone's behalf. Francisco is silent for two seconds then conjures a brutally ironic earful.

"But even though Christians wouldn't eat a man, like cannibals do," he says, staring hard at Hernández, "they tear him to shreds with torture while he's still full of life. In many cases, they char him slowly at the stake, throwing his mortal remains to the dogs. This horror is committed and repeated in the name of piety, truth, and divine love—not so? There is a great difference between Christians and savages because the latter kill their victims first and only eat them afterward. You Christians, on the other hand, devour men alive, just as you're doing with me now—"

Diego Santisteban crosses himself and moves toward the door. Hernández watches him, mouth wide open.

"I want to help him!" he mutters impotently.

Francisco's brow furrows, and the vein in his forehead swells, as if he were writing.

"Excuse me," he says, "I know you want to help me, that you are sincere. But I need other services."

Santisteban addresses the ceiling beams. "On top of everything, he wants to teach us how to help him rectify his soul!"

"I need news of my family," Francisco implores.

The Jesuit lowers his head and clasps his hands in prayer. "I am forbidden to give information to prisoners."

"I need someone to tell my wife that I am alive, that I'm still fighting."

"It's forbidden," he repeats, face clouded. "Doctor," he begins, making his final attempt, "if nothing else, for your wife, for your family."

Francisco waits for the end of this sentence.

The clergyman's eyes fill with tears. He suffers, prays. His voice rises from deep in his chest. "Repent!"

Francisco's eyes fill with tears, too. He would like to avoid mortifying this man. He would like to embrace him.

124

The pages labeled with Francisco Maldonado da Silva's name proliferate like weeds. The notary of the Holy Office oversees this venomous documentation. Five years have passed since the prisoner was brought to the secret jails. From the first day of his arrest in faraway Concepción de Chile, he has stood by his Jewish identity. Despite the overabundance of proof, the inquisitors haven't yet sentenced him and put an end to this enraging case, because the man will not yield, or so much as hang his head.

The course of events has been unprecedented. Captives usually deny all accusations and build an edifice of lies. To demolish these tricks, the Holy Office has its own more efficient ones at the ready. If Francisco had denied his guilt, he would have been promised freedom in exchange for a confession. If they had not achieved a confession, an official would have pretended to be Jewish or to have committed some other heresy to trap him. But Francisco has neither lied nor has he denied the veracity of accusations made against him. He has, in fact, confirmed them, and expanded on them, as if he wished to simplify proceedings. It was therefore not necessary to employ the tools of promises or pretense. He has expressed himself with astonishing frankness and, as such, has broken the tribunal's routine. He has endured five years in a dungeon, isolated, deprived of books, and the tribunal has not been able to make him renounce what he refers to, with demented daring, as the rights and duties of his conscience.

The inquisitors allow several months to pass, so that time, that great persuader, might soften what the theologians could not, but they decide to summon him to read out accusations brought against him by five new witnesses. They must keep beating him down. He has physically deteriorated: the skin of his cheeks is taut across sharp bone, his nose is more pronounced, and his temples have turned to ash. He is not told who the witnesses are, as the Inquisition never does such a thing, and because the captive should only be concerned with recognizing his own guilt. The notary reads the charges as if they were blows from a stone; at the end of each sentence, he raises round glasses to see whether the impact has broken that obstinate skull once and for all. Francisco listens, disappointed, as he hears nothing different from what was already known.

The defense attorney who visited him before in the dungeon, and who had used judicial, theological, rhetorical, and emotional strategies to try to make him abjure, tells the tribunal that he refuses to keep helping such a stubborn man. The quill scratches parchment nervously, as a captive's circumstances change dramatically when even his defense attorney abandons him. At that point, Gaitán's approach gains traction: isolate him further, send less food, no reading, a great deal of darkness, and the suspension of interviews and hearings until clear signs of reformation appear. The tribunal is tired of this maniac who cannot see his own miserable situation, his absolute helplessness.

After seven more horrific months in jail, Francisco decides to launch a new skirmish: he asks the servants to call the warden, and tells him that he desires salvation, for which he requests a copy of the New Testament, Christian devotional volumes, and paper on which he might write down his difficulties. The warden transmits the request with joy. Gaitán smells a ruse and denies the request. The other two inquisitors agree to satisfy it, as perhaps the Lord has decided to rescue his soul. They vote, and Gaitán is left mute with rage.

Francisco receives the requested books, parchment, quill, ink, and many candles—gifts fit for a prince. He strokes the volumes as if they were warm animals, pages through them, and rejoices in the vibrancy of letters that speak. A scent rises from the pages, of open fields, wildflowers, and copses. For days and nights on end he rereads the Gospels, the Acts, and the Epistles. He frequents beautiful spaces that spark ideas and make his heart race. Then he reads the devotional Christian texts, and a text that reflects, in a forced manner, on the seventy weeks of Daniel. When he tires of reading, he starts to write. But he doesn't compose prudently, but rather like a gladiator leaping into the arena with a ready sword. He fills all the pages, concentrating his argument on two themes.

He expresses the first theme at the outset. He notes that Saint Paul said, "Has God abandoned His people, Israel? Not at all! For I too am a Jew, descended from Abraham, of the tribe of Benjamin. God did not reject his people, whom he recognized before." And so, is the Holy Office more powerful than the Eternal One? Can the Holy Office hate and exterminate the people who were so loved by the Lord?"

The second axis of his writings regards the seventy weeks of Daniel, and stabs right at the chest. "When it is convenient to you," he writes, "you take a few verses out of context and interpret them literally, but when this same method does not favor you, then you claim it is a matter of symbolism, allegory, or dark metaphors. If the seventy weeks are to be interpreted in such a rigorous and unilateral manner, then the same must be done with the words of Jesus about the imminent end of the world." He goes on to cite that, in Matthew 10:13, 23, 39, 42, and 49, Jesus announces that it will be at the end of his own century; in Matthew 16:28, Mark 9:1, and Luke 9:27, he assures that some of his disciples "will not die until they have seen the son of man arrive in his kingdom." Has the end of the world occurred? Nevertheless, Francisco accepts that the words of Jesus can be interpreted in many ways, as his message is very rich, but, in that case, the seventy weeks of Daniel are also open to diverse interpretation. This proves that interpretations of the sacred text are made according to one's conviction, and not the other way around. "More clearly put, the objective is to twist my convictions, by any means necessary."

The books and writing materials are taken from his cell. The tribunal gives the writings to the learned men and allows three months to pass before summoning them for another session.

The prisoner appears in an even more physically deteriorated state. He listens silently to the detailed counterargument. The four theologians dismantle his sentences, refute them, crush them, and cast them aside like garbage. Francisco stands up with difficulty, raises his forehead, and responds that he remains loyal to the faith of his elders. In less than a minute, the august room is emptied. The inquisitors, in their secret office, gnaw at their own anger and rebuke each other.

Three months later, Francisco tries to repeat the skirmish. He is granted another hearing, but without books or pages to fill with his false thoughts. For two hours, the learned men show him the dominance of theology, oratory, and their impatience. They bathe him in a cascade of light. But the prisoner is not moved by their sonorous speeches. When they finish, he stands up, swears on the one and only God, and declares his continued loyalty to his roots.

In the following months, he will request more hearings, but they will no longer be granted.

125

On the twenty-sixth of January, 1633, after almost six years of captivity and five days after the twelfth futile theological dispute, the High Tribunal of the Holy Office meets to settle the case. Gaitán, Mañozca, and Castro del Castillo listen to the opinions of the four advisors, though they know beforehand that they will offer no new ideas. The facts have already been proven; the questions have been answered. For all the patience, mercy, and hearings that have been offered, the prisoner has returned nothing but odious obstinacy.

Before the meeting, the officials confess, attend Mass, take communion, and review the rules they must follow in such a grave circumstance. Bernard Gui's *Inquisitor's Manual* says that "love of truth and piety, which must always inhabit a judge's heart, should shine through in his gaze, so that his decisions may never be dictated by cruelty or cravings."

One of the advisors asks whether the prisoner's continued requests for hearings should not first be satisfied. Gaitán's bony hands press together before his face, and he replies that the requests will never be satisfied as they are a ruse for delaying matters. The other inquisitors now agree—no more benevolent gestures. The secretary reads the sentence and the judges confirm it with their resonant signatures.

Simply and brutally, it says that Doctor Francisco Maldonado da Silva is sentenced "to be relieved to the secular branch of justice and to the confiscation of goods." In other words: death and expropriation.

126

But all is not yet said. The prisons are an anthill in which, under severe vigilance and seeming immobility, the captives carve out tunnels of liberty. The correspondence through the walls is unceasing; for hours, every night, it transmits names, anguish, ideas. Communication is more important than air.

Francisco learns that, fifteen yards away, a prisoner used a piece of rubble to vigorously scratch the adobe and open the gutter that connects two dungeons; he pushed two earth-caked fingers through to the other side, like a celestial invasion. Then he could touch the tips of his neighbor's fingers and speak to him without judges or secretaries or tormentors. The information had seemed a flood to them, though all it did was relieve their loneliness.

When the warden discovered the infraction, he made the whip sing, the rack creak into motion, the embers burn. Slaves refilled the holes, and the unremorseful prisoner was taken to a new cell, as gloomy as a tomb, from which he'd only emerge to be burned at the stake.

Days later, Juan de Mañozca unfurls the pages an armed black man was carrying from one prisoner to another. "They contain no messages," the servant apologizes, weeping. Mañozca brings his candle closer to the parchment, and suddenly light falls on letters written in lemon juice. The guard loses a hand in torture, to teach others a lesson.

The inquisitor resolves to increase security in the dungeons. Then he discovers something worse: the seeming complicity of the warden. It's incredibly serious. The knocks on the walls bellow out the news.

The warden weeps like a child at his ferocious interrogation. He is rebuked for allowing the perforation of walls and messages written in lemon juice. Index fingers point at him irascibly, like gun barrels, and explanations are demanded for a recent escape. The warden begins to tremble, and recounts how he himself tried to pursue and catch the young man who'd fled. He falls to his knees and insists that the snitches were lying out of spite. He says it is not true that he took advantage of his own immunity to have carnal relations with a female prisoner, and that he convinced their witness to escape to evade danger to himself. Gaitán takes this opportunity to reproach the warden's greed in pocketing bribes, as he has bought haciendas worth far more than he could afford on his salary. The warden wets his trousers. He has fulfilled two decades of service, has seven children, and is not in good health. So he is given leave in order for them to be rid of him.

The new warden, a tall and surly man, embraces his role with zeal; he works hard to uncover the prisoners' startling schemes, and finds a torn, dirty piece of a shirt in his servant's bag. The look of fright is enough to recognize the crime. The terrified servant confesses that a dying prisoner gave it to him to be thrown in the street of the merchants.

"It's a message, you idiot! Who were you supposed to give it to?"

The servant is not lying. He doesn't understand and is remorseful. "In the street of the merchants," he repeats mechanically.

The official unfolds the rag; a few signs have been marked there with the smoke of candles. He has the man whipped and turns the offending object over to the inquisitors. Mañozca agrees with Castro del Castillo—it's a text in Hebrew. They read it with difficulty, from right to left, trying to intuit its absent vowels. It only mentions the name of the prisoner they just tortured; the message tells his loved ones that he is still alive. But this punctures the secret. It offers up a fruitful fact: in Lima, there are Jews who are still free. Surely, from the lips of this prisoner, names can spill. Those names will provide captives, funds, glory.

Francisco gains partial news of the vicissitudes that ripple through his surroundings. The Jew from Lima who sent the message using candle smoke stops responding to knocks on the wall. A few days later, vibrations announce his death. In the dungeons, death is not distressing news because it means an end to the anguish. It's more upsetting for someone to be taken to the torture chamber.

Francisco lies on his stone bench, gaze fixed on a nail in the door. It joins the crossbar to vertical beams, and its head is sticking out. "What is it reminding me of?" he wonders. "My father's coat hanger in his hovel in Callao? Or is it bothering me that the nail is neither entirely buried nor entirely free?" He gets up and touches it; its thick head protrudes about a half centimeter. An Indian would attribute life to it, would recognize a huaca in the iron and see this being as leaving the prison, slowly, alone. Francisco tries to pull it out and pushes at it with all his might. Useless. For a few days he forgets this attempt, but then that black protruding head calls him again, urges him to persevere. He works at it with a piece of rubble. In the great void of time, any goal can take on grandeur, becoming that inner resting place from which Archimedes claimed it was possible to move the world. Removing a nail becomes as important as defeating Goliath. When at last he achieves it, Francisco basks in a profound relief. A trophy like this one must not be discovered by the ever-vigilant guards; he hides it in the wool of his mattress.

The following day, he starts to file it against a rough stone. As he recites long passages from his beloved texts and composes verses, the nail acquires the form of a small knife, with a sharp tip and blade. Francisco now has a weapon.

"How strange!" he thinks. "This suffocating cell no longer makes me dizzy or dazed. I'm some kind of amphibian that can live where others perish. A mysterious hope is rising in my chest, an unexpected bravery."

Until now he's been able to avoid the new warden's redoubled vigilance, which raises his spirits. He hides away the bones of his food, chooses a chicken bone, and starts to cut it methodically with his brand-new little knife, as if he were a sculptor. The elegant length of a quill is born before his eyes. All he needs is ink and paper to complete his clandestine writing set. It won't be difficult; he can make ink by mixing coal with water. As for paper, he already has it, the most valuable thing that enters his cell: small bags of flour. He will hoard each piece as if they were manna from heaven. He'll be able to write again—he longs for it with the ferocity of a wolf—and he'll violate the fortress of the Inquisition.

127

Paper is scarce, and he must not use more words than necessary. His text calls for solemnity. Francisco concocts a risky plan of communicating with the Jews of Rome through prisoners leaving the prison to carry out their sentences in a monastery. He knows that, in Rome, a significant community has formed since the time of the Maccabees, and that they openly practice their faith and enjoy the relative protection of the popes.

He writes his epistle in Latin and makes copies that reach men about to be released. He has persuaded Simón and Pablo to act as couriers. Both servants have been impressed by the story Francisco told them about Luis, the sorcerer's son. He told them how he was barbarically hunted down in his native Angola, how he was abused in his travels across land and sea, and how his thigh was wounded in an escape attempt in Potosí. He described his musical talents, so powerful as to pull beautiful sounds from the teeth of a mule's jawbone. He made them tear up with the story of the heroic way he hid the surgical instruments. Pablo and Simón said that they had suffered a similar story. Francisco was startled when, one afternoon, along with his food, they brought him a mule's jawbone and an olive branch. The prisoner grasped them as Luis used to do, and there in the damp dungeon, he belted out a rhythm that the men listened to with tears in their eyes.

Francisco's letter was addressed to the synagogue of the Jewish brothers in Rome.

He introduces himself as "Eli Nazareo, Jew, son of Diego Núñez da Silva, master of medicine and surgery, locked up in the prisons of the Inquisition of Lima." He greets them "in the name of the God of Israel, creator of heaven and Earth, with wishes for your good health and peace." He tells them that his father taught him the law of God as bestowed upon the people through Moses, and that, for fear of Christian repression, he pretended to deny this faith. "In this as with other commandments, I confess to have sinned foolishly, as only God is to be feared, and only the truth of His justice should be sought, openly, without fear of men." He refers to his study of the sacred text, and to his memorization of the words of the prophets, every psalm without exception, many of Solomon's proverbs as well as those of his son Siraj, most of the Pentateuch, and many prayers he himself composed in the tomb of a dungeon, in both Spanish and Latin.

He tells them that he is well aware that his destiny will be merciless if he does not abjure. "In truth," he writes, "since the day I was imprisoned, I promised to fight with all my strength and to use all arguments against enemies of the law." He infers that he'll be burned at the stake, his home will be taken away, and his children will be subjected to perpetual shame. And if he abjures, his assets are still taken, and he is harassed with the wearing of the sanbenito and a stigma on his blood and the blood of his children, for generations to come.

He has been chained for six years now. He knows that his thoughts and arguments in the hearings have not brought the results he'd hoped for. "I've worked like someone who plows hard, rocky earth and whose labor in the end produces no fruit." He recounts that he gave "more than two hundred oral and written arguments, to which there still has not been any satisfactory response, despite the fact that I daily ask for resolution. It appears that they've decided not to respond."

He announces his inevitable end and writes moving phrases: "Pray for me to the Lord, my dearest brothers; pray that He may give me strength to endure the torment of flames. My death is close at hand, and there is no one else to help me, except God. From Him, I hope for eternal life, and the soon-to-be salvation of our oppressed people."

His epistle, however, contains the intense elixir of attachment to life: "Choose life for yourselves, my deeply beloved brothers." He reminds them that they form part of a vast community of dignified men, and that they should not abandon hope even if injustice and anguish reign. "Keep to the law, so that the Lord may help us return to the land of our forefathers, so that we may multiply, and so that He may bless us, as it is written in Deuteronomy, Chapter 30." He praises the traditions of solidarity, study, and love.

He folds the pages. First, he turns over one copy. If the walls' correspondence tells him that it has arrived at its destination, then he'll send the second one. One of those will manage to break through the armored fortress and cross the ocean. Then his passion and death will be known. His sacrifice will not be futile, because he will be part of the tragic and mysterious chain unfurled by the just people of the world.

128

In the tribunal's deliberations, the desire grows for an Act of Faith. There are enough prisoners with completed trials. It's not convenient to keep maintaining them in jail and wasting money on their food. Also, an Act of Faith is an exemplary event that reorganizes spirits; it not only punishes sinners or forces them into reflection, but it also reminds the powerful civil and ecclesiastical authorities that the Holy Office keeps watch, works, and issues sentences with great seriousness.

However, Acts of Faith have extraordinary costs, and the resources flowing into the Inquisition's coffers barely cover salaries and minor expenses. The exhaustive confiscations don't bring in enough wealth. It also seems that, in this matter, too, the devil's work is at hand, because instead of tempting rich people whose goods would give this sacred mission plenitude, Lucifer makes poor people fall; most of the accused are humble, immoral monks, black and mulatto sorcerers, austere Lutherans, and Jews devoted to medicine. It would be more profitable to take down rich merchants and a few Indian overseers with vast properties and bags brimming with gold.

In the projected Act of Faith, there will be many reconciled men and women with light sentences, such as public whippings, a few years in the galleys, reeducation in monasteries, the wearing of a sanbenito, banishment. For people to be deeply moved, however, what's needed is the smell of charred flesh. The heat and light of fire cut through sinners' malignant armor. The flames, though they may be lit for a single reptile of a man, fill the whole Viceroyalty with an instructive presence.

The location where the thick stake is placed, its base surrounded by logs that will slowly roast the captive, is interchangeably referred to as the "rocky terrain" or the "burning place." The people fear and avoid it. It is on the other side of the Rímac River, between the neighborhoods of San Lázaro, with its lepers, and the high hill. The didactic clouds of smoke, when they arise, invade all of Lima, and the screams of the condemned sting the ears of all. The inquisitors recall that fire is one of the four elements named by Aristotle, but he didn't know—because he lived before Christ—of its cardinal power to purify. For this reason they consider an Act of Faith without fire to be as empty as a procession without a saint.

The dungeons of Lima already contain the man who will justify their blazes. It's that crazy Jew to whom they offered abundant opportunities for rectification. But—this is inexplicable to them—he has tenaciously rejected the most logical path. He has formulated hundreds of questions that were answered by famous theologians. And at the end of the persuasions, as if to mock them, he repeated a demented right to think and believe whatever he liked. Demanding freedom of thought and belief! Is there anything more grotesque? If one person can believe in whatever comes to mind, then that person's neighbor can, too, and so can the next neighbor after him. These depraved examples would strike at the Lord's temples like catapults. All of humanity would roll into the inferno.

"Francisco Maldonado da Silva is a powerful enemy," Gaitán warns. "He must be eliminated as soon as possible."

"That's why we've already condemned him," Castro del Castillo reminds him.

"If before he managed to change his trial, now he's lost it completely," Mañozca adds, extending a page written in Latin with weak ink.

The judges examine the letter to the Jews of Rome. They pass the coarse paper around between them. The prisoner's audacity is yet another intolerable provocation. Gaitán longs to strangle him with his own bare hands, but he accepts for him to be summoned in order to confess this very grave crime.

Francisco—already condemned to death, and transformed into a specter—responds with his habitual frankness. Yes, he wrote that letter.

The inquisitors tremble with shock again. A sinner so wretched cannot possibly be so simultaneously brave. Something about this doesn't make sense. The only thing they can confirm is that he's possessed by Lucifer, and that this is not a matter of a human being who enjoys free will and his full faculties of reason.

Gaitán bites his thin white lips and says, "We mustn't delay the Act of Faith, as madmen are also weapons of the devil."

—〜〜—

Opalescent light enters through the tiny window. It is late at night, and all activities have ceased, even the correspondence through the walls. Francisco has startled awake, and he stares at that uncertain glow. He recalls the night on which an identical phenomenon took place, when Brother Martín was punishing himself with the help of an Indian man. He doesn't hear the whistle of sticks through the air, though, or Martín's repressed moans, but rather ethereal sandals. They are coming quietly, through a tunnel. Now he hears them better. There's a single person whose tension ripples through the walls, making the tiny window shine and keeping Francisco's eyes open, his ears alert. The sandals stop beside his door. Who's trying to see him at this hour? The bolt rises slowly and a key penetrates the lock. Francisco sits up on his hard bed. The flickering light of a candle slides in between the bars. A familiar figure immediately appears. He closes the door and places the candlestick on the table. He gazes at Francisco with compassion, then pulls up a chair.

The Jesuit Andrés Hernández adjusts the folds of his black habit and speaks in a low, almost whispering voice. To avoid any false assumptions, he explains that he's received authorization from Antonio Castro del Castillo to speak to Francisco privately. The good Hernández has not resigned himself to Francisco's persistence.

"If you lacked intelligence," he says with a sigh, "if you wanted for brains, if you were an unenlightened man—none of that would impede the realization of the pit that awaits you in your terrible destiny. Your attitude is one of futile insolence. Have the theologians' responses not been satisfying to you? They were carefully planned and studied, and well-articulated."

Hernández rubs his throat, tired out by his whispering tone, but still he makes a disproportionate effort to communicate with the prisoner, and to persuade him.

Francisco listens attentively. This priest wishes him well, of course, and he has risked himself to come to this dungeon and offer assistance. He is affectionate, transparent. His presence and his gentle voice act as a balm. He's obviously making a great effort to reach his heart; and yet, he cannot see beyond his own skin. Hernández looks at Francisco, talks to him, and thinks of him without imagining himself in Francisco's place. With kindness and concern he implores only that Francisco cease being who he is.

"Are you not, perhaps, blinded by pride?" he asks cautiously.

"Pride?" Francisco repeats. "No. It's something more precious. I'd say that I'm sustained by an ambiguous dignity."

The Jesuit replies that dignity would not make him be so cruel to himself and his family; only pride could produce such bullheadedness. Francisco is not surprised by such an argument, and he asks about his family, since the Jesuit has mentioned them. Hernández, disturbed, reminds him that he is forbidden from sharing information.

Francisco says, "We were talking about cruelty, weren't we?"

The clergyman despairs, and tells Francisco he can still be saved.

"Only the soul," Francisco completes the prayer.

"If you don't repent, you'll be burned alive. If you repent before they read your sentence, you'll be burned in death."

"They'll kill me no matter what."

"The ways of the Lord are inscrutable—"

The two men stare at each other in the candle's tenuous light, eyes shining. The priest has not been explicit, but he insinuates that the execution could still be lifted. He is offering life in exchange for a modification of belief. Then Francisco puts two and two together starkly, brutally: This kind examiner of the Holy Office doesn't care whether he lives or dies, only that he modify his faith. In other words, he is offering life as a kind of bribe.

Silence, stillness, and tense expectation magnetize the armored dungeon. The damp cold sinks into the bone. Hernández picks up a blanket that's balled up at the foot of the bed and draws it over Francisco's back, then pulls his hood close around his own neck. Francisco shivers under the paternal gesture and can only reciprocate with a wounding frankness. He mumbles a reproach in a grateful tone.

"It's a form of moral violence to demand a change of faith. Some men are taller than others, smarter than others, more sensitive than others, but we are all equal in our right to think and believe. If my convictions are a crime against God, only He is in a position to judge. The Holy Office is usurping God and committing atrocities in His name. To maintain its terror-driven power it even prefers for me to pretend that my beliefs have changed." He pauses and then unleashes the flagrant contradiction. "The Gospel says, 'love thine enemy.' Why can you not love me?"

Andrés Hernández clasps his hands. "Please!" he begs. "Give up your bad dream! Get out of your confusion! Christ loves you—return to His arms! Please—"

"Christ is not the Inquisition, but rather its opposite. I am closer to Christ than you are, Father."

567

Hernández's eyes fill with tears. "How can you be close to Christ when you deny Him?"

"Christ the human being is moving; he is the victim, the lamb, he is love and beauty. Christ the God, on the other hand, for me, for those of us who are targets of persecution and injustice in His name, is the symbol of a voracious power that demands we denounce our brothers, abandon our families, betray our parents, burn our very ideas. Christ the human being perished at the hands of that same machine that may put an end to my days. That is the machine that you call Christ the God."

The Jesuit crosses himself, prays, and asks for these blasphemies to be forgiven. "He knows not what he says," he mutters, paraphrasing the Gospel.

"Isn't it possible that my death sentence," Francisco says, "is related to you inquisitors' lack of confidence in your own faith?"

"That's absurd—please, have mercy, by the heavens. Do not close to the light, to life. I don't want you to be taken to the fires! You are my brother! I have heard you recite the beatitudes from memory with Catholic emotion. Your blind stubbornness, though stirred by the devil, is brave. A person like you should not die."

Francisco raises his hot calloused hands, and places them over the ones grasping the crucifix. He responds with sad irony. "I am not the one who issued the death sentence."

"Your obstinacy issued it."

"The Holy Office, Father! The Holy Office. And it does so in the name of the cross, the church, and God. In the name of all of them. The Holy Office won't even take full responsibility for its death sentences. It tries to act as though its hands are clean, hypocritically clean, like the hands of Pontius Pilate."

Hernández kneels before the prisoner, grabs his shoulders, and shakes him.

"I beg you, on my knees. I'm humiliating myself to wake you up. What more do you need to return to the fold?"

Francisco closes his eyes to keep his tears from falling. How can he make this man understand that he is more awake than ever? The sobs emerge as if from a shameful spring. Both men have reached the limits of their strength, but still their thoughts cannot converge. Both feel overflowing affection and admire each other's respective perseverance. They say goodbye to each other with a gesture that is almost an embrace. Then the glow at the tiny window intensifies, as if it had witnessed an unbelievable act.

129

With swollen eyelids, Andrés Hernández informs the tribunal of his failure and begs them to have mercy on such an illustrious prisoner. Mañozca insists that Francisco has definitively lost his mind, which matters not. The sentence stands: he will be burned alive during the next Act of Faith.

A race then begins between the Inquisitorial machine and its victim. Locked up, disarmed, and debilitated, Francisco appeals to a final resource to mock their spectacle of execution. What can such a wounded and solitary man still do? No one visits him now. He only matters as meat that can be barbecued in public. They provide his meager rations and, every once in a while, empty his chamber pot. Nothing more.

"But I'll surprise them," Francisco mutters. "How long does it take to prepare an Act of Faith? Three, four, five months? That's enough time."

He receives the small bags of food and only keeps the paper, flour, and water. He cuts the paper and shapes a notebook. With the flour and water he makes a paste with which he glues the remaining pieces to make more sheets. He will spend these months writing. But he will not eat. The Holy Office will know that it cannot control everything, that it is terrible but not omnipotent. It will only be partially defeated, but it will be defeated. Francisco's career now consists of dying of his own volition, before they kill him.

He will help God detach his soul from his body before they drag him to the fires. He will not give them the pleasure of final repentance, and he will deny them the pleasure of hearing his moans as he burns. He wants to gain an advantage over his tormentors. His pulse quickens with the insane hope of making it in time for this final contest. Francisco's disadvantage, however, lies in not knowing the date of the Act of Faith. Because of this, his fast must be severe. During the first four days he is hounded by the known discomforts of previous fasts: dizziness and cramps. Then he moves into a paradise of lightness. Hunger dissolves, the intestine's sounds disappear, pain goes up in smoke, and he sails toward another dimension.

The small knife that was once a nail, and the quill that was once a chicken bone, accompany him in his everyday tasks. For many hours he works on his writing materials, and during others he writes down his thoughts. Then he hides the pages.

The prolonged deprivations consume his already emaciated body. He can't stay on his feet for as long as he could before, and his abject fatigue forces him to reduce his hours of work. He is sheathed in a soft, relaxed weakness. His physical deterioration is a counterpoint to his spiritual vigor. He can taste victory. Each passing day is a day gained. When they come to read him his sentence and put on his shameful sanbenito to take him to the altar of sacrifice, they won't find anything more than his insensible remains.

The warden discovers this remarkable strategy late in the game, and runs to confess his guilt before the judges. He is horrified. He fears—and with good reason—that they will punish him in one of those ways that make history. He points out that the prisoner regularly receives his food and that he had stopped asking for hearings. Nothing suggested the need for any special supervision. How could he have suspected such a cursed scheme? How could he have thought that an admitted Jew would be capable of putting himself through such deprivations as have only been recorded in the lives of saints? When the warden entered Francisco's cell, he recounts, trembling, he found a skeleton wrapped in skin as thin as silk.

130

Francisco floats between the veils of half consciousness. His mouth barely articulates his refusal to eat. He is close to his goal and knows he will win. He is offered cakes, fruit, stew, milk, chocolate. A doctor orders for him to be moved carefully so that the broken parts of his skin can be dried out and healed. Even the Jesuit Andrés Hernández and the Franciscan Alonso Briceño are sent to persuade him to interrupt his intolerable fast.

Another event, however, changes the direction of Francisco's life as well as the entire history of Lima's Inquisition. The prisoner's ears, muted by the effects of malnutrition, manage to decipher some of the words: "great complicity," "massive arrests," "Jews discovered." Soldiers, people, cries, and laments fill the gloomy corridors, and new adobe piles on the walls, ditches are dug, the cells multiply. A seemingly minor denunciation had exhumed a vein of secret Jews that sent the zealous Holy Office into a fever. The boredom of long proceedings for the wretched poor is now convulsed by the arrest of notable figures. Rich ones.

Gaitán burns the letter he was about to send to Spain, requesting yet again to be relieved of his duties. These recent discoveries have changed his mood. Now he prefers to stay in Lima, because he never suspected that such plunder would reach his hands. The Act of Faith to condemn a few monks, sorcerers, and repentant Jews will be postponed indefinitely. Now they must work hard on this interminable line of prisoners that's entering the dark cells like a snake. When the Act of Faith takes place, dozens of incredible sinners will be added, and the massive undertaking will shake the world.

What had happened? Very simple. A young man named Antonio Cordero, who had lived in Seville and now worked for a rich merchant in the City of Kings, remarked that he made no sales on Saturdays or Sundays and, also, that he did not care for pork. His boast was passed on to a familiar of the Holy Office. The inquisitors sniffed out their prey and resolved to modify their routine for the first time. They kidnapped Cordero and did not confiscate his goods, to keep his networks from taking precautions. The captive, who was so reckless when free, produced, in the torture chambers, the greatest disaster his brothers could have imagined, informing on his boss and two friends, who were immediately sucked into the grim fortress. The secret Jewish community of Lima did not recognize the danger posed by these people's disappearance, since, without the confiscation of assets, they dismissed the idea that the Holy Office was involved. On the eleventh of August, 1635, however, a surprise raid took place that ripped dozens of people from their homes, sent prestigious families into mourning, and extended a systematic persecution to the far edges of the Viceroyalty.

The inquisitors' enthusiasm was so great that nervous letters were sent to Spain filled with facts and hyperbolic predictions. In one of them, they declared that "there are so many Jews that they could be their own nation," "the prisons are now full," "people go about their lives in shock and do not trust each other because when they least expect it they can find themselves without the friend or acquaintance whom they so valued." They underscored the threat posed by Jews: "This lost nation was taking root here in a manner that, like a bad weed, was threatening to strangle Christianity."

Among the arrested people, there are three women. The judges determine that their diminished physical strength might make them surrender more names. In the first stage, however—before the trials are conducted—it is urgent to capture as many criminals as possible. Some of them have already escaped into the jungle or the mountains, or they have attempted to secretly embark for other lands.

The correspondence through the walls repeatedly transmits a sweet name: "Mencia de Luna." "Mencia de Luna, young-Jewish-tortured." She has not returned to the prison. Her name resounds like a desperate tribute. Francisco strains to count the blows along the walls, to construct words, to come out of his bedridden stupor. Just beyond the walls of his cell, a young woman has been sacrificed. Without realizing it, he drinks a few drops of milk and chews the flesh of an olive. A shaky thought enters his bruised mind: he is surrounded by a multitude of victims and he must not abandon them. What to do? He spits the olive pit into his hand and stares at it in surprise. He's just broken his fast! Why? He rubs his temples and opens his eyes wide as if he could read, on the sooty wall, the message that would explain his sudden change. There must be some explanation. He hasn't done it out of fear. He has done it because of the tragedy sweeping through the Viceroyalty. His struggle should not head toward death, because he'll have plenty of it soon enough. Now he needs to go back to struggling for life, to maintaining the resistance. As he was doing before.

He picks up a piece of bread, breaks it, and chews slowly. His mouth hurts. He has to recover his strength so he can plan his next steps. It's logical to assume that the tribunal would now have postponed the Act of Faith until the new trials have been completed. Another time of action has arrived.

He is astonished to feel a new surge of energy. This change in circumstances demands a change of strategy. But he must think it through. First he has to learn about this catastrophe of which the walls are speaking. What's happened? What will happen? He was almost dead from fasting, but now, as if resurrected, he has to offer help to his brothers in misfortune. How?

131

As always, each new prisoner is forced to denounce others, and all Portuguese people—or individuals who've lived in Portugal—are inevitably suspect. In this manner, the number of arrests grows exponentially. The tribunal decides to increase the number of dungeons. Its success emboldens it to bring a new complaint before the king, regarding that cursed agreement of 1610: "They have our hands tied," they protest, "forbidding us from obstructing anyone's travels, or from requiring a license from those who wish to travel, but the current situation calls for us to have the power to refuse passage to those who lack authorization from the Holy Office."

The prisoners from the first big raids include an extremely prominent resident of Lima. The Holy Office had struck the blow at twelve thirty, when the streets were brimming with people. The officials and their carriages spread out strategically and the operation was completed in an hour. "The city was stunned and amazed," the inquisitors would later say. The highest authority of the Jews of Lima was shackled to the wall of his dark dungeon: Don Manuel Bautista Pérez.

Francisco had heard him spoken of at the university. He was said to be a cultured, generous man, esteemed by priests and laypeople alike, and a celebration was being prepared for him in thanks for his donations. Later, it was discovered that he'd been given a tribute full of praise in the presence of faculty and students. This Manuel Bautista Pérez contributed, with his gifts and initiatives, to the improvement of the City of Kings, and he was held in high esteem by the viceroy and city hall. He behaved like a devoted Christian and was thought of as a moral man with an excellent reputation.

Nevertheless, the Holy Office gathered forced denunciations from thirty witnesses, and the prisoner could not resist against such an avalanche of proof. He practiced Judaism in secret, and was a leader in his abominable community. His people called him "the oracle of the Hebrew nation," and some referred to him as "rabbi." According to the denunciations, he held gatherings in the upper floors of his home, presided over religious ceremonies, and taught the dead laws. In his library, Christian books were discovered that in fact were there to hide his identity. He was, according to informants, "the great captain," who was known, respected, and loved by the other sixty-three people who'd been arrested, including the deceased Mencia de Luna.

The correspondence through the walls transmit Manuel Bautista Pérez's name. His fall into the Inquisition's claws marks the collapse of the last pillar holding up the prisoners' hopes.

Francisco rushes to call the guards and request a change of diet in order to break his fast. The Jesuit Andrés Hernández and the Franciscan Alonso Briceño attribute this news to the success of their own persuasions, and they file a report heralding the start of a long-awaited repentance. The inquisitors receive this news without being moved, as they are sick and tired of Francisco. And now they have their hands full with the big fish who has just been netted.

The elderly rabbi is taken to the torture chamber. He walks with such firm steps that the warden doesn't dare pull on his chain. The torturer, on meeting his gaze, looks away quickly. Without giving him time to realize what's about to happen, he tears the man's groin on the rack. The inquisitors order the session to be stopped immediately; this specimen is too valuable. The man is returned to his cell, unconscious, and a doctor is sent to give him medical attention.

Days later, Francisco learns that something serious happened: Manuel Bautista Pérez had hidden a small knife in his sock, and when he recovered from the torture, he tried to kill himself. He stabbed himself six times in the abdomen, and twice in the groin.

132

For the first time, Francisco receives corn, a ration he requested instead of bread. It's astonishing to see the way the crush of new inmates has overwhelmed the guards and eased the strictures that had reigned throughout the fortress. Francisco looks at the corn enthusiastically and, when he is free of spying eyes, with the door bolted shut, he sets to work. He pulls the husk from each ear of corn and hides the leaves under his bed. With the yellow kernels laid bare, he cooks the corn in a pot he is now allowed to have, over a small stove. He is glad to be recovering his appetite, and he stretches his body. The wounds on his torso are healing. But he can't hear as well as before, and sleeps a great deal. He is stabilizing, like a hurt bird abandoned in the wild.

Francisco ties together many corn husks to fashion a long rope. Nobody pays attention to him anymore. At night, he drags the brittle table to the wall, places the stool on the table, and, holding on where he can, climbs to the ceiling beams. His left hand grasps a beam firmly, while the other uses the tiny iron knife to gnaw at the adobe around one of the small window's bars. He tires and grows dizzy. He knows he's in no condition to overexert himself. He descends, puts the furniture back—though he knows it's unlikely that anyone will come at this hour—and dozes for a while. Then he resumes his task. The small window looks out on an inner courtyard surrounded by cells. Over the roofs, he can glimpse the high outer fortress walls.

At last, he succeeds in moving the bar. He pushes it this way and that, twists and turns it, pushes it again, and finally yanks it out. He smiles at it as if it were a helpless victim and places it on a beam.

Back down on the ground, he picks up his rope and tests each knot to gauge its strength. He climbs up again and ties the rope to one of the immobile bars. He sticks out his head. He feels the cool night air, a crazy caress of freedom. Slowly, grasping the rope, he slides his body out and climbs down the high wall. His dungeon seemed to be in a pit, but the courtyard's firm earth truly feels like an abyss. He can't understand the effect: it's part of the irrationality imposed by the Holy Office. He reaches the ground and crouches in the shadows, glued to the wall. He looks around cautiously. The air carries the scent of the Rímac River. He sees no guards, no servants, no dogs, though they must be lying in wait.

After all these years in prison he has managed to create an imaginary map in his mind of this labyrinth, and he knows there are traps, false doors, and corridors with hidden holes to devour those who try to escape. For this reason, he walks silently, exploring the uneven earth, brushing past bushes. He glimpses the vegetable garden, tended by the slaves of the Holy Office. It is a square in which plant life breathes, deaf to the prison's tortures. The smell of vegetables is intoxicating. He strokes the polished skin of a tomato, presses it gently, and imagines its red color in the daylight; he picks it, bites it, and enjoys its flavorful flesh. How long has it been since he's touched a plant or plucked a piece of fruit? He keeps moving, toward the nearest wall. His imagination has not failed him. He finds the corridor through which enslaved workers reach the garden. A torch languishes at one end, allowing him to reenter the detested labyrinth. To the left, a newly built archway leads to the recently added dungeons. Francisco stays close to the wall, and his hands sense a vibration: someone is approaching. He has to hurry.

The doors along the hall are identical, and he chooses one. He lifts the bolt very slowly. He enters, closes the door behind him, and makes calming gestures to the two prisoners, who spring up, startled. He stays silent with his index finger over his lips, until he is assured that no one has entered the hall. He hears nothing but the frogs out in the courtyard. The silence becomes physical, a thick presence. Francisco lights a candle. He speaks to the prisoners in a whispering voice, expressing solidarity. The captives are stunned. They think they are targets of another trap set by the Holy Office. Is this nocturnal apparition trying to trick them, to make them confess? Perhaps, so they confess: one says he is a bigamist, and the other is a monk who married in secret. Francisco is disappointed, because he's not looking for people persecuted for such reasons, but rather those who will be sent to the fiery altars for loyalty to their beliefs. He blesses them in the name of God and returns to the dim corridor.

He drags himself in the opposite direction. He tries another cell. Two men startle there, too. Francisco introduces himself. He says his name is Eli Nazareo, he who was once known as Francisco Maldonado da Silva. Elijah is the name of the prophet who battled the idolaters of Baal, and the name means "my God is Yahweh" in Hebrew; Nazir, Nazareo, is he who is consecrated to service to the Lord.

"I am an unworthy servant of the God of Israel," he exclaims, with a self-humiliation true to its time.

The captives exchange a glance, full of doubts. Who doesn't know about the spies and provocateurs contracted by the Holy Office to break their resistance? No code or password is guaranteed; the trick can include words in Hebrew, references to feast days, or moving stories. Francisco insists that he is really a prisoner. His presence stirs a sacred fear, with his long, graying beard, and his hair parted at the middle and falling softly over his shoulders. He resembles an aging Jesus. He is tall, perhaps appearing even more so now that he's so thin. His strong nose and penetrating eyes make his voice and words all the more persuasive. Finally, one of the two says that he recognizes him.

"You recognize me?"

The old man nods and invites Francisco to sit down beside him, on the tousled bed. His face is as wrinkled as a nut.

"My name is Tomé Cuaresma," he says.

"Tomé Cuaresma!" Francisco clasps his dry, cold hands. "My father—"

"Yes, your father." He raises his eyes, which are swollen with pain. "Your father knew me, and spoke of me, right?"

In the new section of the secret jails, these two men connect deeply in a belated reunion through the depths of the night. Tomé Cuaresma is one of the most popular physicians in Lima, and yet Francisco, curiously, was never able to see him in person. His father had often spoken of this tireless professional, to whom noblemen constantly turned for help. But he was also the doctor who secretly served the city's Jews.

The old man recounts his sudden arrest on the street, as he was leaving home to attend to a patient. He was assaulted like a common thief; his wrists were tied with rope, and he was forced into a carriage. The warden interrogated him first, and then he was locked in this cell with another victim, as it seemed that there was no longer enough space for solitary confinement.

The other prisoner introduces himself, in turn.

"I am Sebastián Duarte."

"Brother-in-law of Rabbi Manuel Bautista Pérez," Cuaresma adds.

"Of Manuel Bautista Pérez?" Francisco says, astonished. "I have to see him, to speak to him."

"He's ordered me to confess everything." Sebastián Duarte opens his hands in resignation. "And to beg for mercy."

"Confession has no limits," Francisco replies, disturbed. "They want facts and names and then more facts and more names. The rabbi is mistaken, because begging for mercy is futile; it heightens the inquisitors' arrogance, and does not lessen the victims' suffering."

They stare at him in alarm.

"That is what Pérez suggested?" Francisco insists. "He cannot be so naïve. He must have done so in the thrall of torture. It doesn't count."

"He tried to kill himself," his brother-in-law says, by way of justification.

"My father begged for mercy," Francisco tells them. "He asked for mercy, and he was reconciled, but with sanctions, forced to wear the sanbenito. Know this: confession will not erase our guilt, and neither will mercy give us back our freedom. Either we submit to the whims of the Holy Office, or we confront it until God decides. No freedom remains for us except for freedom of the spirit. Let us protect it, and defend it."

Tomé Cuaresma and Sebastián Duarte stare at him skeptically. It is a surreal inspirational speech, spoken by a surreal man. Francisco presses their hands, utters the *Shema Israel,* and recites verses from the psalms. He enjoins them not to surrender. He reminds them, passionately, of Samson's battle against the Philistines.

"If it's a matter of dying, may our deaths weigh heavily upon them."

He blesses them, puts out the flame, and silently opens the door.

He enters the next cell, where the prisoners' fright is repeated, as are Francisco's calming gestures. One of the captives falls to his knees, having confused the visitor with Jesus.

"I am not Jesus." He smiles and helps the man to his feet. "I am your brother. A Jew. My name is Eli Nazareo, servant of the God of Israel."

He encourages them to resist and reminds them that each human being carries a divine spark inside. The Holy Office displays great power, but it is not omnipotent.

"The judges are men, and we are men. We are the same. We are equal."

He returns to the corridor, where the torch flickers and trembles, and he glides toward the inner courtyard. It is enough for one night. He is content, and decides to celebrate his victory with another tomato. Then he moves toward the wall, stays glued to it, and finally reaches the rope that still hangs from his tiny window. He climbs, using his bare feet and knees to grip the knots on the wall, as Lorenzo Valdés had taught him as a child. Before entering the ominous cell, he fills his lungs with night air. He removes the bar he hid among the ceiling beams and puts it back in place. It's essential to cover his tracks, so he can do it again.

No records exist to document the meeting between Francisco and the great captain Manuel Bautista Pérez. But it's notable that Manuel Bautista Pérez sends messages to fellow prisoners that ordered the opposite of what he'd said before. Now he asks them to resist and to retract any confessions made under torture. His brother-in-law Sebastián Duarte reads the coded text that a bribed servant brings him and is stunned to see the same words spoken a few nights ago, in this very cell, by the fantastic apparition called Eli Nazareo: "Do not confess, or beg for mercy! Let us defend our freedom of belief!"

Eli Nazareo moves through the prison like the prophet Elijah visiting the Passover table: almost invisible, like a marvelous mist. If he had not talked, written, and resisted for years, if all his achievements had been reduced to nothing but this reckless stirring of his people, Francisco Maldonado da Silva would have paid his debts to history and to the principles of solidarity. The analogy his father once made between a temple and a human being is put into practice by this man who extracts gold from adversity.

The inquisitors are vexed to find that several prisoners are revoking their confessions, because, in their words, they were made under duress. They are forced to repeat hearings, summon more witnesses, and mobilize spies to dig for hoarded truths.

Francisco is discovered crossing the garden. A servant pounces on him and shouts for help. Francisco falls. Immediately, the eyes of other guards emerge from the walls. With a superhuman effort, the prisoner pulls at the ankles of his opponent, who unleashes blasphemies and a punch that is lost in the empty darkness. The prisoner leverages the missed hit to slip away into the brush, while his pursuers collide against each other.

"Where is he, damn it?"

"That way—he went that way!"

Francisco throws a piece of rubble to distract them.

"That way!" they shout, lurching toward the noise.

He hurls another piece of rubble and rushes toward the rope. He starts to climb, lacking air, lacking vigor.

"I have to get there!" he commands himself, staring up at the unreachable little window, channeling his remaining strength into his hands and feet. They still haven't recognized him.

A guard grabs him by the ankles. Francisco can no longer resist. He loosens his grip and falls on his captor.

—⁓—

Gaitán, fists shut on the wide table, proposes to send him immediately to the torture chamber, with the hope that this will kill him. But in the interrogation Francisco undoes his plan. True to his nature, he acknowledges what's taken place. The notary writes up his account with the fear produced by proximity to demented people.

133

The warden rearranges the prisoners to free up an extremely isolated dungeon in one of the pits reserved for punishing the most perverse captives. It is so narrow that neither a table nor a stool fits, only a stone bench where a dirty straw mattress is laid out, along with a chest into which they press the rest of his rags. In place of a small window, there are three holes through which nothing larger than an orange could pass. The door has a double bolt, the corridor is guarded night and day by the warden's assistants, and a selfless Dominican is obliged to visit him weekly in an effort to break his perseverance, monitor his food intake, and uncover any plans to hatch new crimes against order and the faith.

The prisoner is suffocated by the lack of space and the constant vigilance. Although his olfactory sense has deadened, he can't bear the nauseating sewer smell.

———

Near the fortress, Archbishop Fernando Arias de Ugarte resists the Inquisition's attempts to take his chaplain and majordomo, who are both suspected of having cultivated friendships with the main Jewish prisoners. The archbishop has lived in La Plata, where he met that calm, trustworthy man who, on becoming a widower, studied theology, gave eloquent proof of his devotion, and was ordained as a priest. He is Portuguese in origin, but lived in Buenos Aires and in Córdoba, built a reasonable fortune, and wanted to live and die as a good Catholic. His name was Diego López de Lisboa, and he had traveled in the caravan to Salta with Francisco. At that time, he'd decided to erase his roots. But when the mass arrests of Jews took place, a group of agitators shouted in the cathedral's atrium for the authorities to "arrest that Jew." The bewildered old man sought refuge in the Episcopal residence, but the multitude gathered in front of its windows. "Your Honor, throw that Jew out of your house." The prelate resolved to protect him, but the jester Burguillos, seeing Diego López de Lisboa enter the church wearing the archbishop's skirts, mocked him with words that became popular across Lima: "Even if you grab your own bottom, the Inquisition will get you out." The prelate risked his own life and honor in deciding to protect this man. He knew that Diego López de Lisboa's four children had already renounced their compromising paternal last name and instead used the surname León Pinelo. He would not add any more offenses.

Meanwhile, the tribunal conducts the trials that will culminate in an inevitable Act of Faith, scheduled for January of 1639.

⸺∿⸺

Months before the Holy Office unleashed this turmoil in the Viceroyalty, Isabel Otáñez arrives in Lima with several letters of recommendation and the frightened wish to speak to the esteemed judges. Timidly, she makes her way through the interminable stations of their *via crucis*. She consults with the mother superior of a convent, meets with two familiars of the Holy Office, and finally ventures into the plaza of the Inquisition. The severe building exudes its icy breath, and she is paralyzed before the tall door.

She addresses the guards, hesitantly, and requests an audience. She shows the letters and explains her helpless situation. She is made to wait, then told to return the following day. Then to return the next day, and the next day, and the next. She has been waiting for years, so the wait does not make her angry but drives her to think that all her actions will be useless. They tore her husband away in the middle of the night, then took all the cash they had, later the few jewels she owned, and then the furniture. Her pregnancy progressed, and she was defenseless with her little Alba Elena and the faithful Catalina. Her parents had been scandalized, or else terrified, it was impossible to know which, but they abandoned her. They wanted nothing to do with someone contaminated by heresies and looked upon poorly by the Inquisition. Her tear-stained letters had no effect, neither did her sacrifice of going all the way to Santiago in one carriage after another, because they did not welcome her. She had to return to faraway Concepción, surrounded by the threat of Arauco Indians.

The lieutenant Juan Minaya, who had arrested her husband, returned to take more of her furniture, two trunks full of books, the surgical instruments, and the silverware.

When her son was born, two priests reminded her that contact with her husband was forbidden, and that she shouldn't even think of trying to relay the news. Helpless in the remote Chilean south, she came to wish that the ferocious Indians would attack the city, slit the residents' throats, and put an end to her misfortune.

She received no news from Lima. The local commissioner of the Holy Office helped her see the nature of her tragedy, hard as granite; she had to accept this blow from heaven and grow used to living like a cactus in a wasteland. It was unlikely that her husband would return to freedom and, even if he did, it would be many more years before he'd be authorized to reunite with her. With time, the commissioner took pity on the long-suffering woman. He reread her dowry letter and discovered that Cristóbal de la Cerda, the ex-governor, had taken wise precautions in defense of his goddaughter. The money he held for her, just like the money her future husband had handed over at that time, was not subject to confiscation. If she could recover those funds, she could relieve some of her economic pressure, would be better positioned to raise her children, and could await her husband's uncertain return with some relief. He thought that he was carrying out an act of charity and started preparing her to take her claims to the only place where they could bear fruit: Lima. It was difficult to fund her passage and persuade her to abandon her children for many months. Nevertheless, he succeeded.

In July of 1638, after almost twelve years of anguish, Isabel succeeds in approaching the nightmarish place where her Francisco is locked up. She has traversed the same land and the same stormy waters that he did. If he is still alive, she is only a few yards away from him.

Will they let her see him? Speak to him? Embrace him? Her mind fills with the idyllic moments they enjoyed together from the first time their eyes met, full of surprise and tenderness. Now she would be happy just to hear his voice through a closed door, to read a sheet of paper written in his tidy hand, or to look for one second into his diamond pupils. At the start of their separation, Isabel was haunted by images of the brutal arrest. But later, bittersweet memories took hold, full of nostalgia; their bites were no less painful than the nightmares. Day and night, she wondered what she could do to help him. And the only response that beat in her chest was—nothing! This was confirmed by the few neighbors who didn't turn their backs on her and by her friendly confessor. All she could do was appeal for that which may legally be within her rights and, praying to God, place her trust in miracles.

It is already a miracle for her to be in Lima, so close to Francisco.

At last, the letters of recommendation reach the inquisitor Juan de Mañozca. He takes time to reflect on them and, at the end of Mass, decides to receive her.

The woman is brought in by armed guards. She no longer possesses the beauty of her youth, but, despite the gray streaks in her hair and her early wrinkles, one can clearly see that she is someone who once stirred the lust of men. Her bewildered mind is full of the words she's practiced since leaving Valparaíso. She cannot believe what is happening; in recent years she's been made to feel like a contemptible wife and mother, and now an imposing guard is steering her toward one of the most feared authorities in the Viceroyalty. He is guiding her, taking care of her. When she enters the sumptuous room she falls to her knees, not knowing what posture to take before this grand presence. A clerk invites her to sit and, at a cold gesture from the inquisitor, opens the parchment and, in a weak voice, reads the tremulous request written in her name by the commissioner in Concepción.

The letter says that she is the legitimate wife of Doctor Francisco Maldonado da Silva, and, "in accordance with the law," she begs to have returned to her the confiscated goods that did not belong to her husband, but to her own dowry, "namely the items listed in this text that I present with all the necessary oaths . . . I ask and beg Your Honor to please himself in doing as I request, because I am poor, and suffering due to many needs and having no other assets than the ones that belong to me from the aforementioned dowry."

With his fist, Mañozca stifles a burp that reminds him of the chocolate he just drank and, anxious to get this minor proceeding over and done with, instructs the secretary to name Manuel de Montealegre as "defender of those goods," for his further investigation. Isabel, moved by the swift decision, cannot contain her cry of surprise and gratitude. The judge has listened! He wants to help her.

In a few days, with unusual speed, Manuel de Montealegre gives his verdict: the request is denied. He emphasizes that there is no evidence that the dowry money entered the Holy Office, and, in addition, the main trial, that is to say, the trial of Francisco Maldonado da Silva, is not yet over. With what money are they to keep covering the costs that he still generates? Mañozca reads the verdict and puts it on the table, making a face; Montealegre is a good official who knows how to kill a foggy argument with an irrefutable reply. But in truth, the trial of

Maldonado da Silva finished five years ago, with a death sentence, and the dowry money not only came in, but now belongs to the Holy Office. The Holy Office needs more money than ever for its immediate actions, and it's no time to squander it on refunds to women of questionable faith.

Gaitán finds out that Mañozca turned to Montealegre to satisfy a request from Francisco's wife. In the tribunal's next private meeting, he expresses his distaste. Mañozca stays calm and says he has fulfilled his duties of Christian piety. His adversary reminds him that piety should not confuse soldiers of Christ. Mañozca replies that he is not confused, and at that very moment he decides to grant Isabel Otáñez another hearing to resolve her request "in accordance with the law."

"There are laws that harm the church!" Gaitán yells.

In this manner, then, thanks to Mañozca's need to contradict the severe Gaitán, fragile Isabel is able to meet with him again. The inquisitor doesn't tell her that her cause will end badly, but rather makes a date two months in the future. In the meantime, Mañozca persuades Castro del Castillo for a few meager goods, in his words, "to be sold by public auction in the city of Concepción de Chile, and that, from the proceeds, Doña Isabel Otáñez receive two hundred pesos with which to feed herself and her children, and in addition, that she be given back her house, that she may live in it." Both inquisitors vow to see this decision through, no matter how much Gaitán shouts at them or calls them traitors of the faith.

In the final hearing, Isabel stays on her knees, immobile, before the colossal platform. The result of her petition is incredibly poor. She will return with far less than what the commissioner in Concepción, going over the arithmetic several times, had calculated she would receive. But she's also been unable to express the most important thing. Mañozca and Castro del Castillo retire before she dares to speak. The notary looks at her with contempt as he gathers his papers, and tells her icily to return to Chile, as there is nothing left for her here in Lima. Isabel looks him in the eyes, and her mind fills with the same words as years ago, stronger than ever. Here there is knowledge, here there is power, here destinies are decided. She bites her lips and weeps inconsolably, unable to say what she dreamed of saying, what is so very difficult to say in this place. She clasps her hands in prayer and finally implores, as one might implore God and the saints, to be given one word, just one, a single merciful word on the well-being of her husband.

A dark wind sweeps across the notary's face. Slowly, as if his neck were a toothed wheel, he turns to the clerk and makes a gesture. The clerk disappears, as if by magic. Isabel feels lost, not knowing whom to turn to, surrounded by emptiness. Suddenly a hook hoists her and carries her to the street, as if she were a bag of garbage. Her feet aren't touching the ground, her hands flap like wounded wings. She glides over the evasive paving stones, which seem infinite. In her imagination, the good commissioner reappears, to remind her that she must not offend the tribunal by asking about the prisoner. She has made a mistake that could mean losing the little she has gained. The paving stones seem to flow backward and, suddenly, begin to speak to her. They convey something terrible and marvelous: Francisco walked over them, he raised his defiant voice across them, on them he proved himself to be a hero and a wise man. They tell her that, only a few paces from her, in a narrow underground dungeon, her husband—consumed and aged—is feverishly preparing his final onslaught. He is still alive, and more vigorous than ever.

134

The tribunal confirms the date for the Act of Faith. Never before has the City of Kings witnessed a ceremony of such grandeur. It aims to teach a lesson that will reach the farthest corners of the Viceroyalty. The proceedings are done; all that's needed now are a few statements of repentance from people who will die anyway, an added gain for the true faith. But, in addition to these reasons, the inquisitors need the Act in order to rein in a terror gripping the Viceroyalty—namely, a financial mayhem that has been unleashed, an unexpected consequence.

The same judges have already written to the king of Spain that "with the prisoners we took, there came a large number of claims," and that many suits were filed by the captives' creditors. The mass confiscations interrupted the economic flow of Lima and surrounding areas. "The land is hurt," they acknowledge, "and now, with so much prison and confinement of goods belonging to men whose financial ties reached throughout the Viceroyalty, it seems that the world is ending," because the creditors know that, with time, Inquisitorial secrecy, and the death of witnesses, their rights might go up in smoke. "And although our business is faith," they underscore, the amount of riches they've confiscated and the amount of claims piling up oblige them to alleviate the tension surrounding certain causes "from three in the afternoon to nighttime. . . . We have been paying and are paying many debts because otherwise commerce would be destroyed and irreparable harm would be done." The Royal Court agrees with the Holy Office, but in even stronger terms.

A harsh punishment of the prisoners will appease the creditors' greed—or so the judges hope. They will be glad to see them suffer and quake with fear at the thought of themselves one day enduring such horrors.

The preparations for the Act are manifold and confusing. The first procedure, according to protocol, is to notify the Count of Chinchón, Viceroy of Peru. This honored task is entrusted to the prosecutor of the Holy Office, who appears at the palace and, with grave ceremony, informs the viceroy that the Act of Faith will take place the following twenty-third of January, 1639, in the central Plaza de Armas, "for the exaltation of our sacred Catholic faith and the extirpation of heresies." The viceroy sends a prompt reply to the tribunal thanking it for the announcement. The same message is given to the Royal Court, the city halls, the University of San Marcos, the other tribunals, and the consulate. Before publishing the call for the city's residents to attend, the inquisitors lock up all the black men and women who serve the Holy Office so they won't find out and tell the prisoners, which could cause turmoil.

Nevertheless, the proclamation is delayed due to a stupid incident. It had been decided to adorn the doors of the inner chapel with bronze nails. The sound of the hammers, clubs, and rivets spreads through the labyrinth of cells as if announcing an exceptional construction. The correspondence through the walls associates it with the building of gallows. The prisoners become agitated, some revoke their confessions, and others desperately testify against Old Christians in hopes of provoking a general pardon in the face of a flood of accusations. The tribunal, however, decides to keep the date of the Act and carry out all the sentences. It works into the late hours of the night.

135

A monk, covering his nose with the thick sleeve of his habit, goes to Francisco's stinking cell to insist that he break his obstinacy. Later he tells the judges that the prisoner had begged for another hearing with the examining fathers from the Society of Jesus. It seems that the imminence of the end has softened his heart.

"Has he promised to abjure?" asks Castro del Castillo.

The Dominican says that the prisoner is accosted by many doubts, and that he holds out hope that, if these doubts are resolved, he'll return to the authentic faith.

"A delay tactic," Gaitán declares. "The same as always."

The request is not granted, but the monk returns with the prisoner's insistence. Castro del Castillo reviews his records and points out that this would be his thirteenth argument, an exaggeration that proves how very patient the tribunal has been.

"A good number for something else to be produced," the tired monk says, forcing a smile.

The tribunal takes a few days and, with two votes in favor and one against, decides to summon the learned men of the Society for the last time—Andrés Hernández above all. The session takes place in the austere room whose ceiling composed of thirty-three thousand pieces recently sheltered the distressed Isabel Otáñez. The prisoner is brought in; his thin ankles and wrists are duly shackled. He is Christ descending from the cross, almost blind, lips white, nose sharp, hair sad as rain. His pride seems entirely consumed.

They make him sit, then stand. He already knows, as before, he will have to take an oath. Expectation and curiosity fill the room with an extraordinary atmosphere. He disillusions the judges, swearing in the same way as he did the first time, and the times that followed. Gaitán sweeps his gaze toward the other inquisitors, who consented to this predictable defiance. Mañozca, also irritated, invites the prisoner to express his doubts. The Jesuits lean in to hear him better.

Francisco takes a deep breath. He has to make a great effort for his voice to emerge with enough strength. But his almost servile tone contradicts his biting message. He starts off with a terrifying question.

"Isn't it an arrogant and useless pretension to impose a single truth?"

His physical weakness lends sweetness to his expression, but his words make the room tremble.

"Might the great truth not be manifesting itself? Truth that exceeds the human brain, through partial truths that we can barely apprehend? Might the great truth be so rich and mysterious that we can only be permitted a miniscule approach? And that miniscule approach, isn't it fulfilled through our diverse roots and beliefs? Couldn't it be that diverse roots and beliefs exist exactly for this reason, that we might be more modest and recognize that we've only been given one part to see and feel? Couldn't it be that our convictions, though opposed, can only be resolved in the infinity of the Supreme Being who transcends our own perception? What benefit do you offer the great truth, then, if you wish to convert the miniscule part you recognize and love into the whole that you can't reach?"

The judges and theologians vacillate between rejecting his words as new heresy and considering them the product of a severe disturbance of logic.

"In the heart of each man," Francisco adds in an amiable tone, "there beats the divine spark that no man, no one but God Himself, has the right to assail. If your faith has value, then so does mine."

The judges are scandalized and make great effort to hide their disgust. How can there be more than one truth? It's a sophism, an insanity. These ideas are no inspiration from heaven, but from the devil.

"Since you have urged me to be a Christian, I ask whether being a good Christian includes mutual punishment, the tearing apart of families, humiliation of one's fellow man, and the denunciation of relatives and friends. These are things already suffered by Jesus, who was denounced and tormented. When you repeat his passion on others, aren't you rendering Jesus's own passion useless? If his sacrifice didn't cancel out similar useless sacrifices, then what's changed? What did he begin? To keep persecuting, offending, and killing men the way Jesus was persecuted, offended, and murdered—doesn't that reduce him to one more case in the infinite chain of men who are victimized by men?"

Gaitán drums on his armrest, longing to interrupt the session. This basilisk who will soon be turned to ash is staining the Inquisition headquarters with unacceptable vulgarities. Even Castro del Castillo thinks the same thing when the prisoner spits out, "Where is the Antichrist? Is it possible that you can't see him?" His eyes flash with a light that pierces the men who are present, as his lips smile enigmatically. "Can't you see him? These shackles!" He raises his blistered wrists. "Was it Jesus who put these on me?"

Mañozca murmurs, "He's gone absolutely crazy."

Francisco addresses Hernández, the Jesuit. "Is reason a natural right? Are thought and conscience a natural right? Is care for my body a natural right?"

The theologian assents.

"And yet—" He interrupts as if he's lost the thread. "And yet," he repeats, "the body, my body, is abused, and will be destroyed. Shouldn't Christians respect the body, even more than Jews? For Christians, God was made flesh, in a human body, through the mystery of Incarnation. Christianity, in that regard, is the most 'human' of all religions. But— what a paradox!—its followers, instead of valuing and loving the body as they love their own God, hate it and assault it. I don't believe in the Incarnation, but I do believe that the Only God is in our lives—" And, here, Francisco quotes his father: "To harm a body is to offend God."

"Restrain yourself to expressing your doubts!" exclaims Gaitán, livid and indignant.

Francisco reaches into his clothes and inflicts a surprise on them.

He pulls out two books. The three inquisitors, the Jesuits, and the notary stare, wide-eyed. Where did he steal them from? Then they realize, stunned, that the books were not stolen, but written in his narrow dungeon. The notary takes them with trembling hands, as if touching objects created by Lucifer's magic. The sheets of the two volumes are artistically fashioned out of pieces that are carefully glued together. Each page is full of words as small and tidy as those from a printing press. The notary hands the books up to the impatient inquisitors. Then he returns to his chair and writes, in his amazement, that the prisoner "took two handwritten books from his waist pouch, created with sheets composed of many scraps of paper that were gathered we know not how, and glued together with such subtlety and skill that they resemble whole sheets, and with words written upon them with ink he made from charcoal." He wipes his forehead and adds, "One of the books had one hundred and three pages, and the other had more than one hundred." He records the author's extravagant signature: "Eli Nazareo, unworthy Jew devoted to the God of Israel, known by the name of Silva."

The alarming volumes pass from hand to hand.

"There are my doubts," Francisco says. "And my modest science. He who wrote that has a divine spark, no less than any of you."

"Oh, spark of Satan!" replies Castro del Castillo, disturbed by the audacity.

The inquisitors invite the Jesuits to speak. But it's hard for them to speak. After hesitation and stammering they unfurl unfocused sermons. This unbelievable hearing stretches on for three and a half hours. The theologians manage to unravel Francisco's deceitful declarations, and, to the judges' minds, they again succeed in revealing the path of light; only a capricious, evil mind could refuse to accept the truth, the only truth.

Mañozca addresses Francisco, so he can answer whether he is ready to repent, but before that, he must take his oath again. Automatically, he gestures to the crucifix on the table.

The prisoner rises with the muffled creak of tired joints. Then he utters words that provoke an exclamation of shock and horror.

"Swear on the cross? Why not swear, then, on the rack, or your ropes and spikes, or the brazier that destroys feet? Any instrument of torture would do. The cross was an instrument of torture, Illustrious Ones. Or has it had any other goal? The cross was used to murder Jesus and many other Jews like him. Then Christians kept on murdering Jews, brandishing the cross at them like a bloodstained sword. On the cross, we Jews have died, not Christians. Has any inquisitor died on the cross? Or an archbishop? Someone should finally say it, hurt as it may: for the persecuted Jews, the cross has never symbolized love, but only hate, never protection, but only cruelty. To demand that we venerate it, after centuries of murder and contempt, is as absurd as asking us to venerate the gallows, the vile cudgel, the stake at which you burn us. Christians praise the cross, and they have their good reasons! But we're the ones who carry it, we the persecuted. The cross doesn't offer us well-being; it brings us anguish, offends us, and destroys us." Francisco raises his right hand, and the long chain shines briefly like a filigree of stars. "I swear by God, creator of heaven and Earth, that I have told the truth. My truth."

—⁓—

When the proclamation is spread, on Wednesday, December first, a new atmosphere falls over the City of Kings. The punishment and death of sinners should be cause for rejoicing. While the prisons fill with the poisonous breath of tragedy, the streets grow excited and enthused. While fear rises in the darkness of corridors, the light of the metropolis swells with a longing for the feast. While despair unfurls in suffocating cells, out in the plaza, the spectacle begins. Death on one side, and revelry on the other; the two will unite, embrace, and dance together. Reason will dress up in madness, and madness will adorn itself in reason.

All the familiars exit the Inquisitorial palace in their fearful habits, riding steeds with lustrous harnesses and saddles amid a forest of tall batons, to the sound of lutes, trumpets, and kettledrums. They parade around the plaza then begin their majestic route through Lima's central streets. They are followed by the main officials of the Inquisition, in a rigorously imposed order: the representative of the pope, the head of the treasury, the accountant, the receiver general, the cadaverous notary, and the senior clerk. Colors and sounds inflame the city. Neighbors drop what they're doing, women peer through lattice windows, and noblemen, youths, and servants invade the streets. Such a display stirs great curiosity.

"The Holy Office of the Inquisition," a solemn voice declares, "informs all the faithful who reside in and beyond the City of Kings, that this coming twenty-third of January, the Day of Saint Dominic, we shall celebrate a spectacular Act of Faith at the public plaza of this city to exalt our sacred Catholic faith. All the faithful are called upon to attend, so they may gain the indulgences that our high pontiffs grant to those who witness such acts."

The following day, construction begins on the elaborate stage. A legion of carpenters, ironsmiths, and builders distribute boards, nail stakes, and lay out beams to make steps and walkways hemmed in by sturdy handrails. Several strategically laid-out blocks are made to fit the multitude expected to attend, not only from Lima, but also from surrounding areas. The work does not let up, not even "on the solemn feast days." The inquisitor Antonio Castro del Castillo is in charge of overseeing the work. He sees that neither the many steps nor the strength of fences will prevent chaos from spreading through the torrential crowds, and he orders another proclamation demanding that no person "of any kind whatsoever, except for gentlemen, governors, ministers, and other officials," dare step on the official stage. And, to contain any possible overflow, he calls on many gentlemen and instructs them to patrol the crowd with staffs bearing Saint Dominic's coat of arms. To keep the main platform cool, twenty-two towering trees are brought in and cloth awnings are tied between them with pulleys to create refreshing shade.

Two days before the Act of Faith, the tribunal gathers all its ministers and officials in the chapel of the Holy Office. Juan de Mañozca speaks gravely to them, exhorting that they appear at each of their assigned tasks with love and punctuality. They should dress resplendently, draping their bodies with the expensive liveries they had made for this very occasion.

In the dungeons, security is higher than ever. The monks who selflessly visit prisoners use their last reserves to try to save their souls. They know that in the following days, all will be consumed. Words and prayers vibrate in the gloomy caves during the day and deep into the night.

Meanwhile, the City of Kings is exalted by the procession of the Green Cross, which includes members of religious orders, secular and ecclesiastical officials, noble gentlemen, priests, merchants, craftsmen, soldiers, learned men, students, and women, who fill several streets and crowd on roofs and balconies. Musicians intone rousing hymns. The procession walks majestically to the main plaza and grazes the enormous platforms that will brim with people during the imminent Act of Faith. A chorus sings the verse *Hoc signum crucis*, and lamps are left burning beside the place where sinners will soon be displayed.

136

Francisco has resumed his fast, but now time is not on his side. The days he's spent without a bite of food are only enough for him to feel weaker and more somnolent. A monk and two servants beg him to eat with such a friendly tone that they manage to confuse him about his circumstances. He is growing more and more deaf, and he uses this disability to exempt himself from the Dominican's whining insistence. Staring right at the monk he blurts out, "I'm not trying to get you to stop being a Christian, please—let me keep being Jewish! Don't get tired, don't wear yourself out, please, just stop talking."

The clergyman's eyes fill with tears. How is it possible that he can't break through this man's shell? But, at this point, Francisco is not so different from a corpse. Where is he hiding the source of his pride? His head is little more than a pair of dark eyes, sunken cheeks, and a strangely shining forehead; his long hair is parted in the middle and has gone almost completely gray, as has his beard. His thin lips tend to move as if in prayer. The monk laments that he should pray to a dead law that will take him to perdition. He wants to shake the man like an empty basket and fill him with the substance of his own faith. But the devil has possessed this prisoner's mind. He realizes that he's developed a kind of fondness for this man—a shameful, unspeakable fondness—and he can't resign himself to watching him twist and turn in the flames. He has conversed on other topics with such clear logic that he seems to be a sensible and highly intelligent man. Francisco has told him about his family with such emotion as to reveal pious corners of his soul, where the devil has not yet entered, and these glimpses stir hopes of returning him to the faith. But in matters regarding his abominable roots, he always hardens again, like a lion, and his tender lips let out a sharp, untamable force.

Francisco, for his part, fears that he might soften at the very last moment. Everyone in his family succumbed to terror: his father and brother through torture, and his mother and sisters through their feelings of defenselessness. He knows that they will pressure him until the very last minute. Before the tormentor sinks his torch into the pile of straw and logs, they will shout at him to cede, to save his soul. They will not resign themselves to losing the game.

Someone shakes his shoulder. Has he been dreaming? Several lamps burn in the miserable dungeon, and their flames lick the adobe ceiling. From his horizontal position on his bed, he thinks he sees a multitude. He sits up with great effort, startled. He blinks. There before him, pressed against each other, are soldiers armed with pikes, priests holding up crosses, and, among them, the tired Dominican monk. Suddenly those strong bodies—so numerous that they barely fit in his cell—make way, forming a hole. Francisco rubs his bleary eyes and, when he takes his hands from his face, he sees the metallic face of the inquisitor Andrés Juan Gaitán. He backs against the wall and draws his legs up; he doesn't have the strength to stand, and there isn't space to do so.

The inquisitor avoids his gaze and unfurls a roll of parchment. Slowly and victoriously, he reads the sentence aloud. Francisco doesn't move. He doesn't try to respond, comment, or beg; his eyes are fixed on the inquisitor's eyes, which do not waver from the page. When he is done, he rolls up the parchment and turns to avoid seeing his victim's face. He searches among the crowded men for the Dominican monk and whispers an order.

The cell empties.

Francisco murmurs, "My God! It's happening!"

He will no longer see dawn slide in through the three holes in the wall; in a few hours, they will come to take him away forever. He touches the edge of the mattress he's used for almost thirteen years and asks himself again whether he'll have the strength to keep defending his rights until the culmination of the Act. He lets himself fall against the bed. The candle they left with him emits a light that he appreciates for the first time, soft and pink. The uneven walls are full of pictures, shapes that, even in such a tiny space, are infinite. Through one of the three holes, eyes appear, the eyes of a rat. It's not even coming to say goodbye to him, only to watch his departure. Suddenly, he's assaulted by a flood of memories: the rats in the monastery in Córdoba, the rats in the monastery in Lima, the spiritual director Santiago de La Cruz, his learning of catechism, the biographies of the saints, his confirmation, the enormous Bible in the chapel, his first flagellation, the embrace of naked torsos, the appearance of Luis with his father's medical instruments and the Spanish key. The Spanish key! Where is it now?

The door creaks, and two servants hold out a tray.

"Lunch," they say.

Lunch? At this hour of the night? The Dominican invites him to pray and eat. Francisco understands: those who are condemned to the flames are piously served a feast. It's a morbid courtesy, but more eloquent than the bureaucratic reading of the sentence. For the first time, they offer him food fit for a prince—a late and pointless form of recognition. The Dominican raises his voice to make up for the prisoner's deafness, and tells him—how he longs to reach the man's hidden heart—that the Holy Office has contracted a pastry chef for the past three days to secretly prepare his final meal.

"Secretly," Francisco murmurs. "Always secretly, everything in secret, so abuse may never be brought to justice."

He sits up and walks the few paces he can in that small space. The monk shrinks back to give him room; he wants to help, and to be agreeable. He gestures to the tray again.

"Eat." It is Francisco who makes the offer to the priest.

"Oh God, oh my God," the monk implores, "How can I make you understand that they are going to burn you alive, that your feet will be bitten by hot embers and your skin will be peeled off, your face crushed, charred like meat? How shall I make you see that you're a victim of the devil's tricks and that you'll suffer the tortures of fire only to fall into the endless tortures of hell?"

He falls to his knees. "Save yourself! Save yourself!"

Francisco flees into his inner world. He needs to call the psalms to mind, those words that nourish his hope. He must stay calm so he does not tremble or break at the last moment. As the minutes pass, as the verses raise his spirits, he feels the monsters of defeat clawing at him. In one way, his strength is growing; in another way, his weakness. "Don't repeat my trajectory," his father said to him. Was he repeating it, then? He doesn't think so. His father denounced his fellow Jews, humiliated himself before the judges, and lied about repentance. He mutilated his own dignity. He didn't go back to being a Christian, or a free man, or a dignified Jew; he became a shell of a man, full of shame. He gave his oppressors the most sacred part of his being, for the glory of the Holy Office, and only kept a litany of taunts. That was his trajectory: fear, submission, abandonment of his own truth.

Francisco presses his eyes closed to keep the tears from falling. The image of his defeated father fills him with a terrible pity. He utters psalms as an antidote to that sad, broken image. "I won't repeat your trajectory!" he says to himself. He's at the verge of death and hasn't denounced a single person, hasn't broken before the judges, hasn't faked repentance, hasn't given an ounce of glory to his oppressors.

The monk presses on with his task of persuasion, holding out the tray of delicacies and uttering potent prayers.

At five in the morning, two infantry regiments in their best regalia complete their formations, one in the Plaza de Armas and the other in front of the Palace of the Inquisition. The tall doors of the Holy Office open to let in four huge crosses shrouded in black cloth, brought from the cathedral and accompanied by an entourage of monks, priests, and sacristans in surplices. The "honored gentlemen" are gathered too; they have been chosen to accompany the prisoners and keep preaching at them about the mercy of the Holy Office on their way to the Act. In the bewildering labyrinth of the dungeons, bolts bang open, doors moan, and shouts begin. The firmness of the monks, soldiers, and gentlemen must contain the desperation.

Through the torch-lit corridors, the captives advance toward the chapel of the condemned. There they will be taught another pious lesson.

Francisco is grabbed by the elbows and forced to rise. He doesn't have the chance to cast a final glance over the hole that sheltered him for his last days in prison. He is guided through a threatening hall, up staircases, and through doors. The monk is at his side, blathering nervously, repeating imprecations into his ear and shaking his arm. The gentlemen standing guard keep their gazes forward, puffed up by the powerful implications of guiding a human being to his death. They press him toward a group of officials, without letting him go. Suddenly, a cloth glides over his head. He touches it and looks: a sanbenito. It's a disgusting yellow color, barely reaches to his knees, and is as wide as his shoulders. A big red X has been painted in the area covering his chest, which symbolizes an extreme sinner. The lower portion has been painted with flames pointing upward: an eloquent sign that he will be burned alive. An official picks up a large cardboard cone, a *coroza*, adorned with clumsy paintings of horns, claws, and fangs that bring to mind the devil, and with braided ribbons hanging from its tip like snakes. Irreverently, they place it on his head. Francisco automatically raises his fist to knock it off, but countless hooks hold him back. He feels ridiculous. All that's left is for the soldiers, later, when he's tied to the stake, to mock his clothes the way soldiers did sixteen hundred years ago when the clothes were a purple robe and crown of thorns. He is pushed forward again, into the painful procession heading toward the plaza.

The crosses sway, with their floating black rags, surrounded by copious clergymen. Penitents follow with their heads down, guilty of various minor crimes: sorcerers, bigamists, blasphemers, thieves. Each of them is duly controlled by a guard who prevents them from speaking to anyone. Then come the practitioners of Judaism, the main course of the feast at hand. They are all wearing vulgar sanbenitos. There are dozens of them, arranged into categories: the Jews who repented quickly walk in front, thick ropes at their throats. Those who repented late and will be executed walk behind them with green crosses in their hands.

The torches and candles zigzag across the crowded plaza, making shields flash with light. A hemorrhage to the east announces the stirring of a new day.

Francisco is aware that he is leaving his last confinement; never again will he be shut in between four walls. The dawn air cools his cheeks. He has imagined this instant many times; it is familiar, sinister. A few paces away, he sees the old doctor Tomé Cuaresma, hunched over in his sanbenito and the cone-shaped coroza, painted with flames, snakes, and dragons. Francisco gives back the cross that was placed in his hand.

"You must carry it," he is told.

He shakes his head.

The official opens his fingers and urges him to obey.

Francisco stares at him as if his gaze were a sword. "No."

"You'll go in rebellion!" the Dominican says, alarmed. "Don't make your situation worse, for your own good!"

Francisco refuses to hold the green cross.

"I'll let it fall," he declares.

The monk picks up the cross and kisses it.

Behind the procession, the manager of the Holy Office rides on horseback, carrying a closed silver trunk that contains the sentences. He is followed by the notary, also mounted on a steed draped in green velvet. Alongside them ride the senior clerk and other solemn officials. The streets slowly fill with morning light, and a cautious exultation reigns. Doorways, balconies, and terraces fill to overflowing. The river of people that accompanies the sinners is a wide, long monster that glides lazily toward the main plaza, confined by the building walls. The crosses and candles sway through the arduous march until the river widens as it nears the gallows.

The monks and gentlemen in charge of the captives force them up to the platform in order, arranging them in their reserved places. The murmur of the multitude grows louder as the victims emerge into sight. The fervor grows as the Jews arrive, with their cone-shaped corozas and their sanbenitos covered in painted flames. And it is scandalous, the jeering and booing, when a man steps up whose hair is long and who lacks even the piety to carry a green cross in his hand.

The gentlemen with black batons bearing Saint Dominic's coat of arms now beat back the people, striking them on their shoulders, necks, and torsos to restore the order required by this Sacred Act. On the central platform, the inquisitors are already seated, as is the viceroy. Castro del Castillo gazes happily at the brocaded canopy, fringed with gold, that he had installed at the last moment, on which there undulates an image of the Holy Spirit that represents "the spirit of God that governs the actions of the Holy Office." The viceroy has been given three amber-colored cushions made of fine cloth, two for his feet and one to sit on, while the inquisitors enjoy one velvet cushion each. Castro del Castillo had the good manners to adorn the balcony of the viceroy's wife with banners, standards, tapestries, and plenty of yellow tassels. All around them, as far as the eye can see, the mob swarms and hums. The older people in attendance insist that Lima has never before seen such a crowded Act of Faith.

Francisco holds tight to the verses that exalt freedom, beauty, and dignity, but he trips at the vile spectacle that boils around him. It's a horrific rite that revels in pain and death.

The ceremony begins with worship of the cross, which stands on a central altar, richly adorned with an image of Saint Dominic, silver candelabras, bouquets of flowers, and golden incense burners. Francisco's brow furrows, and he draws back into his dream state. How long will he have to wait? In waves, sermons reach his ruined ears: different voices, but always the same effort to secure glory, truth, devotion. Someone reads, in Spanish, the papal edict of Pius V that supports the Inquisition and its ministers while rebuking heretics and their misdeeds. He peers through the bars of his eyelashes to see the oath of the viceroy, the Royal Court, the members of city hall, and all the city residents as they raise their right hands, faces entranced, and utter "Amen" in a great wave of voices.

Juan de Mañozca reads the resolution of the Holy Office. A vibration of sadistic pleasure runs through the plaza. The spectacle moves decisively into a voracious phase. Those who repent before the implacable words are uttered will receive mercy—so it is said, repeated, implored. Many thousands of pricked ears absorb the cries, the demented pleas. And many thousands of eyes stare at the rows of wretched people displayed on the platform, who will now be subjected to the punishments they deserve.

The warden raises his jet-black staff and turns to the first prisoner. He sinks the tip of his staff between the man's ribs, as if he were a filthy dog, and doesn't speak to him, but rather pushes him cruelly and grotesquely toward a short bridge that is visible from anywhere in the plaza, so that he can stand there, alone and shamed, stripped of protection, as his personal sentence is read aloud. Then the man is pushed back to the sound of suppressed giggles from the devoted mob.

He sinks his staff into the next prisoner. He repeats the task with the third, fourth, seventh, the eighteenth, as one official after another enjoys the honor of reading each sentence as if reciting poetry.

The sun spills heat over the plaza until the crowd can no longer take in any speeches; it longs for action. The captives have been condemned to whippings, prison, and forced labor in galleys. All that's left are the ones to be "relieved" to the secular branch for their execution.

The warden pushes a Jew called Antonio Espinosa, and the staff twists furiously between his ribs because the man is broken, trembling, raising his hands, and begging for clemency. The multitude shouts, waking those who are dozing. Over their closely gathered heads, vague whistles of joy rise and fall when the staff fails to push forward the next Jew, Diego López Fonseca, who must be carried and dragged by the hair so he can stand on the bridge and hear the punishments that will be inflicted on him. Now it's Juan Rodríguez's turn; in jail, he pretended to have gone mad, to make the judges laugh and confuse them; now he recognizes his behavior as evil lies, and he weeps, implores.

It's time for the old doctor Tomé Cuaresma, who is recognized by people throughout the plaza. The staff pushes him obscenely, and nervous coughs arise; the gray-haired victim leans on the handrail, head down, and when he hears that he'll be burned alive he starts to shake and cry. He stretches out his fingers, wanting to speak, but his throat emits no sound. Then something happens that moves the crowd: the inquisitor Antonio Castro del Castillo abandons his seat of honor and walks toward the trembling old man. He gazes at him, holds the cross that hangs on his chest close to the prisoner's face, and orders him to beg for mercy. The disconsolate doctor is on the verge of fainting, and stammers, "Mercy—mercy!" A triumphant roar sweeps across the plaza.

The inquisitor smiles brightly and returns to his place beside the viceroy so the ceremony can continue. Faith has triumphed, although that man will still be executed.

Only a few Jews remain, the worst ones.

The staff pushes Sebastián Duarte, brother-in-law of the rabbi Manuel Bautista Pérez. When he passes his relative, without the guards noticing, the two embrace as a farewell. The scene produces rage among the spectators, who spit out insults and demand more zeal from the soldiers.

Francisco keeps his eyes open and follows each of the condemned men intensely, as if his tranquil spirit had hands that could reach out to those anemic faces and enfold them in tenderness, say how much he loved them, say that they are not alone, that their pain will pass. He has an extraordinary vision of man's precariousness. He has never been able to see it so sharply. Soon he will be dust, and all ambitions and perversions and nonsense will cease to matter. He is sustained—he has been sustained—by what he loves: God, his family, his roots, his ideas, and those pastel-colored memories flecked with blue that moved him so much in faraway Ibatín.

Now it's the "great captain's" turn, the rabbi, the "oracle of the Hebrew nation," as is written in the text read aloud sarcastically by an official. Manuel Bautista Pérez listens to his sentence with majestic bearing. In his brain, another multitude seethes: the martyrs who preceded him and whom he will now join.

There is a pause. There is only one more, the most odious of sinners.

One more—the demented man who dared defy the Act of Faith itself, revealing his rebellion. He is a monster because he knows he'll die for his errors and still digs in his heels. The sweaty crowd stands on tiptoes, having only one opportunity in life to see such a thing.

The prisoner looks vulgar, despicable; he is thin, with long gray hair and a long beard that makes him seem deformed. He doesn't wait for the warden's staff to arrive to humiliate him like an animal. He rises by himself, with obvious effort, and walks, with all the elegance his muscles will allow, toward the bridge where he will hear what he already knows. The cone-shaped hat that transformed him into a grotesque being slips off his head. Suddenly he radiates an unfathomable nobility. Thousands of eyes see something confusing. On the bridge, his images overlap, as an effigy of mist had appeared in place of the man. For the first time on this day bursting with heat and madness, silence breaks out.

Everyone yearns to hear the description of his extraordinary transgressions. The official's voice is streaked with uncertainty, fatigue, and sudden restraint. Francisco's hair begins to rise, like wings. The shameful sanbenito grows light, undulating like silk. The crowd fans its ears, because the words seem to be evaporating. This solitary, upright man evokes something mysterious. A thousand yards away, in the "burning place," the fires are almost ready, but there, on the bridge, softly caressed by the breeze, they do not see a prisoner who will be devoured by flames, but a dignified and just man. His image is brushed with magnificence.

The historian Fernando de Montesinos, respected author of many works, rises from his place in the stands to study the marvel up close. The tribunal has entrusted him with the difficult task of writing down a detailed account of the Act of Faith. He has already interviewed Francisco, has extracted several pages of personal information from him, and was able to write about his studies, travels, offenses, and audacities. Now he must keep his senses alert to record all the details of the Act. Everything matters: the decorations, the sentences, the protocols, the prisoners' behavior, and even supernatural phenomena. The breeze that plays with the condemned man's hair transforms into a wind that swiftly grows strong. The oppressive heat is suddenly fractured by icy stabs coming in from the sea. From Callao, a black mantle advances, swollen and furiously struck by lightning. Attention has been so focused on the spectacle that the storm's beginning has gone unnoticed, and Montesinos raises his eyes in fright; this too must be included in his report.

Suddenly a collective cry of horror accompanies the saber's blow that breaks the awning over the main platform. Montesinos shields his eyes with his hand and manages to hear the words uttered by Francisco, suddenly golden in the light. Later, in his report, he will transcribe it exactly:

"The God of Israel made it so, that He might see me face-to-face from heaven!"

Epilogue

The prisoners sentenced to execution are led to the fire between walls of soldiers to prevent the hordes from attacking them. Monks walk with the condemned men; they hail from all the religious orders and keep preaching to the condemned until the final moment. Among the military officers who oversee the funereal march is the contrite Captain Lorenzo Valdés.

Tomé Cuaresma says that he has no need of the Holy Office's mercy, and dies without repenting. Manuel Bautista Pérez looks at the executioner with disdain and orders him to do his job well.

Francisco Maldonado da Silva doesn't speak, cry, or moan. The books he wrote with such great effort in prison are tied around his neck. Several witnesses observe the moment in which the blue flames reach the pages and a whirlwind of letters spins insistently around his hair like a crown of sapphires.

The officials in attendance—the senior clerk of justice, the notary, and the secretary of the Holy Office—endure the smoke and the smell of human flesh until they can be sure that the condemned ones have been turned to ash.

The historian Fernando de Montesinos covers his nose with his handkerchief and fulfills the Inquisitorial command to write down a complete account of the colossal Act of Faith. His long text is immediately printed by order of the Most Illustrious General Inquisitor. Nobody suspects then that, through this document, the victims will ascend to immortality.

The Central Council of Spain, however, is alarmed by the scale of the massacre, larger than anything the Inquisition has done in all the Americas, and it orders the three inquisitors to transmit "separately" and "in good conscience" their own feelings with regard to what has occurred.

Gaitán answers that the sentences "were justified." Castro del Castillo answers that, before giving his vote, he held Mass and entrusted himself "very much to God, and with great humility." Mañozca does not answer, and that same year his services to the Tribunal of Lima are terminated.

The Act of Faith of 1639 shakes the Jewish communities of Europe, which circulate reports about the martyrology that's taken place in the Americas. In 1650, the famous work *Hope of Israel* appears, written by Menasseh Ben Israel, which narrates the savage event and devotes several emotional paragraphs to the martyr Francisco Maldonado da Silva. In Venice, the doctor Isaac Cardoso publishes another book that expands on the frightening history and extols the heroism of "Eli Nazareo." Later, in Amsterdam, the Sephardic poet Miguel de Barrios writes a poem about the heroic Latin American who fought and died to defend his right to freedom of conscience.

In 1813, the Holy Office of Lima is abolished, and the people plunder the Palace of the Inquisition to erase the terrible proof that still kept hundreds of families on edge. Nevertheless, two years later, it was reinstated, and panic returned. But in 1820, by order of the last viceroy, it was eliminated forever.

In 1822, the most significant blow is delivered to the Inquisition in the Americas: the liberator José de San Martín orders for all the belongings of the dreadful tribunal to be transferred to the National Library, as that is where—these are his exact words—one can find ideas, which are "tragic to tyrants, and precious to those who love freedom."

Acknowledgments

In creating this book, I have been graced by the help of many people and institutions who offered me their rich information, particularly the National Academy of History, the National Academy of Letters, the Simón Rodríguez and Torcuato di Tella foundations, the Library of the Latin American Rabbinical Seminary, and the generous contribution of books and documents by the Cordoban historian Efraín U. Bischoff and the Tucumanian historian Teresa Piossek Prebisch. I dedicate special recognition to Marcelo Polakoff, who, full of enthusiasm for this project, obtained additional information from archives and libraries. The brilliant Peruvian anthropologist Luis Millones offered me orientation, references, and materials from his own archives.

As this is a historical novel, it would be incongruous to name the entire long bibliography that exists, and that I consulted, in order to reconstruct the era and its people, as many minor names and scenes arise from the literary necessity of giving flesh and emotional depth to long-ago or uncertain events. But it is appropriate, at least, to acknowledge my debt to three relevant authors whose research into the colonial era in the Americas and the life of Francisco Maldonado da Silva deserve great praise: José Toribio Medina, Boleslao Lewin, and Günter Böhm.

My wife Marita read and discussed most of the chapters with generous dedication, offering sharp observations that kept me alert in the forest of characters and events. My son Gerardo designed and oversaw the processing of the materials and records of successive versions.

I thank my agent Diane Stockwell of Globo Libros Literary Management for her lucid work and polished efficiency in achieving this edition, as well as Amazon Publishing for launching this book into a broad universe of readers.

About the Author

 Marcos Aguinis is a prize-winning, internationally bestselling author. Born the son of European Jewish immigrants in Argentina in 1935, Aguinis learned at age seven that his grandfather and the rest of his family in Europe had been killed by the Nazis. Describing this as the defining moment of his life, Aguinis says it is what drove him to write, in an effort to repair the "broken mechanism of humanity." He published his first book in 1963 and since then has published thirteen novels, fourteen essay collections, four short-story collections, and two biographies covering historical, political, and artistic themes. Aguinis was the first author outside of Spain to win the prestigious Planeta Prize for his book *The Inverted Cross*, and his novel *Against the Inquisition* was praised by Nobel Prize laureate Mario Vargas Llosa as a "stirring song of freedom." When democracy was reinstated in Argentina in 1983, Aguinis became secretary of culture for his brave fight against dictatorship and the defense of human rights, and sponsored the renowned "cultural renaissance." For more information, visit www.aguinis.net.

About the Translator

Carolina De Robertis is a writer, professor, and literary translator of Uruguayan origins. She is the author of the novels *The Gods of Tango* and *Perla*, as well as the international bestseller *The Invisible Mountain*, and is also the editor of the anthology *Radical Hope: Letters of Love and Dissent in Dangerous Times*. Her own books have been translated into seventeen languages. Her award-winning translations from the Spanish include Alejandro Zambra's *Bonsai*, Roberto Ampuero's *The Neruda Case*, and writings by Raquel Lubartowski, Rodrigo Hasbún, and Pedro Almodóvar, among others. She is the recipient of Italy's Rhegium Julii Prize, a fellowship from the National Endowment for the Arts, a Stonewall Book Award, and numerous other honors. In 2017, the Yerba Buena Center for the Arts named De Robertis to its 100 List of writers and thinkers who are "shaping the future of culture." She teaches fiction and literary translation at San Francisco State University.